SANCTUM
OF THE
SOUL

SHROUD of
PROPHECY

BOOK THREE

SANCTUM
OF THE
SOUL

KEL KADE

TOR

TOR PUBLISHING GROUP
NEW YORK

SANCTUM OF THE SOUL

Copyright © 2025 by Dark Rover Publishing, LLC

Interior Illustrations by Kel Kade
Map by Jennifer Hanover

A Tor Book
Published by Tom Doherty Associates / Tor Publishing Group
120 Broadway
New York, NY 10271

www.torpublishinggroup.com

Tor® is a registered trademark of Macmillan Publishing Group, LLC.

The Library of Congress Cataloging-in-Publication Data is available upon request.

ISBN 978-1-250-29389-3 (hardcover)
ISBN 978-1-250-29388-6 (ebook)

Our books may be purchased in bulk for promotional, educational, or business use. Please contact your local bookseller or the Macmillan Corporate and Premium Sales Department at 1-800-221-7945, extension 5442, or by email at MacmillanSpecialMarkets@macmillan.com.

First Edition: 2025

Printed in the United States of America

0 9 8 7 6 5 4 3 2 1

To my darling daughter, who gives me limitless love and support.
And to my mother, who always believes in me no matter what I choose to do with my life.

CONTENTS

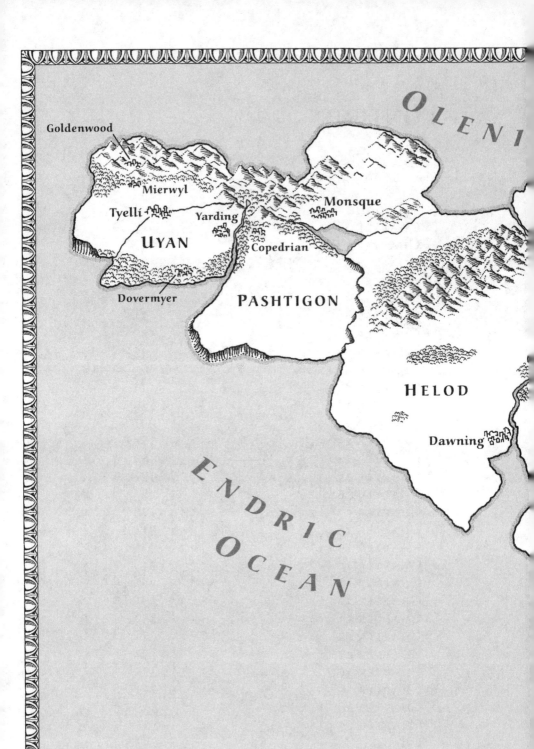

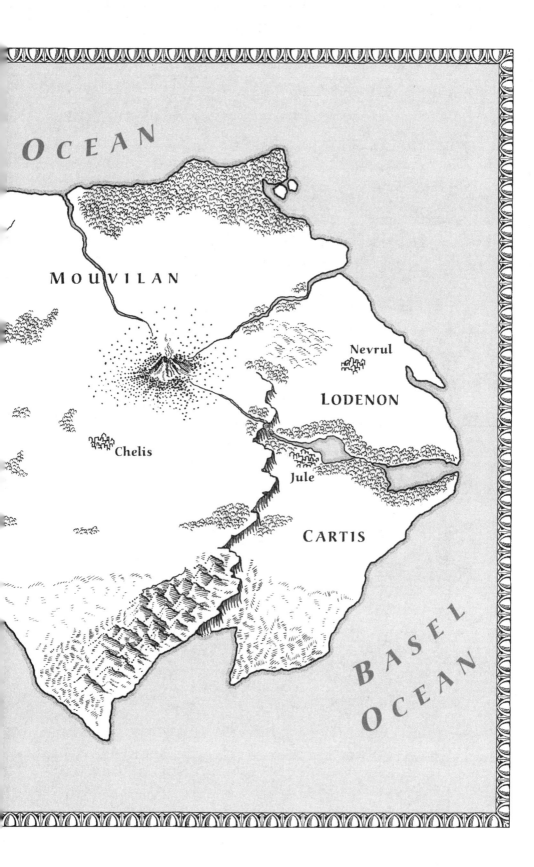

SANCTUM
OF THE
SOUL

PROLOGUE

I LOOKED AT THE ENTRANCED FACES OF EVERYONE GATHERED IN THE community house as I considered that it might be time to turn in for the night. Just then, Aleena entered bearing a tray filled with steaming mugs, which she carefully passed out to the children. I smiled as I watched them blow across the hot milk tea with eager smiles and entirely too much energy. It was obvious they would not be sleeping anytime soon. Beside me, little Corin shifted, and his brother Maydon reached out and steadied the mug before it could spill over the boy. I met Maydon's gaze and thanked him.

Maydon opened his mouth, but his words were delayed as he summoned the energy to speak. Finally, he said, "Thanks not needed. He's my brother."

I blinked back tears as I remembered Maydon as a joyful child, full of mischief and eager for adventure. He had barely come of age when he ran away to join the army, much to his father's dismay. Although it had been nearly 150 years since the Grave War ended, the world was far from safe. With the Berru came death and destruction, and all semblance of organized society in Endrica had ceased to exist for a time. When Maydon returned from his service, he was not the spirited youth he had once been. In fact, he had little spirit at all. His only job now was to safeguard Corin and our small community as best he could.

Aleena turned toward me with a cheeky grin. "Leydah, will you finish the story?"

"Yes," said Corin. "Tell us what Aaslo did with the souls of the *depraved*." This last he said in a spooky voice as a shiver ran through him. Hearing of the depraved always spooked the children a little, as it should. The depraved were a force even the gods would not have unleashed. Aaslo was not a god. He was merely a forester, and he did what needed to be done.

I waited until I had all the children's attention again. "Aaslo didn't do anything with the souls of the depraved—at least, not at that time. In fact, he was so disturbed by the power wielded against the smoke dragon by the single depraved he had placed in the body of the dead magus that he refused to keep the rest. He gave them back to the reaper."

"But why would he do that?" said Jennilee as she tossed her long braid behind her. "The depraved were important."

"Yes, they were," I replied, "but Aaslo didn't know what to do with them at the time, and he wasn't sure he could control them. Instead, Aaslo focused on other matters that were just as important. He set about gathering as many people to his cause as he could find. He traveled through the paths all across Endrica recruiting anywhere he could."

"But he was a monster," said Jennilee. "Weren't people scared of him?"

"Yes, they were," I replied. "And many people ran from him or even attacked him. But that's why he took Teza and the marquess with him. Anderlus Sefferiah, the Marquess of Dovermyer, had a natural way with people that put them at ease, and he was used to being in a position of authority. Teza was one of only two magi who had stayed behind when the other magi left the realm. People were encouraged by having a magus in their presence when so many terrible things were happening in the world.

"You must remember, these people were frightened. Every day they might be attacked by roving lyksvight or one of the Berruvian magi scattered across Endrica when the evergates broke. As more people died, the task of living became more difficult. Food became more and more scarce, and travel between cities more dangerous. Many towns and villages were cut off completely."

"But what about the armies?" asked an older boy named Garus who rarely spoke.

"Well, in the west, the army in Uyan fell apart when the king dismissed them and was later killed. The marquess and Aaslo gathered what forces they could there. In the far east, Pithor's forces destroyed the warriors of Lodenon and Cartis before the evergates were broken. Some escaped to Mouvilan, but most of the Mouvilanian forces were scattered across the expansive kingdom trying to protect people from the roving lyksvight. Much the same happened in Pashtigon and Helod. Until Aaslo came along, Endricsian forces had no central gathering point or governance. Remember, it had been Mathias's duty as the chosen one to unite the armies, and Aaslo had taken up that mantle. It was a difficult task—one to which he was not well suited—but he had help.

"To top it all off, the gods now warred amongst themselves, and Aaslo had captured the attention of more than one of them. Nowhere was safe for Aaslo."

CHAPTER 1

THUNDEROUS HOOFBEATS RESOUNDED THROUGHOUT THE MIST-shrouded forest pathways between realms like an avalanche crushing everything in its path. The cries of the raptors overhead nearly drowned out the shriek of steel and crash of arms, and still the shouts of men and women in despair clung, like parasites, to Aaslo's sensitive ears. The sharp, metallic tang of blood, that of humans *and* of the creatures, scented the air.

Aaslo gathered survivors of the Berruvian campaign against Endrica and took them into the paths between realms. From there, he could lead them from one location on the world of Aldrea to another quickly, but the pathways were far from safe. All manner of creatures from a number of realms found their ways into the paths, trapping themselves where they had no choice but to prey on others to survive. Some used the pathways as a hunting ground, which was apparently the case now. The rear of the column of men-at-arms and refugees had become a battleground. The herd of beasts came upon them quickly, as if the door to the paths had opened directly behind them. Aaslo considered that perhaps it had. This might have been planned. Another of Sedi's traps, or a god's, maybe. Or perhaps it was merely a coincidence, and these creatures resembling the centaurs of legend regularly roamed the paths seeking prey.

The beasts were as large as a man and mount combined. Where the horse's neck might exist, a human abdomen led to a torso, arms, and a head. Wiry fur covered their shoulders, and a mane of brown or black sprouted from their heads and continued down their backs. The creatures wore no clothing, save for the leather-and-steel armor strapped across their chests, and wielded swords, maces, and axes with expertise and savagery. Their hooves bore iron spikes, which they used to rend the flesh of man and horse alike.

Aaslo and his soldiers had already proven that they could bleed as well as any man, and they had already scattered the paths with a number of dead or dying beasts. The losses, however, didn't deter the centaurs. The beasts attacked with fervor, not thinking of retreat. Between the centaurs at their rear and the winged predators overhead, Aaslo wasn't sure his people could survive.

"You're not going to let a bunch of horse people get you down, are you?"

Aaslo was thankful for Mathias's voice filling his head. His best friend, the *chosen one* of whom the Aldrea Prophecy had foretold, had been killed shortly after leaving their hometown of Goldenwood. Aaslo had taken to carrying Mathias's severed and magically preserved head in a sack at his waist. He wasn't sure if he was really hearing his friend from the Afterlife, or if he had simply gone mad. Aaslo didn't know if it mattered.

"Have faith, Aaslo. You are my proxy."

Aaslo appreciated Mathias's support even if he didn't quite believe him. His gut clenched as a soldier was cut down. "I am a poor substitute," he muttered.

"You cannot be the chosen one, but you can *choose to be the one."*

As Aaslo mulled that over, a ball of orange light whizzed past his head to collide with a centaur that managed to elude the undead soldiers blocking their progress. The centaur, a tawny-maned male with a wicked facial scar, stumbled back, crushing the undead soldier behind him. The centaur lurched as he gathered his legs beneath him. His chest was singed and already bubbling with blisters as he raised his mace and swung at the nearest undead. The soldier blocked the swing with his sword, then countered, stabbing the centaur through the ribs. Roaring as the bloody blade slid free of his flesh, the centaur swiped at the undead, bashing in the side of its skull. The undead fought on, distracting the centaur as Aaslo closed the distance and buried his axe in the beast's torso. The centaur flailed as it succumbed to its injuries, sinking to the ground in great heaving spasms.

"He was too ugly to defeat you. You will surely die at the hands of a temptress."

"Already plotting my death?"

"I will rejoice when you join me, Aaslo. You know that."

"That's not exactly comforting considering you're dead."

"It's all a matter of perspective."

Before Aaslo could celebrate, his feet left the ground. Sharp talons, each larger than his fingers, dug into his shoulders. Those on his human side sank deep into the muscles to score his clavicle. Aaslo lost his axe as he was lifted into the air. He tilted his head up to see the raptor, a hideous creature with the body of a vulture and the torso and head of a woman. The horrid feminine face contorted into a sneer with a mouth full of sharp, serrated teeth. A long, thin tongue snaked out to taste his face, and Aaslo swung his claws, scoring its face and drawing four ragged lines of blood.

"This isn't exactly the temptress I was envisioning."

The harpy let go, and as Aaslo fell, he hoped he didn't impale himself on someone's sword. He never reached the ground. The harpy snatched him up again, this time digging into his thighs. The staggering pain roused the powers at his core. The power lent to him by the fae, Ina, swirled, and he was certain he could hear her cackling as she taunted him with the promise of power. It was just beyond his reach. More readily at hand was that of the dragon. The monster roared in his mind with burning fury. Wings beat in his chest against the confines of his human body. Then, with a heaving breath, a gout of flame erupted from its maw. The flame consumed the harpy, feathers burning as her fleshy torso smoldered and dripped with melted flesh and fat.

Aaslo dropped through the air once more. Nothing caught him. He landed atop a centaur in a tangle of limbs and hooves.

"Without wings you're really more of a big lizard than a dragon."

"I'm neither," Aaslo gritted out as he caught his breath.

Aaslo ached and groaned as he rolled to his feet. He noted that he seemed to be in the middle of the herd. Without his axe. The centaur on which he had landed attempted to regain its footing. It seemed unable to control its hind legs, and Aaslo wondered if he had broken the beast's back. He slid Mathias's sword free of its sheath. He lopped the beast's head from its body without guilt.

A sound Aaslo had heard only once before began to emanate from the battlefront. The reaper, Myra, had given him a mystery soul, which he placed in the body of a dead magus. Upon awakening, the new being, the *shade*, exhibited terrifying power over sound that could damage or kill anyone in its path. Without thinking, Aaslo used Ina's borrowed power, and threw up a shield ward. Then he hit the ground, curling into a ball and covering his ears. A concussive wave struck the centaurs, knocking them from their feet. While those close to the front were blown back dozens of feet, those in the direct line of the blast exploded on impact, pieces of their bodies showering the rest in a gruesome, macabre rain.

Aaslo slitted his eyes open. The shade stood at the forefront of their line, its mouth stretched wide. It inhaled as if to scream again, and Aaslo cringed, reinforcing the ward and bracing his body for the impact. Another wave blasted over the battlefield, ripping flesh from bone. When it passed, Aaslo leapt to his feet and rushed to the front line with Mathias's sword firmly in his grip.

"That's right, Aaslo. Run toward the source of power that will shatter you into thousands of pieces."

The shade inhaled again, and Aaslo knew that if he wasn't behind the line by the time the creature released its torrential wail, he would be torn to pieces. His feet pounded hard against the bloody dirt as he leapt over fallen centaurs and dodged their kicks and half-hearted strikes.

One of the beasts snagged his leg, dragging him to the ground as the shade released another flesh-rending scream. Aaslo erected shield after shield as the sound battered his magical defenses. The wail threatened to burst Aaslo's skull from the inside. Hot liquid slid down Aaslo's chin, and he wiped it with the back of a hand. It came away bloody. His ears, ears that no longer heard the sounds around him, had burst. Only Matthias's voice remained, and it refused to stop.

"And me. I'm still here."

Aaslo was both relieved and irritated that among all the sounds of battle, all he could hear was Mathias.

The grip on Aaslo's leg went slack, and he looked down to see that the centaur that grabbed him no longer had a head or torso. All that remained were clumps and pieces steeped in blood. Aaslo got his feet beneath him and surged toward the shade that just might be his demise. As he neared, though, he noted that the shade did not seem inclined to screech again. It swayed on its feet, wrung out, its loose tunic swinging in time with the motion of its body. Aaslo glanced to the grey sky, noting that the harpies had disappeared, presumably due to the shade's wails.

"There went your chance to find your soulmate."

Aaslo chuckled at the thought of wanting anything to do with the wretched harpies. Mathias's taunts didn't surprise him, though. He glanced over his shoulder to survey the battlefield.

The centaurs were likewise defeated, even if they didn't know it. Some recovered and resumed the fight, but this time, they were outnumbered and outclassed. Aaslo's forces barely changed. As the living fell, they were resurrected as the undead wanderers who served him in exchange for a chance to fight again. Between Aaslo, the magi Teza and Ijen, and the undead and living soldiers, they surrounded the centaurs and brought them down one by one until all were defeated. The centaurs never attempted retreat nor surrender. They seemed driven to die for their cause, and yet Aaslo had no idea why. When the last beast was slain, Aaslo retrieved his axe and he and the living retreated a few dozen paces to slump to the ground with fatigue as the wanderers remained on watch.

The partially trained Healer Mage Teza and Prophet Ijen rested near him, both looking the worse for wear. Ijen cleared his throat, and rasped out, "These paths seem to be as dangerous as you claimed. It is a wonder I never saw them in my visions."

Ijen's entire life had been dedicated to prophecies about Aaslo and his role in the Aldrea Prophecy and beyond. According to Ijen, *death* followed Aaslo.

Aaslo ran a hand down his weary face. "Perhaps the paths between realms do not cross with the paths of prophecy."

Ijen appeared thoughtful as he nodded slowly.

Teza said, "I wouldn't have minded a warning about *that*. I thought centaurs and harpies were mere myths."

Ijen tapped his lips and said, "Perhaps the myths began with others who walked the paths."

"They certainly don't exist on Aldrea," muttered Aaslo. "At least, not in Endrica. Perhaps they are native to Berru." The Berru, their enemy, were beholden to Axus, the God of Death, and they intended to end *all* life on the world of Aldrea.

"Maybe," said Teza, "although they could just as easily have come from some other world—or perhaps two different worlds. We don't know that this attack had anything to do with Axus or the Berru. I don't like these paths. Can we get out of here?"

Aaslo nodded. "Yes, the doorway to Tohl Gueron is not far. We've made this trip to and from Mouvilan several times without issue. I didn't expect an attack—at least not a large force like this. We will prepare better in the future."

"That's what you always say."

Sedi slid effortlessly between the realms, an easy feat for one of the ancient First Order magi with over a thousand years of practice under her belt. She stepped into the grand throne room in the palace in the southern continent of Berru, a room utterly unlike those belonging to the Endricsian kings and queens across the Endric Ocean. Bespelled sconces and chandeliers bathed the black stone of the floors and walls in an eerie blue light. Polished columns encircled the throne, accompanied by lengths of grey gossamer fabric hung from the high ceiling. Like insubstantial wraiths, they fluttered in the sea breeze whispering through the arched openings framing the city.

"My sweet, you have come to see me," purred a sultry voice.

Sedi drew her attention away from the domed temples and spired city offices and smiled. She eyed the slight woman who lounged upon the delicate throne. "Lysia, you look well."

The Berruvian empress returned her smile, her black-painted lips curling up over pointed teeth. Her pale, ashen face, not yet touched by the ravages of time, stood in stark contrast to her black mane of braids and nearly black eyes. She lifted a black-lacquered nail long enough that it curled back on itself and said, "You should have come earlier. I sent three to meet Axus for their cowardice. Their refusal to fight in this war was wretched, but their deaths were beautiful."

Sedi stopped a few feet from the foot of the dais and snapped her fingers. A servant draped in only a short, tattered robe rushed to her side bearing a goblet. He bowed low as she took the chalice and sipped the sweet nectar. She carefully considered how to phrase her next words. Sedi knew the empress held no love for Pithor, the fallen leader of the Berruvian army, but he had been favored by the God of Death, Axus, and was a means to an end. The empress raised a sharp eyebrow and tapped her long nails against an armrest. Finally, Sedi decided to just come out with it.

"Pithor is dead, along with many of the forward troops. Those not killed have scattered. General Margus is presently leading the regrouping efforts. Magus Cobin is gathering what is left of the magi. Many died, while others were . . . *misplaced* when they were sent through the broken evergates."

Lysia leaned forward and hissed, "Are you saying that we are *losing*?"

Sedi smirked. "Only that Pithor lost. The greater army will land soon, and the Endricsians are in shambles. The only semblance of a resistance is led by a . . . well, I do not know *what* he is, but he is hardly human. He's the one I told you about. The one I was sent to kill. He's part *dragon*."

Lysia sat back, and the sheer, tattered skirt of her dress exposed her pale, bony legs as she crossed them. She motioned for the servant to bring her a drink as well. As she sipped, she said, "Tell me of him. I wish to know more of this dragon-man."

Sedi smiled to herself as she thought about her attempts to kill Aaslo. "He is a formidable opponent. I have yet to succeed in removing him."

Lysia scoffed. "The way you speak, it sounds like you have not truly tried. You respect him."

Sedi tapped her lips thoughtfully, then nodded. "I do. He is a good warrior, and his power—well, it is different from anything I have encountered. More than that, though, he is driven."

"Oh? What drives such a man?"

Sedi gazed up at the macabre empress and said, "Death. Or, rather, his fight against it."

"A futile effort," said Lysia.

"Of course," agreed Sedi. "In the end, everyone dies."

Lysia's stoic shell cracked, and she gave Sedi a sympathetic look. "Except *you*."

Sedi's muscles tensed as her gaze landed on a magpie that flitted through an arched opening. "Except me," she whispered.

At this, the empress stood and glided down the steps to meet her. She cupped Sedi's face in her hands and turned to meet her gaze. "Do not despair, my sweet. You will have your reward. You will not be left behind."

Sedi took Lysia's hand in her own and gave it a squeeze. "Thank you, my friend. Your words give me comfort."

It was a lie. In truth, nothing the empress or anyone else said would have given Sedi comfort. Sedi had lived for two thousand years, and unless Axus granted her his blessing, she would not die anytime soon—if ever. Sedi was immortal, and that immortality had taken its toll. She wanted nothing more than to experience death's sweet embrace. It was her sole reason for participating in this war the Berru inflicted upon the world. Though recently, something, or rather *someone*, was making her question her decisions. Lysia need not know of the turmoil infesting Sedi's heart of late, but Sedi wondered if she could see it. Lysia was cunning and intuitive. If anyone could understand the smallest grain of what Sedi felt, it would be the empress. Their understanding and acceptance of each other's darkness had blessed them with mutual respect.

Lysia released Sedi's hand and turned toward the single entrance that wound down the tower. She said, "Walk with me. I must see that everything is prepared to my satisfaction."

Sedi fell into step beside the empress. "Prepared for what?"

"For my departure. You will take me through the paths to Endrica." At Sedi's surprised look, Lysia grinned. "Even before learning that the imbecile Pithor was gone, I had decided to lead the army myself."

"*You* will lead the army?"

"You doubt me?"

"No, of course not. It's only that I don't think you have ever left the palace."

"If things in Endrica are as disastrous as they sound, my leadership is needed."

"I am sure Margus will suffice—"

"Margus is a good general. He is a soldier, a brutal one, but only a soldier. He does not possess the people's hearts, their *souls*. I will remind our men and women that they fight for the glory of Death and the Afterlife, for it is only in the everlasting embrace of Axus that we shall find eternal fortune. Pithor, at least, knew this, even if he was blind to the virtues of the blessed journey." She came to a halt on the next landing and turned to Sedi. "Your journey has been longer than any other, and you understand what it means to sacrifice."

"The journey *is* the sacrifice," growled Sedi.

The empress's expression held more pity than sympathy, and Sedi felt a flash of anger. Lysia said, "The journey is not the sacrifice, my sweet. It is the trial by which we earn our places among the gods." She began descending the stairs again as she continued, "The Endricsians do not deserve such a place, so it does not matter that their journeys are cut short. Our soldiers, however, are rewarded with death upon passing of their final tests."

"And what of mine?" Sedi snapped. "Why must my journey be longer by a thousandfold?"

"Obviously, you are to be the greatest amongst the gods."

The way the empress made this simple statement, without a hint of scorn, lent her a sincerity that warmed Sedi's heart. Lysia had a way of looking at things with a clarity that Sedi envied. Time had eroded such simplicities in Sedi's mind, making it as crowded and convoluted as the paths she frequented. It was one more reason to admire and appreciate Lysia as both a friend and an empress. At least, she was the closest thing to a friend that Sedi had or would ever have again. Friendship wasn't worth the loss. And she *would* lose it. Whether through strife or death, it would always be lost.

Lysia had gotten as close as Sedi would allow anyone, though. Her humility led Sedi to feel fond of the woman. Even as the supreme ruler of the Berruvian Empire, a job no one truly wanted, Lysia recognized a superior mind and strength. She listened intently as Sedi explained the expectations of a ruler on the battleground and took Sedi's advice to heart. As she had with most of Berru's leaders, Sedi occasionally served as one of Lysia's tutors during her childhood. She made sure the would-be empress possessed an unmatched strength in strategy and politics. It was for this reason that, although Lysia had never actively led a military campaign, Sedi had confidence the empress could prevail. It was the woman's purpose, after all. Otherwise, Sedi wouldn't have bothered with her. The method of succession made it harder for Berruvian rulers to keep the throne. In Berru, one became ruler by killing the sitting ruler, therefore few wanted the position. Emperors didn't last long, but Lysia had managed to hold the position for a decade, an eternity by Berruvian standards.

Barely more than a week later the two women, followed by a cadre of servants, each touched with the power of the magi, stepped from the paths onto a sandy beach on the southern peninsula of the Endricsian kingdom of Helod. Behind them towered the Argontian Warriors: six massive sentinels carved from stone quarried far to the north and erected on the southern shore to ward off invaders. Sedi smirked at the irony as her gaze absorbed the sight before her. There upon the blue-grey waters of the Endric Ocean were hundreds of galleons, carracks, caravels, and longships cutting across the waves laden with enough trained Berruvian soldiers, weapons, and supplies to wage a dozen wars—or one *terrible* one.

The empress stepped forward, her sandals sinking into the soft sand, and raised her arms. The tattered ends of her filmy grey gown writhed on the breeze, giving her the appearance of an insubstantial specter.

"My brave and vicious warriors will wipe this continent free of the taint of life. Then we shall all rise to the grace of the gods, and I will be the shepherd of death. Axus will be pleased."

Sedi caught the woman's look of elation, and for the briefest moment, felt a twinge of something disconcerting. Perhaps it was guilt, maybe shame. She glanced back to the sea as the first of the soldiers set foot upon the shore, and suddenly she knew what it was—regret.

CHAPTER 2

Dolt nickered then shifted away—again.

"Stop it, you ornery beast, or I'll have you served up as dinner," said Aaslo. He had checked the saddle blanket three times to make sure there were no burrs stuck to it, but Dolt still was not having it. Aaslo had been trying to saddle him for fifteen minutes, to no avail.

"Having a lover's spat with your horse again?"

Aaslo kicked the bucket at his feet and grumbled, "It isn't a lover's spat. Even you couldn't handle this idiot horse."

Mathias hummed in the back of his mind, but Aaslo ignored him.

"Have you tried asking him nicely?" said Myra.

Aaslo looked over at the reaper, who perched on the short wall surrounding the palisade. "He's a *horse.*"

"You have to admit he's odd for a horse."

"An odd horse for an odd man."

Aaslo ran a hand through his hair in frustration. "I know. Some magus must've done a number on him. I don't know why I keep him around."

"He's the only horse that would put up with you."

Myra smiled coyly. "You like him. You just won't admit it."

Aaslo scowled at her. "Don't you have souls to collect?"

Her eyes widened before her expression turned to hurt. "Would you rather I be doing that?"

He released a heavy breath. "No, it's just—why are you here? Should we be expecting trouble?"

"Is that all I am to you? A harbinger of doom?"

"That's not what I meant."

She shook her head and straightened. "No, I understand. I only wanted to spend time with you. It's been a long time since I had companions, and, well, you're special."

"Yeah, you are, just not in the way she thinks."

"Why?"

Myra's mouth hung open, and she shifted uncomfortably. Then, just as she started to answer, they were interrupted.

"The patrol is back," said Mory, coming around the corner of the building. He looked well even if his pants and sleeves were a bit too short. The young thief turned scout had grown since coming into Aaslo's company. "Oh, hi, Myra. It's good to see you again."

Aaslo was glad the boy could also see Myra, since they were the only two who could. The poor boy had had to die, though, in order to claim the ability. Aaslo's process had been a bit more complex, albeit less traumatic. Myra had been pushed into the stream during the transfer of power from the fae creature Ina, and he had inadvertently been blessed with some of her power over death.

Myra smiled fondly at the boy and said, "It's good to see you, too, Mory."

Aaslo cleared his throat. "How did it go?"

Mory returned his attention to Aaslo. "They encountered a small group of lyksvight, but nothing like the numbers we've seen lately. Do you think they've moved on?"

Aaslo suppressed a shiver at the mention of lyksvight. The grotesque creatures the Berruvian magi made from human corpses would never cease to disturb him no matter how many of them he killed. He said, "Hopefully we've killed most of them."

"Success!"

"I don't think so, Aaslo," said Myra, and she appeared doubtful. "There were a lot of lyksvight that scattered when their magi were killed. They've probably gone in search of easier prey."

Mory said, "The patrol did mention they were having a harder time finding game. I think the lyksvight are eating everything that moves."

Aaslo eyed Dolt, who seemed to be staring him down. "This position isn't sustainable, not to mention we're doing little good just sitting here waiting for someone else to attack."

Myra said, "Aaslo, the Berruvian army should be landing soon, if they haven't already. You've gathered a few thousand compared to their five hundred thousand. What are you going to do?"

"We have a few thousand here in Uyan," said Aaslo. "Over the past couple of months I've been practicing using the paths, and we've been recruiting in Mouvilan. Refugees from Lodenon and Cartis have also joined the resistance there. With the way I look, they didn't want to trust me, but Teza and Ijen have been having more success. The people are encouraged by the fact that a couple of magi stuck around."

"I didn't know you've been doing that," she said. "You don't trust me."

Aaslo sighed. "It's not that. I mean, it is, but . . . come on, Myra, you have to admit it's a little difficult to trust you when you're working for the enemy." As a reaper, Myra technically worked for the Fates, but she was assigned to serve Trostili, God of War, who was allied with Axus. While her obligation forced her to serve Aaslo's enemies, her heart was with the people of Aldrea, and she chose to help him as much as she could—or so she said.

"I understand," she said, "but why tell me now?"

"You would have found out soon enough, seeing as how we will be joining the gathering army shortly."

"Oh? That's good," she said, but her expression was pensive. "Things have been . . . *tense* in Celestria. It's never good when the gods fight, but with the Fourth and Fifth Pantheons at war, things are even more turbulent than usual."

"How so?"

"Well, as you know, Arayallen is the leader of the Fourth Pantheon, and Trostili is a member of the Fifth."

Aaslo recalled that Arayallen was the Goddess of the Wilderness and in addition to being the God of War, Trostili was Arayallen's lover.

"How does that work if Arayallen and Trostili are a couple?" said Mory.

Myra tilted her head curiously and said, "Arayallen and Trostili have been together since he was created. I've never seen them at odds. They haven't spoken to each other, they're both in terrible moods, and the realm shudders with the kind of power they wield. Axus is only making things worse, of course. He and Arayallen have each been waging their own campaigns for support among the other pantheons."

"I thought Disevy was the leader of the Fifth, not Axus," replied Aaslo.

"He is, but so far Disevy has been staying out of it. I don't know why. He's been distant ever since he blessed you."

"He blessed *me*? The God of Strength and Virility blessed *me*? How so?"

"*That doesn't seem fair. You get to live my destiny and be blessed by a god, and all I get is this sack.*"

"Believe me, your destiny is anything but a blessing," Aaslo gritted out. Then to Myra he said again, "How am I blessed?"

Myra shook her head. "I don't know. He didn't say."

Aaslo racked his brain trying to think of a time in which he might have been blessed. So far as he knew, blessings were most effective when they were accepted, but he could not think of a time when he had accepted anything from anyone besides Ina. Except . . . he remembered a man with a drink after a battle. Surely not. His gaze slid to Myra. "Why would he do that?"

She bit her lower lip and dropped her gaze to the ground. When she looked up again, she appeared uncertain. "Because I asked him to."

"You did? How did you get him to agree?"

She shrugged. "It wasn't hard. He said he would do it for *me*. He seems to *like* me. I don't know why."

This time, it was Aaslo who was surprised. "You've garnered the admiration of a *god*?"

She breathed out, and the action appeared forced. Aaslo wondered if she even needed to breathe, seeing as how she was dead. "I don't know," she said. "I think I *did*, but I betrayed him when I offered you the six souls he asked me to carry for him. If he found out . . . well, that would explain the distance between us. I don't know what he will do to me for that betrayal."

Aaslo eyed the dangling orbs that hung from Myra's belt. "I'm sorry, Myra. I haven't used the other five yet. Perhaps you should keep them. The punishment may not be so severe if you have lost only one. You may even be able to retrieve that one."

She shook her head adamantly. "No, I did not mean to imply regret, because I don't have any. You need every advantage you can get, and if the other five have power similar to the shade, then they will be of help."

"But you still don't know what they are?"

"They're trouble, is what they are. You should take them all and see what happens."

"Doesn't that sound a little reckless?" said Aaslo to Mathias.

"Come on, Aaslo. Live a little. What's the worst that could happen?"

Aaslo groaned. "I wish you hadn't said that."

Mathias chuckled. *"Superstitious, are we?"*

Myropa eyed Aaslo as if he'd lost his mind, then said, "No, I don't know what they are, only that Disevy doesn't want Axus to get his hands on them. It's very important, Aaslo."

"I know, and I don't intend to give anything useful to Axus."

Myra suddenly groaned. "Oh, I must go now. Duty calls."

Aaslo nodded to her. "Myra . . . thanks."

She smiled at him just before she disappeared. As soon as she was gone, Mory said, "The marquess wanted to see you."

Aaslo looked at Dolt, who had gone back to munching on the feed in the trough, and sighed. He draped the saddle and tack over the wooden fence and said, "Very well. Lead the way."

As they hurried through the streets and alleys of the ancient ruins of Tohl Gueron they kept an eye out for any of the strange creatures that had invaded the city over time through the intermittent rift that opened to the paths. Aaslo didn't know how the rift had gotten there, but he was sure it had something to do with the ancient magi inhabiting the city hundreds of years before. Since then, creatures of all shapes and sizes had inadvertently found themselves in the city, and that had given the place its reputation for being cursed. The previous occupants of the city took to trapping the creatures in amphorae and storing them in vaults beneath the three city towers. One of these amphorae had disgorged the waspy smoke dragon several months prior, thanks to Peck and Mory's meddling. To their benefit, by the time Aaslo and Teza managed to slay the beast, it had damaged their enemies more than their own forces. Since then, there had been no major incidents between the newer city residents and its monstrous inhabitants.

Aaslo and Mory stopped at the front entry of a modest estate near the city's center. The marquess had taken up residence, as it was one of the better-preserved structures. The lower floor of the three-story house, as well as the outbuildings, served as the command center for the resistance efforts, while the upper floors were reserved as living quarters for the marquess and a select few, including Aaslo. The estate had no paddock or stables, though, so Aaslo stabled Dolt with the other horses in what had once been the city's parade grounds.

Crossing the threshold into the foyer, Aaslo could hear the marquess's voice, heavy with frustration, from his study at the back of the house. Aaslo nodded to a few retainers loitering in the hall in anticipation of running any errands. The handful of men and women gave him tentative nods in return, but their eyes made their unease with him obvious.

Although the newest city residents knew who he was, most gave him a wide berth, their gazes tracking the monstrous changes inflicted upon his body. The outward physical mutations had ceased in their spread, leaving him with a dragon arm and scales covering his torso, shoulder, and neck on his left side. While those changes were obvious from afar, closer inspection of his left eye most bothered people. His forest-green iris covered the entirety of his eye, and the pupil had elongated vertically. It was not the eye of a human that regarded others, but that of a dragon—disconcerting if not altogether frightening. Aaslo was glad the scales had not consumed his face.

"It's not that bad, Aaslo. You're stronger now and have special dragon powers, even if you do look like an overgrown lizard."

Aaslo scowled, sighed, and ran a hand through his shaggy hair as he walked through the study doorway and nearly ran into a young woman who was leaving. She squeaked and jumped back, only to trip over her skirts. Aaslo caught her before she fell, but she wrestled away with a shout.

"Don't touch me!"

Then she slipped through the doorway and ran. Aaslo turned his attention to the room's other occupants, all of whom stared. His scowl deepened as he strode across the open space to join them. Anderlus Sefferiah, the Marquess of Dovermyer, sat behind a desk carved from marble, its surface inscribed with a phrase from some ancient language. A man named Hegress, master of the marquess's cavalry and infantry, stood next to the marquess. He liked to call himself a general. Bear, the marquess's training master, stood beside Hegress. Teza and Ijen sat on a sofa across from the desk, while Head Scout Daniga, and Peck, a thief turned scout as well as Mory's guardian, leaned against the far wall. Mory slipped into the room behind Aaslo and went to stand at Peck's side. Broden and Hennis, co-leaders of the Cartisian Yellowtail Clan, lounged in two high-backed chairs, while Aria, former Great Oryx and companion of the late Paladin of Everon, Cherrí, perched on a footstool beside them. It was an odd assortment of individuals, but these were the people making decisions about the fate of the world these days.

The marquess said, "Why do you look so cross? Has something happened?"

Aaslo stopped beside the sofa. "Nothing worth speaking about."

"Well, now that we're all here—"

"Myra's not here," said Mory.

"*Myra* doesn't need to be here," said Teza. "She works for the enemy, remember?"

Mory lifted a shoulder uncertainly. "Well, sometimes she does. She also works for us, though."

Teza lifted a hand toward Mory and scoffed as she looked to Ijen. "See? This is a problem that you need to clear up."

Ijen tapped his book of prophecy and pursed his lips but said nothing.

"Let's just assume Myra is on a need-to-know basis, okay?" replied the marquess.

Hennis said, "Who is this Myra?"

"Never mind her," replied Aaslo. He looked back to the marquess. "What is this meeting about?"

"You know what this is about," said the marquess. "We need to leave. We are doing no good sitting here, and our meager rations cannot support everyone. Every day we wait is another day closer to starvation."

Aaslo said, "What do you propose? We've gathered anyone who is alive who will come with us. Half these people are not equipped for fighting. They're farmers, dockworkers, bookkeepers, and children."

"Every army needs the support of cooks, laundresses, armorers, smiths, and—"

"*Smiths?*" exclaimed Aaslo. "We have no smiths. We have no extra weapons or armor and no raw materials with which to make any."

"We can get what we need," said the marquess, raising a hand to forestall another protest. "*You* can take us through these paths of yours to the cities where we may acquire it."

Aaslo glanced at the hopeful faces and grumbled, "It's dangerous, and isn't as easy as you think."

"*Since when does a forester seek the easy route? Step up, Aaslo. You can do this.*"

Aaslo released a heavy sigh. "Yes, I've been traveling the paths to recruit in Mouvilan, but we've used the same routes every time. What you're proposing is different. It's finding our way through the paths that presents a challenge."

Ijen held up a finger. "Ah, the horse seems to know the way. You did have us follow him *here*, did you not?" Aaslo didn't appreciate the not-so-subtle reminder that he asked them to follow a *horse* through the pathways to the ancient city.

Teza turned to fully face him. "Yes, Aaslo. Why does your horse know the paths?"

"I don't know. He obviously belonged to a magus before me."

"Yes, but that magus wouldn't have had access to the paths. Only the ancients had that power. Well, the ancients and *you*."

"What does it matter?" said Aaslo. "Dolt is a moron who refuses to be understood."

"*Get back on topic, Aaslo. We were talking about your horse, not you.*"

Aaslo growled, eliciting a startled yelp from Hennis. Ever since Aaslo had been joined to the dragon, there were times when he wondered if he wasn't more dragon than man. He gave her an apologetic glance, which received a scowl in return, then he said, "Any explanation we think of for his behavior is nothing more than speculation."

"True, but can he lead us through the paths?" said Aria.

Aaslo turned his gaze on the huntress. Thanks to Teza, her broken leg had been healed, and she looked to be in top fighting form.

"It's possible," he said, "but he's stubborn and doesn't often do what I want."

"Again, we're not talking about you."

"*You're* not talking at all—except in my head," grumbled Aaslo. "If you're going to keep doing that, at least say something useful."

Most of those present were used to him talking to people no one else could see or hear, so they waited patiently for him to stop. Hennis and Broden, however, looked as if they were reconsidering their alliance.

The marquess cleared his throat and said, "Well, with regard to your horse, let us work on that, shall we?"

Aaslo crossed his arms over his chest. "By *we*, you mean *me*."

The marquess smiled. "If you insist."

The rest of the meeting went as expected for an unprepared, ragtag group of refugees. The logistics reports were abysmal: not enough food, not enough weapons, and not enough armor, not to mention not enough *people* if they wanted to put up a fight against the Berru. On top of that, about half their number were already dead—or, rather, they were Aaslo's undead, raised by his power over death to once again walk, and serve in his army. It was pointed out, though, that at least the dead did not require food. They didn't seem to require *anything* so far as Aaslo could tell, and he wondered what mystical power kept them energized. He had the discomfiting feeling that it had something to do with *him*. Teza proposed that they might feed off his own life force, which led him to wonder if he was in for an early demise.

After plotting out which strategic cities they would visit, assuming Aaslo and Dolt could lead them through the paths, the meeting ended, and everyone set about their tasks. Aria caught up with Aaslo as he exited the building.

"Forester," she called.

Aaslo stopped outside the estate doors and turned to find her stalking toward him with purpose. He tilted his head to peer through his dragon eye. She looked different this way. He could see her form and face, but brilliant streaks and blotches of brighter orange and yellow colored her core, which shaded to darker red and black at the edges. A shimmering halo surrounded her like the heat simmering across the horizon on a hot day on the plains. He shifted to look at her through both eyes, and the two images merged to hold a depth of information he was only just beginning to understand.

"Yes?" he said.

Aria gripped a broken spear in her right hand and held it aloft as if it meant something. It was the same spear she had carried since he met the woman, so he thought perhaps it was important to her. She said, "*You* are keeping things from us. I am a Great Oryx, so I understand this is the way of war. It is smart for the leaders to keep things to themselves. But Hennis and Broden do not think this way. They do not trust you, and this is a problem."

Aaslo scratched the scruff at his jaw and said, "Why do you care what Hennis and Broden think?"

Her eyes widened in surprise, and she looked at him as if he were daft. "They are the leaders of the clan. I *must* care what they think."

"Why? Why are they the leaders? Is it their age? Their experience?"

"They have been the leaders since their former clan leader died in a lyksvight attack. Their people chose them."

Aaslo nodded. "Okay, but most of *those* people are probably dead by now. We are at war. Your people need a war leader. From what I can tell, neither Hennis nor Broden are prepared to lead as would a warrior. Perhaps it's time for what's left of your people to choose a new leader."

At first, Aria appeared as if she might agree with him, but a scowl quickly replaced her look. "It is none of your business who we choose to lead us or why."

Aaslo's first instinct was to agree. He was a forester. He had no business telling anyone how to live their lives, but Mathias wasn't having it.

"*Stop being so mule-headed, Aaslo. You're not a forester right now. You're filling my shoes. You are responsible for everyone, including the Cartisians.*"

Aaslo let Mathias's words sink in for a moment. Then he replied, "Actually, it *is* my business. Whether I like it or not, I'm leading the resistance. I need to know my people will follow through when needed. It's better for you all to work this out now than to wait until we're in the heat of battle."

Aria narrowed her eyes and pointed her spear at him. "You need to tell me, who is Myra, and who are you speaking to in your head? I have heard of magi using mind speak. Are there more of you?"

Aaslo brushed her spearpoint aside with a scaly claw. "So far as I know, besides Ijen and Teza, there are no other magi left in Endrica—unless you count the Berru, but I am definitely *not* speaking with any of them."

"What of this Myra? You said she works for the enemy. Is she Berruvian?"

"No, Myra is—*was*—Endricsian."

"What do you mean *was*?"

"She's dead." Aaslo glanced around to make sure no one else was within hearing distance. "She's a reaper."

"What is that?"

"She collects the souls of the dead and takes them to the Afterlife. She technically works for the Fates, but she's been assigned to serve Trostili, the God of War."

"Who you said is working with Axus to kill all of us! And you *trust* this, this *reaper* who works for the enemy?"

Aaslo nodded. "To a degree. I believe she truly wants to help us, but she's also bound in service to the gods. She does what she can, but they hold power over her. That is why it is best if she is not present during our planning meetings."

"What does she look like? How will I know her if I see her?"

"You won't. Only Mory and I can see her."

"That makes no sense. Why only the two of you?"

"Because you're special."

"It's a long story and one I don't really feel like telling. The point is, Myra can travel great distances in no time and carry messages between Mory and me, which is how we knew to find the marquess and his people here."

"So you're using a servant of your enemy as your messenger?"

"We're in desperate times."

Aria seemed to deflate as she said, "Indeed."

Aaslo shifted so that his human side was closest to her and said, "Please consider what I said. We both know Hennis and Broden do not have it in them to do what needs to be done in war."

"Do you know what needs to be done in war?"

Aaslo was struck with the sincerity of Mathias's question. After all, he was only a forester. Even so, he said, "I know enough to accept that death is the lesser of many evils."

"Only a man who walks with the dead would say so," replied Aria.

"Death isn't so bad. Unless someone cuts your head off and stuffs it in a bag."

Aaslo cringed. His guilt over Mathias's death and all that came after would never be assuaged. He could have been done with Mathias's head long ago, but he still needed Mathias. So long as he was on the chosen one's journey, he would carry Mathias with him. He refused to accept Mathias's death. The truth was, he couldn't—*wouldn't*—let Mathias go.

Aaslo looked past Aria to watch the messengers scurrying between the command center and outbuildings, and he wondered how many of those orders would result in the recipients' deaths. He said, "What has become obvious to me over the past several months is that death is not an end. It is merely a passage from one existence to another."

"Which makes me wonder if you still value life as much as our leader should."

Aaslo clenched a scaly fist and met her steadfast gaze. "*Life* is what we are fighting for. Axus has no right to take it from us. Mathias wouldn't stand for it, and neither will I. I will continue to fight for it as long as I am able, even if I must take the fight to *him*."

"*Prouder words were never spoken.*"

"You would fight a *god*?" said Aria, her brow rising in disbelief. "How?"

"I don't know"—he gripped the sack hanging from his belt—"but I have already lost too much. If we are doomed to die, we might as well die fighting."

"*You sound more like a soldier than a forester.*"

Aaslo grunted. Mathias wasn't wrong. Aaslo knew he had changed in more than just the physical sense, and he didn't like it. After a long, calculating look, Aria excused herself and left to rejoin Hennis, who shuffled down the street. Aaslo turned in time to catch a glimpse of someone disappearing into a sliver of light.

A chill suffused him, and Aaslo tensed as he reached for the axe strapped to his back. His vision focused through his dragon eye as he stalked toward the side of a vacant building where the anomaly had occurred. He trained his ears to listen for the scuff of a boot or rustle of clothing, and he inhaled deeply, scenting the air. He felt something shift inside him, like his inner beast was stretching his wings, and a growl escaped before he could stop it. The air held the slightest hint of jasmine and pistachios. At that moment he realized he had smelled the scent before on the paths—not *his* paths, but *hers*.

Sedi.

The ancient magus and assassin had been spying on him, but for how long he didn't know. Had she been in the marquess's office? Had she heard *all* their plans? Or had she only been stalking the outer buildings? More importantly, why hadn't she tried to kill him while his guard was down? He had been preoccupied, and there was opportunity. The fact that she *hadn't* disturbed him all the more. What was she up to?

"Aaslo!"

He tensed before turning at the sound of his name being called. He found Teza hurrying across the street to meet him. Despite the full suit of armor she wore, she moved silently. Even her footfalls were muffled against the cobblestones. The shiny silver armor was sleek and fitted to her form so perfectly it appeared seamless; and, according to her, it was light as linen. Only her head was exposed, and her dark curls bobbed around her face with every breeze. When she smiled, her eyes gleamed with excitement.

"Aaslo, I'm glad I caught you." She paused and glanced around at the empty street. "Why are you over here?"

He shook his head. "Sedi was here."

Teza's eyes widened as she glanced around again, this time with suspicion. "Are you sure she's not here now?"

Aaslo's dragon gaze swept the area. "No, but I think she's gone."

"I don't like this, Aaslo. I don't like not being able to see the enemy."

"What did you need?" He changed the subject. After all, there was nothing to be done, so there was no point in discussing it.

Teza frowned as she glanced around, then she leaned in and whispered, "We need supplies. But I don't like dragging all these people with us. Can't we leave some of them here?"

"No, they wouldn't survive the first lyksvight—or whatever comes through that rift. Besides, the marquess is right. An army needs support personnel."

"You're probably right. I just don't like the idea of putting people at risk. If I'm going to be responsible for them, I want to know the risk is worth it."

"What do you mean, if *you're* responsible for them?"

"Well, when *you're* not around, someone has to be in charge. Seeing as how I'm your second, that's me."

"Since when are you my second?"

Teza balled her fists on her hips and leaned toward him. "Since we met, of course. *I* would be first, but"—she pointed to the sack at his hip—"you're the one with the chosen one's head in a bag." She poked her silver-covered finger into his chest. "You wouldn't have gotten anywhere with the people of Mouvilan if not for me."

"She has a point."

Aaslo scratched the itchy scruff on his face and reminded himself that he needed a shave. He sighed. "Fine. You're right about the Mouvilanians." He examined his scaly fist. "They seem to have a hard time trusting me."

Teza looked guilty for only a moment, no doubt thinking about the changes she'd made to his body. She quickly replaced it with resolve. "I saved your life. I won't apologize again."

"I don't expect you to, and I wasn't blaming you. Just stating a fact."

"You're being as blunt as a forester, Aaslo. You might want to dress it up a little."

"Dress it up?"

Teza tapped her foot. "I *am* dressed up. I have this amazing armor that marks *me* as the warrior queen these people need."

"Warrior queen? And just who is supposed to be your king?"

This time she scowled at him. "If you think it's you, think again. I don't need a king. I'm a force unto myself."

"I wasn't saying you *needed* a king," Aaslo said before running a hand through his hair in frustration. "Look, you *have* been a good liaison. I appreciate your help with gathering the rebel forces."

She grinned smugly. "Well, that's more like it. Why didn't you say that in the first place?" She pivoted on the ball of her foot as she started in the opposite direction, saying, "Now, let's get these people moving. We have places to be, supplies to gather, people to enlist. Well, are you coming? Get moving, dragon-man."

A growl clawed its way up Aaslo's throat and slipped past his lips before he could stop it. "I'm *not* a dragon-man!"

CHAPTER 3

THE LUSH FOLIAGE OF THE GARDEN SNAGGED MYROPA'S DRESS AS SHE carefully stepped onto the path. Although she could not feel the thorns pricking her skin, she had enough sensation to feel them tugging her back to the garden bed she had stepped into upon arriving in Celestria. She only hoped Arayallen would not realize it was she who had crushed one of her glorious blooms. She had not meant to land in the garden. Thoughts of betrayal had distracted her, and she miscalculated.

She straightened and caught sight of the Third Pantheon temple crowning a distant hill. One side of the acropolis sported a gaping hole, still smoking in the aftermath of an attack. The Third had sided with the Fourth in the gods' war and had somehow attracted Axus's ire. Myropa drew her gaze away from the destruction to examine her surroundings. Between the Third and Fourth Pantheon temples sat rolling hills with vibrant green grasses and thick copses of trees. A peaceful stream lent a musical note to the air as it trickled over a rocky bed of polished stones. Vast gardens of orderly plants and flowers intermingled with wild thickets and meadows, and many of Arayallen's smaller creations skittered between branches and bushes to feast upon a copious array of nuts and fruits. So far, the land appeared untouched by the discord among the gods.

Shifting from one foot to the other, Myropa dropped her gaze to her feet. After wiping the soil from her slippers, Myropa hurried toward the steps leading to the goddess's abode in the Fourth Pantheon temple. Like the Third, the Fourth Pantheon temple was a marble acropolis with an intricately designed façade and soaring columns depicting all manner of creatures, plants, and combinations of the two in bas-relief. While the Third Pantheon temple had a flat roof, dark blue glass tiles that came to a peak at the center topped the Fourth. A seemingly infinite set of stone steps led from the gardens at the base of the hill to the acropolis atop it.

Myropa was halfway up the steps when a sharp whistle caught her ear. The air crackled with power, and she looked up in time to leap out of the path of an incoming missile. The knot of power missed striking Myropa by a hair and exploded upon impact with the land beyond the garden's perimeter. An angry shriek emanating from within the structure shook the acropolis, then a massive god clad in shining gold armor came stumbling out of the darkened interior. Trostili took four steps at a time as he hurried down the stairway, but he turned back when he was nearly even with Myropa.

"Come on, Arayallen! Be reasonable," he shouted back the way he had come.

Arayallen, surrounded by a radiant halo, stepped from the entryway. Her long golden locks hung over a pale yellow gown that gathered beneath her ample bosom before draping in folds above her knees. The sunny attire was incongruous with the goddess's fury as she raised her hands and released another of her power-infused projectiles.

Myropa scurried to the side, and Trostili raised a golden buckler to deflect the strike, which exploded in the section of garden Myropa had inadvertently trampled.

"Arayallen, stop this madness!" cried Trostili.

Arayallen's eyes widened. "Madness?! You want to talk about madness?! What madness possessed you to think you could get away with stealing from *me*?!!" she screamed.

Trostili held his hands out in a pleading gesture. "My love, what have I stolen from you besides your heart?"

"You deny it then?" huffed Arayallen. "You did not steal the wind demon from my hall and place it in the human forester's path on Aldrea?"

"Wind demon? Is that what it's called?"

Arayallen screeched, "First you side with Axus in attempting to destroy all *my* hard work on Aldrea, to steal *my* power by killing everything, then you *steal* from me!"

Arayallen cast another bolt of power at Trostili's head, and Myropa decided it best to take advantage of their distraction and find a safe place to hide. She dashed up the steps and took refuge behind a pillar as another explosion rocked the acropolis. Bits of stone fell from the ceiling to crash and crumble at Myropa's feet, and she quickly slipped through the gaping entrance. Since much of Arayallen's power was focused on ensuring Trostili's timely departure, it was dark inside save for the blue-tinted light streaming through the ceiling tiles. Still, she could see enough to determine the place was a disaster. What had once been a detailed fresco now lay in colorful pieces on the floor, and the mosaic that had defined a welcoming path was rent as if by a terrible earthquake.

Myropa wasn't sure why she had been called to the Fourth Pantheon temple, nor could she be certain about which god had summoned her. With both Arayallen's and Trostili's power saturating the air, it was impossible to tease out. She carefully picked her way through the wreckage to the central sitting room. A recessed floor covered in an intricately woven carpet of geometric design contained a number of sofas, tables, and chairs. Most of the furniture was overturned, or in pieces, and nearly all the pillows and cushions had been disemboweled, dusting everything in feathers and fluff like a fresh winter snow. The heavy scents of resin and sulfur hung in the air, but Myropa could not fathom the reason for it.

Myropa's soft slippers did little to protect her feet from shards as she made her way toward a lone cushion that had somehow survived. She swept away the soft down covering its surface and sat to await the irate goddess's return. She dearly hoped Arayallen would take her time to calm down before reappearing, but Myropa wasn't that lucky. Only moments later, the goddess's light filled the space as she swept into the room on a torrent of anger.

"Can you believe him?!" she shouted, throwing her arms in the air but not looking at Myropa. "He steals from *me*. From me!"

Myropa wasn't sure what to say. She wasn't even sure the goddess was speaking to her or had even noticed her presence. She got to her feet and waited to be acknowledged.

Arayallen paced the space in giant form, at least half again as tall as Myropa. She kicked furniture and cushions as she did so and finally grabbed a table and flung it across the room. She roared her fury as the table smashed against the wall, crumbling to the floor in a pile of splinters. The goddess abruptly stopped and turned toward Myropa, catching her in her fiery gaze.

Myropa froze. All that which made her had been stilled, and she struggled to blink. It was as if each and every piece of herself waited to be undone, to be un*made*. Myropa had endured the heavy weight of Trostili's power and the soul-consuming remorse of Axus's, but never had she felt the threat to the very fabric of her being as she did with Arayallen. Myropa's knees became weak, and she lacked the strength to continue standing, yet she could not fall. She froze in an agonizing and eternal moment, standing on the very edge of existence.

Arayallen inhaled deeply then turned from her, and Myropa collapsed. The terror she felt in her bones was nothing beside the desperation she felt in her soul. Her spirit *needed* somewhere to exist—a vessel—and hers had been on the cusp of elimination.

"What do you want?" snapped the goddess.

Myropa struggled to form words. Her lips and her voice did not seem to want to work together yet. Still, she managed, "I was called."

Arayallen frowned at her. "I didn't call you."

Myropa swallowed hard and worked diligently to push herself onto her knees. "It must have been Trostili, then. I will go to him now."

"No!" snapped Arayallen with enough force to push Myropa over. The goddess placed her hands on her hips and asked, "Why are you lying on the floor? Get up."

Myropa's shaky limbs didn't want to hold her as she stood, but she suffered through it. Her journey to stand on two feet again was an arduous one, and she couldn't help the triumph she felt upon accomplishing it. Pleased with herself, Myropa met the goddess's gaze.

Arayallen did not look impressed. She said, "Since you are here, you can help me with something."

Stunned didn't begin to describe the sensation that tore through Myropa. "You want *me* to help *you*?"

"Well, that *would* be ridiculous," said Arayallen with a wave of her hand. "No, not *help* exactly. Just . . . never mind. Come with me."

Myropa followed Arayallen from the sitting room through a maze of passageways. When she was nearly certain they were retracing their steps, Arayallen stopped at a massive door carved with swirling runes, presumably part of some godly language. Arayallen lifted her hands in supplication, and her face held the first peaceful expression Myropa had seen on the goddess for some time. The runes on the door began to glow and move in whirling eddies, and then the doors opened of their own accord.

A flash of light blinded Myropa, and it took a moment for her vision to return. When it did, the goddess already stood inside the room beside a short pedestal. As Myropa entered, she could see there were many such pedestals arrayed around a cloudlike floor, each with a different artifact, scroll, or container crowning it. The one before Arayallen held an unremarkable clay tablet. The goddess, however, regarded it with reverence, and Myropa knew she was looking at something special.

As she turned and walked around the pillar, Arayallen's bright aura retreated, and she shrank to the size of a tall human woman. Her expression was a mixture of cunning and contemplation, and she frequently glanced at Myropa. During one such glance, she smirked in a way that sent a shiver through Myropa's already icy core. Finally, the goddess stopped before her and said, "How are things with Disevy?"

"I don't know what you mean," said Myropa. "He has said nothing to me about your war—"

"I'm not talking about the war," said Arayallen. "I want to know about *you* and *him*." There was a knowing glint in the goddess's eye.

Myropa would have blushed if she could have. The question shook her. Surely Arayallen could not know about Myropa's betrayal. Her fingers itched to grasp the secret orbs hanging at her waist, but she managed to still them so as not to draw attention to the little treasures. She said, "I have not seen Disevy of late. I think there is nothing to tell."

"Oh, I very much doubt that. Gods are nothing if not dedicated to a cause, and I believe Disevy's cause is *you*." She reached out and stroked a lock of Myropa's hair back from her face, then continued. "At the moment, *I* have you, which puts Disevy at a disadvantage."

Myropa's eyes widened. "Am I your prisoner?"

Arayallen's laugh was joyful and sweet, unlike her expression. "Of course not. Even *I* cannot override the power of the Fates. For all my power, I could not keep you here against their will. What I do to you while you're here, though, is my prerogative."

Myropa wanted to run or disappear beyond the veil, yet she was once again frozen where she stood. It was not Arayallen's power that kept her there, but fear—fear for what the goddess might do to those Myropa cared about if she ran. Would the goddess take out her fury on Aaslo just to spite her and Disevy? Myropa didn't dare move, despite Arayallen's conniving smirk.

Arayallen began speaking again as if she hadn't just threatened Myropa's existence. "As you know, I found the wind demon—little thanks to *you*."

"You did? Where is it?"

Arayallen frowned at her and shook her head as if Myropa were daft. "You were *with* me. It's running around on Aldrea with that little . . . what's it called? . . . oh, yes, *forester*."

Myropa gasped and covered her mouth to hide her shock and concern. After composing herself, she casually said, "Really? What is it?"

Arayallen threw her hands in the air. "Can you believe it? Of course Trostili would think to do something like this. All he thinks about is battles and warmongering and weapons and *cavalry*."

It took Myropa a moment to process the goddess's words, and then she was flabbergasted. "*Dolt* is the wind demon?"

Arayallen looked at her, astounded. "I know! That beautiful, realm-defying creature is none other than the forester's *horse*. A horse! I had initially thought the wind demon stolen by Axus, but when I saw what was done with it, I *knew*." She balled her fists and screeched, "Trostili!"

Myropa blinked at the goddess as she waited for the room to stop shaking. Finally, she ventured, "What are you going to do about it? You won't hurt him, will you?"

Arayallen frowned again. "Hurt who?"

"Um, Dolt."

"Of course not. He is *my* creation, after all, even if I didn't intend him to be a horse. The question is, why is he with the forester? What is Trostili up to?"

Myropa shook her head adamantly. "I truly do not know."

"Well, we cannot leave it like this. The forester is all that is standing between Trostili and Axus and the end of all life—all *my* life—on Aldrea. Do you know what will happen if that many lives pass beyond the veil at once?" Myropa shook her head, but Arayallen continued without her response. "You are a reaper. You should know that Axus gains power every time a soul passes through the veil to be taken to the Sea of Transcendence."

Myropa nodded. It had never been so boldly stated, but she had guessed as much. She said, "But once it's in the Sea, he can no longer use the power."

Arayallen pursed her lips. "Yes, and no. I know you have seen them—the whirlpools in the Sea. Souls have been taken. I believe it is Axus's doing, but how he's doing it is beyond me. Still, the fact that only a few are missing means that it is not easy for him. The easiest way for him to gain power is to take it from the worlds."

"So, him destroying all life on Aldrea is part of a bigger picture. It has something to do with his power *here*."

"Precisely. The more he destroys *there*, the stronger he grows *here*. So, you see, my interest in Aldrea isn't just about my ego. Those are my creations, but more importantly, that is *my* power he is stealing—mine and that belonging to every other god who blesses that world. Axus doesn't care about Aldrea. He's making a play for Celestria, and I intend to stop him with or without Disevy's help. That's where *you* come in."

"*Me?* I'm just a reaper. What can *I* do?"

"I have decided to do something unpredictable, and your relationship with the forester is advantageous."

"The forester?"

"Yes, he is Trostili's unwitting champion in all this. Trostili has chosen this forester to wage the war he wants, all the while setting him up to fail. I intend to make sure that Trostili—and, thereby, Axus—doesn't get what he wants. There are only two solutions. Either the forester cannot be allowed to wage this war, thereby limiting Trostili's power; or, he must prevail, which is preposterous given the prophecy." She met Myropa's anxious gaze. "The forester trusts you."

"To an extent," Myropa said cautiously.

"He will once you finally tell him your little secret. You're *going* to tell him, and when you do, you will put my plan in place."

Myropa's heart leapt into her throat at the thought of confessing to Aaslo all that she knew about his past. She had been holding on to the secret for so long, it had started to feel as though she were intentionally deceiving him. If she told him the truth of his origins now, he would probably turn away from her forever. She didn't think the truth would inspire trust. "But I don't think I can. What good would it do?"

"What good? It could save Celestria."

"And Aldrea?"

Arayallen rolled her eyes. "Aldrea is done for. You know the prophecy. You need to get past that. I know your little human mind is probably having trouble keeping up, but listen to me. This is a fight for Celestria. Axus grows in power and allies. Already Axus has the support of the First and Sixth Pantheons, as well as many members of the Fifth. Things cannot continue. I intend to bless that forester in a unique way, and you are going to do it for me."

Myropa's eyes widened. "What?"

"I said listen," snapped Arayallen. "You are going to bless him for me."

"I can't *bless* someone."

"No, of course you can't." Arayallen raised her hands and spun as if indicating the room in general. "*This* is the Fourth Pantheon vault. Every pantheon has one. It is where items, beings, and other *things* of great power are held—things that cannot fall into the hands of outsiders." She circled back to the pedestal containing the clay tablet. "I have brought you here for *this*." She brushed her hand fondly over the tablet. "This tablet contains the power of creation, *my* power. At this time, I cannot go to Aldrea to bless the forester myself. It would leave the pantheon unprotected. Therefore, I am going to bestow upon you the knowledge to read from this tablet—just the tiniest fraction, mind you. Once you do, you will take with you some of my power.

Don't look so terrified. You will not be able to access it. You will carry it within you in the same way you carry the souls you collect."

Myropa furrowed her brow. "I'll put it in one of my spheres?"

Arayallen eyed the spheres hanging from Myropa's belt, and Myropa immediately regretted drawing attention to them. The goddess tapped her lip and said, "Yes, interesting that you should choose that method. You are the only one who does that, you know."

"What do you mean? Using the spheres is how it has always been done."

"No, it is how *you* have always done it."

"How does everyone else do it?"

Arayallen waved her hand dismissively. "Never mind. You will lure the forester onto the paths where you can touch him—"

"You know about that?"

"—and when you do, you will convince him to accept my power into him."

Arayallen made it sound so easy, but Myropa knew it wouldn't be, regardless of whether she told Aaslo the truth. "Why does he have to accept it? I thought the gods could bless anyone they wanted."

"We can, of course, but the blessing is more powerful if it is accepted; and, since *you* will be the one to deliver it, I want to make sure it takes full effect."

"How will I convince him?"

Arayallen sighed. "You are only human, but you are an intelligent human. I know. I created you. You can figure it out. Lean into your relationship with him."

"I don't *have* a relationship with him. He barely trusts me as it is." Arayallen gave her a knowing look, one that said Myropa should have already figured it out, and she *had*. In order to get Aaslo to trust her, she was going to have to come clean. She only hoped that he didn't hate her for it. She swallowed hard and straightened her spine. "I don't know if I can do this—if I'm *willing* to do this. What will your power do to him?"

"What it does is none of your business, Reaper. You *will* do this. If you want any chance at a future with Disevy, you will do this. Besides, you really don't want to find out what the power will do to *you* if you don't."

Myropa clenched her fists to try to keep from shaking. She could tell by Arayallen's smirk she had failed. Arayallen lifted the tablet into her hands and held it before Myropa. Then she pointed at the script and said, "Read."

The sound of the goddess's voice echoed through her mind, and

Myropa became lightheaded and dizzy. She blinked several times until the tablet came into focus. Then she took in the words. Her mind was suddenly filled with knowledge she couldn't access—like words of a language she didn't know. A warm power filled her to near bursting before it settled into a comfortable hum just beneath the surface. It seeped slowly into one of the empty orbs at her belt. Myropa's focus shattered as the power to read the tablet was suddenly ripped away. She stumbled and fell, gasping for air she didn't need. Reeling, she looked up at the goddess. Arayallen stared down at her knowingly before a sadistic grin crept across her face. Myropa began to fear the power filling her, and she despaired at what it might do to Aaslo.

Myropa left Arayallen's temple with a heavy heart and a body buzzing with energy. For the first time, she felt the ice in her veins fracturing and melting. She may not be able to access Arayallen's power, but she *felt* it, despite the fact that it was now contained within one of the orbs at her belt. The energy radiated from the orb to suffuse her body with enough warmth for her to feel her fingers and face once more. She shook as she considered the repercussions if Trostili noticed the difference upon her arrival at the Fifth Pantheon. If he knew she carried Arayallen's power, he would think her a traitor, and there was no telling what the God of War would do to a traitor.

When she arrived, the Fifth Pantheon buzzed with activity. Axus's godly sycophants, mostly lesser beings who hoped to reap some benefit from his growing power, scurried about like rats in a grain mill. Myropa was thankful that Axus himself did not appear to be present, although that could change at any minute. It was bad enough she had to meet with Trostili. She didn't need the scrutiny of *two* hostile gods.

As she neared Trostili's quarters, she turned a corner and ran into a wall of muscle. She lost her footing and fell but never made it to the floor. Strong arms wrapped around her, and she looked up into Disevy's handsome, stern face. As their gazes met, his expression softened, and he smiled.

"Myropa, my lovely reaper. This is a most pleasurable surprise."

Myropa blushed, and he must have noticed because he tilted his head curiously and brushed his fingers across her cheek.

"So warm," he muttered as if to himself.

Myropa struggled to get her feet under her, but it was difficult with the way he had her contained within his grasp. "Oh, I'm so sorry, Disevy. I didn't mean to run into you. I didn't feel your power."

"No? That is fortunate," he rumbled as he set her on her feet but didn't release her.

As he held her against him, Myropa felt his warmth suffusing her core, and she sighed. Embarrassed, she glanced up at him through thick lashes. His eyes glowed with power as he smiled down at her, then his gaze dropped to her lips. For one long moment, all thoughts of betraying Aaslo escaped her mind. She wondered if what Arayallen said was true. Could she truly have a future with Disevy? Would this specimen of male perfection, this god of strength and virility and compassion, truly desire her, and if so, could it ever be more than a fantasy? The tenderness and passion in his gaze gave her the strength to imagine it could be true. He leaned toward her, and she held an unnecessary breath. Just when she thought he would kiss her, he drew back and let her go.

Disevy took her hand in his and raised it to his lips, placing upon it a chaste kiss. He said, "Have you found your truth yet, my love?"

Love? Myropa dared to hope that he meant the endearment as she replayed his words. "My truth? I don't know what you mean."

His expression fell, and he appeared truly saddened by the news. "No, I can see that you do not." He straightened as if to shake off whatever feelings had consumed him and said, "What brings you here to the Fifth Pantheon?"

Myropa held back a cringe. "Trostili called for me."

"Ah, I see. He is not in the best of moods. Perhaps you should ignore him this time."

Myropa's eyes widened, and she gripped her skirt anxiously. "No, I couldn't possibly ignore a god's call, especially that of Trostili. I am assigned to serve him."

Disevy opened his mouth to say something, then thought better of it. He cleared his throat. "Walk softly around that one today, my dear. I do not want to have to destroy him should he harm you." Before Myropa could respond to his declaration, he said, "I will see you soon, my love."

As he moved to step around her, Myropa's courage overtook her. "Disevy?"

He stopped beside her and leaned in as if to confide a secret. "Yes, my dear?"

Myropa glanced down the empty corridor then lowered her voice and said, "Please forgive my impertinence, but I would like to know— why do you support Axus?"

As he stared at her, she wondered if she had gone too far. Then he raised his hand to brush his fingers against her cheek. Although his lips never moved, she heard his voice clearly in her mind. *"Things are not always as they seem, my love."* He turned and walked away, leaving her standing in the hallway in wonder.

A door opened at the end of the corridor, and Trostili's head appeared. The God of War scowled at her and shouted, "There you are. Get in here. I am tired of waiting."

Myropa hurried forward, skirting the thunderous god as she entered the room, to find that Trostili was not alone. Axus, the God of Death, himself, stood in the center of the sitting area, a goblet in his hand and a furious expression on his perfectly sculpted face. He stared her down, then looked back to Trostili, who had closed the door and now hovered over her from behind. Myropa could not force her feet to take her farther into the room, yet she could not retreat. She was rooted in a trap between two apex predators, both looking like they would tear into her.

"Well, have you done it?" barked Axus.

Myropa glanced at Trostili, only to find him staring at her as well. She blinked, realizing Axus had been speaking to *her*, and looked back at him. "D-done what?"

He closed the distance between them in two strides, and Myropa found herself shaking beneath his power. "I *told* you to get Disevy to show you how to enter the pantheon vault."

As he leaned over her, Myropa slowly lowered to the floor until she was on her knees and barely able to hold herself upright.

Trostili said, "Back off, Axus. She cannot speak if you don't contain yourself. Besides, she is only a reaper. What makes you think Disevy would show *her* how to access the pantheon vault?"

Axus's gaze snapped to Trostili. "Do you pay attention to nothing? Disevy has been completely and utterly preoccupied with this wretch. Why do you think he is not here now? He has not set foot in the pantheon in weeks. He is probably off looking for *her*."

Despite her terror, Myropa's curiosity was piqued. Axus and Trostili apparently didn't know that Disevy had been skulking about the halls—if a god could *skulk*. She remembered how he had completely restrained his power before running into her. What had Disevy been up to?

Trostili stepped over Myropa to pour himself a drink at the sideboard, then turned back toward Axus. "She is merely a distraction. Do not underestimate Disevy. He leads this pantheon for a reason."

"Only because he is the oldest of us—"

"And the most powerful."

"He will not be for long." Axus knocked back his drink then

casually threw the goblet against the wall. He leaned down and grasped Myropa's jaw in a punishing grip. Through clenched teeth, he said, "Find a way into that vault or I will issue you a punishment that will make reaping seem a pleasure."

Myropa's eyes watered from the pain, and she briefly regretted being able to feel again. She barely managed to get words past his tight grip. "Perhaps if you tell me what you want from the vault—"

"What I *want*?" Axus shouted as he raised his hand to strike her.

Trostili stopped his fist mid-swing and casually said, "She has a point."

Axus rounded on the God of War. "What are you talking about?"

"Even if he does take her there—which I don't think he will—she likely will not be able to return to it. If you tell her what you want, perhaps she can grab it the first time."

Axus narrowed his eyes at Trostili, looking for some sign of subterfuge. His gaze slid back to Myropa, who lay huddled on the floor, tears streaming down her face. Axus lowered to a crouch and jerked her head back by the hair so she was forced to look at him. "There are six souls in that vault—*six*. They are called the *depraved*. I want them all, and this is important so listen well, Reaper. Disevy must not know you've taken them; and, above all else, he must not know they are for *me*. Do you understand?"

Axus's power spilled over her, and Myropa was suddenly drowning in devastation—all that was light and good and beautiful in every realm had been destroyed. An all-consuming desire to seek the peace and solitude of the Afterlife struck her like a heavy blow, and Myropa would have completely collapsed if Axus had not been holding her head.

"Yes, I understand—the depraved," she mewled, barely able to get the sound past her lips. Pain erupted in her head, and her vision split. When it cleared again, Axus was gone, and only Trostili stood in his place.

The God of War looked down at her, but by his troubled expression, his mind seemed to be elsewhere. After a moment, he quietly said, "Can you do it?"

Myropa whimpered. "I think not."

Trostili nodded once as if relieved and said, "You may go."

Myropa didn't wait for him to change his mind. She inhaled the breath of life and crossed the veil.

CHAPTER 4

MYROPA SAT, WAITING, BENEATH THE TALL REDWOOD, LEANING AGAINST the rough bark with her feet pulled up beneath her. She had left Trostili for the realm of the living out of expediency but had immediately reentered Celestria in search of Disevy. He was not at his temple, and she didn't know where to find him. He had pulled his power in so tightly that even she could not feel it. A breeze blew across her face, and she felt its soft caress on her skin. She lifted her nose to the air and smelled the heady scent of evergreen mingled with a light lilt of lilacs. It had been so long since the senses of touch, taste, and smell had assailed her. Thanks to Arayallen's power running through her, she could experience the world as it was meant to be experienced, to a small degree. Sensations were not as sharp nor as strong as they had been when she was alive. She wondered what might happen if she simply kept Arayallen's power. Then she remembered Arayallen's wrath toward Trostili, and she dismissed the idea. She could not afford to underestimate or anger the Goddess of the Wilderness.

The moment Disevy arrived, Myropa felt it. His power suffused the land and air and forest, imbuing them with strength and fortitude. Myropa sighed with pleasure. She rose and shuffled toward the temple entrance. She found Disevy awaiting her. He smiled, but his eyes looked sad. She wondered what affected him so and hoped it had nothing to do with *her*.

"Lovely Myropa, thank you for coming."

"Hello, Disevy. I, um, was hoping to speak with you. Do you have a moment?"

"For you, I have infinite moments—at least, I would if it were up to me. Unfortunately, events in the pantheons threaten to overcome us."

"That's what I wanted to talk with you about. There are some things I think you should know."

A gleam entered his eyes and he took her hands, pulling them to his chest. "You have secrets, my dear Myropa? And you would share them with me?"

Her eyes widened in surprise. Did he not know how she felt about him? She felt guilty. She had been bathing in his affection for some time yet had shown none in return. In truth, she had not thought herself worthy of showing him affection. He was a *god*, after all. Why should the God of Strength and Virility want affection from a lowly reaper? Still, he seemed to desire it.

She took an unnecessary breath to strengthen her resolve then tugged their joined hands toward her. She placed a kiss upon his knuckles as she searched his eyes for disapproval. She said, "I would share everything with you, Disevy."

Myropa chirped as he swept her from her feet and carried her farther into the temple. He grew in size as he approached a set of steps that each would have reached to Myropa's waist, mounting them with ease as he carried her to the second floor. There he set her down in a room that took her breath away. A mound of cushions and pillows of the finest silks and velvets in an array of colors and textures nestled in its center. Along the walls, tables and pedestals held exotic plants, most of which Myropa had never before seen, including entire trees. Above it all soared a ceiling of glass. Colorful birds flitted between the branches of the trees and filled the air with joyful song.

"This is beautiful, Disevy. Thank you for bringing me here."

Disevy pointed up and said, "Birds are my favorite creations of Arayallen's. I love how they defy the pull to the land, and their songs ease my mind."

Myropa smiled, happy to know such a personal detail about Disevy.

He said, "Please, come sit with me." He tugged her toward the cushions. His size returned to that of a human man, although he was still quite large. Once seated, he pulled her to his side and wrapped his arm around her. "What concerns you, my dear?"

Myropa felt unbidden tears come to her eyes, and for the first time since her death, her body had the power to produce them. Disevy wiped one away with his thumb as it rolled down her cheek. She said, "It's about Axus and Trostili. No, it's about Arayallen." She shook her head as her muddled thoughts sloshed around in her mind. "No, no, it's definitely about Axus."

"Tell me," he said with concern and a hint of an edge.

She met his gaze and then everything tumbled out at once. "Axus wants me to convince you to take me into the pantheon vault so that I can steal something called the *depraved*. Only I think you already gave them to me"—she held up five of the six orbs containing the souls Disevy had given to her for safekeeping—"and I gave one away to Aaslo, and he put it in the body of a dead magus, and now I fear you hate me."

As the tears streamed down Myropa's face, Disevy simply stared at her. After a moment, he pulled away and stood. He rubbed his chin thoughtfully, then looked at her. "You say he actually placed one of the depraved *in* a body?"

Myropa swallowed hard. "Y-yes. It's a disturbing creation with terrible power."

"And he can control it?"

"Yes, he has a connection with it. It does his bidding." After a pause, she added, "I'm sorry, Disevy. I know you told me to keep them safe, and I shouldn't have given it to him, but I was desperate to help him in some way. I just feel so powerless all the time. There are so many things I *want* to do, but I can't, and so many things I don't want to do, but I have to. I'm so sorry I betrayed you, please believe me, but I'm not sorry I gave it to him."

Disevy stared at her again. His broad shoulders and chest filled his shirt, the muscles bulging from the opening at the front and from the short sleeves. His brown hair, gleaming in the sunlight with blond highlights, swept his shoulders, and his chiseled jaw begged her to run her lips over it. He was a sight to behold, and if he was angry with her, he could possibly be the last sight she ever saw.

He flexed his hands then dropped them in defeat before crouching down in front of her. He wiped away the tears on her face again and said, "Don't cry, my little reaper. I am not angry with you. You have been placed in an impossible situation, and I cannot fault you for your decisions, especially where Aaslo is concerned. I know what he means to you. You should tell him the truth about why you care so much for him."

Myropa winced. It was the second time that day a god had told her to divulge her secret. With time, though, the secret had grown, and her fears over Aaslo's reaction had consumed her.

Disevy said, "I admire your strength and courage. My sister out-did herself when she blessed you."

Myropa blinked at him in disbelief. She had never thought of herself as blessed by *anyone*, but especially not the Goddess of Strength and Wisdom.

Disevy raised an eyebrow at her. "You do not believe me? How much courage must it take to freely admit to a god that you have betrayed him and beg his forgiveness? I assure you, you are the first to have done so with *me*, and probably any of the others as well."

He handed her a handkerchief, and Myropa wiped her nose. "You are truly not angry with me?"

He shook his head. "No, my love. I could never be angry with you. But I *am* concerned. The depraved were never meant to inhabit another body—especially not one blessed with the power of a magus. I am also concerned that Axus seeks them, and through *you*, no less. Does he truly think he could turn you against me?"

Myropa shook her head furtively. "I would never. I mean—"

He patted her head with a massive hand. "No, I know you would not, especially now that you have proven yourself."

Myropa gazed up at him imploringly, hoping beyond hope that he truly meant it. Had she proved herself worthy of his affection with honesty? She nearly laughed at herself. Of course, the answer was no. Just because she had admitted her faults, that did not mean she was any better than she was before. She was still a mere reaper, and he was still a god.

He caught her gaze and said, "What of the others?"

Myropa's heart jumped. She had promised the other depraved to Aaslo, but now that she had come clean to Disevy, she would not be able to fulfill that promise. Her priorities were at odds with her heart and her conscience, and she was utterly confused. She held up the strings of dangling, glowing orbs and said, "I still have them. Do you wish me to give them back?"

He rubbed his full lips with a thick finger, drawing her attention to them. Then he said, "No, it isn't safe for me to keep them here. I suspected Axus would come for them, which is why I hid them with you. Now that he has asked you to procure them, however, he may begin to suspect you have them. It is no longer safe for you to keep them either."

"Then what?"

His chest rumbled, and he waved a hand through the air as he said, "Give them to Aaslo." Myropa's surprise was not lost on him. He nodded and continued, "If he can place them in bodies, especially bodies with power, it will make it much harder for Axus to reach them."

"Won't that make Aaslo a target?"

"He's already a target. The depraved are safer with Aaslo right now than anywhere else. Besides, they may be of use to him. If he has already placed one in a body, then he has probably seen that they can be a terrible weapon—*if* they can be controlled."

Myropa experienced a long-forgotten sensation as her gut churned with anxiety. She said, "What *are* the depraved?"

Disevy resumed his seat next to her and drew her in close to wrap her in a godly cocoon. Myropa inhaled sharply and her senses filled with the scent of him—evergreens and lilacs. It suddenly occurred to her that Disevy did not exist *within* his temple. He *was* his temple—or, rather, his temple was *him*. She was once again caught in awe of his power, which sent a shiver through her partially thawed body. Disevy tightened his embrace and rubbed his warm hand over her arm.

"Relax, my sweet, and I shall tell you the story."

Myropa released the tension she hadn't realized she'd been holding and laid her head against his chest. With his other hand, he stroked her cheek and hair as he spoke.

"In the beginning, there were six gods."

"The leaders of the six pantheons?"

Disevy nodded. "Yes—Arayallen, Olios, Enani, Azeria, Bayalin, and *me*. We didn't know how we came to exist. One moment, we just *were*—but we *wanted* to know. We wanted to know how we got here, what we were meant for, and what might become of us. Eventually, we thought to answer this question by creating beings of our own making. We thought it might give us insight into our own existence. So, we did. We created the first new beings, six of them. But we weren't fully prepared for what we had created. We hadn't counted on many problems for which we had no answers. Their bodies were not properly formed or functioning, they didn't have sufficient habitats, they couldn't eat, they couldn't sleep, and worst of all, I think, was that they could not *die*. They suffered immeasurably, worse than anything has ever suffered since.

"We learned much from those first six beings, mostly that we had made mistakes. The problem was, once they were created, we couldn't *uncreate* them. They were doomed to eternal suffering, and it took a toll on them. They became twisted and deranged, and were powerful and demented enough to wreak havoc wherever they were placed. Eventually, they no longer resembled our initial creations. They had been transmuted by pain and madness.

"I believe that watching those beings suffer generated the first sensation of guilt. We took pity on them and worked tirelessly to find a way to end their existences, to relieve their pain. Working together, we found a way to rip their essences, their souls, from their bodies. It was terrible. I will never forget the wails of agony that reached into the very depths of my power."

He took a deep, shuddering breath. "We stored the twisted souls away in the pantheon vault and left them there. We didn't know what else to do with them."

Myropa squeezed his hand. "Why not take them to the Sea?"

"Because the Sea of Transcendence did not exist, at first. But, later, we tried. The Sea would not accept them. Much later, when Axus came to exist, he tried to get us to place them in his maelstrom. Those first six beings were more powerful than anything we have created. We could not afford for Axus to gain control of their power, but, also, as deranged as they are, they did not deserve the additional torment he would inflict upon them."

Myropa could only imagine what Axus would do with such twisted souls, but more importantly, she had to know what their power meant. She said, "Why is it so important that Axus doesn't get ahold of them?"

"They are the original six beings created by the original six gods. They are immensely powerful, but their madness makes them unpredictable and cruel. If Axus could control and direct that power, he could potentially overcome any god in Celestria. We suspected that the combined power of the deranged could *end* a god."

"You mean *kill* you?"

He released a sigh. "Perhaps. We cannot know until it is attempted, and I suspect Axus *would* attempt it."

Myropa was suddenly overwhelmed by the immensity of the danger the depraved posed. She felt horrible about the prospect of dumping it all on Aaslo, then the truth of what Disevy had done struck her. "You entrusted *me* with the power to *kill* you?"

Disevy stroked her jaw, turning her face up toward him. Barely a breath away, he looked down into her eyes. His own eyes gleamed with the golden light of power as he searched her face. "I am sorry for placing you in such danger, my love. Can you forgive me?"

Myropa's voice threatened to abandon her, but she managed, "That's not what I meant."

His lips turned up, and he said, "I know what you meant." Then those sensual lips were crushing hers. His kiss, soft yet firm, sought permission and demanded her affection. His tongue brushed across the seam of Myropa's lips, and she opened for him. Myropa felt the pulse of his power, like a heartbeat, as his tongue plundered her mouth. He tasted of all things sweet and decadent as desire rolled through her, further fracturing her icy core. Myropa's blood began to warm, and she felt tingles of sensation and power dance across her face and through her fingertips. She reached up and dug her hands into Disevy's hair as she pressed closer to him.

Disevy loomed over her, pushing her back into the pillows until she was trapped beneath him, yet he held himself above her so as not to crush her. His fingers slowly trailed down her jaw to her neck, where they stalled over her throat. And then . . .

Thump. Thump, thump.

Ice cracked, and her heart lurched.

Thump. Thump, thump.

He rubbed his thumb across her throat where her pulse would throb if she were alive. The thumping sped up, and Myropa could feel her heart beating for the first time in decades. Disevy renewed his efforts to explore her mouth with fervor. Her blood surged as her heart raced. Myropa drank down his power with every flick of his tongue, and her heartbeat grew steady.

Then he was pulling away. He laid his forehead on her own as they both breathed heavily. "My sweet Myropa, you have no idea what you do to me."

Myropa laid her palm over her chest and marveled at the sensation, of the steady rhythm of movement. She looked up at Disevy with wide eyes. "What have you done to *me*?"

He pressed a soft kiss to her cheek then whispered into her ear, "I have done nothing, dear reaper. That is all *you*." Disevy searched her gaze one last time, then abruptly stood. "I must go, and so must you. Please, stay away from Celestria if you can. I fear Axus will target you."

Myropa sat up and couldn't help herself as the words tumbled from her mouth. "If Axus is such a threat, why do you not stop him?"

Disevy glanced away, and his eyes lost focus as if he were looking into the distance. "To stop him now would be folly."

"But he's barely started. Surely there is time while he is weaker—"

"No," he said firmly. When he spied the look of fear on her face, he softened his tone. "I'm sorry I cannot explain it to you, my dear. I only ask that you trust me."

Myropa closed her mouth and nodded once. "I do."

He smiled fondly then turned and exited the temple. Myropa was left reeling over what had just happened. Disevy had kissed her. The God of Strength and Virility had *kissed* her—*her*, a mere reaper. Arayallen's words began running through her mind in a loop. If she ever wanted a future with Disevy, she had to give Aaslo Arayallen's blessing—or *curse*, whichever it may be, as ordered; and one thing was for sure—she *really* wanted a future with Disevy. But she would have to betray Aaslo to get it.

Aaslo retraced his steps down the foggy path as Ijen followed behind him, pen poised above an open blank page in the book of prophecy. Aaslo grumbled his opinion on the idiocy of his horse then raised his head to squint into the distance. Twisted trees and short, gnarled shrubs dotted the foggy landscape of the paths, and a monstrous shadow shifted in the haze. Cool moisture beaded on Aaslo's brow as he considered his options.

"Serves you right for putting your faith in your disastrous horse to lead the way."

Dolt bolted some time ago, leaving him, his comrades, and two thousand survivors stranded in the pathways without a guide. At first, Aaslo waited, expecting the ornery horse to return, but after three hours he came to the realization that Dolt had abandoned him and taken his supplies. The people closest to Aaslo were anxious. The masses had been told they were stopping for a break, however his inner circle knew they had been following a horse. He *told* them it was a bad idea. Yet they had insisted on putting their faith in a ninny-headed horse with an obvious mental disorder.

Teza spoke into the silence. "You said a goddess showed you how to use the paths. What was her name?"

"Enani," growled Aaslo. "And she didn't as much show me as throw it in my face."

"At least she gave you a map."

"A map?" Aaslo paused in his pacing as he recalled that first mental image of the paths. He had been in a small clearing surrounded by branches; upon each were scenes of places and people. Enani had stood tall over him and explained that the knowledge to navigate the paths was already within him.

"I suppose it *was* a sort of map," Aaslo mused.

"You have a map?" said Teza, abruptly standing from the downed log upon which she had been seated. "Why didn't you say so?"

Aaslo waved her off and closed his eyes as he tried to focus on the image. He felt a shift in the air, then he was looking down upon himself from above. Teza stood staring at him expectantly while Ijen hovered over his book, scribbling something illegible. Aaslo felt himself pulling away, and the scene became smaller. He could see the trail of followers, thousands of them, dotting the path they had traveled. They looked tired and worn and most seemed content to rest. As Aaslo pulled away from the scene, he once again found himself standing in the grove surrounded by tangled limbs upon which were images of innumerable places—too many. He wondered how he would find the path to Monsque, the capital city in the northernmost province of Pashtigon.

From his mere thought about the city, a light began to gleam on a distant branch. Aaslo muscled through the branches, shoving various images aside, until he stood before the illuminated limb. There flickered a city tucked between a great lake to the south and a mountain range to the west. Aaslo had never been to Monsque, and he dearly wished he had Magdelay's maps for comparison, but they had disappeared with his wily horse.

"*You should have memorized the maps.*"

Aaslo said, "Really? All of them?"

"*I would have.*"

"No, you wouldn't have. You didn't bother to memorize a single trail in Goldenwood."

"*That was Goldenwood. This is the world.*"

"Exactly. It's bigger, and you were lazy."

"*Me? Lazy? I trained daily and I walked the forest with you—for no good reason, I might add.*"

"You had a good reason. You wanted to spend time with me."

"*Well, that was a reason, but I'm not sure it was a good one.*"

"Very funny. Why don't you help me memorize *this* path so I can get all these people to Monsque?"

"*You're so good at memorizing paths, you do it.*"

"Obviously, I'll have to, since you're no help. Why have you been so quiet?"

"*Did you miss me?*"

Aaslo huffed. "Like a thorn in my boot."

"*I've been busy.*"

"You're dead. How busy can you be?"

Mathias said nothing, but he continued to hum an annoying tune in the back of Aaslo's mind. Still, after so much silence, Aaslo didn't mind. It reassured him that Mathias was still with him, even if he *was* dead.

Once he memorized the path to Monsque, Aaslo approached the blue door set into the grove's central trunk. He raised his fist and sounded the forester's gong with a heavy *thump*. The door abruptly opened, and Aaslo fell through.

His body shook.

"Aaslo! Are you okay? Hello?"

Aaslo shooed away the hands rocking him. "I'm fine. Stop. Get off."

"Thank goodness you're back," replied Teza. "You weren't responding. It was like your body was here but your mind was gone."

"*So, business as usual?*"

"Very funny."

"It wasn't funny, Aaslo. Stop messing around," grumped Teza.

Aaslo straightened his tunic and met her irritated gaze. "I wasn't messing around. I was getting directions." He turned in the direction he knew he should go, and there in the distance he saw a flicker. After a moment, the pinpoint of blue light grew brighter, and then a thin stream of glistening, golden light lit the trail. "There," said Aaslo, "we follow the light."

"What light?" said Teza.

Ijen paused in his writing and said, "What does the light look like? How big is it? Where does it go?"

Aaslo pointed at the trail, but as he looked, something shifted in the fog—something *big*. The shadowy figure moved closer and took form. Teza spun and set her feet in fighting position, and the nearest guards shouted and drew their weapons. Greylan and Rostus moved forward to stare in the direction of the incoming beast with milky-white eyes. Whether they could see the creature or simply responded to the energy of the moment, Aaslo didn't know. Just as Aaslo reached for his sword, Dolt came into view.

Aaslo immediately deflated. *Of course* his horse would show up *after* he discovered the way. It wasn't until he heard a terrible screech that he realized his relief was premature. He now noticed that Dolt ran faster than ever, and the shadowy figure that loomed behind him was closing. Aaslo drew Mathias's sword and ran toward Dolt in the hope that he would arrive in time to save the stubborn beast from a gruesome demise.

A beastly paw, twice Dolt's size, emerged from the mist to pound into the ground. Its claws, each as long as the horse's legs, ripped into the dirt. A moment later, a second paw joined the first and was followed by the emergence of a head unlike anything Aaslo could have imagined. Its entire face was naught but a gaping maw filled with three rows of razor-sharp teeth. Two red eyes stood out from the mouth on long stalks to either side, and they pivoted back and forth as three sinuous, split tongues snaked toward the horse. A reddish-orange slime coated the creature's leathery skin, and it sloughed off in long globs as the beast lurched toward its prey. Dolt dodged the tongues' attempt to snare him, and equally slimy spittle flew from the creature's throat to splatter Aaslo and his companions. Ijen managed to raise his own shield ward in time to save himself the mess, but Aaslo and Teza weren't so lucky.

"That's a good look for you, Aaslo."

Greylan and Rostus raised their swords, and the guards and soldiers around them prepared their own weapons. Aaslo sensed something shift inside, and when he turned, he saw his undead move as one toward the creature with weapons raised. Dolt ran past them all as the creature following him stomped into the crowd of soldiers and undead. The monster careened forward and snapped up several men in its enormous mouth. Aaslo heard the marquess shout for the remaining followers—those who could not or would not fight—to fall back. Meanwhile, the creature trampled all indiscriminately.

"Aaslo, do something!" shouted Teza. "We need to get out of here."

"The way is blocked," Aaslo replied.

Ijen calmly stated, "With all this fog, there is no way to tell the creature's size or if there might be more."

"We can see that," Aaslo grumbled. "Do you have anything useful to say?"

Ijen pursed his lips, reached over, and daintily plucked a glob of mucus off Aaslo's shoulder. As it slipped toward the ground in a slimy string, he released a spell that caused it to ignite in a sizzling burst. "I might suggest the use of fire."

Teza grinned and raised a palm already filled with flame. "That's the first useful thing you've ever said." She lobbed the fireball toward the slimy monstrosity already chewing its second course. The fireball burst against the creature's knee and a string of fire surged up its leg. The creature screeched and stomped until the flaming slime slipped from its body and smothered beneath a clawed foot. As Teza lit her hands with another round, the flame caught the creature's attention, and it turned to face them. Its tongues arrowed toward them in a squirming mass, and Aaslo raised Mathias's sword. The first of the tongues was severed in a bloody spray that covered everyone but Ijen, while the second and third made a direct line for Teza. She tossed both fireballs in a hurry before the first tongue wrapped around her waist. Aaslo watched the shock register on her face before her helmet covered her head. It did nothing to muffle her scream as the tongue retracted toward the toothy maw.

With a shout, Aaslo ran to catch the retreating tongue. He knew he could not keep up, and in that split second, he made an unconscious decision. He called to his undead minions, and they responded. Half a dozen of the wanderers, led by Greylan and Rostus, fell on the tongue, stabbing, cutting, and slashing at it with abandon. Ijen released a stream of flame at the tongue, which quickly caught alight. The massive creature released a wail and dropped Teza. She clattered to the ground in a metallic jumble before she could regain her feet. Aaslo reached her, and she turned to him with searing anger.

"Fire, Aaslo. Make fire!"

Aaslo nodded once and sheathed his sword. He had made fire before. He could do it again.

"Any day now."

As Ijen and Teza continued spilling flame onto the monstrous creature, Aaslo racked his brain to remember how to conjure fire. The mere thought of the inferno he wanted to create made the beast inside rear up and flap its wings with glee, then it inhaled sharply and held its breath. As the scalding firestorm built within him, Aaslo shouted for everyone to retreat. The darker power he held at bay slipped in and out of his inner beast's legs as it called to his undead to fall back. Teza's and Ijen's fiery distraction prevented the monster from pursuing Aaslo's people as they scurried to safety.

The monster reared into the fog and lurched forward. Before Aaslo could be trampled, he released the torrent building inside him. An immense wall of flame surged toward the monster, engulfing everything in its path, including Ijen and Teza. The inferno enveloped the monster, setting its slimy exterior alight. The surrounding fog burned away, and they saw the monster's entirety in the fire. A beast the size of a city building thrashed as it wailed and screamed in agony. Aaslo might have felt sorry for the creature had it not eaten or trampled so many of his people. The beast ran, flailing, into the fog, and Aaslo did not breathe easy until he could no longer hear its torment.

Breathing heavily, Aaslo dragged his feet toward Ijen and Teza. Teza's gleaming armor appeared unmarred, but the prophet was a little worse for wear. Wisps of smoke wafted off the man's tunic as he plucked at it.

"I'm lucky my ward held," said Ijen as he pinched out a spark. "I was not sure it would. Your flame is more incendiary than the typical fire spells."

"Good to know," said Aaslo. "And thank you for helping us defeat it."

Ijen smiled pleasantly and said, "It was no problem, of course."

Aaslo rolled his eyes. "Of course—because you're always so accommodating."

"I do what I can."

Teza tromped up to the prophet and retracted her helmet. "But do you really?" she said accusingly.

Ijen smiled. "Always."

Aaslo ignored the ensuing squabble between the two magi and chose instead to lead his people through the treacherous paths toward Monsque. The slimy monster was not the only creature they encountered, but it was the largest and most threatening. Aaslo had to split his living and undead forces so that they could protect the column of refugees. By the time they left the paths, more than a dozen people had been killed—ten of which joined his undead forces—and three were lost when they wandered away or ran from predators. Aaslo hoped they would eventually find their way out and that the places in which they found themselves would be hospitable.

After several attacks, it became increasingly difficult to mobilize the column as one. While some people wanted to be free of the paths as quickly as possible, others protested any forward advancement in favor of going back the way they had come. Some were so stricken with fear they could not move in either direction. Reactions toward Aaslo were just as varied. Many clung to him for protection, but others viewed him with distrust or outright hostility, as if he had set them on this dangerous course with the intent to do them harm. When those who had been living suddenly became wanderers, some survivors were comforted that their brethren were still with them, while others acted as if *he* had stolen their lives and refused them rest.

Aaslo met all these reactions with a patience he rarely afforded other people. After all, how could he blame them? He struggled with much of the same inside himself. His no-nonsense forester training encouraged him to lay blame where due and knew he was not responsible for all the bad that had happened. The other part of him, though, the part that doubted himself as a leader and struggled to walk Mathias's rightful path, felt every loss as a failure that lay squarely at his own feet. He wasn't cut out to lead these people, who he had never wanted anything to do with in the first place. These heavy, conflicting thoughts plagued Aaslo as he led his people from the paths into northern Pashtigon.

Aaslo and his people exited the misty, forested paths a few hundred yards from the city gates of Monsque. Aaslo had been informed it was a lovely city, full of a colorful culture and rich with supplies. To his knowledge it remained untouched by the Berruvian forces and lyksvight. Upon arrival, however, it became apparent that citizens had heard of the unrest and were preparing for war. The city was situated in a valley between mountain ranges to the west and east and bordered a massive lake to the south. The air was cooler this far north, and stiff grasses and hearty wildflowers carpeted the windswept meadow between them and the city. The high, cream-colored city walls hid most of the city from view, save for the spires of some taller buildings.

Aaslo saw light reflecting off the armor and arrow tips of the archers dotting the top of the wall between intermittently spaced towers. Two soaring wooden doors at the center of the wall, very firmly closed, barred entry to the city, but a smaller gate to one side released a stream of mounted soldiers that quickly intercepted Aaslo and his people. The squad of brutish warriors was equipped with heavy armor and carrying an assortment of halberds, maces, flails, and swords. The Pashtigonian people garnered a passionate pursuit of both culture *and* war—they obviously left nothing to chance.

Aaslo introduced himself, flanked by Teza and Ijen along with a few dozen dead and undead soldiers. The marquess stayed back to maintain the calm among the people.

"Greetings, I am Aaslo, Forester of Goldenwood in Uyan, and we are the Endricsian resistance against the Berruvian invaders and the evil forces of the dark God of Death, Axus. We seek supplies and recruits."

"That was very well done, Aaslo. Good job dusting off those people skills."

The mounted, helmeted Pashtigonian warriors sat in silence, but Aaslo sensed he was being appraised. As each of their heads turned toward him, their grips tightened on their weapons, and their shoulders tensed. Aaslo did not bother to hide his monstrous side. He figured it was best to keep his differences in the open from the start. If they were going to attack him, they would do so with a smaller squad than with the full might of their army.

Finally, the lead rider gruffly addressed him. "What are you?"

"Only a man—a man changed by circumstance, yes, but I wield the power of the magi, as do my companions here."

"The magi are gone."

"Most, but not all, and certainly not the Berruvian magi. If they have not come here yet, it is only a matter of time. We fight against them and would recruit others who will join us in that fight."

"What are *they*?" said the rider, pointing with his halberd toward a few of the wanderers.

"Careful, Aaslo, they haven't seen what you have. They're not ready for the dead to live again."

Aaslo tilted his head, considering his friend's words, but the truth would be best. "They are the dead, stolen from Axus, risen to once again fight with the living against our enemies."

"They are your doing?"

"They are."

"Then you recruit the dead as well as the living."

"I recruit any who will stand against monsters and gods."

The lead rider chuckled, and his men chuckled with him. "Uyanians are soft. Your king dispersed the army and died a coward's death. I cannot imagine you have found many who would take up your standard."

Aaslo bristled at the accusation of weakness. Although he had not had the occasion—nor the desire—to know much of the lowlanders before the attack, those who stood with him had proven their worth. He said, "Those who have survived the slaughter live to fight, and those who have fallen have sacrificed their afterlives to stand with them."

The lead rider did not respond. Eventually, he removed his helmet, and Aaslo understood why the man had not balked at his appearance. The man was not a man at all, in fact, but a very large woman, broad-shouldered and imposing. Her hair, shorn on both sides of her head but long at the top, was pulled back into a topknot. A mass of scars covered the left side of her face, and that eye was a pale, milky blue and certainly blind. The good side of her face grinned, while the scarred side produced a toothless sneer.

"I am Andromeda, Commander of the Queen's Royal Army. Your living may trade for supplies in Monsque, but your dead must remain outside the city. If you insist on recruiting, however, you will receive no welcome here."

"The Berru intend to wipe out all life on Aldrea. They will not spare Monsque."

"I believe you. That is why you may not recruit here. The Berruvian magi and those *things* we call greylings came through the evergates and decimated the army in southern Pashtigon before we knew we were at war. There are few enough of us to resist now. We need our people to protect the capital."

"Protect the capital? What good will one city be if the rest of the world is doomed to die?"

"The city can sustain itself. We do not need the rest of the world."

"The God of Death intends to consume *all* life. Your people will have no food. Can you not see the futility of your struggle?"

"Can *you*? Reports have been few, but they are all the same. The lands have been overrun with monsters and enemy magi. You will not succeed in your efforts." She narrowed her good eye in appraisal then glanced toward those surrounding him. "You should stay and help defend the city; it will surely remain the last bastion of life."

Aaslo glanced toward the city walls. They were tall and strong, but nothing the Berruvian magi couldn't bring down with a few well-aimed spells. The commander must know this, yet she kept firmly to her orders. And that was what they were—*orders*. She was not the one making the decisions in this city. To change anything, he would need to convince the queen.

"I would speak with your ruler," he said.

The commander barked a husky laugh. "Of course you would, but you cannot. She no longer holds court and refuses to see any but her councilors."

"And *you*."

"Naturally. You are no one. Certainly no one to be demanding an audience with a queen."

Aaslo was surprised when Ijen spoke. "Actually, that is not quite true."

The commander blinked at him curiously. "Who are you?"

"I am Ijen Mascede, Prophet of Aldrea."

Her good eye widened, and she tightened the grip on her reins, causing her horse to bob its head. "A prophet?"

"Indeed. It so happens that Sir Forester Aaslo is also the most powerful magus to walk the land in thousands of years. He is a magus of the First Order, an ancient."

Commander Andromeda's gaze slid to Aaslo. "*Him!* But he is barely human."

Mathias chuckled. *"She's got you there, Aaslo."*

"That would be my fault," said Teza. "I am Healer Mage Catriateza, and I can assure you he is still more human than monster."

"She doesn't truly know you, does she?"

Aaslo cringed. Since the onset of the meeting, he had been holding the beast inside him at bay as it snapped and lunged toward the newcomers. It wanted to dispense with talk. It wanted to hunt, and part of Aaslo was inclined to let it. These people stood in the way of the resources he needed. Ijen was right. Aaslo knew he was powerful. He could simply take what he wanted.

"That doesn't sound like the forester way."

The beast inside him growled.

"This isn't who you are, Aaslo. Take control."

Aaslo shook his head and took a deep breath as he tamped down on the monstrous power of the dragon. In the back of his mind, he heard Ina's light laughter taunting him. Too often, he'd depended on the dragon's power and that of the dark entity in order to avoid her, and he had begun to wonder if that was a mistake. The dragon was becoming too powerful, consuming his mind by increments.

"Wake up!"

Aaslo blinked, and noticed everyone was staring at him. He had lost track of the conversation. Clearing his throat, he said, "Excuse me. What were you saying?"

Teza leaned toward him and spoke softly. "Aaslo, you were growling."

Aaslo shifted the sack at his waist out of habit and scratched the scales on his neck with his claws. He repeated his earlier request. "I require an audience with your queen. I am confident, Commander, that you can make this happen."

She pursed her lips, causing the scars on the left side of her face to pull taut. "Perhaps I can, but why should I?"

"Pashtigonian warriors are famed for their bravery in battle. I think it does not suit you to sit behind pretty walls and watch the world fall."

"I have a duty to my queen and my people. To protect them is the highest honor."

"Except you're *not* protecting them. You're coddling them until the enemy comes in force to overrun your city. While your walls may keep out the roving lyksvight—your greylings—they will not suffice against enemy magi. We must meet the enemy forces en masse. Only a unified front has a chance to change destiny."

"Is that what you're doing? Changing destiny?"

"It's better than succumbing."

"At least we can agree on that. Very well. I will speak with the queen on your behalf, but I guarantee nothing."

"Thank you," said Aaslo. Then he motioned behind him. "I have over two thousand people here. We have few resources and nothing to trade. Still, I ask that they be allowed to seek refuge within the city walls while we wait. They are too exposed here in the open."

Andromeda nodded once. "We can accommodate them so long as they do not make trouble. As I said before, your walking dead must remain out here."

"Fair enough."

ANDROMEDA AND HER WARRIORS RETREATED TO THE CITY TO MAKE arrangements to accommodate the Uyanians. After a couple of hours, she returned, and the long column of refugees and soldiers followed her through the gates. She assigned them to groups that were dispersed throughout the city so as not to overwhelm any one district. Aaslo's wanderers remained outside the city walls in vigilant watch. As he followed the commander through the streets astride Dolt, he plucked at the threads of dark power linking him to the undead.

He felt their presence outside the city, as well as a sense of peace directed at him. He wondered if he would know through their bond if they detected a threat and was determined to hone those senses.

"For someone who prizes solitude, you have a lot of entities sharing your mind and body."

Aaslo nearly laughed at the irony. "Believe me, I am well aware of that."

"You wouldn't know what to do without me, though."

"You may be right. The destiny of the chosen one isn't always clear."

"That's not what I meant. You miss me."

The truth of Mathias's words struck him like an arrow to the chest. He did miss his brother. It had been too long since he had last seen him alive. If not for the head in his bag, he worried that he would forget how his only friend had looked. To his shame, he found himself retrieving the head on occasion, just to gaze upon his dead brother's face. Aaslo pulled the sack into his lap and clutched it to him. He was lost to his thoughts when Myra's voice reached his ears.

"Aaslo, all will be well. You will see him again."

He looked over to see her perched on the back of Teza's horse with the healer unaware. "Are you sure?" he whispered.

Teza glanced over at him but must have realized he wasn't talking to her because she averted her gaze and kept riding.

Myra said, "I have seen it. I release the souls into the Sea of Transcendence, and the others—their friends and kin—swarm around them in a joyful glowing pool. When I step into the Sea, I can feel the warmth of joy and love shared between them. It's beautiful."

Aaslo blinked away unbidden tears and inhaled sharply. "Then I shall strive to not mourn him. Thank you for that, Myra."

She smiled fondly and said, "Of course, Aaslo. It is all I can do to settle your heart. Unfortunately, I am of little use otherwise."

"That's not true. You've been an invaluable fount of knowledge. If not for you, we would be completely lost in this war."

She smiled again and said, "Thank you for saying so. Um, there's something I need to tell you, and it's important."

"You have an audience. Your crazy is showing again."

Aaslo paused when he spied Commander Andromeda scrutinizing him over her shoulder. She lifted an eyebrow at him as if questioning his sanity, then turned back to the road ahead. Aaslo lowered his voice.

"Can it wait?"

Myra's gaze dropped to his frustrating steed. Dolt was gnashing his teeth around the bit and appeared to be trying to lick his own ear. She hesitantly said, "It's most important."

He nodded toward the Pashtigonian warriors leading the way and said, "This is not a good time."

She tilted her head thoughtfully and said, "Yet you can cause time to stop."

Aaslo initially wanted to deny her assertion, then he realized that she was not wrong. Once within the paths, time would stop in Aldrea and he would be able to communicate with her and return before anyone knew he was gone. It took him several minutes to gather the power and focus he needed to open the portal, during which time, Myra moved from Teza's horse to his own. As soon as the flashing rent opened, Aaslo rode through and closed it behind him. With any luck no one would notice.

The gloomy path appeared as it always did, bathed in a perpetual day, but he could not see the sun. The mist and grey clouds obscured everything except the trees and undergrowth. Aaslo briefly wondered if the trees were truly alive or just figments of his imagination made real. He dismounted, stumbling as Dolt turned in circles for seemingly no reason. The horse continued circling as it drifted away, then abruptly paused before chomping on the leaves of a suspicious-looking bush. Aaslo watched for a moment before electing to ignore him, and hoped that Dolt didn't drop dead from some poison.

He turned to Myra, now standing at his side. "What is this all about?"

Myra ran a hand through her dark tresses and sighed. "So many things." For the briefest moment, he thought he saw guilt, or possibly regret, pass over her face, and she added, "But I am not prepared to broach some of them yet." She lifted a handful of orbs that dangled from her belt and said, "For now, I must give these to you."

Aaslo shook his head. "I do not wish for you to anger the gods."

"It is upon Disevy's orders. He already knows."

"Uh-oh. Now a god wants you to have them. You know they're cursed."

"You told him?" said Aaslo.

She looked at him apologetically. "I had to. I could not keep this from him. You must know that Axus wants these dearly. He may begin to suspect I have them. Disevy believes they will be safer with you."

"Did he tell you what they are?"

"He did." Myra recounted the history of the depraved and what they could mean for the future, or rather, the *end* of a god.

Aaslo was shocked. "Disevy entrusts *me* with the power to kill a god?"

Myra's face scrunched in uncertainty. "It's possible. No one really knows what their combined power could do."

"I thought Axus was a member of Disevy's pantheon. Is he not afraid I will use the power against *him*?"

Myra shook her head. "I do not think Disevy supports Axus's cause, but for reasons unknown to me he does not interfere."

Aaslo stared at the glowing orbs for a moment. He could not fully comprehend the power contained in the tiny vessels. Yet, if he accepted them, that power would be his.

"Take them!"

The god's trust humbled Aaslo, and he thought perhaps he should begin to pay homage to the God of Strength and Virility.

A sneaking feeling crept up the back of Aaslo's neck, and he looked around quickly. He was being watched, but he saw nothing in the gloom and tried to shake off the feeling.

Returning his gaze to Myra, he said, "What am I to do with them?"

Myra looked at the orbs doubtfully. "I am not sure. You need to place them in bodies, although Disevy said they must be powerful bodies."

"Magi?"

"Yes, I think so."

"But all the magi are gone except for the Berruvian magi. They will not heed my call. They are the enemy."

With an apologetic shake of her head, she said, "I don't know, Aaslo. You'll have to figure it out. I will help however I can, of course. Disevy's greatest concern besides Axus getting hold of them was whether or not you can control them. You seem to have little trouble with the one you have, so I hope this will not be a problem."

Aaslo wasn't so sure. He felt as though his power over the shade was tenuous at best. He was not sure he could control five more of the beings, especially if they were as powerful and *depraved* as she claimed. Still, he had to keep them out of Axus's grasp, and Disevy seemed to think this was the best way.

Accepting that it needed to be done, Aaslo reached out with his hand. He opened himself easily to the insidious dark power that continually threatened his soul and released it into the orbs. The glowing power suffused the depraved, whose souls were enshrouded in inky blackness. They each pulsed with unrepentant light as they traveled one by one up the smoky tendrils to Aaslo. As they passed the veil separating his own soul from those around him, he felt the entities latch onto something deep within him. He took a shuddering breath as countless eons of suffering and torment ignited in the recesses of his mind. His pulse quickened, his chest tightened. His mind raced. Panic threatened to consume him. An ever-spinning whirlpool of despair drew him deeper into himself; his consciousness sucked into a void. Madness gripped him, eradicating all thoughts of gods and men.

Sharp talons ripped at the demented power that gripped his soul. The enemy pervaded him, and a great and formidable beast clawed and lashed against it. A generative entity joined the darkness, wanting nothing more than to consume him for herself. Ina cackled endlessly as she pulled bits of his soul into her bosom, claiming them from both dragon and depraved alike. The dragon roared and spewed fire against her, causing great gouts of steam to erupt from the green tendrils that embraced him. On and on the battle continued, the powers of the dragon, Ina, and death vying against each other even as they dragged him piece by terrorized piece from the cloying grip of the depraved.

When Aaslo came to, he stared at a cloud-shrouded sky, unblinking. In fact, his body had ceased any and all motion. His lungs did not expand and contract, and his heart had stopped, he was sure of it. His body and his soul were bathed in pain, and he knew that no amount of tears or wails would provide relief. His chest began to burn beyond the torturous ache, and he abruptly inhaled. The breath suffusing his chest was an icy balm that spread to every extremity. He quickly inhaled another soothing gulp and released a pitiful sigh of relief as much of the torment abated.

As his mind began to clear of its beleaguered fog, another presence began to drag at his being. He quickly rose to a seated position, then lunged to his feet as he drew Mathias's sword. Myra jumped back.

As Aaslo's gaze traversed the misty wood, he said, "How long was I out?"

"Out?" said Myra with more than a hint of confusion.

"How long was I unconscious?" he snapped, not at all sure of their security.

"You weren't," she replied. "You merely fell down. I guess the power of the souls hit you rather hard."

Aaslo laughed without mirth at the understatement.

Myra followed his searching gaze. "Are you okay? Did you see something?"

Aaslo knew something, or someone, was there, yet he could not find them. Ever so slowly, he slid his sword into its sheath and returned his gaze to Myra. Before he could speak, she said, "I'm not sure you should carry those souls *within* you, Aaslo. Isn't there some other way?"

He shook his head. "If there is, I don't know it."

"I would say I appreciate the company, but your new friends are rather bleak."

Aaslo ran a clawed hand through his hair. "It is getting crowded in here," he said. "I should find bodies for these quickly."

"Yes, I think that would be a good idea." She looked at him, brows furrowed. "I'm not sure you can handle the rest of what I have for you right now, and neither am I yet ready to share it. I am being called anyway. I must go, but I will return soon enough. Would you release me from the paths? I am not sure I can travel directly from here."

Aaslo nodded once, then retrieved his senseless horse, who seemed to be trying to uproot the bush from which he had been grazing. He mounted Dolt then turned him so that he was once again facing the direction he had been upon entering the paths. With a few minutes of concentration, he was able to open the portal. He nodded toward Myra, who went ahead of him, and nudged Dolt through the opening in reality.

Aaslo exited exactly where he had entered. None of his companions nor any of his followers seemed to acknowledge his absence, and Aaslo wondered if his ability to open the pathways had improved. When he turned his attention ahead, the commander's intense gaze greeted him. He gave his best placating smile, but it was not an expression with which he was well acquainted. Mathias teased him to no end about it growing up, but Aaslo never let his friend's words get to him. The forest didn't require pleasant smiles.

CHAPTER 5

SEDI WAITED, LEANING AGAINST THE WALL BEHIND THE QUEEN'S throne. Of course, neither the queen nor her guards were aware of her presence. She wrapped the light about her in such a way that no one could see her. Not that it mattered. The Pashtigonian queen was not the brightest flare in the spell repertoire. Too many years of inbreeding had taken its toll on the lineage. The woman stared vacantly at the tiled floor as she had for the past half hour. No wonder the queen had never married. She hadn't the sense nor the looks to attract a husband without the promise of a throne, and Pashtigonian consorts held little to no power in court or politics. Sedi had no doubt the woman could have found *someone* to marry her, if for nothing more than a comfortable living, but Queen Tilly hadn't bothered to try. The rotund woman ran her hands down her skirt to smooth the golden silk then resumed staring at the floor.

Sedi rolled her eyes. Such a complete waste. She would never have allowed a useless woman like Tilly to hold the Empress's Seat in Berru. Any number of courtiers would have dispensed with her long ago to claim the Seat. Berru required a sharp wit, cunning, and a certain amount of ruthlessness to maintain power. Sedi had ensured that when designing her empire millennia ago. The present empress, Lysia, was ideally suited to the position, not in small part due to Sedi's tutelage. Tilly wouldn't have lasted five minutes.

The large doors of the great hall creaked open, and Sedi straightened the scarlet wrap twisted about her torso to enhance her bosom. She smoothed her hands over the soft, fitted, black calf-leather of her pants. As she ran her fingers through her dark locks, she silently laughed at herself. Why did she care how she looked? No one could see her except Aaslo. Somehow, he always found her, and in a dark way, that pleased her. She wondered if he would look for her now.

She roused herself from her thoughts as the commander of the Queen's Royal Army strode across the hall toward the elaborately gilded throne. Commander Andromeda wasn't an attractive woman, but she was formidable. Sedi had watched her training in the yard as she awaited Aaslo's arrival, and she had been impressed.

As for Aaslo, it had taken her some time to find him. Luckily, she had seen the list of cities they intended to visit on their way to join the gathering forces in Mouvilan. She knew he would present himself in Monsque, and had found him in the paths speaking with the reaper. The fact that he had nearly caught her spying made her blood rush with anticipation. Of course, once in the city, he would be so bold as to demand a visit with the queen. Sedi liked that. His boldness was one of his more endearing traits.

She grinned when Aaslo appeared. As he strode through the hall, flanked by that pitiful healer and the odd prophet, Sedi considered the many ways she might toy with Aaslo this time. She wasn't ready to kill him, but neither could she allow him to continue trampling the Berruvian forces. Besides, if he led his few thousand against the hundreds of thousands of the Berruvian army, someone *else* would kill him, and that would not do.

Aaslo stopped at the foot of the dais and gave an awkward bow. Teza and Ijen hung back and were a bit more graceful in their presentation. As Aaslo introduced himself to the queen, Sedi perused his appearance. While hardly dressed for court, his clothes were clean and befitting an experienced traveler. His charcoal trousers were tucked into well-worn boots, and his grey shirt was tied with laces at the wrists and up the front, beneath a black leather vest. In place of his usual jacket, he had donned a dark grey cloak affixed with a gleaming cloak pin depicting an ocelot. The ornate piece seemed an odd juxtaposition to his usual homely attire, and Sedi wondered where he had acquired such a thing. It was one more mystery to perhaps the most interesting man she had ever met.

After Aaslo's formal introduction, the queen remained silent. An uncomfortable pause ensued until, finally, one of the councilors standing to one side of the dais cleared his throat. Queen Tilly jumped, startled, then gasped.

"Commander Andromeda, why have you brought this monster before me? Take it to the dungeon—or, better yet, kill it where it stands."

Andromeda's scarred face twisted as her brow rose. "Queen Tilly, this *man* is a sorcerer of ancient power. He is here to fight *against* our enemy, the Berru, *as we discussed.*"

Tilly raised a pudgy finger and pointed at Aaslo. "*This* is the warrior you mentioned? This *thing*?"

Andromeda glanced apologetically at Aaslo, her chin wagging as if she wasn't sure how to respond to her queen. She lowered her voice, and in a stage whisper hissed, "Your Majesty, he isn't a *thing*. You insult him."

Tilly pounded her thick fist on her armrest. "He is a *thing* if I say he is a thing." She fussed with her gown as she tittered her frustration. Then she said, "What do you want, *Thing*? I haven't all day."

Aaslo muttered something too low to hear, and Sedi wondered what invisible entity he was speaking with this time. She knew all about his conversations with the reaper, but what truly intrigued her were those he had with the deceased chosen one. Like his companions, Sedi wondered if he could truly hear the echoes of the dead or if the metamorphosed forester had genuinely lost his mind. She didn't know which prospect thrilled her more.

In his usual crass way, Aaslo replied, "I don't care what you call me, be it thing or monster, so long as you realize that I am what stands between your city and total annihilation."

Sedi smiled at Aaslo's brazenness. Tilly was not so amused.

The woman shouted, "Impertinent beast! I will have your head on a pike outside the gates as warning."

"If you're going to kill me, you'd best get it right the first time. Others have tried. Most of them are dead."

Sedi's feet moved of their own accord as she drifted closer. She saw the shift in his gaze when she stood halfway between the throne and Aaslo. He looked straight at her. Sedi froze. She hadn't intended to draw his attention—not yet. Aaslo tilted his head in acknowledgment, and turned his attention back to the queen.

"You keep interesting company, Queen Tilly. Is it possible you have already sided with the Berru?"

The queen barked a haughty laugh. "*Me?* Side with the Berru? Why would I do that?"

Aaslo glanced at Sedi and frowned. His claw scratched the scales on his neck, and he narrowed his lizard eye. He muttered to the queen, "No, perhaps you don't know she's here." Then he gripped the hilt of his sword and addressed *her*. "You can show yourself, Sedi. I know you're here."

Sedi laughed as the light enveloping her fell away. Commander Andromeda drew her sword and rushed to Aaslo's side. Sedi looked pointedly to Aaslo's grip on his sword. "You need not fret, Aaslo. I'm not here to kill you. Not right now, anyway."

"Who are you?" shouted Tilly. "What are you doing in my court uninvited?"

Sedi turned to the queen with a glare. "Oh, silly Tilly, who I am is none of your concern. Go back to staring at the floor. You're good at that."

Andromeda said, "That is the queen to whom you speak."

Aaslo abruptly reached over and placed a clawed hand on Andromeda's shoulder. The woman tensed but allowed it as she turned. "Do not engage her," he said. "She is a true ancient, and she will kill you without thought. She is also an agent for the Berru."

Sedi tsked at him. "Oh, Aaslo, your faith in me is sweet. I am not an *agent* for the Berru. I *am* the Berru. Or, rather, they are *my* agents. I created them, you know. They are the children of my children's children's children—and so on. Nearly everyone in the empire carries *my* blood."

"Commander Andromeda," squawked Tilly, "take this woman into custody. Place her in a cell."

Andromeda glanced between the queen, Sedi, and Aaslo uncertainly. It was clear she wanted to comply with the queen's order, but she also didn't want to escalate the situation. Sedi gave the commander a knowing and appreciative smile. She liked intelligent people.

Aaslo wiped the shock from his expression, ignoring the queen's outburst. "Then you are their leader?"

Sedi shrugged. "Not precisely. That is the empress's job. I retired long ago. Now, I just dabble in important affairs when I feel like it." Sedi saw several guards had moved closer in her peripheral vision, and Queen Tilly stood.

Aaslo said, "And *this*—destroying all life on Aldrea—is just you dabbling?"

She placed her hand on a cocked hip and watched, pleased, as the motion drew his gaze to her figure. Then she said, "Of course not. You know as well as I that destroying life is Axus's aim. He recruited Pithor, and Pithor convinced Empress Lysia. I had nothing to do with it."

"I don't believe you to be innocent in all this. You've been trying to kill me for months."

Queen Tilly shouted for the guards again, and one of the counselors quietly suggested that Tilly perhaps allow the two powerful magi to finish their conversation.

"Oh, I never said I was innocent," replied Sedi, once again ignoring the queen. "Axus made me a promise of the one thing I can never have in exchange for my assistance. It seemed a good deal at the time."

"And now?"

Sedi smiled coyly and swung her hips as she sidled closer to him. He tensed as she reached out to caress the scales on his neck. They were cool and smooth, just as she had imagined. She said, "Now I have something interesting to play with."

Teza stomped forward and snapped, "Get your filthy hands off him."

With a smirk, Sedi said, "Your girlfriend seems jealous."

Teza growled, "I'm not his girlfriend, but I *am* his friend. You're not welcome here, Sedi."

Sedi glanced over her shoulder toward the queen then smirked. "I'm not sure that you are either."

"None of you are welcome," snapped Tilly.

"That's not the point," said Teza, likewise ignoring the queen. "You are the enemy. Aaslo, kill her now."

Aaslo appeared uncertain, and Sedi knew he lacked the confidence to attack her outright when surrounded by those he cared about. They were both powerful magi, and if they started flinging their power around inside the palace, they would likely bring the roof down atop their heads. Such catastrophic battles occurred often in the early days of the magi. It was the reason for the formation of the Council of Magi. Someone had to maintain order.

It seemed the queen's people had come to the same conclusion: no one appeared ready to interfere. In fact, Tilly huffed and slumped back on her throne and gave intermittent dramatic moans or muttered her frustrations over having lost control of her court.

Sedi tilted her head and looked at Aaslo with a soft gaze. Despite his oddities, or perhaps because of them, he was a handsome man. Her gaze dropped to his sturdy shoulders and broad chest. She especially appreciated his unnatural strength. A small smile graced her lips as she imagined those strong hands caressing her body. It had been a long time since she had bothered with a man. She thought she might enjoy experiencing this one.

Aaslo cleared his throat, snapping Sedi's gaze to his eyes. He appeared both uncomfortable and confused, and she knew he had caught her ogling. She smirked. "The empress would like to meet you, Aaslo. Give up this hopeless fight and join us. We will gladly walk beside you in the Afterlife."

An inhuman growl escaped him, sending a thrill through her core. "I could never be so cruel and evil as to condemn an entire world to death."

Sedi felt a sudden stab to her chest, confused as to what caused it. She swallowed down the unfamiliar hurt and said, "You think me evil? The Afterlife is a beautiful place, Aaslo. How could it be cruel to desire such a blessing upon the world?"

"Is that what you think it is? People getting torn apart and eaten by monsters? Others being consumed by pestilence and blight? Men, women, and children starving or being killed for what little they have left? Is that a blessing?"

Sedi blinked with surprise as uncertainty wiggled its way through her. Something in the way he looked at her made her doubt herself. Of course, she had seen such deaths; but, given the beatific outcome, she had not considered the suffering and gratuitousness. She shook off the tickle of guilt gnawing at her stomach and firmed her resolve. She said, "What's a little pain when supreme glory awaits?"

Aaslo raised a clawed hand, gripping it in a tightly restrained fist. "Axus does not intend to bestow upon any of us *supreme glory*. Our deaths are a means to an end for him. He wants more power—enough power to crush the other gods beneath his boots. That's it. There is no joy or *glory* awaiting *you* in the Afterlife, Sedi."

Sedi internally rolled her eyes at the thrill she felt as he spoke her name and the disappointment that accompanied his use of it for such a miserable sentiment. She didn't know why she cared what Aaslo thought of her. She hadn't cared what *anyone* thought of her in centuries. Sure, he was interesting, but he was only a man, and she was above such concerns. Still, she couldn't fault him for his words. She had long suspected as much about Axus's motivations but had ignored them for want of her promised reward.

She felt a loosening in her chest as she considered the alternatives to her present course of action. For the first time, she wondered if perhaps Axus wasn't the solution to her problem. Perhaps someone else held the answer. Aaslo's emerald gaze bored into her soul as she searched it for meaning. Now, looking at him, she began to reconsider her desires. Perhaps she could suffer to live *a little* longer.

She met his searching gaze and practically whispered, "What do you want, Aaslo?"

His eyes widened in surprise. "What do I want? I *want* you to stop trying to kill me and my friends."

His words reminded her of the other people in the room. Until that moment, it hadn't bothered her to speak so openly in front of the magi, warriors, and councilors. She hadn't cared what they thought of her or her motivations. Now she felt vulnerable, raw. She didn't like it. Still, something within her, some sense of intrigue or curiosity, perhaps—or so she told herself—drove her to assist Aaslo once again.

"I know what you seek," she said.

"And what is that?" he replied.

"Bodies," she said bluntly. "You want the bodies of powerful men and women for a dark purpose. You seek to resurrect the depraved." At his surprised look, she smiled. "I overheard you and the reaper speaking, and I am inclined to help you."

He looked at her skeptically. "Why?"

"Consider it a boon for your consideration of my offer. We need not be enemies." She stroked his cheek with a manicured nail. She quickly pulled back and her manner abruptly changed to one of business. "I know where my former brethren are entombed."

"You speak of the ancients—the first magi?"

She nodded. "Those whose bodies were not consumed by time. I will tell you where they are—for a price."

Teza stepped closer and grabbed his arm. "Don't do it, Aaslo. Whatever she wants is not worth it."

Aaslo pried Teza's tense fingers from his flesh and glanced toward Ijen. The prophet scribbled frantically in his book and seemed uninterested in sharing, or even forming, an opinion. To Sedi, he said, "What would you ask of me?"

She smiled coyly. "I wish to meet a god."

Aaslo blinked at her in surprise. "How do you expect *me* to make that happen?"

She shrugged one shoulder. "I know you have communed with them, and you have the ear of their messenger, the reaper. I know not how it will be done, but if you swear it shall be so, then I will take you at your word. You are, after all, an honorable forester."

At first it seemed he would immediately reject her proposal, but the words seemed to stick in his mouth. His expression changed, and it appeared that he abandoned his first response before he said, "Which god do you wish to know?"

She tilted her head, curious. It had not occurred to her that he might have the influence to convince more than one god to meet with her. She said, "Any but Axus will do. I have questions." Sedi tried to rein in her desperation as she said the last, but she worried she had betrayed herself. The doubts lately plaguing her were mounting, and she was certain only the gods themselves could put her mind at ease.

There was a long silence, though Queen Tilly continued to ramble incessantly to no one in particular. Sedi, and everyone else, ignored the queen as she awaited Aaslo's response.

Finally, he released a pent-up breath. "Very well. I shall do all within my power to gain you an audience with one of the gods in exchange for the information you offer. By the shade of the forest, I so swear it."

Sedi did not smile her triumph. In fact, she barely withheld the tears that threatened her eyes. She soberly reached within the crease of her bosom and withdrew a folded parchment. She brushed Aaslo's hand as she handed over the missive, and the spark that passed between them sealed the pact. Sedi swallowed and firmed her resolve. She resurrected the walls, which seconds ago had crumbled, and steeled her nerves. She laughed with a carefree mirth she didn't really feel and backed away.

She said, "I will see you soon, Aaslo." She stepped into the pathways and left him and his penetrating gaze behind.

As Sedi traversed the crystal-illuminated stone corridors of her pathways, she felt unsteady. Her thoughts, desires, wants, and needs squirmed like a mass of serpents in her stomach. She suddenly despised Aaslo for making her doubt herself. As soon as she had the thought, a pang of regret shot through her heart. No, she didn't despise Aaslo. Despite their enmity, she knew Aaslo was innocent. She despised herself. She had been so certain for so long. She had become weak, but she couldn't comprehend the source of the weakness. She knew what she wanted, and she knew how to get it. It had seemed like such a minor thing—to end life. It was all going to die eventually. What did it matter if that end came a bit sooner? And for what more glorious calling could there be than to answer the call of a god?

But Aaslo was a mere forester. As such, he was the practical sort. He was also intelligent, thoughtful, compassionate, and *so* powerful. If he couldn't see the truth of her reasoning, then perhaps her reasoning was flawed. Was she making a mistake? Had she allowed Axus to draw her people down the wrong path? Was *she* on the wrong path?

Sedi paused as she looked down the corridor that would take her to Lysia. Was *this* the wrong path? She turned and looked back the way she had come—the way back to Aaslo. She blinked several times as a thought loomed. No, she couldn't entertain that thought. She turned and continued down the corridor to rejoin her people.

Lysia wasn't in her chambers. The empress had claimed the residence of the former prime minister of Helod in the capital city of Dawning. The prime minister and his family no longer needed it, of course, because they were dead. Some of the servants had been spared because they could be of use, but it had otherwise been a bloodbath. Sedi was glad she had not been present. While she had hardened her heart to the necessity of death, she didn't enjoy watching it. At least if she wasn't there, she could pretend the blood wasn't also on her hands.

The estate itself was quite fine, as befitted a high-ranking civil servant, but it hardly compared to the palace of Berru—or *any* palace for that matter. It had three wings—east, west, and north—while floor-to-ceiling windows overlooking an expansive orchard dominated the southern side of the building. The east wing had been reserved for the prime minister's family and guests, while the west wing consisted of servants' quarters, the kitchen, laundry, and other functional spaces. The north wing was filled with offices, a sitting room, a study, a library, and a conference room. It was all very organized and utilized the limited space efficiently, but it lacked the grandiose vibrancy to which the empress was accustomed.

Sedi strode past the guards lining the east wing, and they didn't give her a second glance. They wouldn't dare. No one dared question her. Sedi relished status. She lacked a title and position, but she had more freedom than even the empress. She was practically a goddess among her people. She smiled at the idea. Then she remembered her self-imposed servitude to an *actual* god and her grin faded. She turned the corner into the north wing and bypassed the offices and conference room as she headed to the library.

It was an austere space, meant for scholarly learning and not for pleasure reading. A few scrolls and charts, hung with intellectual intent, occupied largely bare walls; the carpet, a plain beige weave, lacked even the most basic pattern; and the chairs and sofa were stiff and uncomfortable, presumably to prevent one from nodding off. The only piece that looked out of place in the ascetic décor was the single high-backed chair near the hearth. It was a recent addition, covered in soft grey velvet and filled with plush down, and it was presently occupied.

"Lysia," Sedi said as she slipped into the wooden chair across from the empress.

Lysia looked up from her book and smiled, her sharpened teeth flashing in the firelight. "Sedi, it is good you have come. I have many things to discuss with you. Will you be staying long?"

Sedi shrugged. "I don't know. I was just checking in. I missed you." She didn't really miss the empress, but it was a game they played. Sedi pretended to care, and Lysia pretended to believe her.

"And I you, my sweet." Lysia crooked a bony finger, and her attendant hurried forward. He poured a second glass of wine from the crystal decanter on the table beside the empress and handed it to Sedi. Sedi pointedly ignored the man, as was custom, except to take the glass. After Sedi had taken a sip, Lysia said, "Have you been to see our dragon-man?"

Sedi paused, wondering how Lysia could have known where she'd been, then relaxed as she deduced it was a general inquiry unrelated to her most recent activity. "I have." She sat back but found no ease in the hard chair. Lysia grinned at her discomfort then snapped, "Bring us another chair."

Sedi gave Lysia a grateful look then sipped her wine as she waited for the chair to arrive. The new chair matched Lysia's. Once she was comfortable, Sedi said, "Aaslo continues to defy me."

Lysia raised a sharp eyebrow. "Oh? Why do you put up with it?"

"Because he *can!*" she replied with enthusiasm. "It has been eons since I have met *anyone* who could stand against me. It's thrilling."

Lysia's black gaze traced the walls as she said, "Yes, I understand completely." She set her book down on the table beside her and crossed her skeletal hands over her lap. "Crisius succumbed to the infection from his injuries. He was a strong man. I expected more from him."

Sedi clucked her tongue in disapproval. Crisius had been the empress's most recent lover, and Sedi knew the injuries he had suffered had been incurred during their lovemaking. It was no secret that the empress was a sadist, and she didn't hold back, even for those for whom she cared. It was one reason she had held the throne as long as she had. If she could be that cruel to her lovers, she could be positively evil with her enemies.

Lysia picked up her glass and tapped a sharpened, black-lacquered nail against it. "Have you taken a new lover, Sedi? If I recall, it has been some time."

Sedi waved a hand in the air. "It is not a priority. I have more important things to consider."

Lysia gave her a lecherous smile. "Like the dragon-man?"

Sedi pursed her lips then grinned. "Perhaps. I find him fascinating. You practically taste his power."

"You should be careful about sleeping with the enemy. We cannot afford for your priorities to get confused."

A shudder ran through Sedi as the empress's words struck a little too close to the mark. She covered her discomfort by taking a long draw of her wine, then lied. "I think he may come to our way of thinking. I hope to gain his trust."

"You mean his affection."

Sedi blinked at the empress. Lysia was shrewd and saw too much. "I am not yet sure how to do it, though. He sees me as the enemy."

Lysia gave a slight sigh and nodded disconsolately. "Yes, trying to kill a man several times will do that. They are so sensitive. Why can they not see it as whetting the appetite?"

Sedi knew Lysia was no longer talking about her and Aaslo. The empress's thoughts were no doubt on her former lover, the deceased Crisius. Or perhaps she was thinking of the one before him. Sedi couldn't remember his name, but she recalled that he had killed himself by jumping off a balcony. Lysia had been severely disappointed; he had robbed her of the opportunity to dispense with him herself in a more pleasurable manner.

"What did you wish to speak with me about, Lysia?"

Sedi's question brought the empress back to the present, and her expression shifted to one of determination. "We are nearly ready to begin the campaign. I thought we could go over some of the logistics. There is some contention between myself and the generals."

"Contention? Since when do you allow contention?"

Lysia fussed with her grey gossamer gown. "I know. It was my fault, I suppose. I told them to speak freely, and they disagreed with me. I want to raze the cities and towns as we go—remove everything at once. The generals, however, think we should decimate those who resist and draft those too cowardly—or too intelligent—to fight us. They seem to be missing the point. As much as I disliked him, I must admit that Pithor would have understood. Our intent is not to build an empire. It is to destroy one."

A spike of guilt wriggled through Sedi. She had to credit the empress with putting it so succinctly. She could not fool herself into thinking this war was about building a glorious paradise, a perfect society. This was about destruction and nothing more. She reminded herself that the end result was the most important element. They would be blessed with either a place among the gods or a tranquil existence in the Afterlife—whatever that was. Sedi had never discovered what happened after death. She only knew that those who had communicated with the gods, like Pithor, assured her there was such a thing as the Afterlife. Once again, a sliver of doubt penetrated her resolve. What if they had been lying? What if Axus had lied? What if they were wrong and there was no Afterlife? Was she contributing to the premature death of *everyone* with no assurance of persistence afterward? Was she robbing people of their one chance at existence?

Sedi put the disturbing notion from her mind and realized Lysia was still speaking. The empress was waxing on concerning troop distribution, tugging every detail from memory like a favorite poem. With Lysia's penchant for death and destruction, Sedi considered, perhaps this war *was* poetry to the empress. Unencumbered sadness filled Sedi at the thought, and she decided then and there: if the prose of death were a sonnet, it was not an ode to the glorious, blessed empire the empress thought it to be. It was a tragedy, a dirge unequaled in soulfulness.

CHAPTER 6

AASLO DUCKED AND SLICED AT THE GROTESQUE CREATURE'S LEG. THE lyksvight collapsed atop the pile of its dismembered brethren, and Aaslo brought his axe down on the monster's face. Then he turned to the next. He hacked and slashed, lopping off both its arms before finally taking its head.

"That's one down. Only about a hundred more to go."

Aaslo glanced back toward the city a mere three hundred yards away and was relieved to see the monsters had not yet reached the gates. A fireball streaked past, barely missing his face. It smashed into a lyksvight that had been approaching from his flank, pushing it back and setting two more around it alight.

"You can thank me later," called Teza. "Is that five now?"

Aaslo hefted his axe and buried it in the flaming lyksvight's chest. It made a *schlupp* sound as he pulled it free. "Five *what?*" he shouted back.

She grunted as a lyksvight rammed her, but her armor protected her from its pitiful knife. She pressed a palm against its chest, and the monster burst apart, sending bits of flesh and bone in every direction. "Five times I've saved your life!" she hollered.

"You're counting?" he said as he migrated closer to her. "How many times have I saved *your* life?"

She turned toward him, but he couldn't see her face behind her silver helmet. "None that I can recall."

"Of course you wouldn't recall it," he grumbled.

"I do recall you allowing me to get kidnapped."

"Yes, that wasn't very gentlemanly of you, Aaslo."

"I never said I was a gentleman," Aaslo grunted out as he removed his axe from a lyksvight's sternum. He seamlessly drew Mathias's sword to meet the next attacker. He turned to Teza as he caught his breath. "I didn't *allow* you to get kidnapped. I tried to stop her, but I had dozens of other people to save. I couldn't abandon them."

Teza spun and kicked a lyksvight in the stomach before slicing it in half with a blade of power. Aaslo hadn't seen her use that particular spell before, and it looked impressive. She said, "I know *that,* but it doesn't change the fact that I was kidnapped."

"She has a point."

It was just like Mathias to take her side. "Yeah, well, you got some amazing armor out of the deal, so quit complaining."

"That's true, but I could just as easily have been killed."

"I think she's still upset."

The Berruvian magus Aaslo had been working his way toward suddenly realized his predicament and turned to run, only to be tripped when Teza caused the ground to explode under him. Aaslo hacked and slashed his way toward the magus, then drove toward the man with his axe in one hand and his sword in the other. In a matter of seconds, pieces of the magus littered the ground, and the remaining lyksvight he had controlled scattered as they went after the Pashtigonian warriors on Aaslo's flank.

Aaslo turned to Teza. "Do we need to have a talk about this, because now really isn't the time. I would have come for you."

Teza retracted the helmet covering her head and met his gaze. "I didn't need you to come for me, but thanks for the sentiment. I'm not mad, so you can tell Mathias to back off."

"How did you know—"

She waved a hand as she replaced her helmet. "A lucky guess. He's always ragging on you."

"It's all out of love, I assure you. I'm still your best friend."

"You're my brother," Aaslo corrected.

Mathias hummed happily as Aaslo lopped off another head. Then Aaslo was tackled from behind to the ground. He struggled against his captor only to realize the woman had saved him from losing his head to an enemy spell meant to cleave it from his body. Andromeda looked down at him and grinned then picked herself up and reentered the fray. Aaslo now owed his life to another woman. A moment later, he returned the favor by chopping a lyksvight in two down the middle as it attempted to stab Andromeda in the back.

The battle didn't last long, but by the end, everyone panted heavily while covered in blood and milky-white gore. As the last magus fell, Aaslo looked across the field. Body parts littered the ground, some still moving of their own accord. Many of his own undead had fallen, too damaged to be resurrected, but he had gained others. Several of the Pashtigonian warriors heeded his postmortem call to arms. As gruesome and morbid as it was, Aaslo was glad for their service. He needed more trained warriors—alive *or* dead. The notion didn't sit well with Andromeda and her comrades, however.

"What have you done?" She stormed across the bloody field. She pointed to one of her fallen brethren, who now stood staring at Aaslo with a hazy white gaze.

"He accepted my offer," Aaslo said. "I forced nothing upon him."

"What offer?"

"I reach out with my power to those who have fallen and offer them a chance to fight again, to visit justice upon their enemies. If they accept, they become my wanderers. He accepted."

She looked at the deceased warrior with wide eyes and said, "This is unacceptable. He fell as a hero. He deserves a proper funeral."

"Don't we all?"

A pang of regret shot through Aaslo, and he patted the sack at his side. "Perhaps he shall have one when he is finished with this world."

One of the other Pashtigonian warriors slowly approached the dead man. He appeared distraught as he looked upon the younger man's sunken face. The white gaze turned to the living warrior, and the dead man smiled. The warrior threw an arm around the animated corpse and released an agonized cry. He turned to Andromeda and said, "Let him fight. Jergus would have wanted that."

Aaslo said, "He *does* want that. He's still in there—mostly." He rubbed a clawed hand over his sternum. "The rest resides in me. I will release the dead when they have fulfilled their destinies."

The man glanced at the undead warrior again then nodded and turned to assist an injured comrade. Andromeda sheathed her sword and said, "We shall discuss this further later. For now, we must aid the wounded and return to the city. It's a good thing we were here. Had we left with you, as you'd hoped, the city might have been overrun."

Aaslo met her heated stare. "Had *we* not been here"—he motioned to himself, Teza, and Ijen—"those magi would have breached the walls, and the city *would* have been overrun. You are seculars. You cannot fight the magi on your own. We would all be better off if you would gather everyone who can fight and come with us to meet the enemy head on."

"And what of everyone in the city?"

Aaslo looked to Teza and Ijen then back to Andromeda. He opened his mouth, but it was Ijen who spoke. "We will construct protective wards around the city as best we can. The wards will hold back the lyksvight, although they will be susceptible to the power of the Berruvian magi. Otherwise, they should hold until we fall. Some might even remain for a time."

Aaslo looked at Ijen, wondering what the prophet knew. He shook his head and dismissed the question, knowing Ijen would never tell.

Teza faced the prophet with her arms crossed over her chest. "How do you expect us to maintain the wards once we leave?"

"Runes," said Ijen.

"What *runes?*" said Teza. "How can we possibly ward an entire city? *I'm* no runemaster, and neither are you."

Ijen pulled his book from his tunic and flipped through the pages. "Here it is," he muttered. He turned the book so they could see the page to which he referred. There was a diagram of a city surrounded by arcane scrollwork. He said, "We shall use the runes in the book."

Her jaw dropped. "You had this all along? Why didn't you say anything?"

"Because Aaslo had not yet designed the runes."

With a huff, Teza said, "He *still* hasn't!"

Ijen turned the book back to read it. "No, you're right, but he *has* convinced the commander, here, to join us. That is a more significant accomplishment."

"What?" snapped Andromeda. "I haven't agreed to anything."

Ijen tilted his head and looked at her thoughtfully. "Yes, you have. You just don't know it yet."

"You're suddenly full of information you're willing to share," grumbled Aaslo.

Ijen shrugged. "This part of the story doesn't matter except that it had to happen for the next part to occur."

"And what is the next part?"

Ijen snapped the book shut. He ran a hand down his tunic and grimaced when it came away sticky with white blood. "*That* I cannot tell you."

"*He's such a tease.*"

As Aaslo turned and headed back toward the city gate, Andromeda joined him. "It will not be easy to convince Queen Tilly."

Aaslo glanced at her through his dragon eye. She looked different to his monster, but he recognized her just the same. The dragon lifted its head and narrowed its focus. It wanted to hunt, to chase. Andromeda would make a worthy prey. She narrowed her eyes, and Aaslo realized he had been growling. He swallowed the sound. "I don't care about convincing Tilly. Her kingdom has fallen, save for this city, and her reign is at an end. We're battling the gods themselves. What Tilly wants is no longer relevant."

"Gods, bah! You speak of them as if they are real."

"They are, and they're waging war against us."

Andromeda released an exasperated sigh. "You just expect us to abandon our posts."

"If need be."

Her back straightened and indignation heated her voice. "We are Pashtigonian warriors. We do not abandon our people or rebel against our queen. What you speak of is treason."

Aaslo rounded on her. "Warriors do not sit on their asses and watch the world die because their queen is scared." His dragon leapt to its feet, and its tail lashed at the confines of his mind. Aaslo felt a wave of fury surge through him. He flicked his hand in dismissal. "Do as you wish. When you die, I shall resurrect your corpses to fight the battles you should have fought while alive. At least in death, you will have honor." As he stormed away, she was left choking on his wrath.

Teza caught up with him. "That was harsh, Aaslo. She's just trying to do her job. These decisions aren't easy."

"You were a bit blunt, brother."

"It was easy for you," Aaslo growled, his dragon still riled for a fight.

"I never got the chance to choose."

"Is that what you think?" said Teza. "You think I wasn't scared—that I'm not scared *now*? You think it wasn't hard for me to turn my back on my family and friends? Yes, part of me wanted to go with them—to go where we would be safe and together. But I *chose* to stay with you—"

"Why?" he snapped.

"Because it was the right thing to do. But my situation was different. My people *were* the cowards. The commander isn't a coward. She's trying to save her people. She hasn't seen the extent of this war. She doesn't know how badly the world suffers."

"Well, while she's figuring it out, the enemy is making progress. We're not staying here any longer. They can come with us or stay, but we're moving on."

"Don't let *me* stop you. I've been wanting to leave since we got here. This place gives me the creeps the way they go about their lives like nothing is happening outside their walls. The whole city is living in delusion."

"At least it's a pleasant delusion," muttered Aaslo. There were times when he wanted to return to his forest and live out his days in peace and solitude. But a forester did what needed to be done, and right now that meant crossing Endrica to meet the Berru in battle.

As they reentered the city there were no cheers or shouts of triumph for having won the battle. The somber, frightened faces of the city's residents revealed the understanding that this was only one battle among many to come, and Aaslo's efforts to rob the people of their protection haunted him. He knew he needed to do something for those left behind, otherwise there would be nothing left to fight *for*. Ijen seemed to think they needed Andromeda in their fight against the Berru, but she wouldn't abandon the city without assurance that the people were protected. It was equally important to prevent Axus from gaining power through so many deaths.

The next day, Aaslo found himself entrenched in a pile of papers with Teza and Ijen working to understand the runes Ijen had shown them in his book. To his dismay, the prophet refused to provide the diagram. He said it was important that Aaslo design the runes as he *apparently* had, or *would*, on that path of the prophecy. As Ijen and Teza drew and explained basic rune sequences, Aaslo tugged at his memories of learning similar structures with Magdelay and Mathias when he was young. At the time, the runes had simply looked like interesting designs that Magdelay said belonged to a foreign culture, and Aaslo hadn't bothered to commit them to memory. Mathias, however, seemed to have absorbed much of what she had said.

"*No, Aaslo, draw the upper line with a steeper pitch and curve it around the side. Yes, like that. This one is for strengthening a material.*"

Aaslo grumbled under his breath as he added the rune to his growing dictionary.

"Good," said Ijen, taking the practice paper from him. "You learn quickly."

"Not quickly enough," muttered Aaslo, glancing around the otherwise silent room. They sat at a large table in the center of the city's library. The soaring, open space held three stories' worth of countless tomes haphazardly stuffed onto shelves and in alcoves. He had no idea how anyone could expect to find what they were looking for without an organizational system, but the attendant assured him anything they needed could be brought to them. Although none of the books or scrolls housed here would help them, it gave him, and his companions, a quiet, unoccupied place to work. Queen Tilly was still irked that Aaslo and Sedi had taken over her throne room on their arrival, and he thought it best to give the flighty monarch space.

Aaslo returned his attention to the diagram in front of him. He glanced at his dictionary, then back to the diagram. Designing something so complex without the most basic understanding of the subject matter felt overwhelming, but Aaslo was determined to succeed. For the next two days, Aaslo benefited from Teza, Ijen, and Mathias's guidance on how to design protective runes for the city and its inhabitants. He didn't know if Mathias really spoke to him or if it was his broken mind's way of drawing information from the recesses of his memory. He appreciated, though, that it at least *felt* like Mathias was with him again.

At one point, Teza cleared her throat and in a quiet, soothing voice, cautiously said, "Aaslo, do we really need *that* to be, um, *out?*"

Aaslo followed her gaze to the head sitting at the end of the table. "Yes," he grumped without further explanation.

A moment later, she ventured, "Well, could we maybe leave it in the bag? You can still hear him, right?"

Aaslo glanced at the head again. Mathias's shining blue eyes stared out of a face with a strong jawline and high cheekbones beneath a cover of golden waves. His expression was peaceful despite the horrible way in which he had died.

Aaslo said, "It helps me to think." At her horrified expression, he added, "When I see him sitting there like that, it feels like we're back home in Magdelay's study learning runes. It's like he's with me again and not just in my mind."

Teza, still severely uncomfortable, said nothing more. Meanwhile, Ijen barely noticed the head as he drummed his fingers on the desk. Aaslo still wasn't sure about Ijen. Being a prophet made him strange by nature, but it was the continual, albeit subtle, manipulation that bothered Aaslo—and was why he ignored him. If he didn't allow Ijen's words or actions to influence him, then he was immune to whatever drove the prophet. Whether or not he succeeded was questionable, and certainly not in this case. Coming up with wards to protect the city seemed an honorable cause, though, so perhaps it didn't matter if Ijen had initiated it with his well-timed revelation.

On the third day, Aaslo's frustration mounted. He had just finished scrawling a set of runes across his page when a bubble of laughter echoed through his mind. This was not his own laughter, nor did it belong to Mathias. This was distinctly feminine, and it had the bitter taste of duplicity.

The laughter became a menacing giggle. *"You've designed a powerful structure, but I do not think it will do what you think it will."*

Ina.

Aaslo gritted his teeth. "How do you know? The fae don't use runes from what I've been told."

"*No,*" said the piece of fae power from a being he had named Ina. "*But I do know power, and that structure will not do what you want.*"

Ijen and Teza both stared at him now, but he ignored them, examining the page before him and focusing on the piece of Ina's will lent to him.

"Well, how do I fix it?" he asked.

She tittered playfully and said, "*I will tell you for a price.*"

"You already exacted your price. I rid your swamp of the blight. Your power is mine now. You agreed."

"*I agreed to lend you* power, *not knowledge. If you want more, I expect payment.*"

"In exchange, you will show me how to ward the city for protection?"

"*I will help you learn the runes, but the design must be yours. Will you pay?*"

Aaslo inhaled sharply. He didn't relish the idea of making another deal with the fae, but they were strapped for time, and he needed to protect the people. "What do you want?"

"*A kiss.*"

Aaslo hadn't expected that. In fact, he couldn't even see how that would work. "I can't do that. I don't have time to go to Ruriton."

"*I didn't say I wanted it now . . . or here. Just one kiss, in the time and place of my choosing. That is all I ask. Surely your precious humans are worth a kiss?*"

Aaslo didn't know what kissing a fae would do, but he was pretty sure it was nothing good. Still, he couldn't sit and work on runes for months on end. Ijen had said that some magi dedicated their entire lives to studying runes and still wouldn't have been able to accomplish what he attempted. Getting help from Ina seemed the only way it was going to happen.

With a heavy sigh, he said, "All right. You have a deal."

The following day, Aaslo set out to inscribe the city with rune designs that he was only somewhat sure would work. He took heart when Ijen assured him his design matched the one in the book of prophecy. The task took all day, as it required him to walk the city's entire perimeter etching runes into the walls every few paces using a spell Ijen taught him. Then, once he was finished etching the symbol, he had to suffuse it with power. Ijen and Teza helped with the lesser-powered runes, but there were some for which only Aaslo had the strength.

The sun neared the horizon when Aaslo sent his power into the final rune near the front gate. It glowed for a moment then went dark again, and Aaslo was devastated. He wasn't sure where he had gone wrong, and it would take forever to reassess each and every rune for accuracy. What if the runes themselves were not the problem? What if the problem lay in the design?

"*Your artwork always left something to be desired. It's not surprising it didn't work.*"

"All these people will suffer for my failure."

"*It's okay, Aaslo. No one can be expected to get everything right the first time. You'll try again.*"

Aaslo appreciated Mathias's efforts at comfort, but the overwhelming task at hand overpowered his words. Aaslo slumped to the ground to think where he had made a mistake. He lay back in the dirt and stared up at the sky as some watchmen on the wall looked down on him with concern. He blinked several times to rid his eyes of the haze in his peripheral vision. Then he realized his eyes weren't the problem; it was the sky. He abruptly stood but kept his gaze trained on the scene above him. A hazy dome stretched across his field of vision. Aaslo's excitement mounted as the dome clearly defined the borders of the city.

"*Congratulations, Aaslo. I knew you could do it.*"

CHAPTER 7

TWO DAYS PASSED BEFORE AASLO COULD GATHER HIS PEOPLE FROM throughout the city. Many of the civilians had decided to stay in Monsque, which he thought was just as well. Those people would only slow them down and provide fodder for the lyksvight. What surprised him, though, was the number of Monsquites willing to join the rebellion, and he had the Pashtigonian commander to thank for that. Despite her protests, Andromeda had actively campaigned for support, and with the rebels' arrival, her followers were eager to join.

Aaslo had just left the throne room where he had met with Queen Tilly when Commander Andromeda caught up with him.

"Well, that went poorly," she said.

"It went as expected," he replied. "Thank you for not arresting me. I would not have wanted to fight you."

She pursed her lips, pulling her scarred flesh tight. "She will divest me of my position for defying her."

"She knows the city's days are numbered, and she knows she needs you."

"It didn't seem that way when she shouted for us all to be thrown into the dungeon."

"It's obvious who holds the power here. The guards wouldn't touch you, yet they jumped to do your bidding when you ordered the queen locked in her chambers *for her own good*."

Andromeda grinned. "We can't have her making trouble if we're going to fight the Berru."

"So you've decided to come?"

Her expression turned severe. "Gods or no gods, it is the only way. As you said, we must unite if we are to have a chance. I am still torn about leaving the city, but now that the protections are in place I feel it is perhaps justified."

The marquess, Teza, and Ijen met them in the grand hall that served as the palace's entrance. Teza smacked her hands together and rubbed them in anticipation. She looked at Andromeda with a perky grin. "So glad you could join us. Just remember that *I'm* Aaslo's second, which means *I'm* in charge when he's not around."

Andromeda raised an eyebrow at the magus. "Are you sure about that?"

Teza clucked her tongue, and her dark eyes lit with an ambitious fire. She ran a hand down her side. "You see this armor? It makes me practically invincible. Plus, I'm a magus—one of only *three* Endricsian magi left on Aldrea. That makes me powerful. But most importantly, Aaslo likes me, and he'll be furious if you don't listen to me."

"I will?"

She grinned at him. "Yes. You will."

"You'd better listen to the lady, or no telling what she'll turn you into this time."

Aaslo shook his head, stepped around her, and exited the receiving hall through the palace doors. The sun was nearing its zenith, and no clouds obscured its scorching rays. As he paused to roll up his jacket and secure it to his pack, he wondered how Teza could stand wearing the full body armor Sedi, of all people, had gifted her. Aaslo still could not comprehend the sorceress's motives, but Teza assured him it was only a boon. She wore the armor everywhere. It flowed with her movements as if she had bonded with it. While the smith who made it had not been a magus, Aaslo knew its true designer to be the God of War, Trostili—also their enemy. According to Myropa, the armor had been meant for *him*, although he could not imagine how it would have fit considering how snugly it conformed to Teza's slender form. Everyone's motives concerned him.

Aaslo led the way to the stables where he collected Dolt, who at first refused to awaken, then the five of them began the long trek through the city to the front gates. Aaslo and Teza rode to the front, mostly because Dolt proceeded to bite any horses in front of him, and Andromeda rode between the marquess and Ijen.

"Anderlus, is it?" she asked of the marquess.

He gave a short bow and said, "Anderlus Sefferiah, Marquess of Dovermyer."

"How is it that you came to serve Aaslo?" she inquired. Aaslo tensed. The hierarchy between them had never been discussed. In fact, they both avoided addressing it directly. Apparently, the commander had no such qualms. Aaslo didn't turn, but he could hear the humor in the marquess's tone as he answered.

"I have always had respect for the forester, but I wouldn't say I serve *him*. Rather, I serve the cause. Sir Forester has taken up the chosen one's mantle, and thus, I am obliged to support him."

"So you allow him to give you orders for the cause's sake."

"Ah, well, I see how you could see it that way. I suppose it's true enough. The forester did me a great service in ridding my lands of a terrible blight. Unfortunately, the damage was done, and events have surpassed us. My homeland was destroyed in an attack. We had to leave in search of refuge and a way to fight the enemy. Meanwhile, the crown fell, and Uyan was overridden with monsters. At this point, any power I might have held is moot."

"Hmm, he seems to be good at rendering powerful people powerless."

"How so?"

"Like Queen Tilly. She currently sits locked in her rooms against her will."

"Was that *him*?" said Ijen from her other side. "Or was that *you*?"

She was quiet for a moment before replying, "I see your point. I suppose it was me, but I only did so because he convinced me of the necessity."

"That is how it is with the forester," said Ijen. "What he does is always out of necessity."

"Is that why you're with him? Out of necessity?"

Ijen tapped the book that was open in his lap. "I follow him because it is my destiny, as it is yours."

"*Mine?* You mean *I'm* in a prophecy?"

"Indeed," said the prophet.

"Well, what does it say?"

"It depends. In one path, you are struck down by an arrow through the heart. In another, you're eaten by a horde of lyksvight. In yet another, you are decapitated by your own halberd."

Aaslo looked over his shoulder to find the commander staring at Ijen in horror. She said, "Are there any instances in which I'm *not* dying?"

Ijen shrugged. "A few. I cannot yet tell you which one will come to pass."

Teza turned in her own saddle. "Why are you telling her *any* of them?"

He looked at her, affronted. "You said I don't share enough. I was obliging."

"Well, don't share that horrible stuff," snapped Teza. She looked at Aaslo accusingly. "You see? This is why I hate prophets."

Aaslo grumbled, "*I* didn't invite him."

"*I wonder if he could have prevented my death.*"

Aaslo gripped his reins tighter, and Dolt tossed his head with a snort. "If they'd known he was an Aldrea prophet, they'd have locked him away, and he wouldn't have been able to help you anyway."

"You don't know that. More likely, they would have seen my death through his prophecies and assumed you had something to do with it."

"They wouldn't have allowed me near you."

"And we wouldn't have grown up brothers."

"And I wouldn't be on this miserable journey."

"And the world would be doomed."

"Unless you lived."

"But the magi might have killed you in an effort to prevent my death."

"So, in order for you to have lived, I would have had to die?"

Aaslo looked back to see Ijen staring at him, and he knew he had hit upon a truth.

Andromeda leaned over and said, "Who, by the gods, is he talking to?"

"He believes he communes with the deceased chosen one," said the marquess. "And sometimes other dead entities."

"So he *is* a necromancer," said Andromeda.

"Aaslo doesn't like that word," said Teza. "He says it has a negative connotation."

"If the shoe fits," muttered Andromeda.

The rest of the ride was silent. When they at last reached the staging area, Peck and Mory greeted them with grins. Peck opened his arms wide. "We gathered everyone." He bowed with a flourish. "At your command, Sir Forester."

Aaslo looked across the ranks. A fighting force of over five thousand living and undead awaited them. For the most part, the undead remained separate from the living, but there were pockets where they had been allowed to rejoin their former family members and comrades. Aaslo wondered if they might gain greater acceptance with time. Time, however, was not a luxury they had.

He dismounted and patted Peck's shoulder as he took Dolt's reins. Aaslo took in the open expanse of land behind him. He closed his eyes and sought the source of power within him—or, rather, the sources. The dragon unfurled lazily, at first, then leapt to the fore. There, it battled against the dark, insidious power of death that also desired to consume him. The dark power lashed out with inky tendrils at the dragon, and the dragon snapped at it in return. Ina, however, was not forthcoming with her power. She held it tight to herself, and Aaslo was forced to wrestle it away. She cackled as it rushed through him, threatening to override the other powers.

Aaslo shoved back against each of the selfish intents vying for control. With the combined powers, he created the doorway to the paths. Once established, a mesmerizing rent in the air filled with snapping surges of energy. New recruits gasped, and a few looked as if they might run. Even though he had succeeded, Aaslo felt frustrated. He needed to be able to access the paths quickly. There was no way he could compete with Sedi, who could come and go on a whim. Granted, he had only been traveling the paths for a few short weeks as opposed to her millennia. He had to admit, her skills were a marvel. Just the thought of the way she danced through the paths from place to place in the blink of an eye sent a surge of admiration through him. She carried herself with poise and wielded power with grace, every part of her sensuous and inviting—except the part that wanted to kill him.

Aaslo shook his head to clear his mind. What had he been thinking? He couldn't possibly be *attracted* to Sedi. He had no idea why such disturbing notions invaded his thoughts.

Mathias cackled in his mind. *"That vixen will bite your head off and spit you out for the lyksvight. Reyla wasn't harsh enough, Aaslo! Are you looking for more punishment?"*

Aaslo swallowed against the memory of Reyla's rejection, the way she had looked upon him with pity while she ripped out his heart. At least Sedi was forthright in her desire to see him defeated. What a sobering thought that was. "I admire her skill. That is all," he mumbled.

"If you say so." Mathias continued humming a tune in his mind. It took Aaslo a few seconds to recognize "The Lover's Ballad." He growled low and moved forward.

Just as he made to step through the portal, someone appeared in front of him. He came to an abrupt halt as he stared down at Myra. She was only a few inches shorter, but for some reason she seemed much smaller at that moment. He noted the way she fidgeted uncomfortably as she looked up. "Hi, Aaslo. I've been looking for you."

He waved his arm toward the city and replied, "I've been here all along."

She nodded. "I know. I looked for you in the throne room, but you had already left. People were talking, though. You made quite an impression. Did you really have the queen locked away?"

"It was for her own good," he muttered.

"Hers or yours?" Myra's light tone held a hint of accusation.

He frowned at her insight. Myra was smart, and he wondered if perhaps she was more cunning than she seemed. "What are you doing here?"

"I told you I had something important to tell you."

"Now is not a good time." He motioned to the thousands waiting behind him. "We are about to enter the pathways."

She glanced back at the surging portal. "Can I come with you?"

Aaslo narrowed his eyes. "You were not certain of spending so much time in the paths before. You seemed to think it might conflict with your power."

"It worked out okay the last two times." She smiled sweetly and added, "I even got a hug out of it once."

Aaslo couldn't forget. That he could actually touch the reaper in the pathways had been a surprise. She had requested a hug, which had felt awkward since he didn't know her that well. But after decades of not being able to touch anyone, it only made sense that she wouldn't be picky about who she embraced.

Aaslo glanced at his companions, who stared at him knowingly. Even though they were aware of his contact with the otherwise invisible reaper, he still noted the glint of disbelief in their gazes. Only Mory smiled happily as he nodded to Myra. The fact that the former thief could see her went a long way in convincing the others that he wasn't crazy, but he knew they still had doubts.

Teza's patience had worn thin. "Well, are we going through or are we just going to stand here all day?"

Aaslo turned back to Myra. "Very well. Come with us."

She smiled and followed him as he stepped through the ominous portal into the paths. Upon arrival, Aaslo felt fortunate that no monsters lay in wait. However, with the number of people that followed, it was only a matter of time before they attracted attention. Aaslo waited with Myra beside the gate as the column passed him. A milky-eyed Rostus was the last to enter the gate, and Aaslo closed it with a thought. He hoped to one day be able to open a gate just as quickly—if he lived that long.

As Aaslo made his way to the front of the throng, people had differing reactions to his presence. Some reached out to touch him, while most shied away. Whispered remarks about the dragon-man and necromancer reached his ears, but he refused to react.

"Embrace your power. There is no shame in it."

"How can there be no shame in robbing the dead of their Afterlife?"

"You said yourself that they choose to follow you."

"Yes, but did you?"

"How do you know you're *not following* me?"

"Because I'm the one carrying your head."

"Yes, you might want to talk to someone about that. It seems a little deranged."

"You wouldn't be here if I didn't."

"Perhaps."

Aaslo found Peck leading Dolt at the head of the line, or maybe it was the other way around. The horse saw Aaslo and rolled his eyes. Aaslo ignored the ornery beast as he kept an eye on their surroundings. The fog was thick among the trees, and Aaslo wondered why *his* paths presented so ominously while Sedi's were brightly lit and orderly. Under normal circumstances, Aaslo would have felt more at home within the fog-shrouded forest, but with the threat of untold creatures from innumerable realms, the setting wasn't ideal.

"Thinking about the vixen again so soon?"

"I don't know what you're talking about," Aaslo grumbled.

"Hey, who is this?" said Peck.

Aaslo turned to see that Peck was staring at Myra. She looked back at the thief-turned-scout with wide eyes.

"You can see me?"

"Well, yeah." He straightened the collar of his jacket and smoothed his hair back. After donning an award-winning grin, he said, "And a very pleasant sight it is."

Aaslo flicked Peck's ear, eliciting a shout. "That's Myra. It seems she becomes more substantial in the pathways. Be polite."

Peck looked back to Myra in shock. "Wait, you're *real.*"

Mory looked at Peck with a hurt expression. "You doubted me?"

Aaslo crossed his arms and said, "More importantly, you doubted *me?*"

Peck glanced between them anxiously, hands raised in defeat. "Look, you have to admit it's hard to believe in invisible people."

Aaslo ground his teeth together, then said, "I didn't ask you to believe in invisible people. I asked you to believe in *me.*"

"I do, I do! It's just that what's real to you might not be real to me—or anyone else."

Aaslo dropped his arms and shook his head as he sidestepped Peck and took a seat on a stump off the path. As he turned his attention to finding the grove that served as a map through the pathways, he heard Teza introducing herself to Myra. He knew Teza was against Myra's help since she thought her to be a spy for the enemy, however Teza remained pleasant and professional. It became obvious that,

contrary to her typically candid attitude, she knew that social nice-
ties were expected among the gentrified magi. He wondered why she
had never felt the need to be so formal with *him*.

"*Maybe it's because your head is full of bark.*"

Aaslo wasn't irritated by Mathias's acerbic words—he only meant
to tease him—and he was glad to hear Mathias's voice. Mathias
wasn't done, though.

"*You wouldn't know what to do with pleasantries anyway.*"

"That's not true," he groused as his mind settled in the grove that
served as the map to the paths. "Magdelay taught me same as you."

"*Yes, but I'm naturally good with people. You only put up with
them when you have to.*"

Aaslo nodded as he searched the tangle of branches for the correct
path. "That *is* true. Since you died, I've had to put up with a lot more
people than I ever wanted."

"*And you're not getting any better at it.*"

"Why bother? They're all going to be dead soon."

"*That's terribly morbid. You're their leader. You're supposed to be
the optimistic one. I would have been.*"

Aaslo sighed heavily as he saw a small light illuminate in the
distance. "I'll work on it. It's hard trying to be you."

Mathias said nothing more, and Aaslo returned to his body, seated
on the stump. His companions gathered around Myra. Some chatted
with her while others, like Aria, watched warily. He stood and began
walking down the pathway, hardly more than a game trail, through
the fog-shrouded forest. He didn't bother to look back to see if anyone
followed. Plenty of people kept an eye on his movements. Seconds
later, he heard the tromps, jangles, and creaks of his followers. His
gaze swept the forest continuously. If the mere presence of so many
people didn't attract predators, the sounds of their passing would.

After about an hour, as they neared their destination, Aaslo heard
his name. He looked over to see Myra keeping pace with him. There
was tension around her eyes, and she worried at her lip.

"What is it, Myra?"

"I still need to speak with you."

"Can it wait until we get to the city? We're nearly there."

She appeared uncertain as her gaze followed Dolt, who was on his
other side. "Where are we going?"

"Indigen. It's a moderately sized town in southern Pashtigon.
We're hoping to acquire more supplies and recruits if any are to be
found. Most importantly, though, it's supposed to be the sight of an
important burial."

"It doesn't sound familiar, although I don't always know where I am when I collect souls. Once you get there, it will take some time for you to accomplish your goal, right? I assume you'll want to camp there as well?"

He nodded. "If there are no enemies bearing down on us."

"Perhaps we could speak alone before we exit the pathways?"

Something in the way she posed the question gave him pause. "Why before?"

"Um, it's like you said. I'm more *real* in the pathways. I prefer it, if you don't mind."

Aaslo wondered if that was truly the reason but decided to give her the benefit of the doubt. To his knowledge, she had always been honest about her motives and had never done anything to warrant his suspicion. "Very well," he said.

Once they reached the terminus of their journey, Aaslo opened the doorway into the world. He stepped through the portal and surveyed his surroundings. He stood in the center of a city square too small to hold all his people. Although he saw some half a dozen passersby freeze at the sight of him appearing out of the rift, the streets were otherwise empty. The majority of his undead minions filed through the portal behind him as a precaution in case any threats awaited them. Those city dwellers who had paused screamed in terror and ran for their lives. Others within the buildings lining the road heard their shouts, and doors and windows slammed shut.

Aaslo groaned. It would be more difficult to recruit followers if he couldn't get them to come out. Aaslo waited a few minutes to see if the city guard would respond, but when no one appeared, he turned back to the portal and stepped through. Aaslo stood to one side as the rest of his people poured into the city. Eventually, he and Myra were alone. He looked at her expectantly.

Myra licked her lips, her gaze refusing to meet his. She swallowed. "I'm not sure where to start. There are several matters of importance, and I need you to hear them all before you get too upset."

Aaslo had figured what she had to tell him wasn't pleasant, but having confirmed his suspicions, his guard rose. "Just tell me." The firmness of the order drew her attention, and he finally held her gaze.

"Do you remember when I mentioned that someone had stolen one of Arayallen's creations?"

He nodded.

"It's called a wind demon. Arayallen said that it is a creature that exists *between* realities, whatever that means. She said it was never meant to exist *here*, but it does—apparently, thanks to Trostili."

The tension mounted between Aaslo's shoulders. "Trostili unleashed this creature on the world? To what end? Where is it?"

She shook her head. "I don't know his intentions, but I do know where it is." She pinched her lips between her teeth, then blurted, "It's Dolt."

Aaslo's eyebrows climbed skyward. "Dolt? *Dolt*—my idiot horse—is actually a creature beyond reality brought here by the God of War for some nefarious purpose?"

Myra gripped her skirt anxiously. "It's more than that. I think he was purposely put in your path."

"That was months ago! That happened long before I even knew about the gods."

"Apparently, they knew about *you*. At least, Trostili must have. Axus seemed truly surprised by you."

Aaslo ran a clawed hand through his hair. "Look, I know Dolt is . . . strange, but he's still only a *horse*. He's never done anything *that* out of the norm . . ." Aaslo's words trailed off as he thought of all the times Dolt had influenced his decisions or played a part in major events. Then he thought about how the horse seemed to instinctively know the way through the interworld pathways. "Well, maybe he *is* that strange," he muttered.

"Just like his owner."

He ignored Mathias and looked back to Myra, who watched as he pieced things together. "What am I supposed to do? Even if I tried to leave him behind, I'm not sure he would stay. He can navigate the paths and probably find me no matter where I am, although I don't know if he can actually open a portal." She remained silent, and he followed with, "You think I should kill him."

Myra scrunched her face. "I'm not sure you *can*. He's not really a horse, and if I understand Arayallen correctly, then Dolt doesn't really exist in this world. At least, not in the way you do."

He sighed with frustration. "So what do I do?"

Myra, at a loss, shrugged.

"Okay," he said, pushing the subject aside for further thought later. "You said there were a few things you needed to discuss. What else?"

Myra's expression shuttered, and she gripped her skirt before smoothing the material again. Guilt passed over her features, but after a moment, she firmed her resolve and she straightened. "I have something for you." She held out her hand, which contained a glowing orb. "Please take it."

Aaslo looked at her skeptically then glanced to her hand. "What is it?"

She pressed her hand forward. "If you take it, you will find out."

"If it's some sort of magic, then I don't know that I should. There are enough powers inside me as it is. How do I know this will benefit me?"

Myra pulled her hand back and gripped the orb to her as if it held something truly important. Then she met his gaze, and something changed. Her face bore immeasurable sadness, a resignation to it. "No, I can't do this," she whispered. Then to him, "You're right, Aaslo. Perhaps you shouldn't accept it. To be honest, I don't know what it is, and it would be a betrayal for me to try to convince you that it is only a boon."

He continued to stare at her questioningly and she added, "It is a blessing from Arayallen, the Goddess of the Wilderness. She sees you as a piece in Trostili's game strategy, and she intends to change that. I don't know her plan, so I don't know if this so-called blessing is truly a curse."

"Yet you would have given it to me anyway?"

At first, she appeared uncertain, then she shook her head firmly. "No, despite my words earlier, I don't think I would have gone through with it." She dropped the orb, which dangled from a string at her waist, then pressed her hands to her chest, curling her fingers inward like claws. "I carry her power in that orb, but I can feel it *inside* me—like it's digging into my soul. But it's not *mine*. The longer it stays, the more uncomfortable it gets. It's already verging on pain, and I know it will only get worse. It needs to come out, but I think only you can take it from me."

Aaslo felt the sting of Myra's attempted betrayal, yet he also felt a sense of relief in knowing she didn't go through with it. Still, he knew Myra was an agent for his enemies, so he was skeptical. "Why did Arayallen not bless me herself?"

"She doesn't want to leave Celestria due to the war. She needs to protect her pantheon."

He nodded. "I get that, but why did she choose *you*? What makes her think I would trust you enough to accept this mysterious gift of power?"

Myra visibly swallowed. "She knows I've been helping you—"

He shook his head. "Not good enough. You work for Axus and Trostili. Of course I would be suspicious. How did she intend to overcome that?"

Tears spilled from Myra's eyes, and she buried her face in her hands. She blurted, "Because she knows what you mean to me. She thinks to use our relationship against you."

Aaslo was taken aback. He had suspected Myra had deeper motives for helping him beyond a penchant for humanity's survival, but he hadn't considered that she thought something deeper existed between them. He softened his voice. "Myra, we don't *have* a relationship—"

"Yes! We do, Aaslo. You just don't know it. I'm so sorry. Perhaps I should have told you from the beginning, but I was scared. I wanted to know you. I wanted you to like me, and I thought you would hate me if you knew."

Aaslo was shaking his head, continuing to deny her claims. "Knew what?"

She wiped her tears and met his gaze evenly as she said, "I'm your mother."

CHAPTER 8

AASLO HADN'T HEARD HER RIGHT. THIS WOMAN, THIS *REAPER*, WHO looked to be no older than he, claimed to be his mother. He couldn't deny it, not outright. He had never met his mother, at least not since he was a babe. After she left them, his father said he had never heard from her again. For a while when he was young, Aaslo had longed to know her, but he had given up that hope long ago. Now, he stared at this woman, this stranger, who claimed him as her son.

"Myra." He paused. Clues clicked into place. "*Myropa*. Your name is Myropa?"

She bit her lower lip and nodded.

For once, Mathias was silent.

"How do I know you're telling the truth? What proof do you have?"

She lifted her empty hands. "I don't have any proof, but I can tell you about myself, about your father, about *you*."

Feelings he had long since abandoned washed through Aaslo, and the dragon woke. "*Me?* What do you know of *me?*" he roared. "You were never there! You know *nothing* about me."

Myra—no, *Myropa*—winced. "Please, Aaslo. Let me explain."

Aaslo turned to pace in front of her. The fury of the dragon compounded his own desire to lash out, and for a moment he wasn't sure he could contain it. He inhaled several deep breaths, and a soothing sensation bathed his frazzled nerves. To his surprise, he felt Ina's power of growth, nourishment, and life flowing around his soul. For once, her tone seemed sincere as she whispered a single word. *Mother.*

Aaslo was still angry, but he was calmer. He turned to Myropa. "Go on. I'm listening."

Myropa blinked away tears and nodded. "Thank you," and she paused to collect her thoughts. Eventually, she said, "When I married your father, I was very young, barely eighteen. I loved Ielo, and I thought nothing could make me happier than to spend my life with him. But the truth was, I wasn't prepared for the life of a forester. The distance and solitude—not just from other people but from him as well—wore on me."

Aaslo started to protest, but she raised a hand. "Let me finish." He nodded, and she continued.

"Ielo was a good man, and he was a good husband. But, as you probably know, he wasn't very attentive. He was often gone for days and sometimes weeks at a time, and when he *was* home, we mostly sat in silence. It wasn't long before I couldn't take it anymore. I wanted a life filled with joy and happiness. I wanted excitement. I thought if I could only see the world, if I could meet people and learn new things, if I could feel the closeness of a human connection, I would be happy. I felt trapped in that little cabin in the woods far from everyone and everything."

The story was so reminiscent of his own misadventure into love that Aaslo couldn't help but feel her words held merit.

"So, I decided to leave," she continued. "I told Ielo I was going to live in the city, and I think he understood. He could see how unhappy I was. Imagine how I felt when I discovered I was pregnant before I could leave. I loved you, Aaslo, but the feeling of captivity was overwhelming. I felt that all hope of happiness had been stripped away from me. It was a selfish feeling, I know, but it was my truth. I didn't appreciate the blessing I had been given. I promised Ielo I would stay until you were weaned, and I did. Then I left."

Aaslo could only stare. He had never known the circumstances behind his mother's disappearance except that she had been unhappy. His father had never talked about her, at least no more than a passing remark when a young Aaslo had pestered him. He could see she was having trouble telling the rest of the story.

"You're dead, Myropa. What happened?"

Her pained expression told him this was the hardest part of the story.

"I went to the city with stars in my eyes. I was so naive." She shook her head sadly. "I found a job as a barmaid working for an older man named Faylon. He had a wife and two grown sons. They were kind at first. They even allowed me to live in a small room in the cellar beneath the tavern with the girl who worked in the kitchen. Her name was Belamny. She was quiet and reserved. I tried to be friends, but even when we were alone, she wouldn't talk much.

"Belamny always woke earlier than I did to start making the bread for the day. Except one morning she slept in late. She was in a hurry to get dressed, and I noticed she was covered in bruises. I asked her about them, but she wouldn't open up to me. In the weeks that followed, she would sometimes stumble down the stairs very late. She would be hunched over and cradling herself, and on a few occasions, she could barely walk. Her wheezing kept me up at night. Someone was beating her, and I sometimes worried she wouldn't make it through the night. One night she didn't. I woke to find her body cold and her eyes empty."

Myropa choked on a sob and blinked rapidly, although Aaslo didn't see any tears. She gripped her arms around herself. Aaslo felt inclined to lend her comfort, but she held herself back, putting space between them.

"Nobody questioned what happened to Belamny. Faylon's sons both worked as city guardsmen. One of them was a patrol leader. They got rid of the body and made it clear that if I didn't keep silent I, too, would disappear.

"After Belamny died, another girl was brought in to help in the tavern. She was younger than me, only seventeen. Her name was Lydia. That was when things got bad for me. Faylon drank *a lot*. At first, he would be friendly and jovial, but by night's end he became angry and vicious. His wife would go to bed early, and once all the doors were locked, Lydia would be sent to bed as well while I helped clean up. That's when the beatings started. At first, it was just a smack. Over time, it got worse and worse. I finally knew why Belamny would come down the stairs with bruises, and my heart ached for her. I knew it was only a matter of time before I ended up dead, like her."

Aaslo was horrified. He wanted to seek out the tavern owner and end his life in the same way he had ended the girl Belamny's. While what had been done to Myropa angered him, to his shame, he also found that he was angry with *her*. His inner dragon's toothy maw snapped, "Why didn't you leave? You had a good, safe life with Ielo, but you left him. You left *me*. Yet you were being beaten and you didn't you leave the tavern?"

Myropa looked as if she had been slapped, and he regretted his harsh words, but he couldn't shake the resentment that accompanied them.

"I wanted to," she said, her voice full of anguish. "I even planned it out several times. I couldn't go to the city guard. I told his wife, and she slapped me for telling lies. But she *knew*. I could see it in her eyes. I knew that if I left, he would only start beating Lydia. If I got Lydia to leave, it would be the next girl. For a while, I tried to convince myself that he had learned after his mistake with Belamny, that it wouldn't get as bad. Even then, I knew it was a lie." She took a deep breath. "I realized that the only way it was ever going to stop was if he was dead."

Aaslo's brow rose. "You killed him?"

Myropa lowered her eyes in shame and shook her head. "I wanted to, but I wasn't sure I could. One night, as he locked the doors, I grabbed a knife. I crept up behind him, raising the knife. But I hesitated. My muscles locked tight in fear. I was afraid of what would happen if I tried and failed—or if I succeeded. If they caught me, they would hang me. In that moment, I froze. He turned and found me there, ready. He laughed at me and grabbed the knife from my shaking hand. Then he beat me until I could barely breathe. The whole time he laughed. Then he said he was going to get Lydia, to show her what would happen to her if she didn't behave.

"That's when I snapped. I gathered the little strength I had left and lunged for the knife sitting on the table. He came at me, and this time when he grabbed me, I plunged the knife into his neck. There was so much blood. So much. He collapsed on top of me, and I didn't have the strength to move him. That's when his son walked in. He rolled his father off me. He said he was going to arrest me, but he would make sure I paid for what I had done before they hanged me. I was reeling from what had just happened, and I was terrified. I panicked. I couldn't let them take me. I couldn't endure any more pain. I grabbed the knife and just—reacted."

"You killed yourself."

She swallowed and nodded once. Even scared and vulnerable, she held his gaze. Aaslo reached out and gripped her hand. "None of that was your fault, Myropa. Why do you look so guilty?"

She met his gaze and said, "Because I was selfish, and I failed. I was too weak. I didn't kill him the first time when I had the chance. I didn't save myself. I might have saved Lydia, but I'll never know. I never got the chance to do right by you or your father. In my whole life, I didn't help *anyone*."

"You *tried*." The denial in her expression told Aaslo he wasn't getting through to her. "Pa never stopped loving you. Neither of us did. You could have come home. They wouldn't have found you in Goldenwood, and Ielo would have protected you."

She looked at him and nodded. "I know he would have. Your father would have done anything to make me happy. I know that now, looking back. The truth is, I didn't think I deserved him. I didn't deserve *you*. I had come to realize my mistake in leaving you, and I couldn't forgive myself for my selfish choices. I see the judgment in your eyes, and I don't blame you." Aaslo started to deny it, but she kept talking. "There is nothing I regret more than leaving you. Seeing you as a man, I can't help but mourn all the years I missed being in your life. I will understand if you don't wish to see me again. Just know that I love you with every piece of my soul."

Aaslo wasn't sure what to say. His mother had lived a terrible life after she had left Goldenwood, one that had come to an end far too soon. She had been so young. She had barely lived, and she had never found the happiness she so eagerly sought. "I don't judge you, and I don't think you were selfish. Is it wrong to want to be happy? I was happy in my forest. I never wanted to leave. If not for Mathias, I doubt I would understand. He always wanted a bigger life than what Goldenwood had to offer. He wanted excitement and adventure. I knew that about him, and I think I always knew we would either be parted or I would have to go with him. I don't blame you for leaving, Myropa. The life of a forester's wife is not an easy one. It's not your fault you weren't able to handle it. Yes, you left me, but Ielo was a good father, and I had Grams and Mathias. I forgive you. I only wish that you had come home when you needed help."

Myropa's lip quivered while tears wet her cheeks. She took a hesitant step toward him. Aaslo opened his arms, and she fell into them, gripping him with all her strength. Aaslo held his mother close; the way he dreamt of as a child. She was slight and appeared no older than he, but Aaslo recognized the truth of her words. Despite her service to the gods who were his enemies, or perhaps because of her willingness to betray that service, Aaslo accepted the bond of kinship between them. He embraced Myropa as she shook with great heaving sobs, clinging to him as though she would never let him go.

"I'm so, so sorry," she murmured over and over. Aaslo hushed her as he gently stroked her hair with his claws. After some time, she pulled away, but he continued to hold her hands. She met his searching gaze. "Thank you. Your forgiveness is all the peace a mother could hope for."

"I can't believe you're really her," muttered Aaslo.

Myropa's expression fell. "You don't believe me?"

"No, I mean, I do. It's just . . . it's been so long, and I never thought to actually meet you. I'd always imagined you, but in my mind you were different."

Uncertainty stole across her face. "Different how?"

"Well, I guess you were bigger."

Myropa suddenly laughed, and Aaslo was glad to have brought a smile to her forlorn countenance. "You're not a little boy anymore, Aaslo, and I'm not one of the gods. You're a big, strong man, and I'm a woman—even if I'm not exactly human any longer."

He nodded with a smirk. "I know. I suppose the image of you in my mind never changed even though I did." He brushed a thumb down her cheek, wiping away a tear. "I'm glad to have met you, Mother." A movement in the fog abruptly caught Aaslo's attention. The dragon inside him lifted its head and sniffed the air. Aaslo caught himself doing the same.

"What is it?" Myropa asked.

Aaslo shook his head. "I don't recognize the scent, and it's getting fainter. I think it's moving away." Myropa turned to scan the area with him, but it seemed that whatever it was had disappeared. The dragon dropped its head and settled, so Aaslo took that as a sign that all was well. Still, he was reminded that they were not in a secure location and people awaited him. With the portal still open, time continued at a normal pace on Aldrea. He turned his attention to his mother.

"This power that Arayallen gave you. If she knew you were my mother, why did she think you would betray me?"

Myropa winced at the reminder then said, "She thinks I desire to be with Disevy, and she all but said she could make that happen if I did this for her."

Aaslo's eyebrows rose. "The god?"

She nodded.

"I see. And she thought that if you confessed to your relationship with me then I would trust you."

Myropa nodded again.

Aaslo didn't know how to feel about his mother being with anyone but his father, but it had been decades since the two had seen each other, not to mention that Myropa was dead. "Do you want him?"

She appeared surprised. "Who? Disevy?" At his nod, she swallowed. "I know this must be awkward for you, Aaslo, but Ielo and I cannot be. Even if we could—"

He held up a hand to forestall her. "I know. That is in the past. Do you want to be with Disevy, though, or is he forcing you?"

"What? No! Disevy is the kindest man—er, *god*—I have ever met. He's strong and compassionate and a complete gentleman. I cannot imagine what he sees in me, but if there is a chance I could be with him, I would take it in a heartbeat." She laid her hand over her heart and said, "I mean that literally. He gave me back my heartbeat."

He ran a clawed hand through his hair. "Okay, give me the power."

Myropa's eyes widened. "You want to take Arayallen's so-called blessing knowing it could be a curse?"

Aaslo released a heavy breath. "Yes. You can't keep it. You said it's hurting you, and I'm the only one who can take it. I don't want more pain for you, and there's no telling what it'll do in the long run. Plus, I could use every advantage available to me."

"But I'm your mother, Aaslo. I would carry this burden forever regardless of the pain if it will save you. You don't know that it will be an advantage."

"It's a gamble. Trostili has been using me to get the war he wants, and Arayallen wants to steal me from him. The best way to do that is either to kill me or give me power to use against him."

"Aaslo, I've seen Arayallen's menagerie, and I've seen her power in use. There are a lot of things she could do short of killing you."

"I know, but I am willing to take that risk if it means the continuation of life on Aldrea."

Myropa shook her head. "I don't think it does. Arayallen is very firm in her belief that Aldrea is damned. She's only concerned about Celestria now."

"All the more reason to accept the power. Let us hope it's a boon."

Myropa sifted through the orbs dangling from her belt. She held one up in the space between them. "Please, be sure of this, Aaslo. I love you."

"You're bolder than I would be."

Aaslo hesitated, wondering if Mathias would have made the same choice. Knowing his brother, he doubted it. Mathias had been adventurous, but not reckless. He took a deep breath and nodded once. "I'm sure."

Then he opened himself to the dark power at his core that suffused him like a miasma. Inky tendrils slapped away Ina's interfering fingers. Then they shot out toward the glowing orb, latching onto it and draining it. A golden power surged up the tendrils and struck Aaslo with enough force to blow him from his feet. The wind had been knocked from his chest, and he landed a good twenty paces from where he had been standing. The power burned through his body as he attempted to fill his lungs with the breath he desperately needed. In that instant, he knew he had made a terrible mistake. The power *gifted* to him by the Goddess of the Wilderness, the very goddess worshipped by his fellow foresters, was killing him.

He blinked the tears from his eyes, and he could see a watery figure above him. All he could hear was a high-pitched squealing and the muffled sound of a voice. His body shook—inside and out. Something heavy struck his chest, and he suddenly sucked in air. He heaved in great gasps as he coughed and sputtered while rolling onto his side. He was still shaking when he regained enough sense that he could see Myropa leaning over him, calling his name.

"Aaslo, please speak to me. Are you okay?"

"Wake up, sleepyhead."

Aaslo shook his head as another round of coughs wracked his lungs. Finishing, he gulped down more air then lay back on the dirt and grass. From that vantage, he could barely see Myropa's face through the fog. She gripped his face between her hands. "Aaslo, say something."

"And stop lying around, you lazy lunk. You have work to do."

The burning embers of his lungs eased to a smolder, and the pain in his limbs became a dull ache. "I—I'm okay. I think. I'm alive," he murmured.

Myropa looked away, then began tugging him upright. Aaslo pulled back. All he wanted was to lie there and sleep.

"Aaslo, please. You're not safe here. You need to get up."

Her harried words tugged at his senses, and Aaslo realized she was right. He didn't know how the shock wave of power had sounded from the outside, but in his mind, it had been an immense explosion. It would attract attention. They needed to leave the paths.

Aaslo forced himself to stand on shaky legs. One glance around told him that he had been thrown onto a completely different path. He staggered over the brush to the doorway that would lead him to his people. Before he stepped through, though, he turned and embraced his mother again. He didn't know if he would get another chance, and he had a lifetime to make up for.

"You're really okay?" she said, brushing his hair back and looking into his eyes.

"Nothing a little dirt and leaves can't fix. Am I right, Forester?"

He nodded. "I think so. I'll sit down and reassess myself when we're in a secure location."

Aaslo grasped Myropa's hand and turned to the portal. He took a deep, steadying breath then pulled her through the gate. The crowd of people, living and undead, who Aaslo had brought with him and no one else, waited on the other side. The shops, homes, and businesses were shuttered, and all was quiet save for the muted drone of the uncertain travelers. When the portal winked out of existence, most turned to look his way, and he was almost certain he heard a unified sigh of relief.

"Whoa," said Teza as she sidled up next to him. "You look different."

Aaslo rubbed his sore chest. "How so?"

She narrowed her eyes thoughtfully and replied, "I'm not sure. I can't quite put my finger on it, but there is definitely something different about you."

"I see it as well," said the marquess, who turned from his duty of organizing the chaos. "It is as if you are suddenly *more*."

"More what?"

"*Stubborn. Mulish. Obstinate. Take your pick.*"

The marquess narrowed his eyes as he scrutinized Aaslo. Finally, he threw up his hands and said, "I don't know. Perhaps it is my imagination."

"What did the reaper want?" asked Teza.

Aaslo looked to Myropa, who stood invisibly at his side. She appeared hopeful, which made Aaslo wonder if she wanted him to publicly claim her as his mother. He tried to take her hand, but his own passed through her to no effect.

He turned back to Teza and the marquess. "We'll discuss it later. Have we found a location to establish a base?"

The marquess shook his head. "Three main streets lead to this square and several alleys. We've secured them all but haven't made additional progress." He nodded toward a towering stone structure that consisted of three levels and windows set behind a row of ornate columns. The long path of steps leading up to the structure traversed a well-maintained lawn. At the base of the steps, a gallows dominated the square. It was solidly built and appeared to be a permanent structure. Several of his soldiers sat atop the platform and leaned against the supports with casual ease despite its intended purpose.

"I thought perhaps we could set up in there," said the marquess. "It's the courthouse."

Aaslo shrugged. "It's as good a place as any. Where are the city guards? Has there been any resistance?"

"No. The city seems to be in lockdown," answered the marquess.

Teza joined in, "It's just as well. At least this way we won't have to fight anyone."

"It doesn't bode well for acquiring supplies or recruitment, though," replied Aaslo.

"What do you want us to do?" Teza looked at him expectantly.

"I don't know," grumbled Aaslo. "What do people normally do when they want others to gather?"

"Throw a party?" Teza gave a bemused smirk.

The marquess chuckled. "These people are terrified. I don't think throwing a party will work. We could go door-to-door and force them out."

Aaslo shook his head. "That wouldn't engender loyalty, plus it would take too long."

"Who needs loyalty?" said Teza. "It's either fight to live or die."

"*That would work, too. You don't need them alive to fight.*"

Aaslo growled. "I'm not killing a city's people to fill my undead army."

Teza blinked back with wide eyes. "Who said anything about killing?"

"Never mind. Send criers through the city. Spread the word of who we are and why we're here. Maybe some people will be emboldened."

Aaslo turned toward the courthouse. Soldiers had already been dispatched to ensure they would encounter no resistance upon entering the building. Several clerks and a magistrate barricaded themselves in one of the ground-floor offices, but they were quickly subdued. Aaslo learned the city had been on lockdown since the magi had abandoned it months ago. After the lyksvight began attacking surrounding villages, nearly all commerce and travel into and out of the city had ceased. Although the magistrate and his clerks had been forthcoming with information, they were not convinced of the army's intentions, particularly given the undead army at its center, which had bypassed the protective walls and gates.

Knowing his presence would only frighten the city folk, Aaslo left the convincing to others and searched out a private place to explore his new *gift*. Myropa silently followed him into an office lined with bookcases filled with thick, dusty tomes. The floor bore several mismatched carpets, and the furniture style was, at best, eclectic. Aaslo took a seat in a chair in front of the dark hearth. Since he was supposed to be exploring his powers, he tugged on a bit of the dragon's influence to send a thin stream of flame to light the logs in the hearth. Satisfied he could at least do that much, he turned his focus inward.

"How can I help?" said Myropa, rousing him from his thoughts.

"I don't know. I suppose you can watch, and if anything bad happens, go get Mory to alert the others."

Myropa gripped her skirt anxiously. "Perhaps someone else should be here with you. Maybe the healer or the prophet?"

"No, I don't need the distraction."

Myropa sat on the floor at his feet watching him as he turned his attention inward. The first powers to strike at him were the depraved, wrapped around his soul in an effort to devour him. With great effort, he yanked each away. They stuck to him like tar, and in their wakes, left messy strings of demented power. He could already feel them slowly migrating back as he turned to assess the other entities that occupied him. He easily identified the three powers dominating his actions thus far. The elusive, yet soft and nurturing touch of Ina, the brazen boldness of the dragon, and the seductive lure of death's dark power were each eager to consume him should he lower his guard. The blessings of the gods, however, were more elusive. Myropa had claimed that Disevy, God of Strength and Virility, had secretly blessed him. While he couldn't remember accepting such a blessing, he had noticed a significant increase in his physical strength.

"You were obviously blessed since infancy with strength of will."

"Another joke about my stubbornness. How refreshing."

"What?" replied Myropa. "I said nothing."

Aaslo's eyes remained closed but he shook his head and continued searching within himself for the so-called blessings of the gods. Other than a general sensation of power, he found nothing. Frustrated, Aaslo was ready to give up when a thought occurred to him. He had gained a great deal of strength with his dragon arm, but of late, it had been more than that. His whole body was affected, and not only in the ability to lift heavy objects or hit really hard. He noticed an increase in his endurance and stamina and even an increase in his strength of will and fortitude. It was as if everything that made him who he was felt stronger. If such was Disevy's blessing, then perhaps Arayallen's was similar. Maybe it was simply part of who he was, and it could not be quantified. Aaslo didn't know if the realization should relieve or perturb him. He needed to know what Arayallen had done to him.

He looked at Myropa—his *mother*—and wondered what she thought of what he had become. Her expression changed when she saw him looking, and he had his answer. No longer restricted to hiding her feelings, she looked upon him with adoration. She did not judge him just as he did not judge her.

"You know," she said, interrupting his thoughts, "there *is* something different about you."

"There's always *been something different about you."*

Ignoring Mathias, Aaslo asked, "How so?"

"I can sense it but not with my eyes. It's a feeling—almost like the feeling I get when I'm near the gods. I can sense their power. It radiates from them unless they pull it in. Not all of them do it very well."

"So you can feel Arayallen's power in me?"

Myropa shook her head. "No, I know what Arayallen's power feels like, and this doesn't feel like her. It's unique to you. It's either well contained or it's too weak to radiate much."

"Will it get stronger?"

With a lift of her shoulders, Myropa said, "I don't know. I don't even know what it is, but it definitely feels like Celestrian power."

Aaslo stood and paced the multitude of rugs as he considered her words. "When Axus wanted to see me, he pulled part of my consciousness into Celestria, but my body remained in Ruriton. Later, when I spoke with Enani in her garden, it felt like more of my consciousness was there, but again my body stayed on Aldrea."

He glanced over as Myropa nodded. "That makes sense," she said. "Humans—the living ones—cannot go to Celestria. They don't have the power to get there. Even if they did, the realm is entirely saturated with the power of the gods. It would overwhelm the body *and* mind. I'm not exactly sure what would happen, but I'm pretty sure a human would cease to exist."

"But you said this new power feels like Celestria. What if it somehow makes me compatible with the power of the gods?"

She looked startled. "You think Arayallen gave you the power to enter Celestria?"

"Perhaps. Arayallen asked Enani to show me how to navigate the paths. What if she wants me to confront Trostili and Axus in their own realm?" He rolled his tight shoulders back and sighed. "I don't know. It's just a feeling."

It was a terrible feeling. Aaslo couldn't imagine going to the realm of the gods. It wasn't open to humans. Sure, Myropa went there, but she was dead and had the power of the reapers. This was different—unless it wasn't. Would he have to die to go to Celestria? Would Myropa carry his soul there? Aaslo cringed. Not only did he not want to die, but he didn't want to put his mother through that kind of anguish.

Myropa's troubled gaze reached him from where she sat before the hearth. "I don't want you to go there, Aaslo."

"Why not?"

She abruptly stood and balled her tiny fists. "Because they're *gods*! They will destroy you."

"She of little faith. You're too dense to be destroyed."

She had a point—one Aaslo had intentionally avoided thinking about because it struck him with visceral fear. How could he, a mere human, fight the gods? The gods were all-powerful. They created *everything*, including him. They had control over life and death. He was an insignificant speck to them, an ant. The grizzly bear did not care about the ant. It was nearly impossible to think about fighting the vast army of the Berru, but at least they were human. He could recruit other humans to fight with him. Him, alone, fighting the gods themselves. An unfamiliar feeling bubbled up inside him. His heart raced, and he broke out in a sweat. It was like the feeling he got before battle, except uncontrolled. He couldn't do it. He would fail, and in his failure would be the end of all life on Aldrea.

"That feeling is panic, brother. Let it go."

"I can't," Aaslo choked out.

"Yes, you can. You're stubborn and resilient. You can do this. If you do nothing, everything will die."

"If I try and fail, everything will die."

"But at least you will have tried. It's better to die fighting. I believe you can succeed."

"How can you say that? They're *gods*!"

"I have faith in you. I will be with you the entire way."

The panic abated, and Aaslo's vision cleared. Myropa stood before him wearing a look of compassion as she said, "Are you okay, Aaslo?"

He nodded as the possibilities fell into perspective. "I am faced with life-and-death circumstances every day. If it's not the Berru who are after me, it's some gruesome monster or lyksvight."

She clasped her hands in front of her. "I know, and I hate it. Those things might only kill you, though. You would die and go to the Sea, and someday I would join you. But the gods can do much worse, Aaslo. There truly are worse fates than death. They could make you into anything they want. They could *unmake* you."

Another thread of panic twisted in his gut, but he pushed it down. "I don't believe the gods have that power," he replied. "I have felt the power of the human soul, and I know it to be infinite. The gods don't have the power to unmake that."

"Perhaps not," she said, appearing thoughtful. "But Axus's maelstrom is a terrible place. You would not wish to go there. Some of Arayallen's creatures are grotesque. She would not hesitate to put you in one should you displease her. I can't even imagine what the other gods would do. Even if you *can* go to Celestria, I doubt they would be welcoming."

Aaslo leaned down to close the distance between them. He tried to take her hands, but his own passed through her to no effect. She looked at him with a sad smile. He said, "I will be careful, no matter what I do. I promise you that."

She blinked as if she might cry. She nodded. "I love you, my son."

"I love you, too," he replied, and he knew it to be true. Even before he knew her, he had always loved his mother. Only now he had a face to put with that love.

The door to the office slammed open, and in walked Teza. Her pristine silvery armor iridesced in the light of the blue flame flickering above her outstretched hand. Aaslo looked at the flame quizzically. Teza took note of the luminous fire in the hearth and extinguished the tiny inferno.

"It's gotten dark in the corridor," she said in explanation. "A storm has blown in, and the sky is nearly black as night."

"That's too bad," Aaslo said, turning toward her. "I don't want to have to search for the tomb in a downpour."

"We can wait until tomorrow. It may blow over."

Aaslo shook his head. "No. I fear things are getting away from us. The gods have been plotting and preparing."

Teza's gaze darted about the heavily furnished room as she said, "Oh? Is *she* still here? What does she know?"

Aaslo waved toward the open doorway. "Go get Ijen and the marquess. There are things we need to discuss. I suppose you should bring Aria and Andromeda, too."

CHAPTER 9

By the time Teza returned with the others, Myropa had departed. Aaslo explained to the group Myropa's true identity as his mother, which intrigued Ijen, stirring him to scribble in his book, and only irritated Teza further. She felt the relation all too convenient for the gods and expressed a renewed interest in keeping Myropa out of their plans. Aaslo understood her feelings, but he was loath to exclude his newfound mother from what little life he had left. He briefly considered taking the paths back to Goldenwood to discuss the matter with his father but ultimately decided against it. Ielo was better off not knowing what had happened to his young wife for the time being. It would only upset him, and Aaslo would not be around to give him the support he would need.

The meeting continued with Aaslo's revelation of Arayallen's blessing and his hypothesis regarding the nature of the power. He received mixed responses, from Andromeda's outright disbelief to Aria's hopeful insistence that he explore the new power to its fullest. When Aaslo brought up the idea that he might travel to Celestria, Ijen became quite animated, and he rapidly flipped through the pages of prophecy.

"Ah-ha!" the prophet exclaimed. "Here it is. Yes, this section makes more sense in the current context. You see, in this line here, you left this world, but never could I find where you reentered it. I initially assumed you had died, but I think now I was mistaken. It is possible you went to another realm; which one, I cannot know. Perhaps it was the realm of the gods after all."

Aaslo didn't want to ask, but he felt it pertinent. "What happens to me on that line of prophecy?"

Ijen tapped his pursed mouth with his pen, leaving a blot of ink on his lower lip. "I suppose it wouldn't hurt to say . . ." He sighed and slammed the book shut. "In this one you leave Aldrea, as I mentioned. Then you are battling a great power. A golden light burns through your core, surrounding you, and then you are thrust into the dark, trapped in a massive storm. What happens next doesn't make sense to my eyes, so I cannot describe it. I don't know if you survive."

Aaslo felt anxiety well up, but the overwhelming urge to lash out at the prophet was buffeted by Mathias's laughter.

"I give him points for creativity, but I wouldn't worry myself overmuch."

"Why? You don't believe him?"

Ijen tilted his head, looking at him curiously.

"Oh, I believe him. I just think it's awfully convenient that he starts sharing now with such vivid imagery."

Aaslo stroked his chin and narrowed his eyes at Ijen.

Ijen looked surprised. He threw up his hands in defeat. "I give up," the prophet announced. "You are unhappy when I don't share, and you are unhappy when I do. Honestly, it never occurred to me that the very subject of my prophecies might think me the enemy."

Aaslo ignored the prophet's outburst. "There's one other thing. It's about Dolt." He explained that his horse was not a horse and had been placed in his path by none other than the God of War. The marquess, cautious in his approach, asked numerous questions without seeming to forge an opinion, while Aria and Andromeda eagerly made suggestions about how to get rid of the beast. It came as a surprise to Aaslo when it was Teza who spoke on Dolt's behalf.

"There is no way that horse—or whatever he is—is a threat to you, Aaslo. You should know that. Ever since I met you, Dolt has been dedicated to you. Sure, he can be a little irritating sometimes, but has he ever done anything to hurt you?"

An assortment of retorts leaped to his tongue, but Aaslo paused. "Not that I recall."

"There, you see? If Trostili did intend for harm to befall you, then he miscalculated with Dolt. He's harmless."

Aaslo regarded her seriously. "Hardly. Myropa saw the body of a man killed by the creature when it came into this world."

Teza held out her hands, pleading for him to understand. "He was a baaaby. He was confused and didn't know what he was doing. But now he's a horse, and he acts horselike—mostly."

Andromeda scoffed. "Most *babies* don't kill people. He obviously isn't to be trusted."

"I am in agreement," said Aria. "It is an unnecessary risk. Just get another horse."

Aaslo turned to the marquess. The man shrugged. "I'm inclined to agree with Mage Teza. I've always thought that you and your horse share an unusual bond."

Finally, Aaslo looked to Ijen. The prophet placidly stared at him, his finger hovering over the book as if waiting for Aaslo to decide.

Aaslo sighed and headed toward the door.

"Where are you going?" said Teza.

"To have a talk with my horse."

Aaslo made his way out of the courthouse to be met by a white sheet of rain. The onslaught had little to no effect on the undead, but the living suffered. Some tents had been erected, but the majority of army personnel were delayed in setting up camp. Aaslo pulled his hood over his head and splashed through widening puddles. He observed gloomy faces as he traversed the open square, and he noted one group of mismatched soldiers from the marquess's guards, the Uyanian royal army, and the Pashtigonian warriors were involved in a heated exchange centered around him and his unwillingness to force the city's inhabitants to accept his soldiers into their homes.

"It's our right to demand entry," said one of the former army soldiers.

"We're not in Uyan," snapped a Pashtigonian. "This is our land, and these are our people. Only the queen can make such demands."

"We serve the King of the Dead," said the first man, "and he rules everything that lives now."

One of the marquess's guards responded, "How would you feel if it were *your* home and *your* family invaded by a foreign army?"

"But we're not foreign—not anymore," said the first man. "We're the army for the living. If these people won't join us to fight, the least they can do is put us up so we don't have to suffer this godsforsaken weather."

"Maybe they should," said the Pashtigonian, "but we can't *make* them."

The first hefted his weapon and said, "I'm the one with the sword. I can make them if I need to."

As Aaslo moved farther from the group their voices were lost in the rain. He wondered if perhaps the former soldier was right. Maybe he *should* force the inhabitants to provide refuge to the soldiers. The soldiers could use that time and proximity to convince the citizens to join the cause. He mulled this over as he approached the picket line where the horses were kept. Hegress, the commander of the cavalry and infantry, had selected this street because of its many overhangs and awnings. Aaslo deduced that this street was probably the city's main market during better times. There were even a few stables dotting the walk, so the horses were somewhat protected from the weather.

After asking directions only twice, Aaslo finally located Dolt. As he entered the stable, he shook the water from his coat. The heavy wool had thus far protected him from the dampness, but it was growing heavier as it began to absorb moisture. It would not be long before he was as soaked as the soldiers. He hung his jacket on a hook beside Dolt's stall and then considered the beast, who dutifully ignored him in favor of the carrots Mory fed him.

Mory glanced over as if just noticing Aaslo. "I got him in here before it started raining. He's been brushed down already."

Aaslo nodded. "Thank you, Mory. If you would excuse us, I need to have a chat with him."

Mory gave him a perplexed look, glancing several times at the horse as if he couldn't quite comprehend what Aaslo wanted. When Aaslo didn't provide further explanation, he said, "Okay, I'll be right over by the door if you need me." The boy exited the stall and crossed the stables to take a seat on a stool by the door at the other end. Although he averted his gaze, Aaslo could tell the boy was watching him carefully.

Aaslo looked to Dolt, who had turned in the stall to give Aaslo his rear. "We need to speak," Aaslo said with only a bit of chagrin. He didn't know if the creature that was truly Dolt could speak or even understand him, but it was worth a try. Dolt abruptly lifted his tail and defecated in a smelly pile at Aaslo's feet.

"This is looking to be an interesting conversation."

"More interesting than some of ours," Aaslo replied to Mathias. To Dolt, he said, "Turn around and listen to me."

Dolt snorted but after a moment did as Aaslo requested. Seeing that they might be getting somewhere, Aaslo continued.

"I know you're not really a horse," he said. "What I don't know is what you want."

Dolt simply stared at him with his mismatched eyes.

"You're a master interrogator."

"I'm talking to a horse," Aaslo ground out. "I doubt you'd be any better." Returning his attention to Dolt, he said, "Are you friend or foe?"

"I see we're counting on the horse to be truthful."

"He's not a horse," Aaslo replied. "And we don't know that he's capable of guile."

"We don't know that he's capable of anything but being a horse. And here you are talking to him."

Dolt snorted then proceeded to nuzzle Aaslo's hair. Aaslo pushed the horse's head away. "Stop that. What are your intentions? Do you mean us harm?"

Dolt shook his head, but Aaslo couldn't tell if he was communicating or shaking off a fly.

Frustrated, Aaslo tried a different tack. He opened his mind to the powers that stirred within him. For this task, he decided the power of Ina would serve him best. He tugged on it, but she cackled to herself as she held it close.

"*You seek my power, yet you do not honor me,*" she intoned.

"What honor do you demand?" Aaslo muttered.

"*Join with me. Allow my power to consume you, and you shall have all you ever need and desire.*"

"I will never succumb to your power. It is lent to me. You must release it."

Ina's laughter echoed as she faded from his mind, and suddenly a thin stream of her nurturing power flowed through him. Aaslo remembered one of the many poems his adopted grandmother Magdelay had taught him and Mathias, which he now knew to have been a spell. She had never told him outright the spell's use, but it seemed to focus on communing with animals. Aaslo whispered the spell now as he suffused it with Ina's power.

The spell unfurled in his mind then drifted through the air aimlessly. He realized he would need to direct it to reach Dolt, so he focused on the short distance between them. The spell wavered then contracted into a stream connecting him to the horse that was not a horse. Aaslo abruptly felt a new presence in his mind. It was altogether alien, seemingly with little sense or reason. Thoughts came to him as senses—images, smells, sounds—and Aaslo tried to collect them in a semblance of order. Beneath it all, he sensed something else, something *other*. Aaslo focused on the foreign entity, pulling it toward him and pressing into it.

Dolt snorted and shook his head, tossing his mane like a willow in a windstorm. Aaslo felt the strange sensation pushing him away, but he persisted. He latched onto it with his will but softened his touch. He tried to coax it into a connection, then it happened. It snapped at him with such force he nearly lost the connection altogether. At the same time Dolt launched forward to bite his face. Aaslo dodged in time to avoid a crippling disfigurement as he backed into the wall of the stall.

Dolt reared onto his hind legs and pawed at the air in front of Aaslo. Just when he thought he would be trampled, Dolt settled onto the ground with heavy stomps and a shrieked whinny.

Aaslo held up his hands in front of his face and said, "Okay, okay. I won't do that again. I'm just trying to communicate."

Dolt tossed his head again then smacked Aaslo in the face with his muzzle. Aaslo sidestepped the horse and backed out of the stall. His heart raced furiously from nearly being trampled by the heavily muscled horse, but he realized they remained connected by the spell. After a few steadying breaths, he brushed his will ever so softly over the alien entity, and Dolt stilled to look at him in warning.

Then, as if in allowance, Aaslo received a new sensation. It was a feeling—a *knowing*. Without evidence, he knew Dolt saw him as part of his herd. Unfortunately, Dolt saw Aaslo, not as the leader, but rather a lesser member of the herd—much like a colt who needed to be protected and directed. With this revelation, Mathias rolled around in Aaslo's mind, laughing hysterically, but Aaslo was confused. He swept his will across the entity again, but this time Dolt was not having it. With a great shove, Aaslo was propelled out of the connection, and he nearly fell onto his rear with the force. When he stumbled, Mory materialized at his side.

"Are you okay, Aaslo?"

Aaslo waved Mory off. "Yes, I'm fine."

"Are you sure? Dolt seems to be in a fit. He wasn't like that before. What did you do?"

"I told you. I needed to talk with him."

Mory looked at him skeptically. "Did you get what you needed?"

Aaslo nodded slowly. "I think so. I'm pretty sure Dolt doesn't mean us any harm."

Mory glanced at the horse with wide eyes. "Why would he? He's a horse."

"More or less," muttered Aaslo. "Just keep him comfortable. I don't know what he might do if he's upset with his conditions."

"Of course, I'll do my best."

"Thanks, Mory."

"He's doing you a favor. Say something nice, Aaslo."

"I did. I said thanks," Aaslo grumped. At Mory's perplexed look, he said, "You'd make a good squire—if I were a knight."

Mory grinned and straightened proudly, and for once Aaslo recognized the wisdom of Mathias's advice.

Aaslo left the stables, and after surveying the hastily erected camp, eventually made his way back to the courthouse. The marquess and Teza were bent over a map laid out on a table in the center of the foyer, discussing how best to acquire the supplies and recruits they needed. Aaslo had not only made a decision about Dolt in the time he had been gone, he had also determined the necessity for action.

"Marquess," he said, approaching the two. "Have the soldiers quarter in the homes of the city's residents."

The marquess looked at him with surprise. "Are you sure? That's an extreme measure."

"I believe it's a necessary measure. Instruct them to recruit whoever they can while there. Willing volunteers only. No one is to be forced."

"I don't think that's a good idea, Aaslo," replied Teza. "Do you know what soldiers do to women in those situations?"

The implication disgusted Aaslo. He hadn't considered his own soldiers might be less than honorable. "Let it be known that anyone mistreating the residents will be hung in the town square."

Teza pursed her lips.

"What?"

"It's just, that might deter *some* but not *all*. Men make threats. They believe they won't get caught."

Aaslo's claws curled into a fist. "Very well, put one of the undead in each of the homes with women who have no protection. I will instruct the undead to protect the women from the soldiers if necessary."

Teza's eyes widened. "The people will be terrorized if they have to quarter the undead."

"They'll get used to them. The undead are a part of our army. They need to understand that."

"You've become a brutal warlord. I did not see that coming."

The marquess said, "This won't be a popular decision with the city's residents."

"No, but it will get the soldiers out of the weather, and will provide the recruitment opportunity we need."

"I see," said the marquess. "I will make it so."

Aaslo nodded once. "Good." Then he turned to Teza. "You and Ijen and I will seek out the tomb of the ancient tomorrow at dawn."

Teza scrunched her face. "Does it have to be so early?"

"The early forester gets the seed."

"What does that mean?" grumbled Aaslo.

"It just sounded like something you would say."

Aaslo said, "Stick to your own sayings. That one made no sense."

Teza crossed her arms. "I'm not a morning person, okay?"

Ignoring Mathias's rebuttal, Aaslo said, "We need all the time we can get. I had considered going tonight but for the storm. It's been more than a millennium since anyone has seen the tomb, and we don't know how accurate Sedi's map is. We must also consider that it might be a trap."

"I don't like depending on the enemy for intel," muttered Teza.

Aaslo nodded his agreement. "Magical armor aside?"

Teza shrugged unapologetically.

"Will you also be taking troops with you?" asked the marquess.

"A few. If Sedi chooses to attack, there is little they could do. They'd probably just get killed."

"There are more dangers than one woman."

Aaslo grunted. "That *one woman* is worse than most of the other dangers combined."

"All the more reason not to trust her," replied the marquess evenly. "I'd say at least five units are necessary."

"I'll take two. We're looking for a buried tomb. It's likely to be cramped. The extra units will get in the way."

The marquess shrugged. "It's your funeral."

Teza shook her head. "If he dies, it's everyone's funeral."

Teza's blatant statement about his mortality struck Aaslo. He knew he was the de facto leader, but he had not thought of it hinging on his survival. Surely if he died, someone else would take his place. He wasn't the chosen one, after all. Anybody could take up the task.

CHAPTER 10

THE SKY WAS DARK, AND THE RAIN ENCLOSED THEM IN A POCKET OF space beyond which it was difficult to see the city. What he could observe looked as though the initial attempts at organizational planning had been thwarted by time and population growth. Smaller homes, some barely more than shanties, interrupted the neat rows of townhomes. On one cobbled street, the homes had been converted to shops, and rows of empty market stalls dotted the lane. Instead of color, wooden carvings with faded paint in a palette of green, yellow, and brown decorated the facades. Some homes had small, raised garden plots in front, containing what looked like root vegetables and leafy greens. Aaslo saw few flowers, and those he did find were edible rather than ornamental.

He squinted up at a window on the second floor of a row of townhomes. The movement of the drapes had caught his eye. The people were curious, even if they hid in their hovels. No elected officials or even self-appointed delegates or nobles approached them. His people had not been confronted by even the smallest demonstration, and it seemed that whatever had passed for the city guard had disappeared. It was eerie, and if not for those curious gazes, he might have thought the city abandoned.

Now, his troops began to invade the residents' sanctuaries upon his orders. He knew he would likely be hated, but it was better to be hated than extinct. That would happen if he allowed them to hide behind their hopes that the Berru would just disappear and leave them alone. Aaslo, or rather the cause for which he fought, needed these people as much as they needed him. It was only a matter of convincing them to stand up for themselves.

Farther down the row, a set of shutters clacked as they were latched, and from farther away he heard the furious bark of a dog voicing complaints his owners refused to make for themselves. The narrow street, barely wide enough for a single wagon, had ruts worn deep into the aged cobblestones. It felt as though the multi-story townhomes on either side leaned into their path, looming threateningly. Aaslo had been buried beneath buildings enough times to feel a shiver up his spine. He averted his gaze from the stone monstrosities and focused on the roadway ahead.

The rain slapped Aaslo in the face, and he realized the wind was picking up. He glanced over to Teza, who rode at his right, and noticed that her wafting dark locks were as dry as desert sand. He frowned and examined her more closely before realizing she was using a magical shield to keep herself dry. It now occurred to him that he might have done the same.

Teza gave a start as she looked at him. "What? Why are you looking at me like that?"

Aaslo shook his head and said, "It's nothing."

"You're a magus now. You need to start thinking like one."

"It's hard. I've gone my whole life without power. I don't see the need to start throwing it around now. Simple tasks can be done by simple men. No power necessary."

Teza smirked. "Are you referring to the rain? You're looking a bit soggy."

"Okay, but you're the one who's soaked."

"I'll dry out—eventually."

"But you'll be miserable until you do," said Teza.

"That's not the point. If you're going to fight magi and gods, you'll need to think and act with all your strengths. You need to practice with your power so that it comes naturally when you need it."

"So I should just spend it frivolously?"

"It's not frivolous. It's training. You understand the value of training. Besides, it doesn't run out—at least, not like that. You can run out in a moment, but it restores itself over time."

"Spend what?" said Teza. "I'm confused. Wait, you're not talking to me, are you?"

"No," he said to her. Then to Mathias, he said, "I dislike depending on something I can't grip with my own two hands. What if it abandons me when I need it?"

Teza frowned at him then turned away as if offended.

"You're extremely powerful. No one knows how much power you have to spend. It would be good to know your limits."

"I suppose you're right, but it feels unnatural."

"Talking to a disembodied voice is unnatural."

"I've always talked to you. Even when I didn't want to talk, you pressed me for it. I don't know what I would do if I didn't have you to talk to."

"Now you have other people to talk to. You're not alone in the forest, Aaslo."

"Must you remind me?"

"You're not limited to one friend. You can develop other relationships. What about love? You don't want to be alone forever."

A vision of dark hair and a sultry smirk rose unbidden, and Aaslo pushed it away. "It wouldn't be so bad. I would have peace. Besides, I tried love. It didn't work out."

"Reyla wasn't right for you, but there are plenty more in the world."

"Not for long if we don't succeed. Besides, there's no time for love. We're at war."

"War is the best time for love. It makes the grisly task of fighting worth it. Besides, I see what you were hoping I wouldn't. I know whom you long for."

"I do not," Aaslo retorted as an image of the alluring Sedi popped into his mind. His protest sounded a little too adamant even for his own ears.

Mathias laughed. *"That vixen will rip your heart out, literally. If she is who you set your sights on, you may be right about love not being for you."*

While Aaslo denied the accusation, he mulled it over as they approached the graveyard at the center of the city's eastern district, the oldest part of the city. A set of ornate iron gates barred the way past the short stone wall marking the front of the graveyard. Behind those, the collection of new and old tombs stretched into the rain beyond Aaslo's preternaturally good sight. Using both his human and dragon vision, Aaslo scanned the area and determined that no signs of life existed within it.

With a sarcastic edge, Teza said, "Of course we would have to ride through a graveyard in a thunderstorm."

Ijen replied, "Where else would you keep the body of an ancient and long-dead magus?"

Teza gave him an irritated look but ignored the remark. "Tell me again why we have to do this *today*?"

"We need to house the souls of the depraved in bodies as soon as possible—before Axus discovers I have them."

"Why does it have to be *these* bodies? There are plenty of other bodies to be had with easier access."

Aaslo patiently responded, "It has to be the ancient magi because Disevy said the depraved needed bodies with power, and the ancients are the only preserved bodies of magi that we know about. *This* is where Sedi indicated on the map that the body was entombed. It's the whole reason we came to this city."

"I guess that makes sense," Teza grumbled unhappily as the rain pattered off her shield ward.

Dolt seemed uncharacteristically subdued as Aaslo reined him in to a halt. A couple of soldiers hurried ahead to open the gates. The squeals of the rusty hinges echoed through the gloom, and Aaslo found himself holding his breath. Releasing it in a rush, Aaslo nudged Dolt forward. The cobbles ended at the graveyard, forcing the horses onto rocky mud and unkempt grass. The newest graves and mausoleums along the perimeter were ordered in neat rows, but farther into the graveyard, the older ones were seemingly placed at random. Smaller graves squeezed into the spaces between the larger ones, and Aaslo wondered if many weren't missing gravestones altogether. As it was, many of the headstones were crumbling or broken.

After twenty minutes of riding through the expansive graveyard, Teza broke the silence. "How much farther is it to the tomb?"

Aaslo shook his head, causing a stream of water to run down his face and over his chin. "I don't know. Sedi's map wasn't specific, but it does note that the tomb is underground."

From behind him, Andromeda said, "The ancient Pashtigonians placed their dead in catacombs beneath the cities. It has only been in the last couple of hundred years that the catacombs were filled and we started burying them above ground."

"Great," said Teza. "We'll be surrounded by bodies."

Andromeda blandly remarked, "Skeletons mostly. Even many of those have crumbled. We might have started using the catacombs again, but the Temple frowns upon it. The deacons prefer to use up much-needed land for the dead who won't appreciate it."

Ijen, who had been silent thus far in the short journey, said, "You are not a fan of the Temple?"

"Few with power are. The Temple's teachings denounce secular authority in favor of religious supremacy. If you ask me, Queen Tilly should have routed them long ago."

"You mean she should have had *you* rout them," replied Ijen.

Aaslo glanced back in time to see her grin. "Are these deacons likely to interfere with us?"

"I doubt it," said Andromeda. "I'm sure they don't care for your undead, and they might pray a bit harder, but they don't have any soldiers."

Aaslo's shoulders tensed. He didn't know if the gods listened to prayers, but he didn't need their attention drawn to what he was about to do. "To whom do they pray?"

"They believe in the One God. They call him Ibris. They believe him to be the *only* god, and he is all-powerful and omniscient."

Aaslo vaguely remembered the name from his studies with Magdelay. He had never heard Myropa mention the god, though, and he wondered if Ibris wasn't just a figment of the Temple's imagination. Either way, he doubted this Ibris would involve himself in the petty matters of men if he was so powerful and all-knowing.

The rain began to let up just as they approached the largest building Aaslo had seen in the graveyard. It didn't look like a mausoleum so much as a temple. He turned back to Andromeda. "Is this one of the Temples of Ibris?"

Andromeda shook her head as she examined the single-story square structure. It had a flat face and roof with no windows and only a single iron door at the center. Aaslo felt it had a dominating presence despite its austerity. She considered. "No, the Temples of Ibris are round, and this looks much too old anyway. I believe this may be the entrance to the catacombs."

Aaslo dismounted, and the others followed. The dead magus bearing the soul of one of the depraved, which they had taken to calling the shade, strode to his side. Aaslo looked upon the only one of the depraved he had placed in a vessel, then turned away from its eerie glowing gaze. He wasn't sure how useful the shade would be underground with its ability to emit a sound that could decimate all in its path. He didn't want to bring down the catacombs on their heads, after all. Aaslo hesitated over leaving the shade behind without his supervision. Thus far, the shade had been fairly docile until attacked, but considering the nature of the depraved, there was no telling what might trigger one.

The rain had finally stopped, so Aaslo removed his sodden coat and hung it over his saddle. His pants were soaked, and his shirt was damp, but at least he would not have to carry the heavy wool jacket. He noted with some chagrin that Ijen was just as dry as Teza, and although Mathias said nothing, Aaslo could almost hear his friend thinking, *I told you so.*

With a wave of Andromeda's hand, several soldiers filed past them to secure the door. Each took a turn shoving against it, to no avail. It would not budge. Aaslo approached the door with Teza on his heels.

"I can try to blow it open," she offered.

Aaslo clenched his clawed fist. "Let me try something first."

Then, thinking to test himself as Mathias had suggested, he sought the source of his strength. The dragon sniffed at his searching mind then crouched as if ready to pounce. Aaslo could sense another power beneath the dragon, deep within his muscles. It did not have its sharp, defined power, but this power felt more diffuse and innate. He focused on it and lifted his scaly arm. He swung at the iron door with all his might, impacting it with a jarring concussive force. The hinges shrieked, and the door buckled as it was thrust from its seat in the stone framework. The force drove the door into the building, where it collided with the rear wall after nearly two dozen feet. A great cacophony echoed throughout the empty chamber as bits of stone settled around the crumpled metal door.

"How did you do that?" exclaimed Andromeda.

Aaslo unclenched his aching fist. "I guess I'm stronger than I thought." Then he stepped into the dark chamber, quickly followed by the shade, who seemed intent on staying on Aaslo's heels. Aaslo's dragon sight had no difficulty with the lack of light, and he searched the space in a matter of seconds. A moment later, a soldier managed to light a torch he had collected from just inside the doorway. The others followed the torchbearer into the temple. A set of steps at the center of the otherwise empty room descended into the floor. The soldiers led the way, and within minutes, a warm light emanated from the subterranean corridor.

Aaslo followed the soldiers down, noting the torches in sconces that now lit the way. The masonry had held against the passage of time, and the steps were solid and easily traversed. At the first landing, a corridor passed into the darkness beyond their torchlight, but the steps continued deeper into the catacombs.

Ijen moved closer to one of the torches and held his book up to the light. Then he looked at Aaslo. "How will we find the tomb? Do you feel its presence, or are you guessing?"

Aaslo scowled at the prophet. He didn't like being accused of guessing, but it wasn't far from the truth. "We'll deduce where it's located. It's probably one of the oldest, if not *the* oldest, tomb in this place. We'll start at the bottom and work our way up."

Ijen nodded and made a quick note in his book. Aaslo rolled his eyes and turned back to the stairs. As he started down, a couple of soldiers darted past him with torches to lead the way. They descended four more levels to reach a fifth, where the stairs stopped. The deeper they explored underground, the closer Teza migrated to him. By the time they reached the bottom, she gripped his arm with surprising strength.

Aaslo looked down at the silver-clad magus. "Are you okay?"

Teza, eyes wide, spoke through clenched teeth. "I dislike being under so much rock. What if it collapses on us? It's very old."

Her words reminded Aaslo of the last time he had been buried, of the feeling of panic that pervaded him at the time and threatened to overcome him again. He shoved it down with the multitude of other feelings he hid, not the least of which was guilt, and pried her grip from his arm. She looked at him with alarm but settled when he retained hold of her hand. Remembering his last escape, he said, "If it collapses, I will move the earth to get you out."

"Aw, that's so romantic."

Aaslo huffed and grumbled, "I meant it literally."

Teza's panicked eyes spoke her doubt, but as he held her gaze, a change came over her. She swallowed hard. "I believe you could." She tentatively released his hand. "I think I'm okay now. Just—just stay close, please?"

"*Everyone* stay close," said Aaslo. "The information regarding this tomb was given to us by the enemy. Assume it's a trap."

The soldiers ahead glanced at each other with unease, but regardless, led the way. They didn't have long to wait before the first trap was sprung. The corridor opened into a wider room with runes etched into the walls. As the first soldier entered, a plethora of light darts streaked across the space and into the corridor. The first soldier dodged most, but one hit his shoulder while a second man took one to his gut. The shade managed to avoid damage, but two of the light darts struck Teza before she could erect her shield. Fortunately, the impressive armor protected her from injury. Aaslo's heightened reflexes aided in ducking before taking a dart to the head. He doubted he would have survived had it landed.

A second volley struck the back of the line, where the undead soldiers brought up the rear, but Andromeda, Ijen, and the other living soldiers had luckily been shielded by those in front. Aaslo knelt beside the unconscious soldier impaled by a light dart to the abdomen, then looked up at the first, who nursed his own injury.

"How is it?" he said.

"I can manage, m'lord, but I don't think Trenton is doing so well."

Aaslo looked back at the downed man. "No, he's not, but the wound doesn't look egregious."

"I can heal him," said Teza as she leaned over the unconscious soldier. She laid her hands on his chest, and after a few moments of concentration, the blistery flesh around the wound began to heal.

Soon, the wound sealed, but the healing left a furious, red, puckered scar. Teza sat back on her heels. "There. That's the best I can do. You know I'm not great with burns. He'll need rest, though, for the healing to continue."

She turned to the other injured man while Aaslo pulled the unconscious Trenton out of the walkway and propped him against the wall. "Will he be okay if we leave him here for now?"

Teza was busy healing the first man as she mumbled, "He'll sleep for a few hours, I think, but he'll be fine."

"Then we'll retrieve him when we return."

Aaslo stood and turned to Andromeda, who was busy examining the room. In one corner a stack of linens lay rotting, and another held several sealed barrels. Beyond that, the room was empty save for the runes etched onto the walls. These appeared to be comparatively recent additions. Whatever power they had stored, however, had been depleted with the two volleys of light darts. Aaslo almost felt disappointed. Either Sedi's heart wasn't really in it or, more likely, she was toying with him.

"Shall we continue?" he addressed the commander.

She nodded and turned toward the opposite corridor. Aaslo mustered his will and crossed.

"I'll lead the way," he said as he formed one of the magical shields he had learned. No one argued with him, and Andromeda took a position directly behind him and the shade. Having anticipated the confined space of the catacombs, she had left her unwieldy halberd with her horse, opting for her short sword.

The roughly hewn narrow corridor beyond the chamber held a multitude of alcoves brimming with skeletons, some with bits of cloth and hair still attached. The smell was dusty and altogether unpleasant as the air remained stagnant. The tight space held fewer sconces, making the space dark and foreboding. Aaslo's dragon sight served him well as he stepped over fallen rubble and alerted the others to hazards that lay in their path.

After a few corners, the ground dipped sharply, forcing them to trudge through knee-deep, icy, and murky water redolent with the scent of decay. Aaslo coughed and covered his nose with his hand, but to no avail. His sense of smell, enhanced by his dragon senses, was too sensitive, and his stomach churned. The scent itself wasn't what made him ill, though. It was the fact that the cloying scent of rotting flesh somehow appealed to him.

A soaked rat, clinging to the corpse of one of its brethren, floated by with a squeak. Aaslo did his best to ignore it, along with several others infesting the water, as he sloshed toward what he hoped was higher—or, at least, drier—ground.

"I think I'm going to be sick," murmured Teza.

Andromeda said, "Breathe through your mouth, not your nose."

"Ugh, I think I can *taste* it," replied Teza.

One of the soldiers shouted. Aaslo turned, and something grabbed his leg. It was large and strong enough to yank his foot from under him, and he toppled into the putrid water. More cries of alarm echoed, along with heavy splashes and the ring of steel. Aaslo grabbed the ropelike cable wrapped around his calf, digging his claws in as he ripped it free. The slippery creature released his leg, but wrapped another coil tightly around his torso.

"Water serpents!" shouted one of the soldiers.

As the air was squeezed from his lungs, Aaslo could almost hear Sedi's laughter ring in his mind. The shade opened its mouth to issue a powerful cry, but Aaslo used the last of his breath to shout, "No! Don't make a sound. The tunnel will collapse." He frantically clawed at the serpent crushing his torso and managed to tear through its body. His lungs expanded, and he surged to his feet. He saw others enduring similar struggles.

Without thinking, Aaslo extended his will, and his dragon dove into the water. Within seconds, the frigid water heated. Aaslo's flames licked at the squirming masses on the surface, and he drew his sword, hacking at the twisting shapes. When the temperature became nearly unbearable, the serpents abruptly withdrew. He didn't know where they had gone, but they obviously didn't care for the heat.

He noted that everyone, save Ijen, was soaked. The prophet, as usual, appeared unruffled, although he *was* holding a rather large, bloody knife. "Is everyone okay?"

"One of them bit me," said Andromeda, holding up an injured arm that had two large punctures.

"And me as well," cried one of the soldiers.

"Let me see," said Teza. After a brief inspection and a bit of healing, she said, "I don't think they're venomous. I don't detect anything in your blood."

"Thank the gods for that," muttered Andromeda.

It occurred to Aaslo they had only one god to thank for that particular boon, and that was Arayallen. He didn't know why it seemed significant, but it felt important that he understand each of the gods' roles in creating their world. Thanks to Myropa, he knew their names and their powers. He didn't know if Arayallen was on his side, but she was still the patron goddess of foresters—he and his forester brethren prayed to her. He had never been particularly devout, but it saddened him to think that his goddess might want him dead.

Their injuries having been assessed and healed, Aaslo and the others continued through the dark tunnels toward the tomb of the long-dead magus. Eventually, they came to a set of ascending stairs roughly cut into the stone, and they climbed to drier ground. The corridor terminated in a vast chamber that appeared to be a natural cavity. Water dripped from toothy stalactites onto equally large matching teeth on the floor, and small pools of clear water were interspersed with striped columns of glistening calcite. In the chamber's center, set between two naturally occurring columns, rested a massive tomb carved directly from the cave itself.

Aaslo cautiously approached the structure, searching for traps with his enhanced senses. Torchlight flickered in warm hues across damp surfaces, causing the glimmers of light to catch his eye. He laid his hands on the formidable lid of the tomb. Nothing attacked him. The soldiers came forward to assist with removing the lid, though Aaslo knew he didn't need the help. The scraping stone against stone echoed throughout the chamber. Everyone gathered around the tomb to peer into the dark pit. Inside lay a box of wood so pristine it might have been placed there only yesterday. An aura of pale blue light suffused its surface, giving it a greenish hue.

Ijen said, "Other than being enchanted to prevent decay, I don't see anything nefarious."

Aaslo pressed his palm to the wood. It felt warm to the touch and almost inviting, as if it *wanted* to be opened. He stood back and motioned to the soldiers. "Pry it open," he said. "Carefully."

With swords and knives, the soldiers eased the wooden lid from the coffin and stepped away. Within the box reposed a woman who looked as much alive as any of them, although Aaslo knew she wasn't. Her vessel lacked a soul. He could feel it. The woman might have been near sixty, and strands of grey streaked her long red hair. The lines of her face hadn't softened with time, and she wore an expression of disapproval. She had been buried in thick ceremonial robes of grey and purple. The ring commonly worn by magi to indicate their status encircled her finger, and a pendant with an arcane symbol hung about her neck.

"Who is she?" asked Andromeda.

"Avra Bouver," said Ijen, dropping the pendant. "This is her house sigil. Plus, I recognize her from a portrait that hung in the grand hall of my family estate. Her family line had always been close with mine.

"Avra believed in an academic pursuit of magic. She advanced the field considerably during her four hundred and eighty-seven years, and nothing was out of the question so long as it provided knowledge. Many of her pursuits were of questionable morality."

"Not unlike your own house," replied Teza, her voice heavy with scorn.

Ijen shrugged indifferently and returned to examining the body.

"How did she die?" asked Aaslo.

"No one knows, exactly," said Ijen, "but some thought it had to do with her studies. In the days leading to her death, she had become quite excited about a breakthrough. One of her students found her early one morning slumped over her desk, her hand poised with a pen, and hastily scrawled notes beneath her."

Aaslo perused what was visible of the body for injuries. "What was she studying?"

"*That* remains a mystery for time, I'm afraid. She wrote all her research in code that not even her assistant could decipher. Many tried to decode her notes over the centuries, but her studies were eventually abandoned."

As Ijen talked, Aaslo searched inside himself for the stored souls of the depraved. "If her body is capable of harboring a soul, I will raise her. Stand back. I don't know what will happen, and the last time it was rather concussive."

The others, with the exception of the shade, moved to the far side of the chamber as Aaslo hovered over the body of the dead ancient magus. He tugged at one of the depraved whose soul had settled in his core, and he immediately became ill. He doubled over, breathing in short pants through his nose, as he tried to hold down the contents of his stomach. As the sensation passed, he straightened and tried again. This time he was ready, pushing past the nausea and drawing the soul up a tether of inky black power. He felt a moment of panic as the depraved struggled to remain in his body, and then it popped free of him. He directed the tendril of power toward the corpse and pressed the deranged soul into the woman.

The soul, however, wanted to return to *his* body, forcing Aaslo to push harder and harder as it approached the still form. By the time the soul reached her flesh, Aaslo was sweating and shoving against the soul with all his will. Just when he thought his strength would give out, it slipped silently into the corpse. Aaslo wasn't finished, though. He had to tether the soul within the vessel so that it would not slip out. He felt certain if that were to happen, and were he to lose control of it, the depraved would attempt to consume him.

Aaslo worked for several long minutes to anchor the foreign soul to the body, and succeeding, his mind ached with the effort. At first, nothing happened. Then, in an instant, a violent force rocked the cavern, and he was blown from his feet. Stone rained down as stalactites broke from their bases. Aaslo fell to the ground, curled into a ball, and covered his head as the shards of rock and mineral pummeled him. When it stopped, he sat up and stared at a new shade. She stood in the tomb, glaring down at him with a sour expression.

Aaslo quickly got to his feet and approached the shade with care. After a moment's thought, he held out his hand. She looked at his claws curiously then placed her own slight hand in his. Her movements were jerky and uncoordinated, and her joints didn't move with the natural motion of a human. As Aaslo helped the shade to the ground, the others joined him. Everyone watched the new shade warily, worrying over what she might do.

At first, she merely stared at them with glowing eyes. Then she moved among them with disjointed motions that made her seem all the more monstrous. She examined Teza with an angry sneer, raising her clawlike hands to Teza's face as if to attack her. A silent but deep drumming force rocked the air. Aaslo felt it in his chest, thudding against his breastbone like a second heartbeat. Aaslo grabbed Avra by the elbow and pulled her away from Teza, and the drumming abated.

"What is she?" whispered Teza. "I mean, what can she do?"

"I don't know," said Aaslo, dropping the woman's arm. Avra barely registered the movement as she slowly lowered her own hands. She looked at everyone else with unblinking eyes, passing over the other shade with a moment's hesitation, then turned to Aaslo. With stuttering movement, she raised her hand once again and turned it over so that her wrist faced upward. She wiggled her fingers. When he didn't respond, she wiggled them again.

"What's she doing?" said Teza.

Aaslo was just as curious, but it was Andromeda who answered. "It's an old Pashtigonian gesture. She's urging you for information. She wants instructions."

"I would give her instruction if I were you," Ijen added offhandedly as he perused his book. "They become quite destructive when left to their own devices."

Aaslo turned on the prophet. "You have information about them?"

"Of course," Ijen said, tucking the book into his tunic. "They play a significant role in the events to come. At least, they do if you acquire them. There are plenty of paths in which you do not, including some in which Axus gets them instead."

"He's been holding back again."

"You didn't think this was worth mentioning?" groused Aaslo.

"I *am* mentioning it."

"But why did you wait?" snapped Teza.

The prophet gave her a flat look that said she should already know the answer then turned his unconcerned gaze on Aaslo. "I had to wait until you were committed to this course of action. Otherwise, you might have made a different decision."

"Are you saying this was a mistake?"

"I said nothing of the sort." He raised a finger tentatively toward the shade, who wiggled her fingers again. "I merely emphasized the need for leadership where they're concerned. And, um, you might want to oblige quickly. She seems to be getting impatient."

Aaslo waved at the first shade he had made. The man stared at the second shade with wide, glowing eyes, and his mouth slightly ajar as if he considered releasing his power on her.

"He doesn't require much instruction," said Aaslo.

Ijen shrugged. "They have different personalities. I would guess they are influenced by both their past experiences as the depraved and by the past personalities of the vessels they inhabit. Avra Bouver was not known for her patience."

Aaslo crossed his arms and thrummed his fingers against his scales. "Very well. In that case, we should name them." He turned to the woman and said, "Your name is Avra. Do you understand?"

The woman turned her hand over and made a fist. Aaslo looked to Andromeda questioningly. She nodded in the affirmative, and Aaslo looked at the first shade.

"Since we don't know your name, you will be called Echo."

"Echo?" said Andromeda with a lift of her brow.

"Very original, Aaslo. You can do better."

"Sound is his power. I'm not sure what else he can do."

His gaze turned to encompass both shades. "You two will not harm anyone in this group, and you will protect us if necessary. You will await further instruction from me. This is Mage Teza. You will take orders from her in my absence."

Teza nodded and grinned happily at the two shades, who looked at her with inscrutable expressions.

Echo turned his head toward Avra and opened his mouth again, but Aaslo jumped in quickly. "You will *not* attack each other." Echo snapped his mouth shut but continued to frown at Avra, who stared back at him and wiggled her fingers, this time with her palm facing downward.

Aaslo looked at Andromeda, who said, "That means to go away or leave her alone."

Aaslo rubbed the stubble on his jaw as he thought about the problem. "These two don't seem to like each other. Since the people who inhabited these bodies never knew each other, it would seem this is a characteristic of the depraved. I hope this doesn't become a serious problem as we raise the others. We can ill afford a war between the depraved in addition to the war with the gods and the Berru." Aaslo glanced at Ijen for a clue, but the prophet wasn't forthcoming.

Aaslo sighed and said, "Let's go. We have four more bodies to find, and something tells me we're running out of time."

CHAPTER 11

TWO DAYS LATER, AASLO STOOD ON THE PLATFORM AT THE BASE OF the courthouse looking grimly at the gathered crowd. Three bodies swung from nooses behind him. Two were soldiers who had abused or taken advantage of the residents housing them, and the third was one of the townsfolk, a man who had attacked a patrol. Nearly twenty-five hundred people occupied the square, a number both impressive and pitifully inadequate. They were all the new recruits the city would provide, but given the residents' reticence, Aaslo had been surprised the number had been so large. Still, in comparison to the Berruvian forces, another twenty-five hundred was a pittance.

Aaslo knew the city's residents still did not understand the gravity of their situation. With heavy stores, they had not yet begun to suffer from the lack of trade, and the high walls had thus far kept the city clear of roaming lyksvight. It was only a matter of time, though, before the Berru arrived in force, at which point the feeble locks on their doors would be useless.

"Perhaps we may return in a few months when their reality has set in," said Andromeda, who stood beside him in a show of support.

Aaslo shook his head. "I doubt there will be time. How many more cities like this will we visit? They will all suffer the same tragedy of fear and apathy."

Teza, looking splendid in her sun-sparked armor, spoke from his other side. "We could stay a few more days and see if any change their minds."

"No, we must be moving. We have bodies to collect. You the living, and me the dead."

"What do you mean?"

"I'm leaving the two of you with the army in Uptony to collect supplies and recruits while I go on to the next tomb. I will return for you once I've acquired the next shade."

Teza's expression was a mixture of hurt and anger. "You're leaving me behind?"

"No, I'm leaving you in charge," said Aaslo, wondering if he might regret it.

"She'll be fine. It's not like she has a history of shunning author-ity or lack of follow-through."

"We're running out of time. What would *you* do?"

"I don't know," said Teza. "I guess I'll do what we did here."

"I wouldn't have to do any of it. People would flock to serve in the chosen one's army."

"Too bad I'm not you," Aaslo said.

Teza nodded. "Oh, I'm sure you feel that way. You're very unpopu-lar with these people. Look, Aaslo, I appreciate your confidence, but I really think I should come with you. You might need a healer or some magical backup. You might not just have to raise some dead people. The last time, it was a trap. It's likely this next one will be too."

Aaslo turned his thoughts to Mathias. "What would you do?"

"Maybe you should stop trying to be me. It's not working for you."

"I don't know," said Teza.

"What, exactly, are my options?" Aaslo snapped.

Teza said, "You could go to Celestria and fight the gods directly. Of course, you'd probably die in the first ten seconds."

"You should listen to her, Aaslo. It's a sound plan."

Aaslo frowned at her but mentally directed his ire at Mathias. "Are you so eager to see me dead?"

Teza shrugged. "I was just saying it's an option."

"There's plenty of room in this bag for one more head."

Aaslo ignored them both as he stepped forward to address the crowd. Teza used her power to amplify his voice so that all could hear. Not used to speaking to crowds, he spoke haltingly at first, but with a few helpful prompts from Mathias, he found his rhythm. Still, no one would accuse him of eloquence or even being well-spoken. He was brusque, to the point, and didn't dissemble over the fact that many of the people who fought for life were destined to die. He pointed out, though, that they would certainly die if they *didn't* fight, which made it worth their effort. In the end, no one looked particularly in-spired, but they followed him anyway, possibly because his undead minions had surrounded the crowd, and the people were wary.

After the speech, Aaslo led his followers into the paths once again. This time, the trail leading to their destination was short, and they traveled the paths without incident. Aaslo ultimately left the marquess in charge of his fledgling army in the Pashtigonian city of Uptony to continue the recruiting and supplying efforts while he retrieved the bodies of three additional ancient magi in which he could house the depraved.

Aaslo took a small contingent of soldiers, along with the two shades, Teza, Ijen, Andromeda, Peck and Mory, and the wanderers Greylan and Rostus back into the paths. He had been hesitant about taking Mory with him, since the boy's ability to speak with Myropa was essential to communicating with the others like the marquess. The army shouldn't be leaving the city, though, so hopefully communication would not be necessary.

The next destination on Sedi's map was a temple in the icy mountain region of northern Helod, and Aaslo had no illusions that the going would be easy or straightforward. Aaslo had never been to Helod, but he knew mountains. After so much time spent in cities in recent months, he looked forward to being immersed in nature. So it was that he found himself stepping onto a wooded mountainside blanketed in pristine white snow, undisturbed save for the deer tracks that led into a thicket.

Aaslo inhaled deeply as he fastened his coat and led Dolt away from the portal. The crisp air smelled of evergreens, soil, and snow— all things he loved and missed. Through the trees ahead, he saw a vast range of snow-covered peaks with sharp ridges and steep slopes. Dolt shifted forward and puffed a stream of frosted air into Aaslo's face. Aaslo gave the horse-not-a-horse a warning look and patted his neck. Dolt might not be a real horse, but he *mostly* behaved like one and seemed to want to be treated like one as well.

A moment of sadness overcame him as his mind turned to memories of Mathias and him, and sometimes his father, scouring the forest for problems to solve and securing the future of the logging communities as they did so. His father's patient gaze would watch him as he learned his woodcraft. He could hear Mathias's laughter— he, of course, having been the butt of some joke or prank. He knew he would not see Mathias again in this life, but he wondered if he might see his father before it was over.

The rumble of voices behind him drew Aaslo from his reverie. Steadying his resolve, Aaslo turned and watched the last of his party exit the portal, then he closed the glowing rift, clearing the air. Avra approached, held out her hand, and wiggled her fingers. Over her shoulder stood Echo, staring down at the female shade with a disgruntled expression.

"Patience," said Aaslo. "I will tell you when I need you to do something."

Avra clenched her fist and huffed with frustration before turning to slap Echo. Echo was incensed and opened his mouth.

Aaslo shouted, "Stop!" When he had the shade's attention, he spoke quietly. "If you release your power, you'll likely bring down an avalanche on us. Stay silent."

Echo slowly closed his mouth but continued to scowl at Avra in a promise of retribution. Aaslo looked at the others and saw Peck and Mory kneeling in the snow with their arms buried in it up to their elbows. They were shivering, but grinning like fools.

"What's wrong with you two?" he said.

Peck yanked his arms from the snow and stared in wonder at his reddened hands. "We've never seen snow before," he replied.

"It's so *cold*," added Mory.

"It should be," said Aaslo. "It's made of ice."

Mory grinned at him. "I had ice once—at the marquess's estate. It hurt my teeth."

Aaslo shook his head. He would have to keep an eye on the two inexperienced travelers lest they freeze to death. "Put your gloves on," he said. "If your fingers get too cold, they'll freeze, and we'll have to cut them off. Tell me right away if your feet get wet. You waxed your boots like I told you to?"

They both nodded as they hurried to put on their gloves. The others looked ready to go, so Aaslo ordered everyone to mount up. Sedi's map wasn't particularly accurate and he was unfamiliar with their location, so they would have to travel a bit to reach their destination. Though Aaslo wasn't exactly sure where they were, he did know exactly where they were going. The map indicated that a temple was located near the summit of the second-highest peak, which Aaslo could see from his vantage between the trees.

After a couple of hours of rough riding, snow began to fall in delicate flurries at first, then harder as the wind picked up, making it difficult to see any distance. Aaslo pulled his scarf up around his face to block the worst of the wind and glanced back at the others. Peck and Mory were bundled up so tightly, it looked as if they had shrunk into their coats.

Peck caught him looking and muttered, "I've never been so cold in my life."

"I don't like snow anymore," added Mory.

"It's not too much farther," replied Aaslo as he pointed ahead. "It should be just beyond that ridge. There's a path. Do you see it?"

"All I see is snow," grumbled Peck, his voice slightly muffled by his scarf.

Dolt suddenly lurched up the incline, nearly dumping Aaslo from his saddle, and Aaslo wondered if it had been done on purpose. The ornery horse had become needy on the ride, and every time Aaslo stopped patting him, the horse found some way to protest.

It seemed an age before they finally joined the path crossing the ridge. They led their horses and picked their way down the steep arete on foot into the bowl a glacier had scraped out long ago. There stood the Temple of Earth and Ash: a grand, six-story affair of grey stone and timber quarried and gathered from the moraines and rock falls so prevalent in the region. A spiral twisting toward the sky formed the front of the temple, and the stone had been laid and carved to appear as if the entire building were wrapped in a massive serpent whose head topped the apex with a gaping maw. The remainder of the temple behind the spiral edifice looked as if it could house an entire village.

"A snake!" shouted Peck. "I hate snakes. Why is it a snake?"

Aaslo had no answer for him, so he remained silent as he led Dolt toward the stables that abutted the cliffside on the outskirt of the temple complex. He paused just long enough to instruct the two shades to wait in the forest. He didn't know how the temple's residents would react, and he didn't want the shades to behave badly. He was a little worried about what they might do in his absence, so he gave them clear instructions not to leave or go anywhere near people while he was gone.

The yard between the forest and the temple complex consisted of a number of outbuildings that appeared to house livestock and farm equipment. Raised garden beds ranged in neat rows along one side of the path, while pens, barns, and stables occupied the other side. People in grey and burgundy robes ambled between structures and among the beds and animals, but they gave Aaslo and his companions only cursory glances as they passed. When he and the rest of the party neared the stables, he saw a woman in a heavy burgundy robe with a deep cowl waiting by the stable doors. She kept her hands tucked into the sleeves and remained still as a statue until they stood before her. Finally, she pushed back her hood, and Aaslo was taken by surprise. Although her face was youthful, perhaps in her early thirties, her eyes were completely white, as was often the case with the aged.

She bowed slightly and intoned, "Greetings to the travelers. May your pilgrimage open your sight and your future be visited upon you." She stepped forward and held out her hands. "I can take your horse. He will be well cared for."

As she said this, several more monks in burgundy robes hurried over to collect the rest of the horses. Aaslo hesitated. There was no telling how Dolt would behave, and he didn't want the woman hurt. Still, she seemed confident, so he released the horse into her care with a warning that made the woman laugh.

Figuring they wouldn't be affected by the cold, Aaslo gave Greylan and Rostus orders to guard the horses. He split the remaining soldiers into units that would rotate guard duty as well. Finally, they walked to the temple, cautiously crunching through the snow drifts, up to the grand double doors of the main entrance. It appeared to be the primary point of access to the remainder of the complex that sprawled beyond the front temple in the vast space between it and the mountainside. Aaslo pulled the door open and stepped through, followed closely by the others.

They entered a large, dark room that seemed to be a ceremonial chamber. There were no windows, a dark fabric covered the walls, and the scent of tallow from the multitude of candles hung heavy in the air. Lines of grey cushions made a neat grid across the floor, and kneeling monks in burgundy robes occupied several of them. They faced the opposite wall, where a plethora of candles and snake statues sat upon an altar.

Before Aaslo could take a step, a man, previously hidden in the shadows, approached from his right. The man's cowl hung limply down his back so that his balding pate reflected the candlelight. He wore a somber expression and thin spectacles rimmed his pale grey eyes.

"Greetings to the travelers," said the monk. "I am Brother Yarrow. How may I assist in your pilgrimage?"

Aaslo considered simply asking about the dead magi, but according to what little information he had about the temple's residents, they worshipped the ancient magi as if they were gods. He doubted the monks would appreciate him stealing their bodies to use in his undead army. Instead, he said, "We seek to honor the magi."

Brother Yarrow smiled, but the expression did not reach his eyes. He said, "Of course. Not many make the journey this time of year, so we are able to accommodate your group within the sanctuary. If you will come with me, I will show you to your rooms."

Brother Yarrow turned and paced to the altar without a backward glance. At the end of the aisle, he turned left and slipped through a doorway hidden by a black curtain. Before Aaslo could step through, though, Andromeda halted him with a hand laid on his shoulder. As she stepped past him, she murmured, "I don't trust him. Allow me to go first."

Aaslo shrugged and stepped aside. It didn't matter to him who went first, and if Andromeda wanted to risk her own safety, then so be it. The woman's hand hovered over her hilt as she pushed aside the curtain and stepped through. Aaslo went next, followed by the rest of the party, single file, as they shuffled into a poorly lit, narrow stone corridor. It occurred to Aaslo that if they were attacked, they would be hard-pressed to defend themselves. The monks, at least, seemed to be peaceful, so he dismissed his concern.

The monk stopped before a squat wooden door and opened it to reveal a small, spartan room with two beds covered in thick wool blankets and a desk that held a variety of writing implements and a stack of paper. Dry rushes covered the floor, and the air held a chill and smelled stale and musty.

Brother Yarrow said, "The women may stay here."

Andromeda and Teza shared a look then cautiously stepped into the room, each dropping a pack onto a bed. Then the monk continued to the next door, revealing a room identical to the first. Eventually, everyone was assigned a room by twos, and Aaslo ended up bunking with Ijen. The prophet seemed to take the assignment in stride, but Aaslo felt anxious. He did not fully trust Ijen; and, since they would be alone, it occurred to him if the magus truly wished him harm, this would be Ijen's chance to act while he slept.

"I'll keep watch over you while you sleep."

"Can you do that?" Although Aaslo kept his voice low, it would have been impossible to prevent Ijen from overhearing.

"I don't know, but it's the thought that counts, right?"

"Not when it could mean my life," Aaslo grumped.

"Are we in danger?" asked Ijen, picking up on Aaslo's side of the conversation.

"You tell me," replied Aaslo.

Ijen opened his mouth, paused, then tapped his chin with a bony finger before shrugging, and sitting on his bed to start rummaging through his pack.

Seeing that their conversation had apparently been dismissed, and since the monk indicated that dinner would not be served for a few more hours, Aaslo decided to take advantage of the warm bed and get some sleep in case he had the opportunity to explore during the night. He lay down on the firm, yet lumpy mattress and closed his eyes. Before he fell asleep, though, a sensation of falling overcame him. He lurched awake and opened his eyes.

Aaslo found himself lying on a mound of cushions considerably more comfortable than the mattress. He felt no breeze nor did he hear the chirruping sounds of night, yet he stared up at a starlit sky. As the little lights glimmered and twinkled like tiny gemstones set into a backdrop of onyx, other images took shape in his peripheral vision. Aaslo craned his neck to take in his surroundings and learned that he was not outside at all, but in a large, round chamber draped in heavy cobalt curtains. The chamber's smooth, domed ceiling soared several stories above him. To his left, in the center of the room, was an ornately gilded circular stand topped with a half globe of what looked to be frosted glass. It glowed a pleasing, soft white light. Aaslo was confused and a bit unsteady as he got to his feet. He approached the plinth slowly and could see a hole in the half globe's center through which streamed a beam of light projecting the image of the universe across the curved expanse of the ceiling.

The clinking of glass from somewhere behind him drew his attention, and Aaslo spun. Near the side of the curved room was a modest round table made of a black material Aaslo could not identify. What held his attention, though, was the person—or, rather, the *god*—seated at the table. And it *was* a god. He was sure of it. The power radiating off the man was undeniable as it suffused Aaslo's flesh to mingle with his own burgeoning power.

"Who are you?" he blurted as he took in the god's unruffled appearance.

"Probably not the best way to greet a god."

The man had a round face with a short brown beard that matched his hair. His shoulders were strong but narrow, and his lean physique was nearly drowned in the soft blue silk of his robes. The man's grey gaze was distant as he smiled faintly.

"It is good to meet you in person, Aaslo. I had not thought I would do so, but it seems I will be dragged into this mess after all. I am Arohnu."

Aaslo crossed his arms as he looked at the seated god. "And you're the god of what?"

"Seriously, Aaslo, did you learn nothing about etiquette?"

Arohnu raised an eyebrow. "So forthright. Are you not sufficiently impressed by my power? By my godliness?" His lips tilted in a wry grin. "No, I suppose you wouldn't be. You are rarely impressed by such a small thing as power, are you?"

Aaslo frowned. "You didn't answer my question."

Arohnu lifted two glasses as he stood from the table and crossed the short distance between them. He held one glass out for Aaslo as he sipped from the other. Aaslo cautiously took the glass. He may not be completely cowed by the god's power, but he didn't want to offend the god, especially not until he knew which side he was on.

The god's eyes twinkled with hidden knowledge as he motioned for Aaslo to drink. Aaslo hesitated. He had no idea what was in the glass or what effect it might have. Still, he felt he couldn't refuse. He tilted the glass up and swallowed a sweet nectar that rolled down his throat with a satisfying light flavor.

Arohnu nodded and said, "I am the God of Prophecy."

"Run, Aaslo!"

Aaslo immediately regretted drinking the tincture. *This* god was not his friend. It was because of *this* god his entire life had been up-ended. *This* god had threatened the world with morbid demise, and it was *this* god who set Mathias on the path that led to his death.

This time Arohnu's smile was sad. "You are unhappy with me. I can see it in your eyes and in your bearing. I think you would attack me if you thought you might survive it. I am used to this reaction from my brothers and sisters, but rarely do I have the pleasure of visiting with one of their creations."

A multitude of responses crossed Aaslo's mind, but one detail stood out. "You said I was here in person. How is that possible? I thought humans couldn't exist in Celestria."

"Ah, that. Well, you are not exactly human any longer, are you?"

"Told you so."

"One of my brethren has seen to that—Arayallen, I think. You have the scent of her power. It is yours now, of course. I have never seen nor heard of such a thing being done. I did not think it possible, but she has surpassed my expectations." He took a deep draft of his drink. "She was particularly unhappy about that little Aldrean prophecy. She seemed to think it was a direct attack on her. That was not my intent, I assure you."

Aaslo narrowed his eyes as he scrutinized the god's apparent disappointment. He didn't believe what he saw in the god's mannerisms. Arohnu seemed congenial enough, but Aaslo wasn't about to be fooled by a friendly countenance. "Do you actually decide the future or just give people glimpses of a future we choose for ourselves?"

Arohnu's gaze was drawn back to Aaslo. "You mean do I control the events of the prophecies?" He tilted his head thoughtfully. "That is a matter of perspective. In truth, I'm not sure. Sometimes I think I am merely watching, while other times . . . well, I am sure I would not engender myself to you if you think I have caused the events on Aldrea to occur. I did everything I could for that little world." With a heavy sigh he said, "I delivered that prophecy for more than a millennia, and I offered many, many paths to choose from, *including* that of the savior. It isn't my fault your people chose poorly."

Aaslo's dragon threatened to burst free. He snapped, "*My* people didn't *choose* to be butchered. That was Axus and the Berru."

Arohnu rolled his eyes and gave Aaslo a long-suffering look. "The Berru *are* your people—*humans*. If they weren't so obsessed with power and glory, they might have heeded the warnings of the prophecy. Instead, they sided with Axus to ensure your world's ruin."

"You make it sound like power and glory are purely human obsessions, when isn't that what Axus seeks even now?"

Tilting his head, Arohnu said, "I concede the point. It changes nothing, I'm afraid."

"So that's it, then? My world is destined to die, and there's nothing we can do about it?"

"Oh, I think you already know that you have some influence over events. You were given a path of prophecy, after all. I sent you my messenger."

"You speak of Ijen."

"Indeed, although I know you keep him at arm's distance. You do not trust him. I can't say I blame you."

"Why is that?"

"I merely deliver the prophecies. I do not choose his motives. But that is neither here nor there. The point is you know you are destined to deliver your world unto death. It shouldn't surprise you, given the nature of your power."

"You mean everyone is destined to become the undead?"

Arohnu shrugged. "That is up to you. Every soul you claim for your undead is another soul you steal from Axus, and the souls *are* the source of his power."

Aaslo mulled over the implication. He had already figured that out, but since the God of Prophecy was underscoring the point, there seemed to be more to it. What were the implications beyond preventing Axus from gaining more power?

"Are you saying that my power over death was part of the plan all along?"

Arohnu raised an eyebrow at him, as if imploring him to continue.

"So, if that was the plan from the beginning, then I was always intended to fight Axus. That means Mathias's path wasn't the only one destined to defeat him."

"I don't think that's what he's saying. I'm still the chosen one."

"I was your backup plan," added Aaslo.

Arohnu smiled sadly. "A morbid one, yes. Truly, I do not know if you can defeat Axus, but I *can* say your world will never be the same. Even if it survives, it will always be touched by death—or, rather, the *un*dead."

"Why are you telling me this?"

"Because you are wasting your time on Aldrea."

"You just said I could win."

"You're not listening."

"I said," the god continued, "I do not know, but I do know it will not be on Aldrea. If you stay, Axus will certainly win. This is a battle for Celestria in more ways than one. I had hoped it would never come to this. Had the chosen one lived, Axus wouldn't have had a chance at winning over the realm of the gods; but, as it stands, we are in danger."

"You're *gods!*" said Aaslo. "Can't you handle Axus?"

Arohnu turned back to the table to replenish his glass. Golden liquid swirled into the cup, then he set the decanter down and looked up. "Although we are powerful, we are not a united people. In many ways, we are just as flawed as humans. Perhaps more so, given how long we live. Axus made promises to many who chose to follow him. This war has already consumed each of the pantheons, many of which are in turmoil simply because their members disagree about which side to take. Arayallen leads the fight against Axus. She is cunning and passionate, but with Trostili on Axus's side, the war will be hard to win. She needs a general." Arohnu gave Aaslo a pointed look.

"*Me?*" Aaslo raised his clawed fist and said, "See this? This is because of *her*. She did this to me when she sent a *dragon* to kill me. She sent my own mother to betray me by giving me some kind of power that also nearly killed me."

Arohnu pursed his lips. "I admit, her methods are unusual, but she has her reasons."

"If Arayallen wants me to be her general, why doesn't *she* ask?"

"Arayallen isn't the kind of woman who *asks*. She demands or she simply manipulates events so that they come out in her favor. That's you, by the way."

"Yes, I got that," muttered Aaslo.

With a grin, Arohnu said, "Just making sure. You seem a bit dense at times."

Aaslo scowled at the god. "I'm not dense. I just refuse to play your games."

"Not the best way to get on a god's good side."

"What is it *you* want from me?"

"Much better."

"I don't *want* anything. I brought you here to give you knowledge. I am telling you now that if you continue to fight this war in Aldrea, you will lose. Axus grows stronger by the day. I know not how he is doing it, but he has already begun taking souls from the Sea of Transcendence to augment his power. You must face him directly, here, in Celestria, before he gains too much power. It may already be too late. Arayallen was gracious enough to give you power, but I've seen that you will never figure out how to use it without help."

The prospect of an even more powerful Axus seized Aaslo's resolve. Arohnu's emphasis on the urgency of the confrontation only instilled more trepidation. How could he possibly face a god? Aaslo swallowed hard and turned his mind to more immediate matters with which he *could* contend. It was his turn to take a chance. Even though Arohnu made it sound like he didn't have much of a choice, he had made a deal with Sedi, and he intended to keep his word. He said, "If I agree to participate in this war in Celestria, I need something from you."

Arohnu appeared genuinely surprised as his eyebrows reached toward the star-studded ceiling. "What is it you ask of me?"

"I need you to meet with someone. Her name is Sedi Tryst."

Arohnu pursed his lips, and again his gaze spoke of unshared knowledge. "I am familiar with the woman. She is your enemy, is she not? Why would you ask this of me?"

"I've been wondering the same thing."

"Because I made a deal with her for knowledge that I needed. This was her price."

"You made a deal with something that was not yours to give?"

"I only promised I would try. Will you do it?"

"I will, but not because of your deal. I must meet with her for the role she plays in the events to come."

"And what role is that?"

Arohnu smiled and shook his head as if Aaslo should know better than to ask, and Aaslo was reminded of the way Ijen did the same.

"Now you know where he gets it from."

"You're going to teach me to use Arayallen's power?"

"It's *your* power now. Its nature has changed since joining with you. It augments what you already possess and gives you the strength to cross the veil and exist within Celestria. You need to know how to get here."

"You're going to show me how?"

"Well, no, not exactly. That's why *she's* here."

Arohnu motioned toward a woman who entered the room through a door Aaslo hadn't noticed. As the door swung wide, Aaslo could see part of the corridor beyond had collapsed, and there were scorch marks along the walls and floor. It was a sobering sight that suddenly brought the war in Celestria into reality.

The woman was just as stunning as the last time he had seen her, with her red mane streaked with golden highlights and strongly feminine physique outlined by a form-fitting red-and-gold dress. Stunning amber eyes peered at him from her dark face.

"Keep breathing, brother."

"Enani," he said as the breath rushed out of him.

She smiled warmly as though genuinely pleased to see him again. "Greetings—what was it you called yourself? *Forester.* Arohnu made a most curious request on your behalf. I did not believe it at first, that he would ask me to teach you to enter Celestria; but I can see now that you possess the power. It pleases me that you have joined us. Have you chosen a pantheon?"

Aaslo furrowed his brow. "You mean I should join one? Why would I choose a pantheon? I am not a god."

Enani looked at him curiously, then, with a glance toward Arohnu, said, "If you will be spending time here, you should belong to a pantheon. You are welcome to join the Third Pantheon if you like. Our members are united against Axus with a few exceptions."

"Stop! Do not say whatever you're thinking. Remember Magdelay's teachings."

Aaslo's first instinct was to reject anything to do with the pantheons, but Mathias was right. He needed to be diplomatic, so instead, he said, "I thank you for the honor, and I will consider it."

Enani smiled and nodded her approval as she reached out and smacked him in the head. When Aaslo awoke, he was once again lying on the uncomfortable bed in the cell-like room of the temple in Helod, and he had a splitting headache. Ijen leaned over him with wide eyes and an open book.

"Where did you go?"

CHAPTER 12

AASLO'S NERVES VIBRATED WITH A NEW SENSE OF URGENCY AS HE SAT in the temple dining hall. Since his meeting with Arohnu, he felt time pressing on him, and his quest to find bodies for the depraved was taking too long. He couldn't face Axus without their power, though: he needed them to defeat him. So Aaslo found himself tensing as he sat at the table surrounded by people who had no idea how close they were to complete annihilation.

"Are you okay?" Teza inquired. "You seem oddly anxious."

"I'm fine." Aaslo snapped a glance at the monks seated near him. He drew his gaze away from the temple's unknowing occupants and returned his attention to his plate. Dinner at the temple was a simple affair of potatoes, onions, and beans. It left much to be desired, but at least it was warm.

Brother Yarrow sat with them for a short time as they ate, though he spoke little. What he did say, however, was of particular interest. He described the sanctuary where the monks conducted most of their rituals. Within the sanctuary were said to be the three tombs of the ancient magi to whom these people prayed. They believed that the ancients had achieved a godlike status upon gaining their power and their magi descendants were revered among them as disciples of those gods—at least they *were* until they had abandoned the world. When Brother Yarrow learned that three of their number were blessed with such power, he was elated. He quickly left them to prepare for some ritual in their honor that would no doubt distract them from their true purpose.

"At least it will gain us access to the sanctuary," Teza stated, a little too cheerfully, as she picked up a chunk of bread and slathered it with a large glob of butter.

"She just wants to be flattered."

"I know that," huffed Aaslo. "But we will be surrounded by monks."

"So?" replied Teza, stuffing the bread into her mouth. She spoke around chewing. "We have power. They don't."

Andromeda, who was seated across from Teza, pushed her bowl

away. She said, "You make it sound like it will be easy to just walk in and steal their gods."

Teza swallowed before speaking this time. "It's not like they can stop us from doing what we need to do."

Aaslo said, "We need to be prepared to leave as soon as it's done. I doubt we will be welcome here afterward."

"Someone had better keep an eye on the horses," said Ijen, staring at his beans and potatoes with distaste.

They all looked at the prophet in alarm. No doubt they each wondered how much of his simple statement had to do with his visions and how much was mere observation.

Aaslo was about to ask when a red-faced Peck appeared at his side. "Uh, Aaslo, we have a problem," the thief whispered. "It's Greylan and Rostus. They're gone."

"What do you mean, they're gone?" said Aaslo. "I left them with the horses." With tension building between his shoulder blades, he grumbled, "We don't have time for this."

Peck rubbed his hands together to warm them as he glanced anxiously at the others. "I know. I went to check on Dolt, and I couldn't find them. I searched the stables."

The others looked at Aaslo as if he could make the two wanderers appear. Perhaps he could, he thought. Aaslo turned his attention inward and searched for the tiny lights that were the two former guards. He had so many lights within him now—hundreds—that it was not easy to parse them out. Eventually, he found Greylan's light, and he tugged on it, searching for a direction. It took some time, but his search led him in the direction of the temple. He summoned the dead warrior, and he could tell that Greylan wanted to respond, but something held him back.

"Well?" Teza asked. "Where are they?"

"I'm not sure," replied Aaslo. "They're somewhere in the temple. It doesn't make sense. They should have stayed with the horses." He turned to Peck. "Make sure the guards are still rotating shifts watching the horses. You and Mory are going on a scouting mission."

Peck stuffed his hands in his coat pockets and muttered, "I hope it's indoors."

"It is," confirmed Aaslo. "We're due for a ritual. If we wander off now, we'll attract too much attention. You and Mory are going to search for Greylan and Rostus. Do it discreetly."

"Of course. Ah, could you maybe point us in the right direction?"

Aaslo hooked a thumb over his shoulder to indicate the remainder of the temple behind him. "They're somewhere in that direction."

Peck smirked. "So somewhere in the temple—the *whole* temple. Thanks."

Aaslo shrugged. "You're the scouts. You figure it out."

"I see you're using those renowned leadership skills."

Peck gave him a salute and exited the modest dining area. Aaslo noted a couple of monks happened to leave at the same time and was about to follow when Teza laid her hand over his, halting him.

"They'll be fine. Peck will shake them. He knows what he's doing."

Aaslo raised his brow. "Since when do you have confidence in Peck?"

She pulled her hand back with a roll of her eyes. "His skills have allowed him to survive this long. I think he can handle a few monks."

Aaslo wasn't sure, though. Something was amiss in the temple. If someone had managed to overcome the two warrior wanderers, then these monks were more than they seemed. After instructing the remaining guards to see that their horses and packs were ready to leave upon completing the ritual, Aaslo returned to his room with the others in tow. When they reached their chambers, which were not far from the dining hall, a cadre of monks awaited them. The eight somber-faced men and women stood in two neat columns, filling the dim corridor. Brother Yarrow was at the fore.

He gave a slight bow, addressing them. "Honored magi, please follow us to the sanctuary so that we may praise the ancients for your presence here and for the power you wield."

Aaslo glanced at Teza, who looked pleased, and then to Ijen, unruffled as usual, before following the monks. They turned about-face and proceeded at a sedate pace. Andromeda and a quiet, stone-faced Pashtigonian warrior named Elias followed at the rear. Elias, a serious man who never laughed at their jests, seemed dependable, and that was all that concerned Aaslo.

As they made their way through winding corridors, Aaslo tried to maintain a mental map. The way seemed convoluted, however, and he wasn't at all sure the monks weren't taking them in circles just to confuse them. On several occasions, they crossed bridges that spanned the icy black glacial river over which the temple had been built. The banks of the river sported a few small boats and fishing piers, mostly populated by men and boys trying their luck with their fishing poles and nets. Aaslo wasn't sure what they could be fishing for at the top of a mountain, but figured they wouldn't be doing it if there was nothing to catch.

The monks led them through multiple chambers and halls, some filled with secular folk engaged in various activities of woodwork or weaving or pottery-making, and others that seemed to serve no purpose at all. One rather large hall served as an indoor market; a variety of goods that might be found in a village were being traded and sold. By the time they reached the sanctuary, Aaslo felt certain they were somewhere near the front of the temple again.

It occurred to him that the temple truly was a city, and he suddenly felt guilty for sending Peck and Mory off to find the errant wanderers without additional assistance. He was also growing concerned that Peck and Mory might not make it back to the stables in time for their hasty retreat.

PECK DUCKED BEHIND A TABLE AS A PUDGY MONK IN PLAIN GREY robes shuffled around the corner. He didn't understand the temple hierarchy, but he assumed this young man, who looked no older than thirteen or fourteen, was an acolyte who hadn't quite reached the status of burgundy robes. He grinned to himself as he targeted his mark, then turned to Mory, who crouched next to him. With a whisper and a few well-worn hand gestures, Peck informed Mory that they would be approaching the young man and that Mory should play along. Mory nodded once, then Peck smoothed down the velvet jacket he had traded for the heavy coat and stood. He sauntered up to the young man, who only noticed him once he had gotten within a few feet.

"Hi ho!" said Peck in a cheerful voice. He kept his motions grand and expressive as he waved at the young monk. "We're a bit lost in these corridors, sir, and we hoped you might oblige us with directions."

The young monk, whose cheeks were rounder than those of a chipmunk preparing for fall, blinked up at Peck in surprise. Then he squinted and leaned forward as if trying to get a better look. It occurred to Peck that the young man was practically blind. Now that Peck was closer, he decided the acolyte was probably a bit younger than he had estimated as well, but his portly size was deceiving.

The young acolyte said, "Ah, I would be happy to help you, but I'm afraid my directions might not do much for you. I have trouble with my sight, you see?"

Peck grinned and rocked back on his heels. "That's okay. What do you do to get around? Count your steps?"

"Yes, mostly anyway. Sometimes I use the sounds around me. Every room sounds different, you know."

Peck ran a finger across his freshly shaved jaw. "I hadn't thought of that. How interesting. Well, you see, we're just visiting here, and something of ours has gone missing. We were wondering—"

"We?" The acolyte blinked at him.

Peck's expression fell. If the boy couldn't even see Mory standing just behind him, then his usual affable mannerisms wouldn't be doing him much good. He slapped Mory on the back, pushing him forward. He said, "This, here, is my brother, Mory. As I said, we're a bit lost—"

"Yes, I remember," said the young man, peering blankly into the space between himself and Mory.

"Right, so we've lost something and were wondering where it might be kept. It's probably locked up somewhere safe. Are there cells or a vault or some such around here?"

The young man looked confused as he nodded absently. "Yes," he drawled. "We have cells for when people get out of hand, but why would anyone lock something—"

"Never mind the why. It's not really important. Could you point us in the direction of these cells?"

"Of course!" replied the acolyte. "They're in the observatory."

Peck looked at the young man skeptically. "No, that doesn't sound right."

"Yes, yes. The cells are back the way you came. Turn at the first right, then take one hundred and eighty-two steps and turn left . . ."

Peck nodded as he noted the directions, trying very hard to remember all the steps and turns. He knew Mory was doing the same, and between the two of them, they would be able to find the observatory—hopefully. He wasn't sure why cells would be located in a place meant for observing the sky, but he would investigate it regardless.

Leaving the acolyte behind, they were well on their way to the cells—*hopefully*—and Mory mused, "Do you really think Greylan and Rostus will be in these cells?"

"Shhh," hissed Peck with a wave of his hand. "I'm trying to remember the directions. Was it two hundred and fourteen steps and to the left?"

"It was two hundred and forty-one steps and to the right," said Mory.

"Right, I misspoke. I remember."

"Uh-huh," muttered Mory.

"You don't believe me?"

"Of course, Peck."

"Good." Peck ran his sweaty palms down his jacket again. "Because I've got this."

"Of course, Peck. We should turn here."

"I know that, but I'm glad you're paying attention. This is good practice. In fact, I'm going to let you lead the way just to see how well you remember."

"Okay, Peck."

Peck grinned to himself. Mory was a good apprentice. Sure, he was a little odd since his brush with death, but he had come a long way since Tyellí. He had matured in ways that Peck didn't understand. Sometimes he had a look in his eyes that seemed much older than his fourteen years. On occasion, it felt as if he wasn't leading Mory anymore. It was as if Mory led *him*, and Peck didn't particularly like that. It was *his* job to take care of Mory, not the other way around.

After a long jaunt through the temple, they finally found the room they sought, and its function as an observatory became apparent. The large hall contained several rows of wooden benches and a short pulpit to one side of the room. On the other side, two monks flanked stairs leading to a recess in the floor large enough to hold several dozen people. Only a handful were actually present, however, and they did not mingle with each other. Instead, they watched or shouted to the people in the center of the room. Those people, disheveled and worn, were on display for the world to see, trapped in a series of open-barred cells.

"I see why they call it the observatory," said Mory. With a shiver, he added, "I wouldn't want to be imprisoned in front of everyone. Can you imagine the shame?"

"I think that's the point," Peck mumbled as he scanned the space for the two undead warriors. He sighed. "They're not here. Looks like we're back to square one."

"Maybe not," said Mory, pointing across the hall. "Look. That monk has a lot of keys."

Peck noted the heavy key ring dangling from the monk's belt. "Yes?"

"He's probably someone important. We could follow him. If he doesn't lead us to Greylan and Rostus, then we can, you know, *question* him."

Peck nodded slowly then brightened. "Okay, here's what we do. We're going to follow that man with the keys. He's bound to know more than the acolyte. I bet he can tell us where the wanderers are."

Mory nodded. "That sounds like a good idea, Peck."

Satisfied with himself, Peck motioned for Mory to follow him as he moved surreptitiously around the perimeter of the room toward the corridor where the monk had disappeared. No one took notice of them, as the preoccupied temple residents had their own interests. The two thieves padded down the corridor on silent feet, as Peck had taught Mory to do since he could walk, and they eventually caught sight of the monk's robes as the man turned a corner. The corridors were dark here, with fewer torches, but Peck was reasonably sure it was the same man.

Peck peeked around the corner, staying in shadow as much as possible. He watched as the monk unlocked a door on the opposite side of the corridor, then entered, closing the door behind him.

"What do we do now?" whispered Mory, who crouched beneath him, watching.

Peck held his breath as he considered their options. He had no way of knowing what was beyond the door. It could be a room, or it could be another corridor leading deeper into the temple. If he was a daring man, he might attempt to follow the monk through the doorway. Daring, however, hadn't kept him alive on the streets of Tyellí. Sure, Peck took chances every time he targeted a mark, but those were calculated risks with a good chance of reward. Plus, he always had an exit strategy. This wasn't one of those times, so Peck elected for caution.

He said, "Now we wait."

Mory didn't question his decision. The boy rarely did. Mory's complete trust did as much to cause him distress as it did to bolster Peck's confidence. His greatest fear was that one day he would lead Mory into an unescapable situation and be the cause of Mory's death. A shiver ran through him as he remembered the day Aaslo had caught them. He had thought they were both done for, but Aaslo turned out to be a good man worthy of their loyalty. Such was the reason for their present task.

Peck had almost changed his mind about waiting when the door finally opened again. The same monk exited, this time empty-handed, and locked the door. He turned in their direction.

"Go back," Peck whispered urgently as he jerked his head back. Mory scrambled to his feet, and they both hurried down the corridor to the closest intersection. Mory tried a door, which opened easily, and they ducked inside. The small storage room was dark but afforded a view of the corridor. They peered through the crack in the door as they waited for the monk to pass. The man seemed lost in thought as he strode by, and Peck had no problem sneaking up on him. He struck the man in the back of the head with a candlestick they found, then he and Mory quickly dragged the barely conscious monk back into the dark room. Peck used rags to tie the man's hands and feet and gagged him. Then they waited for the monk to rouse. Once the man started struggling, Peck figured they could start the questioning.

Peck wasn't a violent man by nature, but he knew from his years on the streets that instilling fear was the best way to get information. He grabbed the man's hair and yanked his head back. He could see very little in the dark, but as the man whimpered, he figured that only added to the sense of doom.

With his best impression of Aaslo, Peck gruffly said, "I'm going to ask you some questions, and you're going to answer. Otherwise, there will be consequences. Understand?" The man struggled against his bindings, and Peck knew this wouldn't be easy. He said, "Two guards are missing from the stables. Do you know who I'm talking about?"

The monk jerked against Peck's hold on his head, and he took it to mean *yes*.

"I'm going to remove your gag, and if you shout there will be pain. Tell me where the guards are."

As he removed the gag, the man bit at him. With a growl, the monk said, "Those monsters are an offense against nature. They deserved what they got. I'm not telling you anything."

Peck groaned, "I didn't want to have to do this, but you're giving me no choice." He balled his fist and socked the man in the gut. The monk curled over and retched from the impact. Peck didn't think he had hit him that hard, but while the monk wasn't overweight, his middle was soft. He clenched his teeth against his own nausea over what he had to do and yanked the man up by the hair. Then he slapped the man across the face. "Tell me where they are or this is going to get a lot worse." He really hoped it didn't have to get worse.

The man spit at him. Peck pulled his arm back for another hit but hesitated when Mory spoke. "How about I go get Aaslo?"

Peck was confused. Mory knew Aaslo was busy. Why would he suggest getting him in the middle of their interrogation? He started to say as much, but Mory interrupted him.

"You know, so Aaslo can turn him into one of his undead. Then he'll be forced to answer our questions."

"No!" blurted the monk, his voice heavily laced with fear. "You can't turn me into one of those things. I'd rather die."

Peck, catching on to Mory's plan, added, "Oh, you will die. Then you will become undead and will cooperate."

"Okay, okay, I'll tell you. They won't do you any good anyhow.

Just don't turn me into a monster. We locked them in one of the storage rooms in the vault. Take my keys. It's around the corner. You'll have no problem finding it."

After obtaining specific instructions, Peck and Mory left the monk bound and gagged in the storage closet and ran down the corridor toward the vault. Peck pulled the keys from his pocket and made short work of the well-oiled lock. He opened the door just far enough for them to slip through before shutting it behind them.

The vault was a massive storage room that rivaled any warehouse in Tyellí. The room was well lit by mage lamps, many of which had already lost their glow, presumably because no one had replenished the spells. Several empty carts and wheelbarrows sat beside the door, lined up and ready for use. The orderly open space beyond held stacks of goods, shelves, crates, barrels, sacks, and pots organized into rows with enough space between for a cart. At the end of each row, posts bore painted wooden signs indicating which items might be found in that row. Unfortunately, none of those signs read *Dead People*.

Mory eyed the room skeptically. "I don't know, Peck. This doesn't seem like the kind of place to hide some guards."

Peck rubbed his chin thoughtfully. Mory was right, but he didn't want to admit that. "There are doors around the perimeter. Maybe they're the cells the monk meant—you know, the kind they don't want everyone seeing."

Mory didn't sound convinced but said, "Okay, hopefully they're unlocked. Being in here makes me anxious. I feel trapped."

Peck led the way to the first door. The keys jingled as he sifted through them to find one that fit the lock. It took too long, but they managed to unlock the door and walk in. Shelves lined the walls of the small chamber, each holding items that looked more valuable than anything else in the warehouse. Seeing that their guards weren't present, they moved to leave the room when something caught Peck's eye. A sheathed knife lay on the shelf beside the door as if it had been dropped there.

"We're on the right track," he said, picking it up. "I recognize this. The knife belongs to Greylan. See? It has his initial on the pommel."

"He wouldn't give that up willingly," noted Mory.

"No, this isn't looking good," Peck said as he tucked the knife into his belt. "But if we don't find them, at least we won't have to go back to Aaslo empty-handed."

They were two chambers over when a sound reached their ears. Someone had entered the warehouse, and they weren't quiet about it.

Peck closed the door to the small chamber as much as he could and peered out of the small gap. Several people moved into view in front of him, one woman wearing burgundy robes and three others in grey.

The woman said, "Get the carts, and load up quickly. The ritual will be over soon, and the others will want to be ready. They're magi. We won't be able to handle them without the enchantments."

"I don't understand," said one of the acolytes. "If they're magi, shouldn't we honor them?"

"They're not *our* magi," said the woman. "They want to take what's ours. They're the enemy."

Mory whispered, "Are they talking about Aaslo?"

"Shhh," hissed Peck. "I'm trying to listen."

The monks said nothing more as they gathered items from the warehouse. As Peck watched, he began to get the creeping feeling that he was being watched in turn—like someone was in the room with them. A muffled rustling reached his ears, and the hairs on his nape stood on end. He turned around slowly, scanning the dark chamber with wide eyes. There was barely enough light coming in through the crack in the doorway to see the opposite side of the small room. Peck saw that Mory was watching, too, and the boy jumped when a heavy *thump* echoed through the chamber.

Peck glanced out to see the monks moving toward the exit, then he turned to listen for the sounds that were much closer. They seemed to emanate from two heavy chests nestled against the wall at the far end of the room. Once the monks were gone, he opened the door for more light. Drawing his belt knife, he moved cautiously toward the trunks with Mory at his side. As they drew closer, another *thump* came from the trunk on the left. Mory jumped, but Peck steeled his nerves.

He crouched before a heavy trunk wrapped in dark green leather and examined the lock. A simple mechanism, and thanks to his trusty lock-picking set, he had it unlatched in a matter of seconds. He turned to the side and poised himself to strike as he lifted the lid with one hand. He jumped back, startled by the trunk's horrifying contents.

There, inside the unassuming trunk, were body parts—those of a human—butchered such that the arms, legs, and head were removed from the torso and tossed in carelessly. Despite the grotesque appearance, there seemed to be very little blood. What unnerved him was the fact that the body parts *moved*. The hands clenched and unclenched, the knees spasmed so that the feet kicked against the sides of the trunk, and the face—oh, the face was the worst of all.

The corpse's features were carved into a grotesque vision of fury and anguish as the milky-white eyes blinked back at him.

"It's Greylan!" whisper-shouted Mory.

Peck swallowed down his initial fear and startlement and inched closer to get a better look. It *was* Greylan, and even though he was cut into a number of pieces, he was still *un*dead. Peck briefly wondered exactly how much damage would need to be done for him to be rendered *dead* again. Peck jumped when a scratching sound emanated from the other trunk, and he made quick work of unlocking it as well. Sure enough, Rostus lay within, and had endured the same harsh treatment as had Greylan.

"What do we do?" said Mory. "We can't just leave them like this."

Peck clucked his tongue as he considered their options. He said, "Perhaps we can leave them here and Aaslo can make them dead again from wherever he is."

"Maybe," said Mory, appearing uncomfortable. "But we don't know that, and I think we need them. They're good warriors, and they're loyal to Aaslo."

"But they're in pieces," said Peck.

"Maybe one of the magi can put them back together."

"They're not dolls," Peck grumped. Then he sighed. "You're right, though. Aaslo should decide. We'll have to take them with us, but these trunks are too heavy. You go get one of those carts by the door, and I'll find some sacks to put them in."

The two of them went about their tasks quickly and quietly, mindful of the door and the possibility that they could be interrupted. As they emptied the trunks into the sacks, it occurred to Peck that someone might come check on the corpses. He and Mory gathered sacks of grain and potatoes, filling the trunks and locking them. If someone tried to lift the trunks, they would at least feel heavy enough to contain bodies.

"There," said Peck. "Hopefully no one will look inside. Now we just have to get through the corridors with this cart without getting caught."

"I have an idea," said Mory, rushing from the small room back into the storehouse. A moment later, he came back with a couple of grey robes like those worn by the acolytes. "We can disguise ourselves, and maybe no one will pay attention to us."

Peck took the grey robe as a surge of pride washed over him. "That's a great idea, Mory. You're doing well."

Mory grinned at him as he donned his own grey robe. "Thanks, Peck. You're the best teacher."

Peck shook his head. "You remember that the next time you get the harebrained idea to join the army."

"I don't need to anymore," replied Mory. "Thanks to you, I'm a scout."

Peck was satisfied with that. Being a scout was a much safer bet than being on the front lines of the infantry, and a better use of Mory's skills. Plus, he could keep an eye on the boy.

As Peck pushed the cart toward the warehouse door, the sacks' contents continued to shift as if the bags were filled with demented squirrels. Peck finally slapped one of the bags and hissed, "Stop moving. People will notice."

The sacks abruptly stilled, and Peck was once again unnerved that animated corpses were still so full of life.

CHAPTER 13

AASLO SAT ON HIS ASSIGNED FLOOR CUSHION AS HIS GAZE SWEPT THE room. While sitting there, he wondered how many souls Axus had stolen from the Sea. How many souls had escaped Aldrea to power the death god's maneuverings? He was anxious and didn't want to be sitting doing nothing. He wanted to get the bodies of the dead magi and be away from this place. With a deep breath, he forced his hands to relax and glanced to his right.

Teza and Ijen sat on similar cushions. Both appeared distinctly uncomfortable, particularly Ijen, which unnerved Aaslo. It was disconcerting *anytime* the prophet expressed an opinion regarding their circumstances. Andromeda and Elias had been separated from them, and the commander now sat four rows back in the midst of the monks. Elias was not far from her, among those seated on cushions arranged in neat columns that filled the vast chamber. Everyone faced a large pit built into the floor at the front of the room. Smooth stone tiles lined the pit's wall and within was a pool of burning oil, the scent of which seared the nostrils and stung the eyes. Every so often, one of the monks presiding over the ritual would toss a bundle of herbs into the fire, causing it to smoke with a pungent aroma. The smoke permitted Aaslo to relax, and he could feel himself becoming lightheaded.

Mathias began nattering in the back of Aaslo's mind, but he ignored it as he attempted to refocus. He sharpened his gaze and surveyed the room with a critical eye. The windowless chamber was lit with a number of mage lights. Some had gone dark in the absence of the magi and had been replaced with torches, adding to the irritants in the air. A second-floor balcony surrounded the room, and beneath it, burgundy curtains of the same fabric as the monks' robes draped the walls. Sixteen statues stood evenly spaced around the perimeter of the room, each representing one of the original magi, and each bearing a placard at its base inscribed with the magus's name. Front and center was a statue that needed no placard. Aaslo immediately recognized the likeness, and it sent a shiver through his bones. It was without a doubt Sedi Tryst, and these monks seemed to worship her above all others.

The ritual continued, the monks' voices droning, monotone, and Aaslo could hear Mathias speaking to him. He seemed to be warning him against the present circumstances, but Aaslo could see little reason for alarm. Pushing the voice aside, he felt quite pleasant and a bit dreamy as he examined the likeness of Sedi in a way he had never been able to in person. Her eyes were wide and cunning, her nose and chin were narrow and sharp, and her high cheeks gave her the appearance of a raptor, a hunter. Her bearing was sure and powerful with her head held high and her shoulders back. She stood with the poise of a queen, and although this statue lacked motion, he knew she moved with the grace of a dancer—or an assassin. With his mind swirling in a miasma of dreaminess, he could admit to himself that Sedi was a handsome woman, beautiful even, in an exotic kind of way.

Mathias's voice broke through the calm. *"Aw, Aaslo, are you smitten with Sedi?"*

"I'm not smitten," he murmured. "I can appreciate beauty when I see it."

"Just keep in mind that the vixen you're fawning over is the enemy."

"I wasn't *fawning* over her. I was just—never mind. There's no point in arguing."

"You're right. I'm inside your head. I know your thoughts. You can't hide your little crush from me." There was a pause, then, *"I don't feel so well."*

"You're dead. You can't *feel* anything."

"But I'm in your *head. Are you okay, Aaslo?"*

Mathias's voice drifted to the back of his mind as Aaslo's focus waned. He wondered what had driven Sedi to side with Axus. Was it simply a matter of apathy, a longing for an end to an infinite life, or had it been something specific, something so terrible that she could no longer bear to live? He didn't think she was evil. In fact, she seemed to think she was doing the world a favor. She believed that everyone who died *here* was destined for some glorious future in Celestria or the Afterlife or wherever they ended up. He wondered again at what had driven her to assist him and her desire to meet with a god *other* than Axus. Was she beginning to question what she had been told? Had her intelligence finally overcome her single-minded death drive? If so, what compelled her? Had *he* played some role in her potential change of heart? Sedi was a conundrum he often found himself contemplating. He wondered if perhaps there was more to her than being an enemy.

"You're enraptured by a woman who wants you dead, Aaslo."

Mathias's snide comment roused Aaslo from his thoughts again. He shook his head, trying to dislodge the voice as the lead monk approached to stand before him, blocking his view of the statue. In his haziness, he found that he was disappointed he could no longer see the enchanting magus's effigy.

"The vixen is enchanting, now?"

The monk was less interesting. He was a tall, thin man with a beaklike nose, bulging brown eyes, and a scraggly beard covering only the point of his chin. Aaslo had not gotten the man's name before the ritual began, but in his mind, he nicknamed him the Rat.

The Rat held a large goblet before Aaslo's face, imploring him to drink. Aaslo obediently opened his lips, but the voice in his mind shouted at him, and he cringed, clamping his mouth shut when the Rat presented him with the goblet. He reminded himself that he didn't know or trust these people, and he cared nothing for their ritual. A second man joined them as the Rat pushed the goblet toward Aaslo's face, and Aaslo tensed, ready to fight back. He had no reason to suspect they would fight him, however. Thus far, the monks had been pushy at times, but they hadn't been inclined to attack. The irritating buzz of Mathias's voice in his mind kept Aaslo alert enough to refuse the drink a third time, and the monks muttered their frustration to each other before offering the beverage to Teza.

Teza's eyes drooped, and a small smile played at her lips, but she refused the drink as well, as did a wide-eyed and overly alert Ijen when it was his turn. The frustrated Rat spun and threw the goblet into the fire, causing burning oil to splash the floor outside the pit. Several gasps sounded throughout the room, and the Rat glanced around irritably, daring anyone to speak. Then he tossed several handfuls of the pungent herb into the flame and continued with his tasks as if nothing had happened.

When the ritual was, presumably, complete, Aaslo and the others stood. He glanced back to see that Andromeda and Elias watched the proceedings with sharp gazes and tense shoulders. Unconcerned, he turned from them, his attention once again sweeping the room. Aaslo began to feel a bit giddy, and it didn't alarm him when the monks presiding over the ritual disappeared behind the curtains that draped the walls. It didn't surprise him when a majority of those who had been seated followed them. And, after a few seconds, when the monks reappeared, he didn't really care that this time they held an assortment of odd items that included what looked like tools, weapons, sculptures, and rods. The Rat carried a staff topped by a sphere that glowed with a silvery light that entranced Aaslo, and he barely noticed the cruel smile that played across the man's face.

Teza rubbed her eyes and shook herself as she backed up to take Aaslo's hand. She yanked him toward the rear of the room to the doors.

"We need to get out of here," she said with alarm. "Those are enchanted items, and I'm pretty sure they intend to use them against us." When Aaslo didn't move, she jerked his arm again. "Come on, Aaslo. Snap out of it. They drugged us!"

That got his attention. Aaslo had inadvertently drugged himself once. When he was fifteen, he had stumbled into a veronia patch while looking for a good place to plant a sapling. The veronia plant's thorns had scored his skin and infected him with their toxin. He had been dizzy and absent-minded for days afterward. This time was different. It took him a moment to assess what it was he felt. The constant nattering of the voice in his mind began to grate, and he realized his placid feelings of peace and joy were unnatural.

Aaslo reached down to his waist and found that the sword that should have been there was missing. Blinking away smoke and mental fog, he searched those nearest him for the thief. He found a wide-eyed acolyte backing away with Mathias's sword in hand. Aaslo lunged after the young man, and chaos ensued.

The Rat monk shouted, "You shall not take our ancients, Defiler! She warned us you would come. You must die and take the corpses who walk with you into the ground!"

Monks muttered words of power and swung their rods and staffs with purpose. Spells were slung through the air and erupted from the floor and dripped from the ceiling. The spells collided with magical shield wards erected by Teza and Ijen, and in his mental haze, Aaslo realized he should probably shield himself as well. Before he could establish a shield, though, something struck him from behind. The force thrust Aaslo forward into a hooded woman wielding a long dagger that glowed a furious red. Unable to save himself, Aaslo shouted as the blade slid effortlessly into his abdomen. Aaslo raked his claws across the woman's throat as he jerked back to find the handle jutting out just beneath the ribs. He knew he should leave the knife inside him until Teza could heal the wound, but he couldn't breathe. He grasped the handle with his clawed hand and jerked the dagger free. At first, blood gushed from the rupture, but it quickly stopped as Aaslo lunged in the direction of the acolyte in possession of Mathias's sword.

A spell zipped by his head, but this time, he was prepared. The spell deflected off his shield and struck an approaching monk, who held a long rod snapping with power. The monk dropped the rod as he fell back, and Aaslo swiped it from the ground, grunting from the pain the effort produced in his abdomen. He swung the rod at another monk. The monk jerked and collapsed in convulsions. Aaslo looked at the rod with a new appreciation as he used it to clear a path toward the sword-stealing acolyte. The young man had, unfortunately, backed himself into Andromeda's fighting range. The Pashtigonian warrior did an admirable job of dodging magical attacks as she engaged several sword-wielding monks.

Aaslo pointed toward the young acolyte. "Stop him! He has my sword."

"You die once, and suddenly everyone is claiming your belongings."

Andromeda took a staff to the jaw as she turned to look where he pointed, and Aaslo felt guilty. She shook off the attack and shoved the nearest monk into the path of the retreating acolyte. The two monks fell over each other, tangled in their robes, as Aaslo closed the distance. Aaslo reached down and grabbed Mathias's sword, striking the young man in the temple with the hilt, rendering him unconscious. Aaslo helped Andromeda and Elias clear monks from their immediate area then looked over to see Teza and Ijen engaged in a battle of magics with the staff-wielding Rat.

Aaslo started to cross the space toward them when a patter of light darts struck his shield. He turned to find Sedi leaning against her own statue with her arms and feet crossed, and Aaslo couldn't help but note the accuracy of the likeness.

"Your girlfriend is here."

"She's not my girlfriend," Aaslo protested.

Stalking toward her, Aaslo said, "What are you doing here, Sedi? I thought we had an understanding."

She shrugged one shoulder. "I said I would tell you *where* the bodies were located, not that I would make it easy for you. Besides, I was only getting your attention. If you were so easily killed, we wouldn't be having this conversation." She abruptly tugged his shirt up to reveal the already healing wound in his gut.

Aaslo slapped her hand away. "And what conversation is that?" he said, standing directly in front of her.

She reached up and brushed a lock of hair from his face, then looked startled as if she hadn't intended to do it. She recovered quickly. "Did you come through on your end of the deal?"

"I did, so call off your monks." He pointed to where the others were still engaged with their attackers.

Sedi rolled her eyes. "It's not as if they're much of a challenge for you."

"They don't need to die. Besides, they're your worshippers. Don't you want to protect them?"

She sighed and looked at them sadly. "They don't worship *me*, specifically. They worship the ancients, and they're zealots. They do what they think is best. They wouldn't stop fighting even if I ordered them, which I *did*, by the way—right after I got here."

"You did?" Aaslo was genuinely surprised. Perhaps Sedi had a conscience, after all.

"Yes, but they just keep fighting. I'm afraid you'll have to kill or incapacitate them if you want the bodies."

"Where *are* the bodies?" he said.

She waved toward the burgundy curtains. "Behind there. There are three of them." Then she looked at him slyly. "How did you get a god to agree to meet with me?"

"I asked," said Aaslo. "Why do you want this so badly?"

She straightened. She was nearly of a height with him, and merely tilted her head slightly to look in his eyes. "I know what you think of me, Aaslo, but I'm not a bad person. I want to know the truth as much as you do."

"It doesn't seem to me that the Berru are interested in the truth."

Sedi shook her head. "They're not, but I'm not the Berru."

"You said you were—"

"I know what I said. Perhaps I oversimplified things. It's true that I created the Berru and that I've guided them throughout the millennia; but, dogmatically, they went their own way a long time ago. I have little influence over what they believe, and if I tried to refute it, they would castigate me, perhaps even banish me."

Standing so close to the fire, Aaslo's head began to swim again, but he looked at her skeptically. The woman standing before him was not the self-assured leader she had been in their previous meetings. His murky mind wondered what might have changed her. He could almost hear a voice in the back of his mind, and it might be crying out in warning. He was nearly certain it was Mathias.

His voice sounded like an echo to his own ears as Aaslo said, "Why are you doing this?"

She looked at him with interest. "Doing what?"

"Speaking to me. Telling me this." He wasn't sure he had spoken aloud.

Sedi's gaze, beautiful and sultry, regarded him from beneath thick lashes. At first, he thought she wouldn't answer, then she smiled knowingly. "Maybe I want you to like me."

"The vixen's toying with you again."

A cloud of smoke wafted over them, and Aaslo felt his mind spin. He stepped toward the beautiful enchantress, bringing them only inches apart. He said, "It's too bad we're on opposite sides of this war."

She blinked up at him, and he noticed her pupils were dilated and unfocused. Her voice was breathy. "Are we?"

He reached up and brushed his fingers across her cheek. As he caressed her soft skin, a second voice whispered to him—inviting, intriguing. In his fevered state, he heard one word—*kiss.*

Aaslo leaned forward and pressed his lips to Sedi's. She stiffened at first, then melted into him, wrapping her arms around his neck and digging her fingers into his hair to deepen the kiss. Pleasure, unlike any Aaslo had known, swirled across his senses as his hands traced her hips, gripping them to pull her closer. The soft voice of Ina was pleased, and he knew he had paid a debt. Aaslo shoved away Mathias's insistent, loud taunts as the herbal smoke and Sedi's arms held him.

Sudden pain chased away the fog, his heart in a vise. Aaslo pushed away from Sedi and looked down to see a knife hilt sticking out of his chest.

"You should have listened to me, but no, you were too busy tonguing the enemy."

Sedi's laugh held such joy, but her eyes glinted with something else. Guilt? Surely not.

Behind him, a throat cleared, but it wasn't until someone barked out, "Aaslo!" that he snapped from his trance. Practicality warred with desire as he turned to see Teza, Ijen, and Andromeda standing behind him. Each appeared to battle their own thoughts about his actions. He turned back to Sedi, but she was gone, disappeared from beneath his fingers.

"What was *that?*" snarled Teza. She stalked forward and took his face into her hands, examining his eyes. Then she wrinkled her nose and glanced at the fire. "He's standing too close to the smoke. He's *really* drugged. It's the only explanation."

"If you insist," said Ijen cryptically. "That isn't his only problem, though."

"What are you talking about?" snapped Teza.

Ijen spread his hands. "Well, I am no healer, but I don't think *that,*" he pointed to the knife handle in Aaslo's chest, "is good for his health."

Teza's eyes widened. "Oh!" She reached out and yanked it from Aaslo's body. He jerked and blood spurted across the floor, stopping nearly as quickly as it started.

Tugging his shirt up, Teza examined the wound. Aaslo waited for the tingling sizzle of her healing power, but it didn't come. Instead, she continued to stare at his gaping wound. "Well, are you going to do something?"

Teza shook her head. "I don't think I need to. It's healing on its own."

Aaslo looked down to see that the wound had, in fact, nearly healed.

Teza met his startled gaze. "Aaslo, that knife struck you in the heart. I couldn't have healed that wound. You should be dead."

He tugged his shirt down. "Well, I'm not." He took a step and wavered. Teza lent him a steadying hand.

"You've lost a lot of blood and you're still drugged. It'll probably take a while for you to come down from this," added Teza. "Hopefully you can raise the magi before the people out *there* find out what we did in *here*."

Aaslo blinked several times as he took in the aftermath of the fight. Burgundy and grey lumps littered the floor, and spatters and smears of blood splashed across much of the room. The monks had not fared well, which for some reason saddened Aaslo. Teza took his hand and pulled him to the far side of the room, away from the fire. The others stood talking around him for some time before his mind finally began to catch up. On several occasions, he caught the words *Sedi* and *kiss* and *mental*.

Mathias had plenty to say as well. *"I can't believe you kissed her. What were you thinking, Aaslo?"*

"I wasn't thinking. It just happened."

"But you wanted it to happen?"

"Did I? I guess I did at the time. You're going to hold this over my head, aren't you."

Mathias hooted. *"You have to ask? You should probably stop thinking about your vixen and get on with things, though. Perhaps you can use your power to clear your mind."*

Aaslo ignored Ina's pleased purring as he tugged on her power. He sent a tendril of it washing over his thoughts, and his mind abruptly focused. He pointed to the curtained wall. "There," he said.

The others stopped mid-conversation, and Teza said, "What?"

Aaslo coughed and rubbed a hand over his face. "The tombs of the magi are behind the curtains."

"How do you know?" asked Andromeda.

"Sedi told me."

Teza smirked and remarked dryly, "I didn't realize you two had taken the time to *talk*. You seemed rather busy with *other* things."

Aaslo's jaw clenched. While the smoke had apparently affected his inhibitions, it hadn't damaged his memory. Everything that had happened was quite clear in his mind, as were his reasons for doing it, and he was utterly confused. Had he really kissed Sedi?

"Yes, brother, you did, and I'm never going to let you hear the end of it."

Aaslo's head wasn't so foggy that he felt like talking about it, so he instead strode to the curtain. He wrestled with the fabric for a moment before finding an alcove. Nestled within that alcove was a tomb. According to a plaque, it belonged to Loris Deretey.

Peering into the tomb, Ijen said, "She was known for her work in health and wellness. She was the first healer."

"There's another over here," said Teza from farther down the wall. "Aen Ledrian."

"The first prophet," said Ijen with a hint of surprise.

"And here," said Andromeda from across the room. "Jillian Mascede."

Ijen smiled. "Ah, my kin. Known for her disregard for ethical experimentation."

They opened each of the tombs to ensure the bodies were present. The corpses were all magically preserved and bore a likeness to their statues. Aaslo rubbed his temples as he moved to stand in the center of the room between the tombs. He said, "I don't know if I have the focus or he energy right now to do this twice, much less three times. I'm going to try to raise them all at once."

Andromeda said, "Is that wise? The last time you did this, things exploded. I'm not sure we'll survive *three* awakenings."

Aaslo nodded. "I think doing all three will help distribute the power."

Andromeda looked at him skeptically. "How sure are you about that?"

Aaslo didn't reply as he turned away from her. The voice in his mind was getting louder, and he was pretty sure Mathias was laughing at him. It didn't matter. Mathias wasn't the one who had to make things happen. Aaslo raised his arms; not because he needed to, but because it helped him concentrate. He wrestled the dark power from the clutches of Ina, who had wrapped it in her own power and wanted to play, and focused his will to connecting with the corpses. He latched onto Jillian first, then Aen, and finally Loris. It was not difficult to hold all three within the dark embrace. He had done this so many times now, often with even more bodies than just three. The hard part would be what came next.

Sifting through the many souls he harbored, Aaslo found the three he intended for these bodies. Simply connecting with the depraved made him feel ill, and he could sense his rising irritability. The souls of the depraved were different from the human souls he had claimed. They were just . . . *wrong* somehow, a twisted parody of what they should have been. Aaslo tried not to think about them too much, for he was pretty sure he could lose himself should they attempt to devour him. Connecting with three of them at once was like drowning in an ocean filled with sharp-toothed, writhing sea monsters.

Aaslo separated the three tormented beings and sent them each along a path to the body of a long-dead magus. Keeping them separate seemed to be the key, because two of them appeared to want to join with each other. The third one, bound for Aen, seemed to repel the other two, and it was less inclined to cooperate. The first two slipped seamlessly into their awaiting vessels, but Aen's soul resisted. As Aaslo pushed against it, it lashed out with an unusual power that struck Aaslo's gut. He doubled over, clutching his abdomen, as nausea and cramps caused a wave of heat to wash over him.

A whisper reached his mind. *"You're stronger than it, Aaslo. You can do this."*

Aaslo was thankful to hear Mathias's words of encouragement; they meant much to him. He gritted his teeth and shoved against the stubborn soul, thrusting it into the body against its will. He felt only slightly guilty. It *had*, after all, agreed to do his bidding when he took hold of it in the first place. A soldier could not be choosy about his duties.

When all three souls settled in their bodies, Aaslo tied off the links and withdrew his power. As soon as he disconnected, a pulse of energy shook the room, causing them all to stumble and lose their footing. Then a second pulse knocked them from their feet and part of the ceiling crumbled. It was immediately followed by a third pulse that rocked the room and toppled a few of the statues. Somewhere beyond the chamber they heard the thunderous crash of a structure collapsing, and Aaslo hoped no one had been harmed. It appeared he had been wrong about the backlash of power.

As the dust settled and Aaslo and his companions regained their feet, all three shades sat up at once. They looked around the room in curiosity, and Jillian and Loris climbed from their tombs and ran to each other, clambering over the debris without concern. They wrapped each other in an intimate embrace and forgot everyone else as they cooed and nuzzled each other. Aen's shade was slower to rouse. He seemed to be in no hurry, and as he looked at the other two shades, he curled his lip in disgust. When his gaze landed on Teza, however, his expression faltered, and he fell to his knees in front of her. He stared up at her, adoration in his glowing green eyes.

Teza took a quick step back and looked at Aaslo in alarm. "Why is he looking at me like that?"

Aaslo slowly straightened as the cramps in his stomach finally subsided, but it was Ijen who answered. A small smile played at the prophet's lips. "He seems smitten with you. Aen Ledrian was well known for his popularity with women, and he wasn't above using his power of prophecy to *encourage* their affections."

Teza's eyes widened, and she appeared shaken. "Well, I'm not interested. He's dead *and* depraved. Those are two red flags in my book!"

"You could learn from her, Aaslo. She knows how to set boundaries."

Ijen grinned more broadly and tapped his chest where the book of prophecy lay beneath his tunic. "I shall be sure to note that."

Teza looked at him pointedly and narrowed her eyes. "You do that. And tell *him*"—she pointed at the shade who still stared at her with awe on his admittedly handsome face—"that it's not going to happen."

Ijen nodded. "I don't think he'll listen to me, just as he doesn't seem to be listening to your rejection. I think you're stuck with him for a while—at least until he finds someone else to moon over."

Teza scowled at the prophet, then gave the shade an uncomfortable glance. "Well, at least he's pleasant to look at—if I'm going to be stuck with him, that is." She placed her fists on her hips and leaned over the shade, addressing him directly with her usual assertiveness. "You are not getting any of this. You hear me? I'm not interested, so you can just forget it."

Aen smiled at her and rose. He towered over her as he held out his arms for an embrace. Teza held up a hand and shook her head. "Ah, ah, not happening! I do *not* give you permission to touch me."

The shade appeared hurt and disappointed as he dropped his hands, then he looked at Aaslo pleadingly.

"Don't look at me like that. She's an independent lady. I have no control over who she does and doesn't have an interest in. You will respect her wishes, though, and you will *not* touch her." Aaslo noted Teza's pleased grin and added, "Unless she gives you permission."

Teza's grin evaporated as she scowled at him.

The shade's agonized expression slowly morphed into resolve. He straightened and nodded once with a solemnity Aaslo wouldn't have expected from one of the depraved. These weren't the depraved anymore, though. These were something new—something unknown. They were the combined essences of the depraved and the magi who once inhabited these bodies, and no one knew how the changes would affect them.

Aaslo gave the three shades the instructions not to use their powers unless they were under attack and to follow Teza's orders in his absence. Even though most of the monks were probably dealing with the fallout from the awakening, Ijen placed a temporary ward on the door so no one would find the bodies that filled the room until they were long gone. Then Aaslo opened a portal directly to the stables so they wouldn't have to navigate the labyrinth of corridors. When they arrived in the stables, their guards were breathing heavily, and several dead monks lay about in bloody puddles. Peck and Mory awaited them as well. They both wore acolyte robes, and hovered over a cart filled with two large, lumpy sacks.

Aaslo commented, "It looks like you had some trouble out here."

One of the guards said, "Yes, m'lord. They tried to kill the horses." He pointed to the crumpled body of a monk who bled from the head. "Your horse took out that one, and we took care of the rest."

Aaslo nodded with a frown, then looked at Peck. "Did you find Greylan and Rostus?"

"Ah, about that . . ." said Peck, opening one of the sacks exposing Rostus's head and a twitching foot, and Aaslo briefly wondered at his mental state since he was not sickened by the sight. Peck added, "We found them chopped up and stored in some trunks. We thought maybe someone could put them back together." He looked pointedly at Teza.

"What?" she blurted. "Oh, no. They're corpses, and they're in pieces. That's not what I do."

"But, they're still moving," Mory pointed out. "And they're good warriors. Don't you want to help them?"

"Dealing with the dead is Aaslo's job. I just heal the living," replied Teza, crossing her arms as if that would put an end to the discussion.

Aaslo opened the other bag and lifted out one of Greylan's arms. "I don't see how this is any different from what you did for me. You just reattach everything."

Teza held up a finger. "First of all, it doesn't work that way. Sure, I can do little things to one of your undead, but healing requires energy from the body—a *living* body. Maybe if we had several healers all working together—"

"What about her?" Andromeda pointed at Loris. She looked at Ijen. "Didn't you say she was the first healer? She has a lot of power as a First Order magus, *plus* she's one of the depraved." Then she addressed Teza. "Can't you work with *her* to do it?"

Teza's mouth hung open as she glanced between the bodies and Loris. Resigned, she released a heavy breath. "Yes, that might work."

Aaslo got Loris's attention. "You help Teza heal these bodies."

Loris disentangled herself from Jillian with a nod and looked at Teza. While the two of them went to work, Aaslo and the others kept watch for aggressive monks and prepared the horses to leave. They claimed two additional horses from the stables for use by the three new shades. It was all they had, but Aaslo didn't think Loris and Jillian would mind sharing a mount since they seemed to have no desire to be separated. Teza and Loris successfully pieced the two undead guards back together, and Greylan and Rostus didn't seem worse for wear. They were, perhaps, even better than they had been.

Everyone mounted up and returned to the woods to collect the two shades they had left behind. When they arrived, they found that the trees in a good twenty-yard radius had been obliterated, and an outcrop that had once stood strong was reduced to gravel. Echo and Avra were fighting. Echo's nose was broken, and Avra's hair was wrapped around his fingers. They both grimaced as Aaslo snapped at them to separate.

The five shades all stared at one another. While most seemed curious, Aen made it clear he wanted nothing to do with any of them. When the five neared each other, Aaslo felt a deeper power vibrating along the strands that bound the depraved to him. He hadn't noticed it when he had only two of them, but with all five, the energy was undeniable. With that power came a deep-set discontent, an irate turmoil that spread through him like blood in water. It brushed against his sanity at the edges of his mind. Aaslo resolved not to use the power of the shades until he absolutely had to.

After collecting his thoughts, Aaslo told the others to prepare for travel. They needed to be away. He didn't know if it was some blessing of Arohnu's or just his taxed mental state, but he could *feel* time slipping away. He gathered his power at his core and opened a portal back to his army.

CHAPTER 14

THE SEA OF TRANSCENDENCE TOSSED AND CHURNED AS MYROPA gazed across the choppy waves. It was as unsettled as she was after having received a summons. There were more whirlpools in the Sea now, places where souls had been stripped from their Afterlife. She knew Axus had stolen them. There could be no other explanation. What he used them for was the mystery. But if Axus gained power from the crossing of souls across the veil, then what possible power could be had by taking souls directly from the Sea? If what she believed was true, then Axus had already grown more powerful than they knew, and they had run out of time.

She dug her feet into the warm sand as the cool water sloshed around her ankles. She was stalling. Soon enough, Axus would tire of waiting and rip her from her present existence back to Celestria. She didn't want to go. She didn't want to endure Axus's dominating gaze or his relentless, uncompromising questions. There was no choice, though. Axus called, and she was obliged to answer.

Myropa took one last look at what had been a placid Afterlife and pulled her feet from the sand. As she stepped onto dry land, she crossed into the realm of the gods. Her path took her directly to Axus's maelstrom, that dark, foreboding place within the endless cavern. Sentinels of floating rock hovered like islands in the surf, and in every direction beyond the central core all Myropa could see was the black, empty space. At the center, Axus's power swirled in a tumultuous whirlwind of suffering, but again, Myropa's inability to feel anything buffered her. Having Arayallen's power stripped from her relegated Myropa to the frozen, unfeeling existence that had plagued her for the past two decades. The only difference now was the slight patter of her heart in her chest, thanks to Disevy.

The ledge against the cavern wall on which she stood was too narrow for two people to pass safely, but somehow the massive God of Death occupied it with her in all his hauntingly stunning splendor. Myropa abruptly fell to her knees as his strength overpowered her. His energy pulsed around him in aggravated waves, and Myropa sensed his anger even before she saw his scowling face.

Axus was beautiful, enchanting in a way that could effortlessly draw a person in and not recognize the danger until death claimed them. But with the furious expression he wore now, that beauty promised terrifying and horrible things to come. Myropa's entire body shook as ice crackled in her veins.

"What took you so long?" His voice was a whiplash.

At first, Myropa could only wag her chin, sound refusing to escape her lips. Axus leaned over her with a vicious command. "Speak!"

A cry jerked from her chest, and Myropa whimpered. His power was too strong, and she couldn't make her voice work. He growled in frustration then closed his eyes as he inhaled deeply. Slowly, ever so slowly, his power receded, and Myropa found that she could once again move of her own accord.

She said, "I was at the Sea—dropping off souls. I came directly here."

He raised an eyebrow. "Oh? What does it look like?"

At first, Myropa was surprised he didn't know, then she chided herself for the oversight. Of course he didn't know. He was barred from approaching the Sea, which made the missing souls all the more mysterious. How was he stealing them? She didn't mention the missing souls, however. She merely said, "It's turbulent."

"What is the cause?"

Hedging, she replied, "I can only guess."

"What good is *your* guess? You're a pitiful reaper, nothing more. I have no idea what Disevy sees in you." He abruptly switched topics. "Did you do as I asked? Did you get the depraved?"

Myropa's heart lurched and she gave a furious shiver. She had hoped Axus wouldn't ask about the depraved directly. With his power so heavy in the air, she was incapable of an outright lie. She tried to think of something, some way to dance around the truth, but the words slipped from her mouth before she could stop them. "Yes, I did."

His eyebrows rose in surprise. "You did? How did you manage that? No, never mind. It doesn't matter. Give them to me. Place them in my maelstrom."

"I—I can't," said Myropa. Her chest heaved with several deep breaths, trying and failing to cross the veil into the realm of life where she could escape him. She thought, once, she might even succeed, but she remained cowering on the ledge just out of range of the raging maelstrom.

"Why not?" he growled.

"Because I no longer have them." She gulped out a tearless sob.

She knew where this would go, and she had no idea what would become of her once he found out she had betrayed him.

"Where are they?" he shouted down at her, his power pulsing through her with fury.

Try as she might, she could not stop them. The words were ripped from her mouth. "Aaslo has them."

This brought him up short. "Aaslo? That human that has been a thorn in my side?"

"Yes," Myropa cried.

Axus clenched his teeth. "And how did he *get* them?"

"I gave them to him," she murmured, knowing her fate.

"*You* did this? All on your own? You defied *me*?"

Part of her wanted to tell him that she had done it on Disevy's orders, hoping that would shield her from Axus's wrath; but she would not betray Disevy if given a choice. She grasped at the one truth that might prevent her from exposing him. Although Disevy had ultimately given her the order, *she* had made the decision long before that.

"I made the choice. I offered the souls to Aaslo. I wanted to help him, to help the humans—people like me."

Axus shouted, his godly voice echoing throughout the endless cave even louder than the maelstrom. "*You* are *not* like them! *You* are a reaper. You serve *me*!"

"I serve Trostili," she shouted back. She wasn't sure why it should make a difference, but something told her it did.

Axus appeared to grow even more infuriated before he abruptly stopped and turned from her. "Curse the Fates," he snarled. "I will take this up with Trostili." He leaned down and took her chin in his hand with a firm grip. "Do not think this will deter me. I have nearly reached the power threshold that I need to take Celestria, and then even the depraved will be no threat to me." He spun away from her and stormed out through a fissure that led to the rest of Celestria.

Myropa shook beyond her ability to stand. Somehow, she had escaped the confrontation unscathed—so far. She didn't know what Trostili could do to her for her betrayal, but it would be terrible. Myropa didn't have time to dither over her fate, though. Thanks to her, Axus now knew that Aaslo had the depraved. The angry god would brutally mete out his vengeance on him. She had to warn him, but first she needed to see Disevy.

Gathering her strength, Myropa managed to get to her feet. She swallowed hard, tamping down the buzzing of her nerves, and focused on Disevy's energy. When she found him, though, she wished she hadn't. She stepped into a scene from the most terrifying of epic tales. The Second Pantheon was under attack, and Disevy fought in the thick of it. The God of Strength and Virility wore armor—similar to what Trostili might wear, except that somehow it appeared far more glorious on Disevy. A multitude of creatures that should never have been able to exist in Celestria engaged him in battle. The sword he effortlessly wielded was larger than any weapon Myropa had ever seen, and it glowed with the golden light of a god.

Beside him fought the most stunning woman—*goddess*. She wore splendid indigo armor that seemed to expose more than it covered. Her very being was a weapon. In her hands she wielded a scimitar with expert grace, and a violet power that seemed to originate from the goddess herself emanated from the blade. The goddess's straight, jet-black hair brushed the tops of her shoulders, and her violet eyes seemed too large for her face. Her perfect, heart-shaped mouth grimaced as she sliced cleanly through one of a horde of vights attacking her, and without stopping, she turned to dispatch another.

Above both of the gods towered a creature Myropa could only have conceived of in her nightmares. She had no name for it. Two stories high, with thick and strong muscle corded beneath its leathery, rust-colored skin. Its long and agile six limbs moved like those of a cat, and on each of its toes, a talon scored the earth with every step. Deep, dark eyes looked out from sockets in a sharply angled face, cheeks hollow and bony. The gaping, fang-filled mouth opened, descending on Disevy, and Myropa's heart leapt as she clutched her chest in surprise.

Disevy wasn't consumed. The god swung his blade, catching the creature in the chin, opening a gaping wound that oozed with thick, black blood. The creature reared back with a screech that shook the ground, and a bolt of light soared into its mouth. Myropa searched for the source, only to realize that Disevy and his female companion were not the only gods on the field. At least five others also engaged in the battle, some in the fray and others taking refuge behind toppled statuary and columns. These gods struck at the creature using a variety of ranged weapons.

Myropa wondered at these gods. If they were truly immortal and all-powerful, why would they hide? Why would they need armor? She looked again at the gods and noted several streaked with blood, and painful-looking injuries hobbled a few. Myropa considered: if gods could be injured, then it held to reason that they could also be killed. And if they used weapons rather than magic, then their powers must be limited, at least against these monsters.

Goose bumps prickled Myropa's flesh as a hiss reached her ears. She spun in time to see her attacker before it leapt upon her, bearing her to the ground. The horrid little vight snapped and clawed as she struggled against it. The little beast was stronger than its size would suggest, and its claws sliced into her arms. Myropa had power of her own, however; power ideally suited for dealing with creatures of the Alterworld. She opened herself to it and implored the Fates. Power flooded her, spreading out through her limbs and, for the briefest moment, she was warm and energized. All too quickly, or perhaps just quickly enough, the power leaped from her to wrap around the vight, ripping it away and forcing it through a rent that opened in the air behind it.

Myropa scanned the area for more attackers, and she saw the battle had shifted. The horde was closer to her, and the monstrous creature had moved nearer to the pantheon. Disevy and the raven-haired woman attacked its flanks and rear as several of the other gods faced it from the front or held off the vights. The creature lunged for the gods, snapping one of them up in its maw and chomping him in two.

A wave of nausea swept through Myropa as another vight leapt for her. On impulse, she opened herself to her power again, and again the vight disappeared from Celestria's plane. She sucked in a deep breath, hoping to ease her heaving stomach. She needed a moment, but she would not get it. More of the little monsters came at her, and access to her power was too slow. With so many attacking at once, she would be overwhelmed in seconds. Myropa delved into her power's source, her connection to the Fates, hoping to find some way to speed the process. Unsure what might happen, she left the connection open. Power poured into her, filling her, and she struck out at the vights. Bindings of light ensnared those nearest her, stalling their progress even as more pushed past them. One by one, Myropa's power gripped the creatures, and this time, when the path to the Alterworld opened, a multitude of vights were banished at once.

Thrilled with her newfound ability, Myropa seized upon the opportunity to help Disevy. She held on to the power, the sustained connection to the Fates, and sought out the beasts she had the capacity to purge. With each vight she dispatched, Myropa moved deeper into the horde and closer to the center of battle. At first, the gods took little notice of her, but as she skillfully removed enemies, they migrated to a protected sphere around her. With the lesser threats subdued, the gods could focus their collective attention on the larger monstrosity that began to crush the entrance to the pantheon.

Myropa searched frantically for Disevy, who had disappeared

moments before, and her heart lurched when she finally found him. He stood beneath the beast, dodging its six limbs as he struck at each with his colossal sword. The creature limped on one of its legs and another seemed completely useless, but it still moved with determination—and frightening speed. The beast reared back and leapt, spinning in midair and landing to face Disevy. The raven-haired goddess evaded being trampled as its huge, taloned claws slammed to the ground. She struck its foreleg, her radiant scimitar digging deeply into the hairless hide, and it screeched and kicked at her. This time, the blow landed and tossed the goddess a good twenty paces.

Disevy, now towering larger than Myropa had ever seen, slashed at the beast's throat. The monster avoided the strike and snapped back, engulfing Disevy in its mouth. At the last moment, Disevy raised his sword, lodging it between the creature's jaws, trapping himself within the creature's maw.

Myropa couldn't take any more. Disevy was in trouble, and she needed to help him beyond her current effort. Without thinking, she lashed out with her power at the monstrous beast. At first, a single glowing band of power wrapped around the monster. As she struggled with it, pushing more power into the attack, additional bands began to encase the beast. The fighting suddenly shifted as the other gods abandoned their attack on the monster and redirected their efforts against the vights Myropa had held back. Now *they* protected *her* as she struggled against the monster threatening to consume Disevy.

Thanks to Myropa's distraction, Disevy managed to free himself from his predicament and re-engaged with the offensive, but Myropa didn't let up in her attack. She continued to tighten her hold on the creature as she allowed the infinite power of the Fates to pass through her. Then, she shifted her focus to the portal she would need to exile the monster from the Alterworld. With a resounding *crash* the air rippled and tore the space between the monster and the damaged pantheon. Myropa directed the bands of light to pull the monster into the rift. It howled and jerked, gouging massive furrows in the ground as it slowly slid toward the opening.

Disevy slashed the creature's face, enraging it, but distracting it long enough that it lost some of its grip on the earth. The raven-haired woman began hacking at the creature's paws, separating its talons from its body, causing it to lose more ground. Myropa watched Disevy with her heart in her throat as he sprang toward the beast. Just as he thrust his sword into its chest, Myropa jerked the creature with a surge of power. The monster wailed as it lost its footing on Celestria and was sucked into the portal. With the creature suddenly gone, the extra power flooding Myropa had nowhere to go. It gushed from her, wrapping vight after vight in its glowing clutches and wrenching them through the portal before it finally collapsed.

Myropa immediately subdued her power, closing her connection to the Fates. With the monster gone, the beautiful raven-haired woman thrust herself at Disevy, wrapping herself around him in a firm embrace, and he held her just as dearly. Myropa stood, cold and empty, as her heart shattered, and the other gods finished off the remaining vights. Myropa wanted to run, to escape as quickly as possible, but she had a duty to Aaslo. She needed Disevy's help, so she stood her ground and waited for their intimate moment to end.

It felt like an eternity before Disevy pulled himself from the goddess's arms, although in truth it was only a few seconds. He turned and walked to Myropa, his gaze burning with purpose. Upon reaching her, he said nothing. He merely swept her from the ground and kissed her soundly and deeply, filling the joining with enough passion to melt the ice in Myropa's chest. When he released her, Myropa was startled and confused. The raven-haired goddess regarded them with a knowing smirk. Myropa didn't know what to think, but she definitely wanted Disevy to kiss her again. As if reading her thoughts, he did just that, pressing his lips firmly to hers as he opened to her.

When he released her mouth and placed her on her feet, Myropa felt dazed and dizzy with emotions she couldn't process. Disevy's gaze raked her, pausing at the gouges on her arms. His frown turned to relief as he took in the rest of her. "I am pleased that you are relatively unharmed." After a lingering look, he said, "Have you found your truth yet, my dear Myropa?"

Disevy had asked her that before, but she still had no idea. "What does that mean?"

His expression filled with admiration, but a sadness flitted past his gaze. He said, "Your power was superb today." He placed his hand on her cheek and stroked his thumb across her skin. "You are nearly there, but not quite." Then, he held out his hand to the raven-haired goddess, who took it and stepped closer. He introduced her, "This is my sister, Azeria, Goddess of Strength and Fertility. She has been wanting to meet you."

Myropa blinked in surprise. With all the fright and excitement, she hadn't considered that the goddess, who led the Second Pantheon, would be there and might be close to Disevy. She didn't know how familial relationships worked, since the gods weren't actually *born*, to anyone's knowledge, but he considered Azeria his sister, and that was all that mattered.

Belatedly, Myropa bowed low. "It is my honor to meet you, Goddess Azeria."

Azeria's eyebrow arched. "Oh, that wasn't how it seemed a moment ago."

Myropa was mortified that her feelings had been so transparent. She would have blushed had she been capable of it. She couldn't meet either of their gazes as she dropped her head.

Azeria reached out and took her hand, and Myropa forced herself to look up. "I only jest," said Azeria. "It pleases me that you have such feelings for my brother. His strength must be matched by a woman of his equal."

Myropa's tongue tangled around itself. "Oh, but I'm not—I mean, I can't be—It's just that I'm not strong—not at all."

Azeria smirked again, dropping Myropa's hand. "I know that to be a lie. You were strong even before I blessed you. I know your strength better than you do."

"What? You blessed me? When?"

Azeria waved offhandedly. "When you were born."

Myropa glanced at Disevy to find him staring fondly at her. "But what I did—to become a reaper—I wasn't strong."

Azeria gave her a knowing look. "Do you think all people who kill themselves become reapers?"

"Well, I assumed—"

"You know what assuming does," said Azeria with her characteristic smirk.

Myropa didn't know what to say. Was she being punished when others like her weren't? Azeria made it sound as if being a reaper was a good thing, but Myropa couldn't see how that could possibly be so. She deflated and replied, "I don't understand."

Disevy's voice was kind as he said, "Have mercy on her, Azeria. She may be strong, but she is also soft, and I mean that in the best of ways."

Azeria tilted her head and looked at Myropa appraisingly. "You were not finished living and so you refused your reaper when he came to transport you to the Sea of Transcendence."

Myropa's eyes widened in surprise. "But no one can refuse a reaper."

Azeria's gaze softened. "You chose to continue living beyond death. Only the strongest are able to do so."

"You're saying I *chose* to become a reaper? I thought it was the Fates."

"The Fates are not what they seem," Azeria responded cryptically.

"Azeria," Disevy admonished his sister.

Azeria glanced at him, then closed her mouth and shrugged. "Fine. Do things your way, Disevy. It only slows things down."

"She must find her truth on her own." Then he looked at Myropa. "I have told you before not to underestimate your strength. Surely you have seen by the power you wielded today that you have much of it."

"I only wanted to help you. I was worried . . ." Myropa's voice drifted off in embarrassment that she had been concerned over the battle's outcome. Disevy was a god, after all, and the God of Strength at that. He would surely have prevailed without her help.

He took her hands in his. "Your concern for me is heartening, my love. Come, let us escape this destruction, and you can tell me why it is you found me here."

"But what about the pantheon?" Myropa waved at the damage around them.

"It belongs to Azeria," said Disevy. "She will take care of it."

"But this was Axus's doing, was it not? Shouldn't *you* do something about *him*?"

As soon as the words left her mouth, she realized she had overstepped. Azeria grinned and slapped a hand on Disevy's shoulder. "I see she is perfect for you, brother. Let me know if anything else goes awry." Then the goddess joined the other gods standing over their slain brethren in mourning.

Myropa murmured, "I thought gods couldn't die."

Disevy didn't answer. Instead, he said, "Come. We shall speak privately."

Myropa offered a weak smile and walked with him. They strode down the hill to a glade where wildflowers grew naturally amid knee-high grasses, and buzzing insects flitted on wafts of balmy air. Puffy white and pink clouds intermittently hid the bright golden disk of the sun. The scent of the air eluded her, thanks to her frozen nature, but she imagined it smelled like toasted wheat and crisp dew. Myropa felt a sense of peace and serenity wash over her that was incongruous with the battlefield atop the hill and the news she carried.

She turned to find Disevy spreading a blanket out on the ground. He took her hand with a pleased grin and pulled her over to sit beside him. He looked at her and said, "Now tell me what brought you to me."

Myropa, now in anguish, didn't want to admit to the weakness that caused her to betray both him *and* Aaslo. Instead of answering, she asked, "Please, Disevy, tell me how it is that you can be killed."

He sighed. "There are very few things that can kill a god. Among those are the creatures of the Alterworld—the larger ones, at least, which are rare and cannot be controlled. The vights have little chance of doing serious damage. This was completely unexpected. It is forbidden to bring them here to Celestria, and it takes an immense amount of power, even more so than to the other realms like Aldrea. I suppose that explains what Axus has been doing with the power stolen from the Sea. I would not have believed even *he* would do this."

"Axus seems to have no limits," mused Myropa. "Will you do nothing to stop him?"

Disevy averted his gaze, and she saw a flicker of frustration. "I cannot. It was agreed that it is best for me to allow events to happen as they would with only minor intervention."

"Agreed? With whom?"

He looked at her as if imploring her to understand. "Arohnu."

A surprised chill ran through her. "The God of Prophecy?"

With a nod, he said, "It is possible that with a bit of help I could bring Axus to heel. But let us say that is not the optimal outcome."

"What *is* the optimal outcome?"

"I cannot say."

"And this *optimal outcome* is not guaranteed?"

"No, far from it."

"Is it truly worth risking everything, risking Aldrea *and* Celestria, for this *optimal outcome*?"

Disevy reached out to stroke his finger along her jawline. "Arohnu wasn't certain, but I believe it is." He leaned toward her. "It is pertinent that Aaslo face Axus here in Celestria. You must make this clear to him, and it must be done before Axus gains enough power to overcome the power of the depraved."

Myropa relaxed into his warm hand as her body shook with fear of the mounting threat. Then, steeling herself, she said, "I've done something terrible. I tried not to, but I couldn't stop myself. His power was too great." She paused when Disevy's shoulders tensed, and he frowned. He did not interrupt, so she continued. "Axus confronted me about the depraved. He asked me directly about what I had done with them. I didn't want to, but I *had* to tell him that I gave them to Aaslo."

Disevy's shoulders relaxed, and he leaned back. "You mustn't fret over this, Myropa. He was bound to find out. I am only glad that you are well and unharmed."

Myropa's brow furrowed with confusion. "He was so angry. I thought it was surely the end of me, but he did *nothing*. He acted like he *couldn't* hurt me."

Disevy reached out to absently twirl a lock of her hair around his finger. "You are a reaper. You are not his to command or control."

"So he has no power over me?"

He carefully considered his words. "Yes and no. His power is not absolute, and my sister was not wrong. You are stronger than you think. How strong you are remains to be seen."

Myropa's expression fell. "He said he's going to take it up with Trostili. What can *he* do to me?"

Disevy's deep and knowing gaze captured her own as he asked, "What will you allow him to do?"

"*Allow!*" she exclaimed. "It's not as if I have a choice."

He looked away from her, struggling with his thoughts. Then he sighed heavily. "You are not yet ready to know the truth, my love. But you will get there. I have faith in you and in us."

Myropa's eyes widened, her voice catching in her throat. She managed to croak, "*Us?*"

Disevy turned to her, took her shoulders in his hands, and pulled her closer. "I have made no secret of my feelings for you, Myropa. You must know that I care for you—deeply. I wish to keep you with me, always."

Myropa's heart leapt. She felt it pounding in her chest in a pool of warmth that heated her core but did not reach her limbs. Her soul begged her to accept Disevy, to tell him that she would be his forever, but she shook her head in disbelief and denial.

"I can't," she said. "I'm a reaper. I serve the Fates for as long as they require it, and I am assigned to Trostili. How could we be together?"

Disevy brushed her hair from her face and placed a soft kiss upon her cheek. Then he whispered, "You must find your way to me, my love." She started to protest again, but he took her chin and lifted her face to meet his gaze. "When you do, you will be mine, and I will be yours."

With a sob, she begged, "How can you think that *I* can somehow make this happen?"

"As I said, I have faith in you."

CHAPTER 15

TEZA WATCHED THE PORTAL CLOSE BEHIND HIM. IN A FIT OF URGENCY, Aaslo left her. He. Had. Left. *Her.* Not just her, of course. He had dropped off Peck and Mory and the shades as well. Teza shivered as she watched the shades move through the camp to the tent erected for their use. Some of them seemed perfectly content in each other's company, while others appeared outright hostile. Although Aaslo had instructed them to follow her orders, she was not at all sure they would do so. Besides, it was not her place to make use of their power at this point. In fact, Aaslo had decided *not* to use them unless absolutely necessary, in an effort to keep Axus from finding out they had them.

Thinking of Aaslo infuriated her again. Not only had he left her, he left her in charge of the army! At least, that's what she decided as she stalked toward the command tent with Peck and Mory on her heels. When she entered the large tent erected outside the gates of the modest Pashtigonian city of Uptony, the first thing she noticed was how busy it was. Many people hurriedly ducked in and out, and they often held scrolls or folded missives. Other people stood about at their leisure chatting and, sometimes, shouting over each other. Many of these wore the colorful robes of the rich and officious, and they seemed to care only that *everybody* heard them. In the middle of it was the marquess, sitting at a table with his head in his hands. A man in a full suit of armor loomed over him talking in a voice that held the ring of command.

The knight puffed up as if he had made some point, and the marquess abruptly dropped his hands and looked up at the man. As Teza neared, she heard him clearly over the crowd. "As I told you, Sir Elridge, the men will be absorbed into the ranks of the army."

"But these are *our* men!" the knight protested.

"They must become *our* men," retorted the marquess, his exasperation evident. "It will do us little good to have many tiny armies. We need one unified force. You will have a command position, of course, if that is what's bothering you."

"That's not—"

"What's the problem?" interjected Teza as she marched up to

stand at Sir Elridge's side. The grungy knight—scruffy faced, brown hair mussed—perused her armor with a scowl and dismissed her.

"This doesn't concern you." As he turned back to the marquess, Teza smacked him in the chest, adding a touch of magical force as she did. The heavy knight fell back in a clatter that drove everyone in the tent to silence. Sir Elridge looked up at her from where he lay, dazed. "What was that?"

Teza leaned over him with her hands on her hips and informed him, "I'm Mage Teza, the general of this army, and everything that goes on here is my business. You will treat me with respect, and you will treat the marquess with respect, or I will make it my business to teach you what respect is."

The man got to his feet, with great difficulty and noise given the bulk and weight of his armor, and Teza smirked at the sizable dent that now adorned his breastplate. Sir Elridge ran his hand across the spot, which had to be sore, and complained, "I'll need to get this hammered out, thanks to you."

Teza nodded once. "Remember it or next time I'll do that to your head."

The man swallowed hard, turned, and left the tent. Teza looked to the marquess, who hadn't moved. He appeared worn and haggard as he commented, "That kind of treatment won't win you any friends nor will it aid in our recruiting efforts."

Teza's shoulders dropped as she sighed. "I know. I couldn't let him stomp all over you, though. It makes us look weak."

The marquess responded dryly. "I appreciate your concern."

Teza waved her hand toward the crowd occupying the tent. Most had returned to their discussions but threw glances her way. "Who are all these people, and what do they want?"

"They're from the city, and they're here to negotiate."

"Negotiate what?"

"For the recruits—or, rather, what they'll receive in exchange for donating the services of their vassals."

Teza's eyebrows rose. "They're hoping to *profit*? Don't they know everything and everyone is doomed to die if they don't fight?"

"Oh, they know that. They're trying to negotiate for their best outcome in case we *win*. This city is a major trading hub. Most of the city's elite are wealthy merchant nobles. They don't mind offering their people to our cause so long as it means more money or status in the end."

"So what's the problem?" Teza said. "Just promise them whatever they want."

The marquess shook his head in dismay. "We cannot follow through on those promises."

Teza rolled her eyes and leaned in to speak in a harsh whisper. "You forget that Aaslo isn't really a king or even a noble. He doesn't have the authority to promise *anything*. We just need people to fight *now*. Let the kings and armies figure out the rest later. At least they will be alive."

The marquess blinked several times, and a slow smile crept across his face. "Shrewd."

With a satisfied grin, Teza sat back as, one after another, the marquess made ridiculous promises to the even more ridiculous people who proposed them. Soon enough, nearly an entire city's worth of able-bodied men and women had joined their ranks. They also had deals for food, supplies, weapons, and armor, each based on promises that would never be fulfilled. Teza might have felt bad about lying to all of them if they weren't so greedy in the first place.

She sat at the table listening to the marquess haggle over the grain prices for appearances' sake when Head Scout Daniga entered the tent. She glanced between the marquess and Teza, unsure of to whom she should report.

Before the marquess had a chance to speak, Teza said, "What is it, Daniga?"

Daniga looked at Teza. "The scouts from the east have returned. They report an army moving this way. They'll be here by nightfall."

Teza leaped up, and the marquess followed. She said, "How many?"

"Perhaps a few thousand," reported the lead scout. "Mostly infantry, some cavalry. Some of them are lyksvight, so they have at least a few magi with them. I've sent more scouts to get a better look."

"Thank you, Daniga," said the marquess. He turned to Teza. "We should prepare the troops. I'll alert Hegress and Bear."

When Daniga didn't immediately go, Teza looked at her questioningly. Daniga spoke. "Ah, there is one more thing. Peck has an idea he wanted me to approve, but I thought he should run it by you first."

Teza looked past Daniga and spied a couple of no-good thieves puttering about doing nothing of use.

"All right. I see him now." She made her excuses to the marquess, then stalked across the encampment toward the two scoundrels. The two were engaged in a game of dice with two soldiers when she approached. Peck explained to Mory how he had somehow come out on top despite the odds, and the soldiers eyed them with suspicion and no small amount of irritation.

"You two!" she barked, making them jump.

Peck straightened and gave her a winning smile. "Why, Mage Teza, so lovely of you to join us. Perhaps you'd care to place a bet?"

Teza crossed her arms. "I don't gamble with thieves."

With a start, one of the soldiers said, "Thieves?"

Peck donned a hurt expression and brushed his hand across the leaf patch over his breast. "We're no thieves. We're scouts who do an honest day's work."

"Is that so?" she replied. "Well, I can find some honest work for some men with questionable scruples."

Peck tugged on his ear as he mulled over her statement.

She leaned forward. "I'm talking about you two."

He nodded sagely. "Yeah, yeah, I know that. I'm just not certain I want to accept a task from *you*." He smiled again and winked. "No offense, of course."

Teza leaned back with a roll of her eyes. "Right. Consider me not offended. Daniga said you have an idea. Do you want to tell me about it or should I just say no?"

Peck opened his mouth, but Mory piped in excitedly. "We have a mission, but, ah, it's a secret."

Teza glanced to the two soldiers. "It's a secret mission? Come with me." Then she turned on her heel and strode toward the edge of the encampment. She assumed they would follow. Once they reached a spot beyond the last row of tents where they wouldn't be overheard, she addressed them.

"Now tell me. What's this grand idea of yours?"

Peck straightened and brushed his hands down the lapels of a velvet jacket that had seen better days. She had watched him do this hundreds of times and knew he was putting on a brave face for Mory's sake. "You know we're dedicated to Aaslo, right?" said Peck. "We're his men."

Beside him, Mory nodded enthusiastically. Teza glanced at the boy, then nodded curtly.

"Well," said Peck, "Aaslo's trying to fight a war with very limited information. We know almost nothing about the enemy, and what little we do know comes from an agent who is admittedly working for them."

"We know that," confirmed Teza. "What can *we* do about it, though?"

He grinned broadly. "I'm glad you asked. The two of us are *scouts*," he said with pride. "We're supposed to gather information ahead of the army, right?"

Teza eyed him suspiciously. "Yes, that's right." Her mind worked quickly, trying to suss out his intentions.

"So, we're going on a mission to do just that."

"What do you mean?"

"I mean, I want to infiltrate the enemy and send back information to Aaslo."

"You want to *what*?" deadpanned Teza.

"You heard me. We're going to get captured and forced into service with the Berru. Then we'll send back information to you about their numbers, inner workings, intentions, and what they're doing. We'll try to get as high up in their command as we can."

"Why *you*?" said Teza.

Peck held up a finger. "One, we're used to this kind of subterfuge—"

Teza shook her head. "No, you're not. You were thieves before, not *spies*."

"We're used to sneaking around." Peck held up a second finger. "Two, and most importantly, Mory can communicate with the reaper to send information to Aaslo."

"Wait a minute," exclaimed Teza. "Your logic doesn't make sense. You said you don't want to depend on the reaper."

"I don't," he huffed, "but we may have to for now. We don't have any other sources with the Berru."

"But why not just ask the reaper about the Berru, then? Why do you need to go?"

"I don't think Myra knows much about troops and arms and that kind of thing. With us in the middle of it, we can get more detailed information."

Mory seemed enthusiastic but a bit pale. Teza continued, "But what if they don't recruit you. What if they just kill you?"

She didn't want to be responsible for their deaths, especially Mory's. He was just a boy, after all. But these were desperate times, and life on Aldrea was at stake.

He said, "The latest reports all say that the Berru steal able-bodied fighters for their army, they don't kill them. Look at us. We're young and strong. They definitely won't kill us."

Gritting her teeth, she said, "I know the consequences of losing this war, and I know we're at a huge disadvantage militarily speaking, but what you're asking is akin to suicide. Aaslo would never approve."

"That's why we're asking *you*," said Peck.

Mory said, "Technically, we asked Daniga."

Peck ignored him. "We want to help Aaslo, to help win this war. We want to do something important. We can do this. I know we can."

WHEN PECK AND MORY SLIPPED AWAY SEVERAL MINUTES LATER, TEZA was angry and, if she admitted it, a little frightened. They seemed committed to the task assigned to them, but Teza swallowed the acid that had made its way up her esophagus. She knew sending Peck and Mory to the enemy was by far the worst thing she had ever done. Part of her wanted to call them back and cancel the whole thing. She had claimed the burden of authority, though, and she knew Aaslo would never send the two thieves on such a dangerous mission. It was up to her to make it happen.

Teza strolled through the camp, which was already abuzz with preparations. Everywhere she looked, men and some women were sharpening weapons, donning armor, preparing bulwarks, and digging trenches. The newer city recruits filed out of the gates in a long line, many already armed and armored. Others were without weapons, and she assumed without training. It was up to Bear to sort them out and send the most seasoned fighters to the front. In an effort to boost morale, Teza mingled here and there with the troops, using spells to reinforce armor and weapons, more so that they would recognize the presence of a magus in their ranks than for the effects themselves. Knowing they had magic behind them would hopefully make the troops feel on equal footing with the Berru, who surely had magi of their own.

The Berru arrived in late afternoon, when the Endricsian army had the advantage. Already dug in and with the sun setting behind them, the Berru would be looking into the last glaring rays of the day. The Berru didn't attack immediately, though. They began to set up their own camp several hundred yards from the city. Teza wasn't inclined to let them prepare. She found the marquess in conversation with Commander Hegress, Bear, and Aria, who had taken over command of their small Cartisian contingent along with a good number of the Uyanian and Pashtigonian soldiers.

Without preamble, Teza commanded, "Prepare the troops for attack."

"What?" said Hegress, surprised by her sudden appearance.

Teza continued, "We go in now, before they have time to entrench themselves, while we have the advantage of the setting sun."

Hegress protested, "It looks as if they're preparing for a siege. It would be better to wait a few days so that we can better integrate the new troops."

Teza's short locks bounced around her head as she shook it firmly. "No, we're not waiting. It appears that our forces are evenly matched, or nearly so. We could sustain heavy losses in this fight. If we attack now, before they've prepared, we could force them into retreat."

Hegress rubbed his jaw and nodded slowly. "Perhaps, but what good is a retreat? They'll just join back up with the main army and come back at us."

"Hopefully Aaslo will be back before then, and we'll no longer be here."

"What about the city? When we leave, the people will be unprotected."

Again, guilt ate at her as she flatly stated, "This battle isn't important. This isn't the battle that will decide the fate of the world. We must preserve the army we have so we can meet up with our own larger force in Mouvilan. It's the only chance we'll have at taking on the main force of the Berruvian army. I will use the time after the battle to set protective runes about the city like we did in Monsque."

"Alone?"

"It will take some time, and it will be tiring, but it must be done if we are to save these people. Aaslo can power his portion of the runes once he gets here. It'll also give you time to move troops inside the walls in case the Berru do return for a siege before Aaslo arrives."

"I can't say that I like the idea, but it has merit," said Bear.

"It's necessary," Teza emphasized. "That's one of the reasons I'm in charge. We must keep perspective. If our intentions were to occupy the city, you would be right in waiting. But that's not what we're doing. The final battle is all that matters."

After a brief discussion about the advantages of attacking immediately, the consensus found Teza in the right.

"At least we have the shades," said the marquess.

Teza's heart fluttered at the thought of using the shades. Aaslo had said the shades were a last resort and warned against using them when he left. Their powers were unknown, unpredictable, and potentially volatile in ways that could be detrimental to their own forces. Plus, he wasn't sure that he would be able to control them once they began unleashing their powers. If Aaslo couldn't control them through their connection, then Teza certainly wouldn't be able to. No, she wouldn't use the shades unless there was no hope of prevailing otherwise.

LITTLE MORE THAN AN HOUR LATER, TEZA'S TROOPS PREPARED FOR the attack on the fledgling Berruvian encampment. The Berruvian supply line had not yet arrived in full, the trebuchets and other heavy artillery remained dysfunctional, the cavalry mounts were winded, and a goodly number of infantry were preoccupied with setting up camp. The Berru made a concerted effort to respond to the threat, but by the time they realized they were under attack, it was too late. The Endricsian troops clashed with the lyksvight and soldiers of the front line. The Endricsians had closed so fast that the enemy archers only managed to loose a few volleys, and the cavalry delayed just long enough for the pikemen to gain a foothold.

Teza was there, in the thick of it, mounted so as to see over the fray and identify her quarry. Men and women fought around her as she scanned the field for the telltale signs of magic. The flash of fire and glow of power drew her attention to the two magi among the Berru. Both focused on controlling their lyksvight, but once Teza targeted them with a blast that sent them toppling from their mounts, they allowed the lyksvight to run amok in favor of attacking her.

The first spell detonation took her by surprise. Smashing into her, it knocked her off her horse and threw nearby soldiers to the ground. Thanks to her hastily erected ward and godly armor, she survived the vicious attack. By necessity, a path between her and the enemy magus opened as friend and foe alike cleared the way. The enemy magus, a blond woman with streaks of grey running through her tresses, pointed with a black-lacquered nail. A sizzle of energy surged toward Teza. She easily blocked the attack with a shield ward and sent a return volley of explosive sparks. The attack ricocheted off the blonde's own shield ward, and the magus grinned at Teza as it struck a cluster of soldiers engaged with lyksvight near her. Even from across the expanse separating them, Teza could see that the woman's teeth had been filed to points nearly as sharp as her attacks.

The second magus, a willowy man with shaggy brown hair and deep creases across his long face, injected himself into the battle. A glowing red whip lashed Teza, snapping through her ward. She leapt away as it impacted her armor. Teza knew that most of the Berruvian magi were stronger than she was, and now she had two to withstand. With Aaslo and Ijen away, she was the army's sole magus, so it was up to her to bring these two down. Once again, she wished she could use the shades to her advantage, but she had intentionally left them behind.

As she recovered her feet, Teza began a new spell. She hadn't employed this one in battle yet, but she was excited to see it in action. As she released it, the ground began to rumble. An earthen wave surged toward the two magi, evading their shields and throwing them from their feet. Then the ground began to swallow the two spell casters as they frantically struggled against the dirt that consumed them. Several ineffectual spells erupted from the flailing magi, but one spell burst the ground, releasing the woman from her confines. As the woman turned to help her downed comrade, Teza sent volley after volley of magical attacks, exhausting her trove of spells as most splattered uselessly against their shield wards.

Teza's stomach clenched with anxiety. She was almost out of spells, and most did little more than irritate the superior magi. Her nerves told her to flee, but her stubborn nature wouldn't allow it. She *would* overcome the two magi, if not for her own satisfaction, then for the sake of the army surrounding her. She had a feeling, though, that she was about to die horribly.

Teza considered calling the shades into the fray, when the enemy magi turned to attack Teza once more. Just as they began to focus their power on her, someone slid surreptitiously from the throng of fighting soldiers. They got behind the shield ward and stabbed the male magus in the back with a long dagger. The woman hadn't noticed the assailant, but the male magus's body sliding lifelessly to the ground effectively distracted her. The woman's shield wavered, and Teza got a spell past her ward. It was a simple spell that Teza never thought to use against a person, but it had deadly consequences. As it struck, it began to draw all the water from the woman's body. The magus struggled against the spell; her own spells partially formed and collapsed around her. Clutching her chest, she fell atop her fallen compatriot as a withered, dusty husk.

Teza shared a look with Peck, who stood behind the two downed magi with a bloodied dagger. He bore a look that would surely haunt her forever. Then a throng of enemy soldiers swallowed him and Mory, who fought beside him, and Teza lost sight of them. As Teza fought off the enemies that turned toward her, she couldn't shake her worries over Peck and Mory. In the thick of battle, they were unlikely to be taken prisoner. Had they been overrun? Were they dead already? Tears sprang to her eyes as she thought about Mory. He wasn't a fighter. At only fourteen, he wasn't even supposed to be here. But Peck brought him because they believed in Aaslo and *she* had allowed it. Had she betrayed the thieves?

No, not thieves.

Scouts.

Yes, they were scouts. They were part of the army, and she was a general. Generals had to give tough orders, and sometimes the people who carried out those orders had to endure difficulties. Peck and Mory were no different, and besides, it had been Peck's idea. It was her job—no, not just her job—her *duty*—to see that her army had the information necessary to carry out a successful campaign. *Everyone* depended on her. Suddenly, she wondered why she had ever wanted to be in charge.

The need to believe that she had done right sustained Teza for the remainder of the battle. She fought with vigor, striking those around her with spell after deadly spell. She kept her attacks small and precise, but when it was over, she was entirely drained. Still, she managed the mop up efforts with cold calculation. While they permitted the retreat of a number of the Berruvian forces, they did not take prisoners. Teza ordered a thorough search of the bodies for Peck and Mory, but the two scouts were not to be found. That they were probably still alive heartened her, but the realization they had likely been captured sent a spike of fear racing through her. That was the goal, after all, and like good soldiers, Peck and Mory had followed through.

CHAPTER 16

PECK STUMBLED AS HE WAS SHOVED FROM BEHIND. HE GLANCED OVER at Mory, who somehow did a better job of keeping his feet. He narrowed his eyes, realizing in that moment that Mory looked older than his fourteen years. Guilt consumed him as he considered what he had done. He led Mory into a battle with the express intent of getting captured; and now, having been successful, he didn't know what would happen to them. He considered that he had made a mistake. He knew Aaslo would never have allowed them to go through with it, but Teza hadn't been difficult to convince. She had only ever seen them as worthless thieves, but that was no longer who they were. Peck had bigger aspirations now. He fought for what was good and right and honorable. He was devoted to a cause bigger than himself. It was because of that devotion that he and Mory found themselves in this predicament. Aaslo needed information on the Berru, and they had no spies in place to deliver it.

He looked at Mory again with silent regret, then his gaze moved past the boy. They weren't the only Endricsians who had been captured. He saw a half dozen prisoners, and he would bet money there were more. In fact, capture seemed to have been the goal all along. The Berru obviously hadn't anticipated encountering an army in Uptony. They probably planned to overthrow the city guard, claiming those who could fight for their own, and killing everyone else. When he and Mory had become separated from the rest of their army on the battlefield, he had expected to be cut down, but that hadn't happened. Almost immediately, they had been bound and delivered to a grueling task master, who began their march long before the official retreat sounded. Now they moved quickly as the rest of the Berruvian force followed behind them.

Several hours after dark, they stopped for the night, and the prisoners were forced to help set up the camp. Peck helped erect the few tents that hadn't made it to the camp before the attack, as well as start campfires, although it turned out they would not be permitted use of them. When most of the troops turned in, Peck and his comrades were bound together and picketed within a ring of guards. He briefly wondered why they didn't use lyksvight to guard them as he had seen the Berru do in other camps, then he realized that without any magi to control them, the lyksvight had either been slaughtered or escaped.

Sleep was nearly impossible that night, as it was for the next several nights. They walked for four days with little food or rest, and Peck would have given anything for a skin full of water. He and Mory hadn't been separated, thankfully. The Berru kept the captives together, and he had been able to remain at Mory's side. To his credit, Mory never complained, but Peck could see the misery in the boy's eyes. A pit deeper than hunger gnawed at Peck's stomach as he considered that he was responsible for putting Mory in this situation. Sure, Mory had wanted to be involved, but he was only a boy. Boys should not be making such decisions. Peck dearly hoped any knowledge they might gain would be worth their sacrifice.

On the fifth day, they climbed the escarpment marking the Helod border. Crossing the alluvium was difficult enough, but once in the ravine, the going became treacherous. The dry riverbed held sharp, loose boulders, and cactus or some other pointy plant life adorned each crevice. The light armor Peck had been issued certainly didn't feel light as he scrambled up the incline, and the sharp talus underfoot made him realize he sorely needed new boots.

When they reached the top of the plateau, he viewed what looked to be a long-term encampment beside a small lake with great relief. A number of large white tents were interspersed with smaller tents and wagons, and while most people busily carried out their duties, others milled about as if they had nothing to do. A horde of lyksvight guarded the perimeter, so Peck knew at least a few magi had to be present.

As they were led through the throng, Peck kept an eye out for the officers and magi. He took to studying the soldiers, their numbers, their arms and supplies. He didn't know how the reaper, Myra, would find them or even how she might know to look for them, but if she did, he wanted to provide her with useful information for Aaslo. He hoped Mory was doing the same, and that they would be together when the reaper showed up. Otherwise, all of this would be for nothing. That thought made his gut churn as he accepted that this plan probably hadn't been as well considered as he'd thought.

Peck followed the line of captives being led into a large tent, when a woman stepped forward and stopped him with a hand to his chest. She was tall with a mane of silky dark hair and sharp features accentuated with lip stain and rouge. She didn't dress like a soldier or magus. Her fitted leather pants and wrap-around blouse emphasized her curves but would do little to protect her in the event of attack.

She snagged Mory by the shoulder as he started to shuffle. "Hold it. Not these two."

One of their guards said, "Is there a problem, m'lady?"

The woman smirked. "No, everything is just right." It took a moment for Peck to realize who she was. Although he couldn't remember ever seeing her up close in person, the description was undeniable. This was Sedi, the assassin who had pestered Aaslo for months. "I'll be taking these two with me. The empress will want to meet them."

Peck swallowed hard. He had intended to spy on the Berruvian forces, but he hadn't expected to encounter the empress herself. Sedi effortlessly opened a portal to the paths. Hers, however, were different from Aaslo's. Instead of a mist-shrouded forest, they found themselves in a warren of brightly lit corridors with a luminous river of power running through it. Peck blinked at the river, dearly wishing it contained water he could drink, but he instinctively knew this river could be deadly.

"Follow me," Sedi sang as she strolled ahead of them. When they didn't move, she glanced back. "Believe me, you don't want to be lost in here. You'll never make it out alive."

"You know who we are?" asked Mory.

"Of course. I've been watching all of you for a long time. You're Mory and Peck." She looked at each of them. "You're a couple of thieves Aaslo adopted and turned into scouts."

"Where are you taking us?" asked Peck.

She smiled sweetly. "Don't worry. I don't intend to harm you—for now." She tilted her head thoughtfully and added, "I can't speak for the empress, though. Her choices of entertainment tend to be painful." She perused each of them before wrinkling her nose. "You both look and smell terrible. How did you end up in that encampment, anyway?"

Peck said, "We were captured during a battle."

"Oh? Where did this battle take place?"

Peck saw no reason to keep the truth from her, as she could easily find out for herself. "At Uptony in Pashtigon. We've been marching for nearly a week."

Sedi tsked and shook her head. "The empress will not want to smell you. She may have deviant tastes, but not like this. You'll need to bathe." Mory's stomach chose that moment to rumble, and Sedi huffed. "Might as well put some food in you, too. Can't have you passing out at her feet. Unless she wants you to." Ominous last remark aside, the promise of food and a bath beckoned, so when she turned and began walking down the corridor again, Peck and Mory followed.

Upon exiting the paths, they were alone in a large chamber containing three recessed pits filled with water. The closest to them steamed and smelled of soap and oil. Sedi looked at them expectantly. "Well, get to it."

Peck and Mory stood staring at the three pools. Their baths had always been taken with a rag and a bucket of rainwater or some soap in the river. Neither of them had ever been in a public bath—or any sort of bath, for that matter—and Peck wasn't sure of the protocol. Were they supposed to just . . . pick a pool? Were they to undress in front of her? Peck was loath to admit that he didn't know how to do something as simple as taking a bath, so he was glad when Mory piped up.

"Uh, what do we do?"

Sedi hummed under her breath then pushed Mory into the first pool. As he came up sputtering, she chuckled. "This is the first bath. Wash quickly with the soaps and oils that are lined up there along the side. You don't have time to soak." She pointed to the second pool. "Then, get into that one. It's not as warm. It's just for rinsing. Finally, you get into the third bath. It isn't heated, and it will cool you off before you dress."

Peck drew his gaze away from the bedraggled Mory and looked down at his clothes and leather armor. All of it smelled horrible and was covered in sweat, blood, and filth. He was wondering if he should just get in the bath with his clothes on when Sedi informed him, "There are robes over there. We'll find you some clean clothes when you're done. You won't need the armor. You won't be fighting anyone."

Peck removed his armor and empty belt and was once again saddened by the loss of his knives that they'd taken from him upon capture. He removed the rest of his clothes, feeling no shame in undressing in front of the woman. Mory, on the other hand, bright red in face and ears, tried his best to cover himself as he piled his sopping clothes on the tile beside the pool. Peck wasn't sure if Sedi was being kind or simply practical, but he found that washing away the blood and nearly a week's worth of grime felt cleansing in more ways than one. He reclaimed something in his soul—that hope wasn't lost. Sedi hadn't killed them, and she even provided them with basic necessities. That surely had to count for something.

Once they were clean and wrapped in plush robes, Sedi led them down a short corridor. They encountered several guards on their way to their mysterious destination, and with a snap of Sedi's fingers, a couple of the armed men followed. She led them to a room filled with garments, stacks of fabric, spools of thread, ribbons, lace, and other baubles. A willowy man and a rotund woman, both of middling years, bent over a table in the center of the room examining some creation. They both looked up at the same time, blinked in surprise, and fell into deep bows.

"My lady Sedi, what may we do for you?" said the man.

Without preamble, Sedi said, "These two need clothes to see the empress. See that it's done." Then she turned to the guards. "Watch these prisoners until I return." With that, Sedi disappeared down the corridor. Peck and Mory were subjected to a series of invasive measurements before being told to wait in the corner out of the way. Peck watched the seamstress in fascination as she picked through an assortment of garments and began altering them to fit. The two guards appeared bored but alert as they awaited Sedi's return. When she finally came back, Peck wore the finest clothes he had ever donned. The soft, thick fabric felt luxurious and the deep blue of the tunic was brilliant set against the rich grey of the pants. The lengths of both were perfect. Still, he missed his velvet coat. Mory's clothes were of similar trim, but his tunic was made of a vivid vermilion and his trousers were black.

Sedi eyed them critically. Peck couldn't help the feeling that he had been garbed for his funeral pyre. Sedi sniffed. "Hmm, something's missing."

The tailor cleared his throat. "My lady, the leatherworker is down the hall."

Sedi rolled her eyes. "Of course."

She led them to the leatherworker, who provided them with belts, then to the cobbler where they were fitted with boots that Peck could only have dreamed of owning. Peck looked at Mory, who could easily have passed for a noble youth, and wondered what he himself looked like. He had never thought to wear such finery and would certainly never have expected it to come from their enemy. The clothes were not proper for a battlefield, but Sedi had said they wouldn't be fighting, so Peck knew they wouldn't be sent back to the army. Sedi mentioned the empress's deviant tastes. Perhaps she liked her prey clean and full before she reduced them to ashes.

Suitably clothed, Sedi took them to a dining hall where they were served plates of fried chicken, potatoes, and steamed greens. Peck eyed the food with suspicion momentarily before his stomach growled loudly. Then he dug in, and when he could eat no more, he filled the remaining space in his stomach with a tankard of cool water. Mory ate well, but Peck knew something bothered him. With a glance toward Sedi, who spoke to a man in long robes on the far side of the room, he whispered, "What's wrong, Mory?"

Mory looked up from his plate, his expression troubled. "What if she kills us? The empress, I mean."

Peck rubbed his abdomen. "If I die today, I'll die with a full stomach."

Mory shook his head. "I mean it, Peck. I don't want to die."

Peck wasn't at all certain of their fate, but he donned a brave face for Mory's sake. "She won't kill us. We're valuable."

"How are we valuable?" said Mory skeptically.

"We're Aaslo's men. She'll know that. She might try to use us as hostages, and she'll probably want information."

"What kind of information? What will she do to get it?"

Peck leaned toward Mory and caught his gaze. "You listen to me, Mory. You're a brave lad, but there's no need to be brave here. You don't know anything important, so there's no need to endure torture. Tell her what she wants to know. Just don't tell her about Myra."

"But what if she asks?"

"She won't. She doesn't know enough to ask about that."

"But, if I don't know anything important, then how am I valuable to her?"

Peck opened his mouth to respond. Mory had a point. In the face of Mory's fear, though, Peck grinned. "Don't worry about that. Aaslo needs us, and she'll know that, too. You worry too much."

The question continued to plague Peck, though. What good were they to the empress alive? Peck had a suspicion that, having been dressed and stuffed, it was time to feed them to the empress.

After a while, the robed man departed and Sedi returned her attention to them. She grinned with a satisfied smirk. "Now it's time for the entertainment. Come with me."

Mory's voice wavered as he said, "What's the entertainment?"

Sedi looked at him with a raised brow. "You."

Peck swallowed all his food a second time as he got up to follow the ancient magus. Sedi was a strange woman he didn't understand at all. She toyed with Aaslo between attempts to kill him, and seemed almost kind amidst her playful threats of death. She was their enemy, yet she also helped them at times—like with Teza's armor and the locations of the ancient magi. Peck just couldn't figure her out.

Although he expected to be taken to a throne room, she led Peck and Mory to a library. At least, it was what Peck imagined a library looked like from the descriptions. He had never actually been to one, but the numerous books and scrolls stacked on shelves along the walls seemed right. Two high-backed chairs sat near a blazing hearth. Sedi threw herself into the one on the left, because a strange, frightening-looking woman occupied the other. Small and thin, she wore a gauzy dress that ended in tatters around her pale legs. She wore no shoes, and her talon-like fingernails were painted black. She looked up and smiled. A shiver went through him as he noted her pointed teeth, and Peck wondered at the amount of pain one had to endure to achieve the effect.

Sedi gestured to them. "These are the two I told you about, Lysia."

The woman, who must have been the empress, perused Peck and Mory with a calculating gaze. She spoke. "You serve the dragon-man. You know him personally?"

Peck considered lying, but he knew Sedi watched them long enough to know the truth. He steeled his shaky nerves and straightened. His hands unconsciously attempted to adjust his lapels, but he wasn't wearing his customary velvet jacket, so he smoothed his tunic instead. He courteously replied, "That's right. We're Aaslo's men."

The empress smiled, but she wasn't looking at him. Her gaze fixed on Mory, who stood beside him showing less confidence. In fact, Mory appeared downright terrified, and Peck felt a stab of guilt. The empress abruptly rose from her chair and moved toward them. She looked to be floating, as if her feet barely touched the ground. With her gossamer threads and ashy appearance, she looked more like a wraith than a woman. It sent a shiver up Peck's spine.

Mory's shaking stilled as the empress ran a black-lacquered nail along his jawline. She gripped his chin between dexterous fingers as she turned his head to and fro, examining him closely with narrowed eyes. She practically hissed, "*You* are special. *You* have seen death. I can see it in your eyes."

Mory swallowed, but no words passed his quivering lips.

Peck quickly interjected, "We've both seen death. We were in a battle just a few days ago. Many people died."

The empress released Mory's chin, and her fingers began a sinuous dance in the air in front of her. As she moved, dark tendrils of power slipped along her arms and down her fingers to mingle in a riot of smoky forms in the air between them. Then, like sand falling through an hourglass, the black power funneled to Mory, wrapping him in a delicate veneer. Some of the power stuck to his skin like soot, and it re-formed into strange, inky glyphs. Mory blinked rapidly, pupils growing to nearly eclipse his irises, as his mouth went slack.

Peck wanted to intervene. He wanted to erase them, to release Mory from whatever the empress was doing. At the same time, any interference might cause the boy more harm. Peck had seen enough magic to know that an interrupted spell could have disastrous consequences. Still, he couldn't just watch as this wretched woman did who knows what to his only family.

"Stop!" shouted Peck. "Leave him alone. He's only a boy." Then he jostled Mory in an attempt to wake him from his stupor. The inky glyphs slipped from Mory's skin like autumn leaves, and the empress ceased the dancing gestures.

Pain erupted across Peck's cheek and down his neck. The empress stood poised with a short black rod that had materialized from nowhere, and the tip dripped with his blood. She hissed through sharpened teeth. Then she composed herself as if nothing had happened. *"Never interrupt me."*

Peck wiped up the blood running down his cheek with a shaky hand then gripped Mory to his chest as he had when Mory was a small child. He gave the empress a furious scowl, but she no longer regarded them. She had turned back to Sedi, who carelessly lounged in the chair beside the hearth.

Lysia stated, "This one has the necessary connection to death. I will use him. Thank you for this generous gift, Sedi. Axus will appreciate your dedication, as do I."

Sedi gave the empress a sharp look as if those words held a hidden meaning. Peck had the feeling these two were not always so gracious with each other.

Sedi's tone was light as she inquired, "Do you doubt my dedication to Axus, Lysia?"

"Not at all, my sweet. I only doubted one so useful existed in this world. I had thought to resort to *other* means."

Sedi gave the empress a knowing look. "You planned to power it yourself."

Lysia took her seat across from Sedi and picked up a goblet from a small side table. "Yes, it would have been necessary, given the power Axus bestowed upon me, but now I need not make the sacrifice."

Sedi leaned forward and gripped the empress's free hand. "We all make sacrifices for the cause, Lysia." Her tone was placating as she added, "Still, I would not want to lose you."

"We will all be gone from this world soon enough, Sedi, but you may take heart in knowing that we shall rule together in the realm of the gods."

Peck noted a flash of doubt in Sedi's eyes that the empress didn't see as she tipped up her goblet. Sedi rose from the chair with the grace of a cat and sauntered, hips swaying, to stand before them. "I'll see that he's situated. What do you want to do with the other?"

"We will keep them together for now," Lysia replied. "They share a deep bond and will be easier to control if they don't have to fight their fear of separation. Plus, that one"—she pointed to Peck—"can be used to convince the other to cooperate."

"Very wise. I will see that it's done." Sedi snapped her fingers for them to follow.

Peck and Mory filed out of the room behind her, but the ancient magus didn't remain with them long. She instructed a woman, who Peck assumed to be a maid, to provide them with a room and commanded several guards to keep watch over them. As they followed the maid, Peck noted every twist and turn, every room and hall, every corridor and stairwell, in an attempt to create a mental map. He felt torn between trying to find a way to escape and remaining there to accomplish their spying mission.

They ended up not in the dungeon cells Peck had expected, but at a suite that included two modest bedrooms and a central sitting room, much to his surprise. The furnishings and décor were simple, even austere, in comparison to their quarters at the marquess's estate in Ruriton, but still far better accommodations than Peck typically enjoyed. He noted that none of the rooms had windows, nor did there appear to be a second egress, so they were effectively trapped so long as the guards remained outside their door.

As soon as the maid left, Mory turned to Peck. "What are they going to do with me, Peck? What was the empress talking about? What's she going to use me for?"

Peck gripped Mory's shoulders and gave them a squeeze. "I don't know, and I'm pretty sure we don't want to know. I think this whole mission was a mistake. We never should have come here. I'm sorry, Mory. This is my fault."

"No," said Mory, meeting his gaze. "I wanted to do the mission. I wanted to do something important for Aaslo. It just didn't turn out the way we expected. But, we're still alive and together."

"For now," Peck sighed. "But I think we should try to escape."

"Okay, Peck. If you think that's best."

Peck did think it best, for Mory's sake. He didn't say that to Mory, though, as he set his mind to the task of planning.

CHAPTER 17

SEDI WATCHED THE CHILD SCURRY INTO THE ALLEY AND THEN FOL-
lowed her. Like so many children without parents or homes, pain
and hunger afflicted this child. She could see it in the way the girl
moved, clutching her side and gingerly ducking around obstacles.
Ever since the Berruvian army descended on the city of Dawning in
southern Helod, the shops and markets had largely closed, and the
street rats suffered the most for it. With no one shopping and selling
goods, there was no one to donate to their plight nor was there anything to steal. *This* girl had ventured into the army camp looking for
food and had, unbeknownst to her, garnered the guard's attention.
No telling what soldiers would do with a young girl like this should
they catch her. Well, actually, there was. Sedi had seen it before. In
countless towns around countless battles, men took from girls and
women what did not belong to them, or they killed them outright.

Death might be a blessing for one such as this child, destined
to starve. The child was young, though, and Sedi figured she had
much potential. So Sedi found herself trailing the girl into the war-
rens that existed behind, between, above, and below the buildings of
Dawning, lugging a sack she snagged from the stores meant for the
army. The food was a peace offering, a bribe of sorts, because while
brutality was efficient, especially among the upper echelons, Sedi
had always leaned toward kindness when it came to the needy. The
girl, only a few dozen steps ahead of her, ducked into a hole in a wall
covered with a length of tattered fabric. Sedi had to turn to the side to
fit through the small space, and what met her on the other side was
anything but welcoming.

A man stood beside the wall. Although he was slouched, Sedi noted
that he was easily one of the largest men she had ever seen. She narrowed her eyes to get a better look in the dim lighting and realized
he was not, in fact, a man, but a boy. His youthful face and vacant
gaze belied his mature stature. He raised his fist to strike her, but
a high-pitched shout from farther in the room stopped its descent.
Sedi glanced over to see several young people occupying a space that
should have been condemned for all its cleanliness. Broken furniture
and refuse scattered among the youths like flies in a stable.

The shout that stopped her assailant came from the young girl Sedi had followed into the hovel. The girl, who could not have been much older than ten, pushed past the others, many of whom were much older, and came to stand in front of Sedi.

She wore a wrinkled and stained brown dress with a grey smock, both of which were a bit too large. She cocked a head with mousy brown hair in two messy braids, placed her grimy hands on her hips, and said to the hulking boy, "Keep an eye on her while I figure out what she wants." Then to Sedi, "Why did you follow me?"

Sedi tossed her sack at the girl's feet, and several root vegetables and a loaf of bread fell out. Sedi said, "I thought to feed you."

The girl's eyes widened, and several of the other children surged forward to gather the foodstuffs. Before they could lay their hands on them, though, the girl bit out, "Stop! No one touches anything until I say so."

The others eyed each other warily and kept their distance.

The girl looked back to Sedi. "Why would you help us?"

Sedi raised one brow at the commanding, jaded young girl. "Children should be cared for, *fed*. They should not have to fend for themselves."

The girl crossed her arms and gave Sedi a skeptical look. "We don't owe no one nothing. We're not owned, and we can't be bought."

Sedi clucked her tongue. "I'm not trying to buy you. I'm just feeding you, free of charge."

"What's in it for you?"

Sedi spread her hands. "Nothing, but if it makes you feel better, I didn't pay for the food either. I took it from the army."

"You stole it?" said the girl, glancing at the food.

"I . . . *acquired* it," said Sedi.

The girl looked at the food again, and Sedi saw the moment she caved. The girl temporized, "Well, I guess that's okay, then." She waved at the others, who scurried forward to gather the food. Then all but the girl and the overlarge boy disappeared into the next room.

When the girl looked at Sedi again, there was a gleam in her eyes that hadn't been there before. The girl's stance became relaxed and sure, and her voice was level and mature as she said, "That was well done, Lady Tryst."

Sedi stared at the girl in surprise. "How do you know my name?"

The girl shrugged. "Names are not difficult when you have watched and listened to all that has happened and all that will be."

Sedi caught the gleam in the girl's eyes again, and she would swear her eyes glowed. "Who are you?"

"My name is Arohnu," said the girl, "but *who* I am is not as important to you as *what* I am, I think."

Sedi didn't know the name Arohnu, but she was certain the name did not belong to the little girl. She said, "And that would be . . . ?"

The girl laid a hand over her chest. "I am a god. Or, rather, I am a god in possession of this vessel."

Sedi's jaw dropped. "How is this possible?"

"Ah well, you see, I am the God of Prophecy, and this girl has the gift."

"But all the Endricsian magi left," protested Sedi, "including the prophets."

"Well, you know these humans are always misplacing their offspring. At times, they do not even know they exist. This one has gone unnoticed. It is lucky for us both that I am capable of speaking through her."

Sedi didn't know what to say. If this being was truly the God of Prophecy, then Aaslo had made good on his word. She was suddenly far less embarrassed about having kissed him than she had been a moment ago. She had to know for sure, though, before she could give such credit to her enemy. "Why are you here?"

The girl said, "You requested an audience, did you not?"

"Well, yes, but I didn't expect to get one," muttered Sedi. Then, before she lost her nerve, "I need to know if Axus is lying to me. He has made certain promises, and—well, let's just say I'm not as confident in his word as I once was."

"You want to know if Axus will grant you a place among us," clarified the girl.

"Not just for me, but for *everyone*. He promised me a place in Celestria and a glorious Afterlife for everyone else, an Afterlife where no one dies, where there is no more loss, no more pain and suffering."

"Axus does not have that kind of power. He cannot control the destiny of the soul."

Sedi swallowed hard against the bile in her throat. "He *promised* that the glory of the Afterlife would be greater than the suffering of this world."

The girl nodded slowly. "There is some truth in that, we assume. However, we do not really know what happens to the souls once they enter the Sea of Transcendence. It seemed a peaceful place until recently. *Someone* has been stealing souls from it."

"Axus?"

"So it would seem."

"Then he *is* a liar." Sedi's doubts struck her like a punch to the chest.

The girl looked as if she chose her words carefully. "Axus has always tried to make his own truth, even if it is only to suit his needs."

For the first time in centuries, tears sprang to Sedi's eyes. She told herself that Arohnu's words were the confirmation she needed, but in truth, Aaslo had already convinced her. Axus was a liar, and he would never—*could* never—keep his promises. Sedi could barely swallow past the lump in her throat, and she didn't know what to say anyway.

The little girl continued, "I didn't bring you here to talk about Axus."

"What do you mean?" inquired Sedi. "I requested this meeting."

The girl shrugged. "It was an easy request to grant when I already intended to meet with you. You see, the prophecy has hit a snag. I cannot stand back and observe this time. Unfortunately, I must become directly involved—just a bit."

Direct involvement by the God of Prophecy didn't seem to be in Sedi's best interest, but neither did she know what that interest was anymore. Knowing Axus wouldn't deliver on his promise, Sedi felt no regret for not serving him—quite the opposite, actually. A deep-seated anger started to fester at her core, and vengeance had a sweet ring to it. But which side was Arohnu on?

Arohnu addressed her. "I can see the wheels turning in your mind, Lady Tryst. You should know that I do not intend to harm you, but I do intend to *change* you."

Alarm shot through Sedi as she considered the many ways in which the gods could change a person. Aaslo was the perfect example, and while she found his uniqueness appealing, she did not want to end up like him.

The little girl's laugh sounded far too bold for her age as Arohnu assured her, "Don't worry. The changes will be of a magical nature. The changes do not come entirely from me. Enani had a hand in them as well."

"Who is Enani?" she asked as she unconsciously took a step back.

"She is the Goddess of Realms, and it is through her power that the most important change will occur. I, of course, have seen the many futures ahead of you, and let's just say those I prefer to occur require something of you that you are not capable of at the moment."

"And what do you prefer to happen? Whose side are you on? You've been forthright about Axus's abilities, but you haven't denounced him."

"Neither have you," said the little girl with a sneer. She shook her head. "I see *all*. I need not confine myself to one side or the other."

With suspicion, Sedi continued, "What is it you want me to be able to do?"

"You need to be able to enter Celestria." The little girl held out her hand, upon which lay a golden leaf. "Accept this blessing and walk the path of your greatest destiny."

Sedi looked at the golden leaf with apprehension. She didn't know Arohnu's motives. At this point, she didn't even know her own. If she accepted the blessing, would she be betraying Axus? He had lied to her. She wouldn't be receiving the boon he had offered. If she did turn on him, she would be on her own. Sedi smiled to herself. She understood being alone. She had been alone for millennia, so this wouldn't be any different.

The leaf glinted in the dim light, and Sedi considered. Vengeance was not the only reason to take the offer. There was no reason to do as *this* god asked either. Once granted the blessing of the gods, she could do with it what she pleased. If Sedi was certain of anything, it was that she couldn't depend on anyone else to serve her best interests. Like Arohnu, perhaps she didn't need to take a side. She could set her own destiny, and she could do so in Celestria. Sedi crossed the space between herself and the girl and looked down at the golden leaf. She plucked it from the girl's palm. "For me."

In the week he had been away from the army, Aaslo slept very little. Time was running short. He tried—and failed—multiple times to find the path to take them to the final tomb. This one had been a particularly difficult quarry—as if it had been hidden. He didn't think Sedi had the power to do such a thing, though. He didn't know why finding the path had been such a challenge, but his failures hadn't engendered confidence in his abilities for the soldiers in his retinue.

"I've never known you to get lost."

"We're here now," he grumped.

Aaslo folded Sedi's map and tucked it back into a pocket, while his narrowed gaze took in the desolate terrain. As far as his dragon-sighted eyes could see stretched a bleak, blackened landscape filled with sharp fragments of stone and glass. These intermixed with long, twisted ropes of black stone stretching across wider swaths of smooth lava flows. There, on the slopes of Vol Hedrix, nothing green and thriving filled the barren space. Fresh lava flowed in molten streams, and Aaslo felt completely out of his element.

"It's not that different."

Aaslo nearly laughed at Mathias's jest.

"I'm serious. At least it's a mountain."

"It's a volcano, and, yes, it's completely different. This is worse even than the plains. *Nothing* grows here."

"That's not true. I see something green right over there."

Aaslo shielded his eyes against the grit in the air and noted a tiny fleck of green standing out against the black backdrop. "That's not growth. It was stuck to my boot when we came through the portal."

"Sir?" One of the soldiers he had brought with him, a man named Brent, drew his attention.

"Shhhh," a second man hissed in a forced whisper. "He's not talking to you." Aaslo thought his name was Merc. Or perhaps that was his profession. Either way, that's what everyone called him.

"Then who's he talking to?" said Brent, just as easily heard by Aaslo's sensitive ears.

"Just shut up," said Merc.

Aaslo ignored the two but turned to the soldiers anyway—six of them plus Ijen and Andromeda. Aaslo hooked a thumb over his shoulder indicating the tunnel leading into the flank of the volcano. It appeared to be a massive, hollow lava tube that had been reinforced and preserved with magical runes carved into the tunnel's entrance. Aaslo couldn't sense any power, so he figured the spells protecting it from collapse or new lava had dissipated. "We're going in there. If you don't think you can handle it, speak now."

Some of the soldiers sent anxious glances between themselves and the tunnel. The volcano rumbled beneath their feet, and Brent started to raise his hand, but Merc slapped it down with a grunt. "Soldier up," he growled. Brent wiped his palms on his trousers but didn't raise his hand again. Aaslo nodded and turned toward the entrance. They picketed the horses near the tunnel's mouth, but Dolt was being ornery as usual. The horse kept pulling up his picket stake and trying to follow Aaslo into the tunnel. After several harsh words and vulgar gestures, Aaslo nearly gave up, but Dolt laid his ears back and gnashed his teeth at Aaslo before turning around and flicking him with his tail.

Aaslo knew he had somehow angered Dolt, and he didn't want to return to find him missing. "Dolt, damn it, it's for your own good. You have to stay here."

Dolt's ears twitched, but he didn't turn around.

"Fine," Aaslo huffed in frustration. "Act like a child if you want, but at least you won't be following me into the tunnels."

When Aaslo turned around, Andromeda stood behind him. "Do you always let your horse get to you like that?"

"He's . . . difficult." As Aaslo passed her, he added, "And he's not a horse."

"He *looks* like a horse," she said. "An ugly one, but still a horse."

"Well, he's not. Don't let him fool you. He has secrets."

"Your horse has secrets," she repeated. One more nail in Aaslo's mental coffin.

A couple of soldiers snickered, and Mathias joined them, although he was much more obvious in his good humor. A few minutes later, the echoing clack of hooves followed them into the tunnel, and Aaslo groaned.

It was dark, but Ijen used a spell to produce enough light to ignite their torches. In the enclosed space, the burning pitch stung Aaslo's nose, though one more foul odor added to the noxious air hardly mattered. The vile odor of sulfur and burning gases made breathing unpleasant, but the route's heat and the steep incline made deep breaths necessary. The black basalt and gabbro walls of the tunnel were narrow, and at times, Aaslo was sure Dolt would not fit, but somehow the stubborn beast managed to keep up with them.

After an hour of climbing the steep grade, the heat increased to a point well beyond uncomfortable.

"We can't keep going like this," panted Andromeda as she leaned against the wall. She pointed back to a few of the soldiers who looked woozy on their feet. "This heat will kill us."

Aaslo wiped sweat from his brow. He was hot, but not terribly so. He certainly felt much better than the others looked. He realized the dragon in him must be keeping him from overheating. Inside, he could feel it basking in the heat of the volcano. Most of the others, though, appeared as if they might collapse. Except for Ijen.

Aaslo stared at the prophet. "You're using a spell to keep yourself cool, aren't you?"

Ijen tilted his head. "Naturally."

"Well, can you do it for the rest of them?"

Ijen pursed his lips as he looked at the others starting to succumb to their fatigue as they slumped to the ground. "Perhaps one other," said the prophet. "I don't have the power for more."

Aaslo rumbled impatiently, "Then show me. I'll do it."

A few minutes later, the others guzzled water as they recovered their wits. They weren't exactly cool, but they were cool*er*. Aaslo would have extended the cooling protection to Dolt, but the horse seemed perfectly content.

"Horse, indeed," Aaslo muttered. "It's like you're not even trying anymore."

Dolt snorted and swished his tail happily.

Moving once again, they didn't have far to go before the tunnel opened into a large chamber brilliantly illuminated by magma that bubbled and popped in a massive pool a dozen yards below. The golden-red light glinted off the vitreous crystal faces in the gabbro, illuminating a narrow path that spanned the chamber. It led to a sheltered alcove on the other side.

"I don't like this." Brent's voice wavered.

Merc gripped the other man's shoulder and pushed him forward. "Come on. We'll lead the way. That way you'll get to the other side sooner."

The two men started across the stone bridge, and the rest followed, with Dolt bringing up the rear. Everything went well until Aaslo looked down. It took him a moment to realize what was wrong. The realization struck him with the force of an axe to the face. They were sinking. No, that wasn't right. The magma was *rising*. Where before it had been a dozen yards below, now it was merely a dozen feet away. What's more, the tranquil churning of its crusty surface became an erratic surge, and small mounds of magma began to pool at the base of the bridge.

As Aaslo watched, the mounds grew taller, elongated, and took on new shapes. A head formed, one possessed of eyes and long, sharp teeth. Then limbs sprouted as the magma formed a body. The four long limbs ended in massive paws tipped with tachylyte claws. It used these to climb the remaining feet between the magma pool and the top of the bridge. As the monster half stalked, half flowed toward them, Aaslo couldn't help but think that it looked like a molten dire wolf, nearly the size of Dolt. Worse, he counted five more creatures, each different, converging on them from either side of the bridge.

Aaslo urged the others to pick up their pace, but the soldiers in the lead were already running for their lives. Their mad dash was so frantic that before the threat could even reach them, Brent tripped over his own feet and fell over the edge into the bubbling magma. Instant incineration cut his agonized scream short.

"Well, damn," grunted Merc as he pulled back from the edge, where he had tried to catch the falling Brent. "I guess he should have stayed behind."

Aaslo added another death to his conscience as the dire wolf stood before them. A lion of lava followed behind them. With escape cut off, Aaslo and his party stalled. Aaslo pushed past the terrified soldiers to face the dire wolf, and Ijen maneuvered around Dolt, who spun to meet the attacker behind them.

Aaslo drew his axe from its belt loop and gripped the haft with dragon strength as he swung at the molten dire wolf. The beast lunged, and Aaslo's axe sliced through the monster's face. The strike had little to no effect. Magma filled the crack, and the face re-formed.

"Well, that was disappointing."

Aaslo grunted with the effort as he struck fast again and again to weaken the monster and knock it from the bridge. With great strides, he swung his mighty axe furiously, rending magmatic flesh from the beast in front of him. As chunks of magma sloughed away, the beast re-formed but diminished in size with each round. As Aaslo continued hacking at the animal's magma body, his axe glowed red with heat and the haft began to char. When the monster was the size of a large dog, Aaslo took one last mighty swing and threw it from the bridge.

The way was now clear, but he had no respite, as more of the monsters had reached the pinnacle. Aaslo turned to cover the others as they slipped by him at a run for the alcove on the other side. As Aaslo's axe bit into the arm of a molten bear, he noted Ijen and Dolt still battling the lion. Ijen cast spell after spell, and the not-a-horse seemed to take no ill effects as his hooves struck the beast. If Aaslo had needed confirmation that Dolt was not a real horse, this was it.

Aaslo chopped away at the bear, ducking and rolling to avoid its heavy strikes, when a giant serpent slithered up from behind. Hot magma dripped from its fangs as it hissed and struck. He managed to avoid the serpent's lunge, but Aaslo's scales sizzled as he took a hit from the bear, nearly throwing him from the bridge. He slid; sparks erupted from the stone as he dug his claws and axe into the ruts to slow his momentum. His legs dangled helplessly over the magma. His boots heated as he clung to the bridge by his claws.

"I don't think even the dragon can save you from magma, Aaslo. Use your strength. Use your magic."

The bear and the serpent converged on him, and Aaslo drew on his power. He called upon Ina and the dragon as he began to absorb the heat from his surroundings. Then, just as the bear raised its arm to swipe him from the bridge, Aaslo directed the cooling spell at the monster and *pulled* as hard as his will would allow. Poised in its deadly pose, the bear instantly turned to solid stone. Aaslo redirected his will to the serpent, but it had already descended on him. Without warning, brilliant beams of light erupted from its eyes and mouth, and its head burst before the rest of it crashed to the bridge and exploded in a shower of rocky fragments. Pieces of volcanic glass tore Aaslo's exposed flesh, but he did his best to ignore the pain as he clung to the bridge. Where the serpent had been stood a different creature, one even more powerful and just as inclined to kill him.

Sedi.

"Your girlfriend is back."

The ancient magus stood over him with a sultry half smile as Aaslo pulled himself onto the bridge. He kept one eye on her as he proceeded to draw the heat from each of the remaining creatures, including the lion that, thanks to Ijen and Dolt's efforts, was now not much larger than a house cat. When all the remaining magma monsters had been reduced to a stone menagerie, Aaslo stood panting and searching for more enemies. Ijen, appearing disheveled for once, stood beside Dolt, staring at Aaslo. Still breathing heavily, Aaslo motioned behind him. "Go. Get to the other side with whoever is left."

Ijen tilted his head, then pointed behind Aaslo. "Might you do something about *those?"*

Aaslo glanced over his shoulder and blinked through the blood dripping into his eyes. To his shock, waves of flame wafted from him like two giant wings. No, not *like* two giant wings. They *were* wings. Two enormous, flaming wings extended from his back and into the cavern. Aaslo flinched. The wings arched over him, then flapped, creating spiraling eddies of heat, sparks, and ash.

"Look at that. You're becoming a mighty dragon-man. Your vixen must be impressed."

Aaslo felt the flesh on his face and neck knitting together as he looked back to Ijen. "How do I get rid of them?"

Ijen shrugged, withdrew his book from his tunic, and stood with pen poised to write as he looked at Aaslo expectantly. Aaslo grumbled and turned his attention inward to find the mechanism that had created the wings. With the adrenaline from the battle still raging through him, and his dragon still on the hunt, it was hard to concentrate.

"You absorbed the heat."

Aaslo jerked as he noted Sedi standing beside him. In his shock, he had forgotten her. "What?"

She eyed the wings with a lifted brow. "You absorbed the heat and magical energy from all those magma monsters. It had to go somewhere."

The wings shuddered and stirred of their own accord, as Aaslo's irritation with her cavalier attitude grew. Sedi's tendency to come and go as she pleased had evolved into such comfort in his presence that she no longer feared attack. He briefly considered using one of his newly formed wings to toss her from the bridge, straight into the magma. But what he hated even more than her confidence at that moment was his own distress at the thought of her death.

"It's sweet that you care, Aaslo, but you keep forgetting that she's the enemy."

Aaslo couldn't concentrate on his wings with Sedi standing so close. She was the enemy. At least, that's what he told himself. "What are you doing here, Sedi? Have you come to stop me? Have you forgotten that *you* sent me here?"

She brushed her luscious dark locks from her face and shrugged. "Not at all."

"Maybe she just wanted to see you."

Aaslo ignored Mathias's needling as he tried to focus on the present. "And while we're discussing it, what's with the lava and monsters? Was this a setup?"

Sedi tsked as she stared at him without answering. Then she raised her hands placatingly. "Well, yes, it *was*, but I decided this wasn't the most opportune time for you to die, so I came here to help you. Only, you already took care of it, so call me impressed."

Aaslo's wings shifted as he clenched his fists and jaw. "What were those things? How did you create them?"

Sedi's laughter filled the chamber. "I may be powerful, but I am not a god. I didn't *create* those things. They're fae, and they were here when I chose the place to keep the tomb. They're not dead, by the way, so I suggest you hurry."

Aaslo could appreciate the need for haste, but Sedi's incessant meddling irritated him. "*Why* are you doing this, Sedi?"

Sedi glanced at Ijen, who scribbled in his book with a pleased grin. Aaslo didn't like that grin. Nothing good could come of a prophet's smile.

Sedi looked back at Aaslo and clasped her hands in front of her, wringing them as she bit her lip. For the first time since Aaslo had met the woman, she appeared uncertain. He knew it to be a ruse. Sedi wasn't the anxious type. He allowed her to go on with her act, only to see what she would say. She didn't disappoint.

"I've decided that serving Axus may not be in my best interest."

Aaslo barked a full-bellied laugh. "Oh, you'll have to do better than that."

Sedi's grin fell. She straightened imperiously. "What I do and why I do it is none of your concern."

"Of course it's my concern! It's *my* life, and you are a threat to my cause."

Sedi sidled closer, close enough that his dragon could scent jasmine and pistachios over the noxious fumes of the cavern. "Perhaps, but the only cause I'm concerned with is my own."

Her words verged on hostile, but something in how she looked at him reminded Aaslo of their kiss. One of Aaslo's wings inched its way toward Sedi. It seemed to be trying to embrace her. Aaslo struck out at the offending appendage with his fist, trying to force it behind him. He wasn't sure if it was an effort to protect *her* from the flames or prevent himself from getting too close. Either way, he didn't want his wings anywhere near the woman—or *at all*, for that matter.

"They seem to want you . . . and her."

He did his best to ignore her sultry gaze. "You are an infuriating woman."

Aaslo took a few steps back, creating a modicum of distance between them, and closed his eyes. He focused inward on the energy he had absorbed. His first instinct was to push it away, to dispose of it in the magma.

"Power absorbed is power gained. You'd be a fool to part with it so easily."

Mathias was right. If he needed to fight a god, every bit of power counted. Instead of dispersing it, he pulled the energy into himself. As he did so, the dragon inside him grew. It reveled in the heat of the flames and their power, and it roared its delight in the cavern of his mind. When Aaslo opened his eyes again, the wings had gone, and he was growling furiously.

He abruptly stopped, and at their inquiring look, said, "What?"

Sedi observed him curiously, though. "You have an aura all around you now—like *them*."

"Like who?"

She shook herself. "Never mind. You might want to pull that power in, though. Right now, you are a beacon for anyone with eyes."

Aaslo's breath whooshed out as he drew the power in even tighter. His entire body felt strained as if he'd finished a heavy round of training. He noted his muscles began to ache, the aura Sedi pointed out faded into nothing. Aaslo motioned toward the recess where the others waited. "If you're truly interested in helping us—"

"For the moment," she interjected.

"—then, tell me, are there any more traps?"

Sedi shrugged. "Not that I recall."

Aaslo ground his teeth together as a low growl escaped him.

Sedi licked her lips and smiled, her gaze appreciative. "You have no idea what that does to me."

Aaslo choked down his surprise at her brazen remark. He turned on his heel and headed for the recess where Andromeda and the soldiers stood anxiously watching.

The tomb sat upon a short plinth made of the same black gabbro throughout the chamber. It simultaneously reflected and absorbed the light generated by the magma. Aaslo shoved the top of the tomb aside with ease, briefly caught off guard by his own strength. The tomb held a body wrapped in a scarlet shroud encircled by several golden chains, each clasped with a heavy lock.

Aaslo looked over his shoulder to Sedi. "What's this? None of the others were wrapped or chained."

Sedi brushed her silky hair back from her face. "It's Peter Sereshian. I didn't particularly like him. He only wanted to use magic for profit. I thought it fitting that he should be bound by his gold in death."

Aaslo grunted. "How poetic."

Sedi gave him a suggestive wink. "What can I say? I'm a romantic."

"Lucky for you. She probably expects you to give her flowers or chocolates. Wait, no, that's not right. Hmm. What would Sedi want? Probably a sword for backstabbing you. Maybe a jar to put your head in. It would be a step up from this bag."

"Will you stop talking?"

"Just trying to help."

"I'm not courting her," Aaslo retorted, not quite low enough to avoid Sedi overhearing.

She said, "Courting who?"

"No one. I am courting no one," he replied.

She raised one eyebrow. "Okay, but I don't remember asking. Is this about the k—"

"We don't need to talk about that." He turned his attention back to the task at hand.

He didn't bother with the locks. He simply snapped the chains as he yanked them from the corpse. Andromeda came forward to help unwrap the body, but he noticed her suspicious gaze returning to Sedi.

She whispered, "Why is she here? What does she want?"

"She says she wants to help."

"You believe her?"

Aaslo glanced at Sedi, and her gaze met his for a brief moment. "Not particularly, but I *want* to." Andromeda looked at him in disbelief. He quickly added, "She would be a powerful ally, and she has copious information on the Berru."

Andromeda scoffed but said nothing more as they finished unwrapping the long-dead magus Peter Sereshian. The man was thin with a narrow face and deep-set eyes. His dark blond hair brushed his shoulders, and his mustache and beard were of the same color, if not texture. His rich silk doublet was probably too tightly fitted for him to don without assistance, and his neatly manicured nails were surely the work of a manservant.

A chuckle shook Aaslo's chest, and Mathias joined him.

Andromeda gave him an annoyed look. "The man is dead. Why are you laughing?"

Aaslo didn't answer, but he did find it darkly amusing that such a fastidious and vain man would end up a shade for the depraved in his undead army. Though, the fact that he found any humor at all in the situation gave him cause for concern. The world had become a morbid and demented place, and he was at the crux of it.

Having practiced reining in his power, this time Aaslo raised the shade without releasing the concussive force that might have brought the entire chamber down on their heads. The shade turned his nose up and sneered at them all as if they were not worthy of being in his presence. He paid particular attention to Sedi, who returned his curiosity. Aaslo wondered how much of Peter's memory remained in the vessel and if he recognized Sedi. She had said she didn't care for Peter in life, but that didn't mean she wasn't above using him against Aaslo if she could manage it. Had she done something to the body? Was she merely waiting for it to turn on Aaslo?

Peter followed Aaslo as they returned to the surface, and Aaslo glanced back regularly to make sure he stayed in line. Aaslo remained close to Sedi as well, primarily to keep an eye on her and be able to react if she should cause trouble. At least, that's what he told himself. It didn't matter that her presence always elicited a thrill in him.

"Are you seriously crushing on the woman who has tried to kill you multiple times?"

"I'm not," Aaslo barked.

Sedi slid him a questioning look. "Not what?"

Aaslo glanced back at the shade, following him obediently. Although the depraved seemed contained at the moment, his shifty eyes and sidelong glances in their direction made Aaslo nervous.

"Not what?" repeated Sedi.

Aaslo redirected his attention to the threat at his side. He didn't know why Sedi remained with them. She didn't seem inclined to leave, and he wasn't prepared to break their tenuous, unspoken truce by forcing the issue. "I'm not understanding something. Why is it the other ancient magi are all dead, yet you still live?"

"Ah, *that*. I suppose it doesn't hurt to tell you. You're one of us, after all." She flashed him a predatory grin that wasn't exactly welcoming. "You know how we got our powers, right?"

"I've read a bit in the histories, but why don't you tell me?"

"A great war that lasted for decades, nearly a century, actually, spanned the entire Endricsian continent and every level of power. The kingdoms and factions broke treaty after treaty over and over again. It seemed the bloodshed would have no end. There was one faction, though—academics, mostly—who didn't care about *winning* the war. We just wanted to *end* it. After multiple efforts of diplomacy failed, we decided that if the war was ever to end, we would need to do something drastic. That's when Louis Flourent presented the idea to seek aid from the fae. He had made it his life's work to understand the fae and all manner of magical creatures. He believed that the survival of humanity depended on *them*. Not everyone was convinced, of course, but some of us were desperate enough to try.

"So we sought out the fae. Louis had already made contact with a few, and from them we found others. Each of us made a deal with a different fae. The fae *lent* us their power in exchange for some boon. I didn't understand it at the time, but, apparently, I traded my mortality."

"And the others?"

"They each had their own price to pay. Most didn't talk about it." She looked at him curiously. "What was yours?"

Aaslo absently scratched the scruff along his jaw. "I had to rid Ruriton of Axus's blight."

Sedi wore a small smile as her gaze turned toward a memory. "Ah, that was an intriguing event. You seem to have gotten off easy, then."

"I'm not so sure."

"Why is that?"

"It was something Ina said."

"Ina?"

"The fae creature with whom I made the deal. She said, 'You will rid my land of the blight. That is *my* price. *Your* price will be greater still.'"

"What did she mean that *your price* will be greater?"

"I don't know, but I think it had something to do with—" Aaslo cut off his statement as he remembered to whom he was speaking. As far as he was concerned, Sedi was still the enemy, but a piece of him wasn't convinced of that. It was the piece that had taken her into his arms and kissed her soundly. It was the piece that continued to draw his thoughts back to her even when she wasn't around. The piece that admired her strength and skill and appreciated the beautiful woman who winked and smirked as she toyed with him. Part of him wanted to confide in her, to pick her mind and see what she thought of all that had been happening to him. She had endured so much, lived for so long, that somehow he felt only she could truly understand him.

"It had something to do with what?" she said.

Aaslo struggled against the idea of telling her and ultimately decided that he had no reason to trust her. It hadn't been that long ago that she had tried to kill him.

"Less than an hour, in fact. She set you up to get incinerated by lava monsters."

"Never mind," Aaslo grumbled as he considered that he had probably lost his mind. How could he be having sentimental thoughts about Sedi when she had done nothing but antagonize him?

"At least you're using your head again."

"I see," Sedi answered her own question. With a mirthless chuckle, she added, "You don't trust me. As well you shouldn't. I would think you were an idiot if you did. But if it's any consolation, I'm sorry for exploding the manor on top of you."

The hairs on the back of Aaslo's neck rose. Sedi was apologizing? That wasn't like her. He gave her a sidelong look. "Are you? Sorry, I mean."

She appeared to mull it over before saying, "No, not really. It was a lot of fun. And you survived, after all. That's what intrigued me."

"This doesn't sound good."

"What do you mean?"

"Your fortitude impressed me. It had been a long time since I failed to kill someone." She seemed to want to say more but held her tongue.

"What is it?"

She pursed her lips and stared at the dark rock beneath their feet, picking her words carefully. Finally, she sighed, "I probably shouldn't admit this, but I think your ability to continue to survive makes my own longevity seem more bearable. At least it gives me something to do."

"So killing you is a hobby."

Aaslo could understand how she might feel a bit of camaraderie with someone who had a difficult time dying, but he questioned her motives for revealing something so intimate. Was she exposing her vulnerability in a bid to gain his trust?

"She's nearly two thousand years old. She'll outwit you, Aaslo."

Aaslo grunted his agreement. Mathias was probably right. No matter how much thought he put into it, it was unlikely he could outsmart the ancient magus. If she was truly immortal, then he wouldn't be able to kill her either. Sedi switching sides would be the best outcome he could hope for. According to her, though, she was only interested in one side—*hers.*

CHAPTER 18

AASLO AND SEDI SAID NOTHING MORE AS THEY MADE THEIR WAY TO-
ward the tunnel entrance. At one point, the path narrowed, and
Sedi brushed against him. He knew she did it on purpose, but why?
Even more concerning: he *wanted* her close to him, which made
no sense. He had excused, if not justified, their kiss because he had
been drugged, but now his mind was clear. Aaslo wasn't sure what
role, if any, Ina had played in that kiss, but he knew the fae woman
had claimed *a* kiss as the price for her information. Ever since, his
thoughts, even his dreams, had been riddled with Sedi, and in most
of them, she was not his enemy. He knew that when dealing with
the fae the true price was not always the obvious one. Was this the
true price for the kiss? Was Ina pushing him toward Sedi? To what
end? And if it wasn't Ina, then what could possibly be driving it? He
wondered, not for the first time, if carrying the depraved beside his
soul had left a mark on his sanity.

*"I'm sorry to tell you this, but you left your sanity behind long
ago."*

Aaslo knew it to be true. He was not the man he had been back
in Goldenwood—physically or mentally. He wondered if his father
would even recognize him. He thought of Ielo, moving through the
forest with the surety only a forester possessed. He would be at peace
among the trees and shade. Aaslo longed to join him but knew it
would likely never be again.

His gaze slid to Sedi, and he wondered what life she had longed
for—before time jaded her. She had been honorable once, in her pursuit of the end of the war, the end of suffering. It occurred to him
that perhaps she had not changed so much. If she could be believed,
she followed Axus for that very reason. In her despair, she deemed
that her actions would lead to a better existence for everyone. Was
it her fault that she had been deceived? Axus was a god, after all.
Myropa had said his power was seductive. Perhaps Sedi's choices
had not been entirely her own. Axus's power might have consumed
her mind, if not her soul. As he looked at her now, he saw that she
struggled against some inner turmoil. In the darkness of the cave,

her self-assured confidence slipped, and she seemed exposed, emotional, *vulnerable*.

She glanced over to find him watching her, and her face abruptly hardened. She smiled coyly then winked as if nothing had been amiss.

"You see what she wants you to see."

Was Mathias right? Was he being played? Was he making excuses for Sedi's actions just because he *wanted* her on his side? Aaslo didn't know what to think, so he resolved not to think about her at all. He lasted all of five seconds before he glanced her way, again. Fine. Instead of avoiding thoughts of her, he would get as much information out of her as possible.

Feeling the pressure of the monumental task, one that would in all likelihood mean his death, he asked, "The world is going silent, Sedi. How many have died? Tens of thousands? Hundreds of thousands? How close is Axus to gaining enough power to take over Celestria?"

She looked at him with surprise. "How should I know? I know little or nothing about what Axus is doing. Contrary to what you may believe, Axus does not confide in me. I've only ever met him the once, when he offered me the deal."

Aaslo felt disappointed that Sedi had nothing to share with him regarding Axus, but he believed she was being truthful. Now that he had all six shades, he was as prepared as he would ever be to face the death god. He could feel that it was nearly time. A squirming sensation in his mind felt as though it had been placed there to alert him to the danger. He had convinced himself that the drink Arohnu had given him had blessed him with an internal countdown to the final battle with Axus. Somehow Aaslo knew that if he didn't face Axus by the end of the countdown, all would be lost. Axus, however, was not the only threat. There were other matters with which Sedi could help.

"Tell me about the empress," he said as they passed through a larger cavern. Heavy breathing and the crunch of boots and hooves over hard stone was all that could be heard.

Sedi's shoulders tensed, then relaxed. "Lysia is brilliant. Her wit is as sharp as her tongue, and her passion drives her. She won't be easily defeated."

"But you're close to her."

She gave him a cutting look. "I'm helping you now because it suits me. Don't expect my help against Lysia."

He wasn't familiar with the empress in any way. As far as he knew, before the invasion, no one in Endrica had ever heard of the Berru or their ruler. That Sedi was being less than forthcoming made him all the more suspicious of her motives. Sedi was trying to play both sides.

"What are her plans?" he continued.

Sedi stopped walking as they neared the horses, and turned to him. "It's not a secret. Her plans are what they've always been. To kill everyone."

"And when she's done with Endrica? What does she plan to do with the Berru?"

"They will die as well. It is their destiny to serve her in the realm of the gods. At least, that's what she believes. I know, now, that Axus does not plan to follow through on his promises."

"But *how* does she plan to kill everyone? I can't imagine so many people would willingly lay down and die."

Sedi shook her head. "She doesn't plan to give them a choice. She has a way."

"What is it?"

She smiled sweetly. "Why don't I take you to her, and you can ask her yourself?"

"That's not helpful," Aaslo chided. "You need to pick a side."

With a hard look, Sedi said, "No, I don't. I'm not concerned about Lysia. My focus is on vengeance against Axus. Now that you have all the shades, you have the power to defeat him—in theory—but you need practice. You depend too much on physical strength, which, while impressive, isn't your greatest weapon against a god. You need to learn to use your magic."

"For once, I agree with her."

"I know that," Aaslo sighed. He looked into Sedi's eyes. "Are you going to help me?"

She pursed her lips, and Aaslo's gaze dropped to her sensuous mouth. *"Not again."*

He returned his gaze to her eyes, and she had read his thoughts. A rosy flush colored her cheeks, and her pupils had expanded. She cleared her throat and laughed. "I'm not your friend, Aaslo. Perhaps next time we meet, I'll finally kill you. For now, I have more important things to do." She winked, then slipped through a portal and disappeared before he could reply.

"At least she put you in your place. Now you can stop mooning over her."

"I'm not mooning," Aaslo contradicted as he pursued Dolt in circles around the other horses. Dolt pranced, flicking his mane and tail as if he were on parade while the other horses snorted and shifted out of his way. Andromeda reached out and snagged Dolt's reins as Aaslo was about to give up.

"Thank you." Aaslo took the reins from the commander.

"You're welcome. At least that woman's gone. She *is* gone, isn't she?" Andromeda's eyes widened when she looked around, as if that might help her to see the ancient magus who could become invisible.

"Yes, she's gone. Hopefully she will stay that way," he muttered darkly.

"I doubt we will be so lucky. She seems obsessed with you, and not in a good way."

"I've noticed."

Aaslo took a moment to open the portal back to his army in the Pashtigonian city of Uptony. As he stepped into the foggy wood of the pathways, he wondered at how Sedi might try to kill him next. A messed-up piece of him actually looked forward to it.

They arrived outside Uptony's gates and knew a battle had taken place recently. While human bodies had been collected, the field was still strewn with blood and gore being addressed by all manner of scavengers. Only the white-blooded pieces of lyksvight were untouched, some of them still moving. The army encampment was gone. Another, partially erected camp, bearing the Berruvian sigil of a flame within an ellipse, had been abandoned a few hundred yards away. It had been picked over quite thoroughly. As they approached the city's entrance, Teza appeared upon the wall. She waved at them, then disappeared as the gates opened to permit their entry.

As Aaslo crossed the threshold into the city he was inundated with people wanting to speak with him—or rather their servants and aides who attempted to make appointments. They couldn't have known when he would arrive, so they had to have been waiting for some time. Aaslo wasn't in the mood to speak with anyone, and he didn't see why it should be his responsibility anyway. He may be the leader of this army, but he wasn't a king. He wasn't even a noble. The only duty he had was to the forest. Given the marquess and Teza here, he didn't know why anyone wanted to speak with him. Surely, they had taken care of everything that needed to be said.

Teza pushed her way to the front of the crowd. "You're back! What took you so long?"

Aaslo scowled. "I traveled through uncertain, deadly paths in search of a depraved soul cursed by existence and abandoned by the gods, hidden beneath a live volcano booby-trapped with fae magma monsters. I think a bit of patience is warranted."

Teza raised an eyebrow. *"I* wasn't worried, but the marquess was starting to think you'd gotten yourself killed."

Aaslo huffed and turned his attention back to the crowd. "Who are all these people? Why do they want to see me?"

Teza's cheeks flushed, but she shrugged. "Don't worry about them. They're not important."

Aaslo eyed the people, many of whom wore opulent dress with an air of conceit. "They look like *they* think they're important," he muttered. "What do they want?"

Her shoulders dropped, and with a defeated sigh, Teza pulled him through the crowd until they had more room. She erected a sound-blocking ward around them. "They want to make sure you intend to follow through on the deals we made."

"Maybe it was a bad idea to give Teza *authority."*

"What deals?"

Teza pursed her lips, then pointed to one of the officials wearing a long, purple silk robe. He spoke to a squat, rotund fellow wearing a yellow velvet vest and dark green trousers. "The tall one there wants ten gold per recruit, on top of the usual pay. The shorter one wants a large parcel of land in the south country to start an orchard. The woman in blue, over there, wants an exclusive deal with Lodenon for silk imports."

Mathias cackled. *"She's mistaken you for someone important."*

She pointed to another, but before she could say anything, Aaslo interrupted, "What are you talking about? I can't pay that!"

Teza rolled her eyes. "You don't have to. You're not a king or even a lord. You don't have the authority to make most of these deals anyway."

"Then why are you telling people I do?"

"Because we need fighters. This is how we get them. None of it will matter if we lose, which is certain to happen if we don't get more recruits."

"And if we win?"

"Then you'll go back to your forest and never hear from any of these people again. Probably a lot of them will be dead anyway."

Aaslo's stomach soured. It went against everything in his forester upbringing to make deals he didn't intend to honor, but it felt morbid to make deals with people under the assumption they would be too dead to collect. Teza started to tell him about more of the deals, but Aaslo raised a hand. "Don't tell me. I don't want to know."

Ignoring the officials and their representatives, Teza led Aaslo through the cramped streets to the staging area, located in a relatively disused square in the older part of the city. Some of the heavily rutted cobbles were missing, the faded signs on the buildings hung askew, and the largest buildings were boarded up or occupied by the homeless. It stood in stark contrast to the busier part of the city where shops shone with colorful goods, men and women sparkled with gems and precious metals, and stalls were piled with fresh cuts of meat, fruits, and vegetables. Aaslo wanted to be offended by the inequity, but as he looked at the destitute, huddled in corners and alleyways, all he saw were potential recruits who would likely be glad to serve for a hot meal.

He directed some of his men to recruit the homeless, then turned toward the command center in the largest of the boarded-up buildings. The marquess greeted him with a worn but pleased grin.

"Sir Forester, I am heartened by your return." He peered over Aaslo's shoulder to see the new shade hovering behind him. "It seems your mission was successful. Is it true, then, that we now have what we need to succeed?"

Aaslo unclenched his jaw. "I hope so. With the power of all six shades, there is some slim chance of prevailing against Axus. I hope to do enough damage that he won't have the power to follow through with his plan. For a time, at least."

The marquess nodded, his grin not as wide as it had been. "Well, that is *something*."

Aaslo glanced between Teza and the marquess. "Are the recruiting efforts here finished, then?"

"Yes." Teza spoke first. "And we collected a goodly number of supplies as well. Enough to sustain us for a few weeks, anyhow."

"Very well," said Aaslo. "It is time to move. We have a few more stops before we join the main encampment in Mouvilan. The greater army has surely garnered the attention of the Berru by now. Since the Berru operated out of Dawning in Helod, I anticipate we will meet them west of Chelis."

Teza said, "If I remember my geography lessons, that's hill country."

Aaslo nodded. "It is, and we can work that to our advantage."

The marquess commented, "Won't the Berru think of that?"

"Perhaps, but they are the aggressors. It will be harder for them to maintain the high ground."

"You're assuming the Berru choose to meet us at all," Teza pointed out. "What's to stop them from fanning out and wreaking havoc wherever they go like they did in the last wave?"

"For one, their army is made up of mostly seculars. They could not use the broken evergates even if they wanted to hazard them.

Also, because our army is the largest gathering of life left on Aldrea. To meet their end goal, the Berru must face us."

The marquess nodded. "There's one more thing you should know." He looked at Teza expectantly.

Teza was anxious, which immediately put Aaslo on edge. "It's about Peck and Mory."

"What about them? Don't tell me they're dead."

"No, not dead," Teza said in a hurry. "They've been captured."

"Captured," Aaslo repeated, unable to process what she was saying.

"Yes, they wanted to contribute something to the war effort. They thought we needed more information about the Berru, so they got themselves captured so they could spy."

Heated rage overwhelmed Aaslo, and the dragon reared its head. Flames erupted on his skin, licking up his arms. "You're telling me they got captured by the Berru *intentionally*?"

Teza straightened her spine and lifted her chin. "Yes, that's what I'm saying."

"And you knew they were going to do this?"

"I did."

Aaslo's anger was overshadowed only by his anguish. No longer were Peck and Mory the simple thieves that had stolen Mathias's head in Tyellí. They were *his* men, honest and loyal and always supportive. They had wedged themselves into a crack in his armor and become something more to him. His imagination ran rampant as he thought of all the things that could be happening to them at that very moment. His instincts screamed at him to go after them, but rationally he knew they could not. The two scouts were on their own.

DESPITE HIS FURY OVER PECK AND MORY'S CAPTURE, AASLO SLEPT like the dead that night. The fact that all six depraved were now joined with magi to create the shades gave him some relief, both mentally and physically. Although he retained a connection to the shades via their bond, their souls were no longer completely housed within him. He hadn't realized how much turmoil he had been harboring until it was lifted. Through trial and error, he learned that he could draw on the powers of the shades through their soul-bond regardless of their proximity to him. Although they possessed individual personalities and autonomy, so long as he maintained a tight hold on the bonds, they were, in essence, powerful extensions of his will.

Aaslo could feel each shade's power as well as the essence that made them unique. For the most part, their powers were much like those of any magus, but there was also something intrinsic to the depraved within each of them. The shade known as Echo could emit a blast of sound that it could obliterate everything within its immediate vicinity. With a thought, Avra could disassemble anything down to its most minute level, including the living. Jillian could absorb the energy around her, freezing everything to devastating effect, while Loris agitated any energy, ultimately causing it to ignite and even explode. Peter's power induced a state of decay, and anything he touched was reduced to sludge or ash in a matter of minutes. Aaslo thought that Aen's power was the most disturbing, however. He could bend a mind to his will causing homicidal madness or mindless frenzy.

The shades were revoltingly destructive in nature, and it sickened Aaslo to have such terrible powers at his call. Nothing in his life as a forester had prepared him for the gruesome brutality of the life he now led, but knowing he had six immense sources of power to call upon in the battles ahead gave him some respite. Despite their destructive natures, the shades were sure to play a significant role in the fight to preserve life on Aldrea.

Upon awakening, Aaslo called for his forces to march. Thanks to Teza's and the marquess's efforts (and lies), their numbers had grown significantly. As they departed the city, they left much of it abandoned. The larger the army, though, the slower they moved, and Aaslo was anxious to get through the paths to join the main encampment outside Chelis. They endured a few skirmishes with creatures in the paths, but their people were armed and prepared to fight so their losses were minimal. Overcoming the new recruits' apprehensions about traveling mystical fog-shrouded paths with a bunch of undead soldiers proved the greatest challenge. Ultimately, desperation prevailed. No one wanted to be left behind when death was a surety.

They arrived at the sprawling army encampment outside Chelis after several hours marching through the paths. Time had not progressed on Aldrea, so it was still morning when they exited the rift. Even though Aaslo had visited the greater army a number of times, he still received wary looks from those who saw him as a monster who raised the dead. Luckily, the leaders had gotten past their prejudices.

"Welcome, friend dragon," called a deep voice laden with the North Mouvilanian brogue.

"Ah, someone knows you."

Aaslo recognized the voice even before he saw General Vincent Regalis striding toward him from the massive command tent on the encampment's eastern flank. Regalis was a great burly man with as much hair on his chin as on his head and arms, strong enough to strangle a bear. His weapon of preference was the massive broadsword swinging comfortably at his hip, and he wore full mail even with no immediate threat of battle.

"General," Aaslo greeted him as Teza sidled up on his right.

By Mouvilan custom, General Regalis saluted Teza with a finger to his brow. "Mage General, it's a pleasure to see you again as well."

Teza gave a satisfied nod. "And you, Regalis. What are we at now?"

Regalis's golden tooth sparked as he grinned. "It seems your efforts didn't go as badly as you thought. Looks like with those you brought we're up to near a hundred thousand. I expect we'll just break that with your final efforts in the coming weeks."

Aaslo scratched the scales on his neck. "A hundred thousand versus half a million. Those aren't good odds."

"No, I've been thinking about that," Regalis explained. "It's not good if we intend to meet them in open ground, that's for sure, but I have an idea. Come with me."

Regalis waved them toward the command tent, a large structure draped in red canvas. A constant flow of messengers walked in and out with reports, requests, and orders. One overburdened messenger hefted a heavy stack of papers onto a table before scurrying out.

"Over here." Regalis indicated the table holding a large map of Mouvilan. Aaslo joined Regalis and Teza in peering at the drawing. "You indicated we should meet the Berru in the hill country to the west. That's not a bad place to start, but we don't want to go up against them in the open, high ground or no. There are just too many of them. We'll be overrun in no time."

"What do you suggest?" asked Aaslo.

Regalis thrust a thick finger to point at the border of Helod. "I say we make our stand here. It's slightly farther north and west than what you proposed, and it's on the river. It's not on the map because it's old, abandoned nearly a century ago, but there's a fortress here— Rendvik Tower. Unique. Impressive. It was originally built during some great war over a millennia ago to protect an evergate. The evergate was somehow destroyed, though; some say to prevent it from falling into enemy hands. After the war, peace reigned between Mouvilan and Helod, so the fortress was no longer necessary. Makes sense as a strategic position if the Berru are at Dawning as you say. There's no place to cross the river with a large force north of Dawning until you reach the fortress, and there's a series of rapids along here, so they can't come up by boat."

Aaslo scratched the scruff on his chin as he thought about the general's suggestion.

"Go for it, Aaslo. It's just like when we were kids. You can be king of the castle."

"You were always king," Aaslo remarked. "And it's a fortress, not a castle."

"Excuse me?" said Regalis.

"What is the condition of the fortress?" Aaslo ignored his question.

"I haven't seen it myself, but I've asked around. A few have seen it in their travels. It lies along a common merchant route. They say it's in good repair. They built their strongholds to withstand the magi back then." He looked to Teza. "Mayhap you'll even find a few built-in enchantments to charge." He turned back to Aaslo. "With a force this large, we can have it in working order in a matter of weeks."

"Very well," Aaslo agreed. "I'll take some scouts through the paths to check it out."

"All hail King Aaslo of Rendvik Tower."

Ignoring Mathias again, Aaslo addressed everyone. "We should be back in two, maybe three days. Then I'll finish the recruiting in the east." Aaslo rubbed his chest where he felt the squirming of the countdown with which the God of Prophecy had blessed him. If he wasn't mistaken, it was speeding up.

Regalis gave a decisive nod. "It's a sound plan. Will you be taking the magi with you?"

Mathias hummed in Aaslo's mind. *"What need have you for magi? You have the chosen one."*

Aaslo tapped the table with a claw as he considered. "I'll take a small contingent of soldiers and Prophet Ijen. They can begin preparing it for the army's arrival, and Ijen can work on any enchantments that might still be usable. Teza will stay here to help prepare the troops. They need to see her as the mage general, someone to be depended upon and trusted during the coming battle."

"Very well," replied Regalis. "But I suggest you take more soldiers than you think you'll need. The tower is massive. I'll put together a contingent."

Aaslo absently rubbed his chest again. "We have to move quickly.

We are running out of time. And it's important that Teza be seen as the leader of this movement since I will not be at the final battle."

"What?" Regalis and Teza spoke at once.

Aaslo lifted his gaze to Teza. "You knew this. Why does it surprise you?" Then he looked to Regalis. "While you face off against the Berru under Teza's leadership, I will battle Axus in Celestria. If I cannot defeat him, then the outcome against the Berru will not matter."

Regalis stared at Aaslo with eyes of flint. "I have to say, I heartily protest this plan. *You* bear the power of the ancients and the blessings of the gods, not to mention all these people have gathered under *your* banner. You *must* lead the army."

Aaslo shook his head. "It is not possible for me to be in both places at once. Besides, if I defeat Axus *before* the battle, then the Berru have no reason to fight, and we may spare the lives of all these men and women. Teza and Ijen will be here, as well as the shades. They can inspire the army."

Regalis didn't look happy, but regardless, he turned to Teza. "I think the troops will be emboldened by your presence. We expect the enemy magi to be many, and it helps to know we have at least one or two on our side."

A flash of doubt crossed Teza's features before her expression turned hard. "I'll do whatever I can to spare these men and women from the Berruvian magi."

Aaslo laid a hand on her shoulder and gave it a gentle squeeze. "You will not be alone. You will have the shades until I need them, and their powers are far greater than the magi you will be facing."

Teza raised an eyebrow. "I'm not sure who I fear more—the Berru or the shades."

Regalis asked, unsure, "Are they that dangerous?"

"They are," Aaslo confirmed. "And they can be unpredictable, but they will be a necessary weapon in the coming battle. They are bound to me, to my will, and they have instructions to follow Teza's orders in my absence. Unfortunately, they do not discern friend from foe, and neither do their powers, so it is dangerous to use them around our own troops. You will need to consider this when strategizing."

Regalis stroked his beard thoughtfully. "Hmm, I'm not sure if you've left us with a great weapon against the Berru or ourselves." He glanced at Teza. "We will have to plan this carefully."

Teza grinned, and it was anything but reassuring. "Of course. I wouldn't think of doing otherwise."

"Why don't I feel any better about this?"

"There's one more thing." Aaslo hefted his pack onto the table. After rummaging through it for a moment, he withdrew a small but thick tome. He held it out to Teza with a warning. "Take this. It is a book of rituals Peck and Mory liberated from some Berruvian magi. As far as I can tell, most of it is dark blood rituals that I wouldn't in good conscience use, but you might find something useful. At the very least, you may be able to counter some of their spells."

"You've had this all along, and you're just now showing it to me?" said Teza.

Aaslo gave her a hard look. "I was hesitant to show it to you at all. That's dark magic in that book."

"There's no such thing as light or dark magic. It's only how you use it that matters."

"I feel like the magic that killed me was pretty dark."

Aaslo winced at the reminder. "I think you'll change your mind after you see what's in this book. We are *not* sacrificing people for the sake of spells, no matter how powerful they are."

Teza snatched the book with a scowl. "You think I would do something like that?"

"I think your moral compass spins a little freely when you're desperate."

"That's an understatement."

With an irritated sniff, Teza replied, "I take offense to that."

Aaslo crossed his arms. "And Peck and Mory?"

Teza's expression fell. "That wasn't my fault. It was *their* idea to get captured."

"But you didn't stop them," he replied with a heavy dose of accusation.

She huffed. "They wanted to be scouts, so they're off being scouts."

"No, Teza. Getting intentionally captured is not being a scout. It's being a spy. I never would have put them in that position, and you know it."

"There was nothing I could do to stop them."

Aaslo reached out and gripped the book Teza held as if reconsidering giving it to her. "You call yourself the Mage General, but you couldn't stop a couple of scouts from going off on their own and endangering their lives? Not to mention what they know. Did you think of that? They could be tortured for information. They knew too much for this kind of mission, and Mory's only a boy. You should have stopped them."

Teza yanked the book away. "Okay, I get it. I made a mistake. I'm truly sorry. I should have talked them out of it, but there's nothing I can do about it now."

Aaslo slammed a fist onto the table, causing it to crack. He was still fuming about the loss of the two scouts, two people he dared to call friends, but he forced back the dragon that wanted to lash out. He steadied his nerves. "I know. But in the future, you need to think things through. Regalis and the other commanders have experience. Listen to them. You don't have to make all the decisions on your own."

Teza glanced at Regalis, who looked at the map, riveted, as he stayed out of their argument. "I'll do better," she said. "I'm not stupid. I know I've never led an army or really been in charge of *anything*. I'm depending on them to make sure things get done the way they need to."

Regalis drew his gaze from the map to meet Aaslo's stare. "We'll give her all the support she needs, but with her and her God-given silver armor in the lead, the troops will rally."

"Let's hope."

Aaslo released the book into Teza's care. He clenched his jaw as he held her gaze. A silent agreement passed between them, and his shoulders relaxed. He said his farewells and left them to their plans as he exited the command tent. His own tent was not far away, but it held very little since he carried his belongings with him. When he arrived, a young soldier hurried out, stopping short upon seeing Aaslo. He raised placating hands.

"I'm so sorry, Sir Forester, but I've tried everything. He won't leave!"

Aaslo's attention turned to his tent and the uninvited guest. He groaned inwardly as he considered who might be awaiting him and what they might want. He pushed the tent flap aside and stopped, abruptly faced with the rear end of a horse. Since he wasn't prepared to endure another of the beast's kicks, he sidestepped and rounded the front. There he met Dolt's steady gaze.

"What do you want?" Aaslo attempted patience.

"I think he missed you."

Dolt swished his tail then dropped his head and closed his eyes.

Aaslo stared at him for several seconds before realizing Dolt had fallen asleep. Aaslo debated the merits of trying to force the horse to leave versus ignoring him and finally settled on the latter.

Dolt was no longer in his tent when Aaslo awoke the following day, although his smell lingered.

"That smell isn't coming from the horse, Aaslo."

"How would you know?" Aaslo sniffed his own clothes only to realize Mathias was right. "Never mind." He grabbed some fresh clothes, a cake of soap, and a drying cloth. Then he stalked through the camp toward the designated bathing area at the creek. Men openly stared as he performed his ablutions, and he heard several comments on his dragon form.

"You're a curiosity, nothing more."

"They think I'm a monster."

"Maybe you are, but you're a good monster, and you're on their side."

"Do they know that?"

"Nobody's attacking you."

"Just give it a minute," Aaslo muttered darkly as he pulled on his trousers.

"You don't give people enough credit."

Aaslo bristled as a man cautiously approached him. The man was tall and broad of shoulder and fully armed with a long sword at his hip, a large dagger, and a hatchet secured to his belt. He had a scar above his left eyebrow, and wore a hardness that spoke to experience. "I think you spoke too soon," Aaslo commented to Mathias.

The man's ardent gaze took in every detail of him as Aaslo flexed his claws in preparation for a fight. He stopped a few paces away and, to Aaslo's surprise, he pressed his finger to his brow in a traditional Mouvilanian salute. In a smooth, melodic brogue, he began, "Sir, I'm Captain Evan. I've been selected to lead your contingent to Rendvik Tower." He nodded toward the men, dressing on the shore. "These men here and several others back at camp will be joining us. We'll be ready to leave within the hour. Is there anything you require of me before we head out?"

Aaslo eyed the men watching the proceedings. He lifted his dragon arm and flexed his claws. "Is this going to be a problem?"

Evan's gaze flitted to Aaslo's fist before turning steely. "Not for us, but if it is for you, we can work around it." He hooked a thumb over his shoulder and added, "My men are professionals. We've worked jobs in the far northern wilds *and* in the southern frost mountains, both of which are known to house the fae. We've seen a lot of strange things. This is different, but nothing we can't handle."

"I told you you were being overly sensitive."

"I'm not sensitive," Aaslo murmured sotto voce. Nodding toward a wanderer trailing along the creek, he jerked his chin in their direction. "And them?"

Evan didn't flinch. "It won't be a problem. We've all signed *The Contract*."

"Contract?"

For the first time, Evan showed a hint of surprise. Whatever this contract was, he had expected Aaslo to know of it. "Perhaps it'd be best if you spoke with General Regalis about that. If there's nothing else, we'll be preparing the horses and supplies." As Evan turned on his heel and joined his men to head back to camp, Aaslo wondered what kind of *professionals* these men were and what contract they had signed.

Aaslo finished dressing and returned to camp to find Regalis in the command tent once again. The man spoke to himself as he calculated figures into a notebook. He looked up at Aaslo's approach.

"Good morning, General. I've just spoken with Captain Evan. What's this about a contract?"

"Ah!" The general snapped his book shut. "Not *a* contract. *The Contract*." He pointed toward the large stack of papers Aaslo had seen the day before. The stack had doubled, and as Aaslo watched, a young man walked in carrying a third stack, which he placed gently on the table before hurrying out of the tent.

Aaslo walked over to the papers and thumbed through them. Each was an exact copy of the previous with the exception of the signature at the bottom, and in some cases, a simple *X*. Below each signature was a globular reddish-brown stain. Upon closer inspection, Aaslo realized it was a bloody fingerprint. Then he read through the short statement, utterly shocked. He looked up at the general. "What is this?"

The general graced him with a golden grin. "*That* is exactly what it looks like, and it is our secret weapon. Every person who has signed that contract has agreed to become one of your wanderers upon his or her death, and I intend to make sure everyone in this army signs it. We may be at a disadvantage in numbers, but at least our people can keep fighting after they're dead."

"*Brilliant. It will truly be a corpse corps.*"

Aaslo stared at the stacks of papers. If the general did as he said and things didn't go well, Aaslo would have to hold as many as a hundred thousand souls within himself to ensure they could rise and continue fighting. Aaslo didn't know if he could carry so many. At times, he felt half mad with the powers he already *had* within him. Could he truly contain tens of thousands of souls without losing himself?

"Don't underestimate yourself, Aaslo. You're doing fine."

"Am I?" Aaslo wondered. "If I was doing fine, I wouldn't be talking to you."

"That's not a sign of madness. It's a sign of good taste."

Aaslo turned to the general. "How am I supposed to manage this? I won't even be here, and I can't flip through these contracts every time someone dies to see if they signed it."

General Regalis raised his hands. "That I can't help you with, but I know someone who can, and he'll be here any minute."

Just then, as if summoned, Ijen stepped into the command tent. He seemed to be aware of their conversation already. Aaslo chose to attribute it to the thin tent canvas and not some prophetic vision. "I have already solved your problem," said the prophet. "A spell."

"What spell?" said Aaslo.

"Actually, two spells that I've combined to do the job. One is a simple cataloging spell called a mind vault. It will create a vault in your mind linked to these pages. It will store the pages within the vault and allow you to recall them faster than thought."

"That sounds useful. Why do people spend so much time learning things if you can just create a mind vault?"

"It's a simple spell, but it's dangerous. It has the potential to break one's mind. I think you will do fine, though."

"Because your mind is already broken."

"Why will I be fine?"

"First Order magi commonly used mind vaults, but the spell became more dangerous as the generations passed. They presumed that the greater one's power, the more stable the spell."

Aaslo wasn't sure if he was willing to put his trust in this volatile mind vault spell proposed by the sketchy prophet. Mathias was right. His mind was already broken enough. He cleared his throat. "You said it was two spells. What of the other?"

"The other is a blood magic spell."

"From the Berru's spell book?"

"No, this one is common enough in Endrica, often used to certify contracts, and it's the reason for the bloody print. It will link the contract with the body. When someone dies, the first spell will find the contract, and the second will link it to the body. They should be able to rise again almost instantaneously."

"But I won't even be in this realm."

"It shouldn't matter. Blood spells are powerful. That's why the Berru use them. They act independently of space or time."

"What if the contracts are destroyed?"

Ijen waved toward the stack of papers. "As far as *The Contract* is concerned, these pages are no longer necessary. Upon signing *The Contract*, a third spell was activated—another blood spell. *The Contract* is bound to the person's blood, not the page."

"So once I cast these spells, the contracts will be added to my mind vault, and these people will become wanderers when they die?"

"Exactly."

Aaslo shivered. A hundred thousand people were going to sign away their Afterlife in favor of binding themselves to *him*.

Ijen wasn't done, though. "We can use this"—he produced a wand—"to add contracts to your vault after you have already cast the spells, but the truth is, I believe all of this to be unnecessary."

"What do you mean?"

"It's purely theoretical, of course, but I believe anyone anywhere could *choose* at any time to become a wanderer after their death, whether you are present or not."

"What makes you think that?"

"As I said, it's theoretical, but it has to do with the nature of the soul and your link to it. Some scholars propose that all souls are connected, perhaps by the veil between life and death itself. I posit that, if this is true, and you can touch one soul, then you can touch *any* soul. That means that if someone in Lodenon vows to serve you, then you will be able to raise him once he has passed even if you are not aware of the oath."

Alarmed, Aaslo said, "How would he make such a vow?"

Ijen shrugged. "A simple promise to himself."

"Like a prayer?" said Regalis.

Ijen nodded. "A prayer would suffice."

Aaslo scowled at the two men. "I am not a god. People don't pray to me."

Ijen raised one eyebrow. "I think you would be surprised."

Aaslo huffed. "I've had enough of this. Show me these spells and be done with it."

Aaslo repeated Ijen's spells several times before activating them. Curiously, when it came time to cast them, Ina's power was eager and willing to participate. Aaslo had no problem casting the two spells, but when they finished, he felt a certain heaviness in his chest.

"It's all in your mind. You're panicking over the responsibility of carrying so many souls."

"You're probably right," rumbled Aaslo. "I wasn't prepared for this."

General Regalis took the wand from Ijen. "Don't worry. We'll add the rest when the contracts come in. Prophet Ijen says this wand is bespelled for even a secular like me to use. It's truly a wonder."

"A great wonder," bemoaned Aaslo. He looked to Ijen. "Are you ready to travel?"

Ijen nodded. "I am, indeed."

"Then let's be off. I'd like to get there before nightfall."

"Might I remind you that time doesn't pass here while in the paths?"

"That's not the point," barked Aaslo as he exited the tent.

CHAPTER 19

THE PATHWAY WAS SHORT BUT TUMULTUOUS AS THEY TREKKED TOWARD Rendvik Tower. It took them only a few hours to cross a distance that would have taken weeks in Aldrea, but the attacks were numerous and their foes strange and unpredictable. One group came upon them from an adjacent path and looked like children with cherubic faces and short statures, but they wielded bladed weapons and moved like lightning. Even with small numbers, their effectiveness would have been disastrous if not for the shield wards erected by Ijen and Aaslo. Still, Aaslo couldn't help but feel remorse for the deaths of the childlike creatures. On another occasion, their shield wards proved ineffectual against large beetle-like creatures, but save for one soldier who broke his arm after being thrown from his horse, their injuries had been minor.

Between battles, Aaslo led Ijen and the eighty soldiers, plus horses and three wagons of supplies, toward a doorway that, to his surprise, happened to open directly into the overgrown Rendvik Tower bailey. Aaslo wondered if his arrival point had been more precise by coincidence or if he was getting better at using the pathways.

"You'd better have improvement. You've been doing this for nearly six months. You'll never keep up with your vixen at this rate."

"Sedi has been doing this for millennia, and she's not *my* vixen."

"But you want her to be."

Aaslo did not respond as he took in the sight before him. To call Rendvik Tower massive would be an understatement. Sitting atop a rocky motte, it was five times the size of any tower Aaslo had ever seen and easily the tallest structure ever built. It had multiple limbs sprouting from its sides from the base to the pinnacle, lending it the appearance of an enormous stone tree. Each limb terminated at what looked like a cistern. A waterfall spilled from each cistern, crashing to the rocks in the moat encircling the tower's base beyond the bailey walls. The spray of water filled the air and the gleaming sun bathed the fortress in rainbows.

A grand staircase of stone led from the bailey up the motte to the base of the tower. At several intervals were resting areas with stone benches, overgrown gardens, and even a gazebo that looked to be in good repair. The bailey itself held barracks to the left of the main roadway, along with several support structures including a large one that housed a smithy, an armorer, and a farrier, and the nearby stables looked recently maintained. Poorly preserved homes and shops nestled to the right of the roadway. Some of the nicer buildings looked to have been lived in not long ago and bore the evidence of travelers and vagabonds.

Still in awe, Aaslo muttered, "I can't believe this place is abandoned."

Captain Evan replied, "We are far from an evergate, and the river is hardly navigable. Sometimes travelers use these outbuildings, but the tower itself has been locked and warded for centuries. Only the magi could enter, and I don't imagine many of them had cause to come here."

The soldiers abandoned the wagons in the middle of the bailey, spreading out to scout the area and inspect the disused stables and barracks. It wasn't long before shouts of alarm followed by the telltale screeches and howls of lyksvight reached Aaslo. A handful of soldiers came running from the barracks followed by the once-human, grey monsters. Crossbow bolts and arrows flew before the squelch of weapons in flesh filled the air. The soldiers, well trained and methodical, were obviously experienced fighters. With an axe blow, Aaslo lopped the head off one lyksvight that had gotten past the soldiers, then headed for another. Soon enough, over a dozen lyksvight lay scattered across the ground in quivering pieces.

"Be on guard for a magus!" shouted Captain Evan as his force fanned out once again.

Ijen joined those scouting the barracks as Aaslo moved toward the motte and rounded back toward the stables on the other side. After a while, Captain Evan approached. "The bailey is secure." He nodded toward the gaping hole in the wall where a gate once stood and added, "As secure as it can be, anyway. We'll need a new gate."

Ijen joined them. "There are no signs of a magus. I believe these lyksvight were a roving band without a leader."

Aaslo looked to Evan. "Send scouts to the south and across the river to the west. I want to make sure there wasn't more to this, considering its strategic location. This won't be viable if the Berru are already on the move from the south." Then he turned to Ijen. "Can you set a stationary ward on the portcullis to keep anyone out until we can rebuild the gate?"

"It won't be a problem." Ijen started to move away, still talking as he went. "In fact, most of the protective runes are still visible.

I will repair those that are broken or missing and then power the enchantment."

"Look at you, being all commander-like. You're getting the hang of this."

"No thanks to you."

"What does that mean?"

"In all of our games, you were always the king or commander."

"You preferred it that way."

"You're right. I did. I still do. But that's no longer an option, is it?"

Mathias said nothing as Aaslo and the soldiers regrouped and returned to the motte to ascend the steps to the tower keep. Overall, the bailey had been in decent order. The sturdy stone structures had a little wear here and there. The battlements and towers stood tall and would only require minor repairs. The buildings would need new doors and thatch, and the wall would require a new gate, but everything was usable. While the open spaces and the moat outside the walls were overgrown, water flowed freely from the tower waterfalls. Aaslo had no idea where the water came from or how it got into the tower, but he assumed it had something to do with magic.

The walls of the tower keep looked to be in better shape, and the keep itself appeared to have been lived in recently. The original furniture had long turned to dust, but newer items had been brought into the great hall. There were a few stacks of empty crates, a couple of mismatched chairs, as well as a table composed of tree stumps and what looked to have once been the bed of a wagon. Clotheslines hung between sconces, clumps of clothing and blankets were scattered like dunes, and one lonely boot lay in the middle of the aisle.

"It feels homey in here. Kind of like living in your mind."

"My mind isn't full of refuse," muttered Aaslo.

"What would you call all that useless information?"

"Any useless information in my mind was forced upon me by you and Grams."

"Vagabonds," said Captain Evan. "Sometimes merchants or other travelers. They use this place to stay over during their travels." He kicked a barrel, which gave a hollow echo. "Sometimes they stay longer."

"And brigands," added one of the soldiers.

"Those too," affirmed Evan with a nod. He toed a bloody mound of fabric near one wall. "But I'm fairly certain the lyksvight took care of anyone who might have been staying here."

Aaslo pointed to the opening at the back of the hall that led to large double doors. These were sealed just as the captain had said they would be. As the soldiers waited behind him, Aaslo inspected the ward that barred entry to the rest of the keep. Aaslo had little experience with wards such as this, and he considered waiting for Ijen.

"Nonsense, Aaslo. You're a big boy. You don't need someone to hold your hand."

Aaslo shook his head as he used a bit of Ina's power to prod the ward. He applied a bit of pressure, and the ward pressed back. When he pressed harder, his power rebounded with equal force. The magi who constructed it had to have been powerful for the ward to have lasted this long, and he wondered what might be so important that it had to be protected in such a way. When he sent his power skittering across the ward's surface he got a sense of its construction. It was an intricate web of power, woven in such a way as to be impenetrable. Aaslo couldn't begin to make such a thing, and he didn't know how to unlock it, so he thought of the next best thing. He would pull it apart piece by piece like untangling vines choking a sapling.

Aaslo used Ina's power to begin plucking at the threads of power making up the web, but for each one he pulled away, another grew in its place. He became frustrated when after ten minutes he had made no progress.

"Tsk, tsk, Aaslo. If at first you don't succeed, have another drink."

Aaslo wasn't much of a drinker, but he suddenly had a craving for ale. "Stop that," he groaned, and a couple of soldiers gave him wary glances.

Turning back to the task at hand, Aaslo once again picked apart the threads, only this time instead of letting them go, he held them and wove his own threads between them so that they would not come loose. He was pleased to find that when he did this, the ward threads did not grow back. After a while, Aaslo's head began to ache, and his eyes burned from the extended focus. He stood back and stretched his neck as Captain Evan walked up beside him.

The captain looked at him with concern. "Sir, are you well?"

"Yes," Aaslo replied, rubbing at his tired eyes. "How long has it been?"

"You have been at this for over an hour."

Aaslo blinked at him in surprise. He had been so focused on his task that he hadn't realized it had been that long. He glanced over as someone else approached, and he recognized Ijen.

The prophet examined Aaslo's hard work, appearing perplexed. "You have constructed a ward. Why?"

Aaslo turned back to the web and realized Ijen was right. He had replaced every thread of the ward with one of his own. "I wasn't trying to construct a ward. I was trying to *de*construct one. The threads kept growing back, so I had to replace them with my own."

Ijen tilted his head curiously as he examined Aaslo's work. "This was an interesting method of doing so. I have never seen anyone do it this way, and I did not know it could be done. It looks successful. Now that you have replaced the ward with one of your own, you can dismiss it."

"Great," said Aaslo. "How?"

Ijen shook his head. "You can replace an ancient ward but can't dismiss your own. Sometimes when I see how much you have progressed, I forget how new to this you truly are." Ijen demonstrated the ward dismissal, and Aaslo followed suit. Then Aaslo stepped through the space where the ward had been and opened the doors.

Within the keep was a massive circular chamber beautifully adorned with mosaics, gilded carvings, and statues of beasts and maidens and warriors. Many doors, set around the perimeter of the chamber, presumably led to other chambers and passages, and interspersed between the doors, tall windows permitted brilliant shafts of sunlight to bathe everything in a warm light. Oddly, no stairs were to be seen, leaving Aaslo to wonder how in the world he would get to the upper levels. Most riveting, however, were four platforms at the center of the room, which attached to a series of cables. Each platform had a railing around the edge and was covered in a mosaic of runes.

"What is this?" said Aaslo.

Ijen examined the odd constructions. "I have read about this place. These platforms are lifts similar to what we used back in Yarding. They are enchanted to rise to different levels of the tower."

Aaslo tilted his face up and realized he couldn't see the top of the tower, but crisscrossing pathways at each level filled the keep and would allow for the lifts to pick up passengers. He dropped his gaze down to his level, and realized there were stairs that descended into darkness below.

"A couple of men should stay here to keep an eye out for lyksvight or other intruders. I'll take a unit down. The rest of you spread out and check the rest of the rooms on this level. Keep an eye out for anything that looks like runes or enchantments."

One soldier asked, "How will we know what an enchantment looks like?"

"Look for symbols carved into the walls, ceiling, or floor. Take special note of any metal or wood inlays."

Captain Evan assigned the units, and Aaslo headed for the stairs behind them. The stones, worn with use, appeared to be in good condition. Still, Aaslo led his men with caution as they descended. His enhanced dragon sight allowed Aaslo to see in the dark, but a few men behind him lit torches collected from the wagons. Shadows danced along the narrow winding shaft as they descended, and a cool breeze wafted up from below. Its low whisper lent the stifling space an eerie chill.

When they reached the lower level, they found a few small rooms, mostly empty, but for one that contained the instruments of torture hanging from the walls. Chains and items with spikes, clamps, and rusted blades hung lifelessly around a raised stone slab stained brown. A series of cells lay beyond the torture room: some enclosed by the natural stone of the hillside; some with broken or missing doors; and others lined with rusted metal bars and filled with shackles pinned to the walls. A few of the cells contained skeletal remains in piles or scattered. At the end of the row, a final stone cell contained walls dotted with runes.

"Poor bastards," grumbled the unit leader. "Are these the markings you were talking about? The runes?"

Aaslo surveyed the carvings around the door and along the walls. He didn't know what they all meant, but he could pick out a few from his limited experience. "Yes, I believe this was a cell used to keep magi. These runes would stop them from using their power."

"Do they still work?" asked the man.

"Maybe, if they're filled with power by another magus."

"Could we use these on the whole fortress? Keep the Berruvian magi from attacking us?"

Aaslo presumed that if it were that easy, the ancient magi would have done that. He wondered how much power it took to prevent another magus from using their power and resolved to ask Ijen. He didn't want to dishearten the soldiers, though, so he temporized, "I'm not familiar with these enchantments, but we'll see what we can do."

"Now you sound like a politician."

"There's no need for insults," groused Aaslo as he made his way back through the dungeon.

He took a hard right into what looked like a natural crevice and was the source of the cool draft. A broken metal grate sat discarded to one side. Aaslo had to turn sideways to fit through the narrow fissure. The constant flow of air chilled his nose and cheeks, and after a few minutes of walking, the fissure became damp with moisture. The passage opened out into a modest chamber. The torchlight sparked off an icy subterranean river, which flowed through the room, and threw reflected light onto the rune-speckled walls. Other than the passage they had taken and the tunnel through which the river flowed, there appeared no other way into or out of the chamber. A stone plinth, smaller but not unlike the one he had encountered at the Citadel of Magi, stood at the chamber's center beside the river. A maze of grooves carved into the floor flowed out in an ever-widening labyrinth from the plinth. Iron inlays within the grooves had somehow not rusted despite the moisture.

"What is this place?" wondered the tattooed unit leader.

Aaslo laid his palm upon the plinth. It was cool and empty of power. The power within him rose to the surface, and Ina whispered promises better left unclaimed. He ignored her bemused pout. "This is good. I had not expected to find this. This chamber powers the enchantments, wards, and protective spells of the fortress. It will be easier to bring them to life after we check them for damage."

The angry fire in the man's eyes belied his outward calm. "I will never understand the magi. There are places like this, places with protections and weapons, yet they left. They abandoned us in the time of our greatest need."

Aaslo nodded in commiseration. He could understand the sentiment. He felt the abandonment most personally and bitterly where Magdelay was concerned. It did little good to dwell on what was or might have been, however, so he simply said, "Those of us who are left will power what we can."

As Aaslo made his way from the chamber, he could hear the men muttering behind him about the magi and the fact that they had only three compared to the great many of the Berru. There was little he could do to reassure them, though, so he remained quiet. Mathias, however, had taken to singing a merry tune in his head, and a singer Mathias was not. Off-key and with lyrics that neither rhymed nor made sense, it grew into an irritation Aaslo could have done without. Unfortunately, the song continued for the next two days while Aaslo worked with Ijen, to repair runes and enchantments, and activate the plinth to power them all.

When Aaslo left the fortress, the small contingent remaining was well protected against magical attacks coming from the outside. Preventing foot soldiers from entering the bailey proved more difficult, since Aaslo knew of no way for the spells to distinguish between the Berru and his own people. If the enemy magi got inside the walls, the enchantments would do little if anything to protect them, making it vital for the Endricsian forces to keep the attackers from breaching the wards. Intriguingly, one set of runes in the pinnacle of the tower keep hinted at enabling some kind of magical attack. Aaslo didn't want to attract attention to their efforts to occupy the fortress, so he didn't dare test it.

Aaslo traveled alone with Dolt through the pathways back to Chelis and their main forces. Being a single rider, it was easier to avoid the threats of the pathways, but he still had to fight a few particularly observant predators. A creature that looked to be a cross between a lion and a bear thought to attack but Aaslo projected a stream of fire at the beast, scaring it off. Somehow, his return to camp didn't take as long as the pathway from it, so Aaslo reached his destination in just over an hour.

For the next few days, he ferried troops and supplies through the pathways to Rendvik Tower, where they prepared for a siege. Aaslo figured it wouldn't take much to draw the enemy into a fight once the Berru learned of their presence. The Berru, after all, wanted to kill them, and gathering their inferior force all in one place would be an irresistible lure.

After that, Aaslo and the marquess undertook recruiting efforts from city to city in the south and east, making stops in Cartis, Lodenon, and southern Mouvilan. A few skirmishes with creatures of the pathways broke out but were quickly subdued. He had gathered another ten thousand by the time they joined the greater army at Rendvik Tower, bringing their number to just over a hundred thousand able-bodied men and women willing to fight for the right to live. Recruiting for an army combined of people from across Endrica was not easy. Many were already dead, and survivors were too frightened or skeptical to join the army. Still more did not trust a man who claimed the dead as well as the living. The dead were an integral part of Aaslo's army, though. They required no food or sleep, and they could continue fighting even after sustaining the most egregious wounds. Abandoning them was not an option.

Joining the greater army had its own set of problems. Even though Aaslo, Teza, and the marquess had worked for months to gather recruits, some individuals in power still failed to see the appeal of relinquishing that power once Aaslo arrived. General Regalis was a reasonable man who understood their circumstances and approached them with sense rooted in reality, but some of the generals, believing they knew better than a forester how to manage a war, were particularly difficult to convince. Aaslo would have been glad to turn the whole business over to the generals, but Teza was persistent. In truth, she had proven herself to be a capable commander, and as one of the last magi in Endrica, she, in her god-inspired silver armor, stood as a symbol of strength and power behind which the army could gather. The title Mage General spread through the ranks as Teza ascended to the position of the army's top commander after Aaslo.

Aaslo didn't mind sharing power with Teza. He had other things to worry about, and he would not be with the army during the final battle anyway. His future was in Celestria, and he had no reason to believe he would return.

CHAPTER 20

PECK PRESSED HIS BACK AGAINST THE WALL AS THE DOOR SWUNG OPEN and the guard strode into the spacious suite. "What is it?" the woman scolded as her hand hovered over her hilt.

Mory stood at the center of the room, wringing his hands. "Ah, I was wondering what I'm supposed to do."

"To do?" the woman said with irritation.

The boy shifted his weight uncomfortably, studiously avoiding glancing at Peck. "Uh, yeah. I'm bored. There's nothing to do in here."

The woman looked around the room but did not turn. If she had, she would have seen Peck slipping toward the open doorway.

She asked, "Where's the other one?"

"Uh, the other one? Oh, you mean Peck. He's sleeping. The empress's questioning was a little much for him."

Peck stifled a mirthless laugh. Mory wasn't lying. The empress wanted to know all about Aaslo and his plans, and Peck's mottled chest had the scars to prove it. He had given her some information, nothing important, to give her the illusion of cooperating. He had otherwise claimed he hadn't been privileged to attend Aaslo's war meetings. He knew the empress suspected he was lying, and there would be quite a bit more *questioning*. He suspected she did the questioning herself simply because she enjoyed it. Peck suffered through the torture for two reasons: one, he didn't have much choice at this point; and two, he took his spying task seriously. He was determined to prove that he was more than just a thief—if not to Aaslo, then to himself.

The guard looked toward the closed bedroom door where Peck supposedly slept, but she didn't move to inspect it. Peck slipped through the open doorway and sprinted down the corridor. As he went, he checked several closed doors, finding them locked. About halfway down, he found one that wasn't and slipped inside just as the guard returned to her post outside Mory's door. She didn't look as if she would be providing Mory with entertainment, and he hoped the boy hadn't endured any abuse for wasting her time.

Peck turned to inspect the room he darted into and found that it wasn't a room at all. To his delight, he had entered the servants' passages. Peck had never stolen from any place opulent enough to have servants' passages, but he had heard of them from his former colleagues in Tyellí. If what he had heard was right, the passages should allow him to move virtually unseen throughout the estate. He would need to avoid any *actual* servants, of course, but servants were better than armed guards.

The passages were easy to navigate, if a bit dusty. Peck didn't know his way around the Helodian estate the empress had commandeered but found tiny bore holes in many of the passages through which he could spy into rooms. Between the map he had drawn in his mind and the spy holes, Peck found the empress's wing after only a few hours of searching. Along the way, he found a store of Berruvian servant livery and threw the robes on over his clothes to fit in with any servants using the corridors. It was unlikely anyone would recognize him since he had only encountered a few guards, the empress, and Sedi. Peck didn't know what happened to Sedi, but she hadn't been seen since dropping them off. He assumed she had washed her hands of them now, having deposited them with the empress.

Peck managed to find the library the empress frequently used, but she wasn't there. He began searching other rooms along the servants' corridor, hoping to get lucky. When he finally happened upon an occupied room that he could see into, it wasn't the empress he found but three men, each wearing a decorated uniform that made them seem important. Their heated conversation was loud enough that he clearly heard them but not loud enough to make out what they said. Peck needed to get closer to learn anything, but he could see no easy way into the room from his location.

He followed the walls with his eyes, searching for any weaknesses. His pulse quickened as he noticed a shadowed part of one wall that had broken away near the ceiling, creating a space large enough to slip through unseen. He searched the servants' corridor for access to the adjoining room, and around a corner he found a disused cupboard. There, he scurried up the shelving into the crawlspace above the room. Then he silently crawled through the hole in the wall, entering the maze of rafters and creeping across the room until he was overhead of the three mysterious men. He could see that they stood over a table covered with papers and scrolls. One with a booming voice stood facing him. He had short, dark hair, an old scar across his cheek, and he wore the uniform of a high-ranking military official. Another man stood beside him wearing the long tunic and loose pants of a Berruvian magus. His long, dark-blond hair was neatly parted down the center. As he spoke, he pointed at the papers on the table with a black-lacquered nail filed to a point.

"General Margus, I've explained to you that we can no longer use their evergates. We will have to continue with the campaign the old-fashioned way—on foot."

The military man, apparently General Margus, clasped his hands behind his back. "Look, Cobin, I hear what you're saying, but there has to be another way. Endrica is a huge continent. A campaign on foot will take years—decades, even."

"It was always to be expected," replied the magus named Cobin. "You can't take the regular troops through evergates anyway."

"What about Sedi?" Margus countered. "She can take the troops through the paths."

Cobin chuckled anxiously. "Good luck convincing her to do that."

"She is as dedicated to the cause as any of us," argued Margus.

"Sedi operates by her own rules and on her own schedule. I doubt she would take kindly to being asked to ferry our troops around the continent. Trust me. You don't want to irritate that one. She could kill both of us with barely a flick of her finger, and she wouldn't feel the least bit bad about it. That one is as cold as the northern range."

Peck caught himself nodding in agreement with the magus, but he wasn't sure everything he said was true. Sure, Sedi had attempted to kill Aaslo on a number of occasions, but she hadn't succeeded, and she hadn't taken out any of his companions. Plus, she had almost been *kind* to him and Mory when she took them prisoner. He thought perhaps there was more to the woman than the magus gave her credit for.

"You make it sound as if she can't be trusted," commented Margus. "Is she even on our side? What does the empress say about her?"

Cobin shrugged. "The empress keeps her own council. Sometimes I wonder if the empress doesn't rule at Sedi's discretion."

The third man, who had his back to Peck, interjected. "You're riding awfully close to treason, Cobin. You'd best watch your tongue." The man spoke with authority, and although his black garb had the look and cut of a uniform, Peck could not place it.

Cobin raised his chin. "Forgive me, Spymaster. I forget myself. But my point stands. This campaign will be waged on foot. I suggest we gather as many horses as we can find."

General Margus released a sigh of frustration. "Good luck with that. Your lyksvight have cleansed the countryside. Most of the herds have surely been loosed, if they haven't been eaten."

"Then we will have to make do with those we brought," the spymaster patiently observed.

"What of those beasts of the Alterworld?" suggested Margus. "Can you not summon more of those?"

"Of course. We have enough prisoners to perform plenty of rituals. We will bring through as many Alterworld creatures as we can. I think a few flocks of flying *vizens* are in order."

Margus groused, "Just keep them away from my men. Last time you brought vizens into Aldrea, I lost five units before we took them out, and that was only two of the creatures."

Peck shivered at the thought of not only being attacked from the ground but from the sky as well.

"We couldn't control them properly at the time," Cobin reassured him. "We know how to deal with them now. It won't be a problem."

Peck wanted to know more about how they *dealt* with these vizens. They could be a valuable asset if they could be turned against the Berruvian troops. The magus said nothing further, though.

The spymaster pulled a scroll tube from his belt and removed its contents before spreading the rolled paper on the table. "Back to the point. I don't think moving on foot will be an issue. The Endricsians have gathered a sizable force at a fortress to the north. I don't know how they're getting their troops there, but reports say they've accumulated over a hundred thousand."

"Pff. A meager show." Margus dismissed the information as he leaned over the table, surveying the paper. "We will crush them in a matter of days."

"Exactly," said the spymaster. "They are gathering as many as they can in one place. We can take them all out at once and make our jobs that much easier. Then we collect the dead, make as many lyksvight as possible, and release them on the continent while your troops mop up."

"It's less work for the empress's machine," Cobin pointed out.

Peck's ears pricked at the mention of a machine. This was the first he had heard of any such thing, and it would certainly interest Aaslo.

"The machine was never meant to cleanse all of Endrica," said the spymaster, stepping back from the table.

"No," replied Margus. "It is meant to cleanse Berru once the campaign on Endrica is finished."

"She doesn't have the power for more," explained the spymaster as he poured himself and the others some drinks at the sideboard.

Cobin interjected, "Have you not heard? She has a new source of power for the machine. There is a boy—an Endricsian boy with the necessary link to death."

"I had not heard. I have been away. She has this boy now?" asked the spymaster, returning to the table.

"Yes, he's guarded in one of the rooms."

"He should be in the cells," said Margus, picking up his drink.

"You question the empress's decisions?" said the spymaster, a sharp edge to his voice.

Margus bowed his head toward the man. "No, of course not. I only worry that he will escape."

"Not to worry about that," said Cobin. "He is only a boy and has no magic of his own."

"We do not want to underestimate anyone, especially if he is so important to the cause. I will talk to her about more *appropriate* accommodations for the boy."

"And what of his companion?" inquired Cobin.

"Companion?" Margus searched his memory. "Oh, yes. He is insignificant and has revealed little. He will be killed, of course."

Peck jerked and nearly lost his balance.

"The empress wanted him to ensure the boy's cooperation," said Cobin.

"I'll make sure the boy cooperates, have no doubt about that."

Cobin shrugged. "If you say so." Peck swallowed hard. If he returned to Mory, he would be killed. He quelled his shaky nerves as Cobin continued speaking. "With this new source of power and the information about the gathering Endricsian troops, the empress may change her plans. A great battle means much death. With that much death concentrated in one place and with the boy to power the machine, the machine could wipe out all the remaining life on Aldrea in a matter of days."

"That soon?" Margus seemed surprised.

A chill suffused Peck as Cobin nodded. The empress would use Mory to power a machine to destroy all life. Peck couldn't allow that to happen. Getting captured to spy had been a terrible mistake. He had to get Mory away.

"What would we need to do?" said the spymaster before taking a swig from his goblet.

"It would not be difficult," explained Cobin, setting down his own drink. "Scattered skirmishes like we've had won't work. We need to lure the Endricsian forces into one massive battle and kill as many as possible while the machine is operational. The machine would need to be in close proximity to the battle, which means the empress will need to be present."

"I don't like the empress being so close to battle." Margus's voice was tinged with concern.

The spymaster replied, "She desired to lead the troops to victory herself. This will allow her to do so."

"Of course." Margus gave a slight bow, although he looked as if he still didn't agree.

Peck didn't agree, either, but not because he cared for the empress. He didn't want Mory near the battle, and he certainly didn't want him powering some kind of life-ending machine.

The spymaster shoved papers aside and began tracing his finger over the map beneath. "If we are to meet the Endricsians in Mouvilan, we will need to cross the river. My people have scouted to the north and south and found the nearest viable crossing here a little over two weeks' march to the north. This location is also ideal, since it is located where the Endricsians have gathered at the old fortress on the opposite side of the river."

"How is that a benefit? They're guarding the crossing," General Margus observed.

"The Endricsians will think they're safe there. They have walls and fortifications, and they'll know exactly where we'll be crossing."

"Again, how does this benefit us?" Margus seemed skeptical.

"One, it isn't too far. Our troops will be relatively rested, and it gives us a good place to cross the river close to the site of the battle. Two, the land there is soft hills and valleys, some forested, and it is near a water source. It would be easy to occupy and the hills south of the fortress would give the empress a good place to set up her machine. Three, we could implement a siege. Our enemy would be gathered in one place, ripe for the picking. We could draw out the death or increase it as needed to power the machine."

General Margus drummed his fingers on the table. "Hmm, I see your point. It is a good plan, and not a bad site for a final battle."

Cobin rubbed his hands together. "I didn't think the end would come so soon."

Peck heard the grin in the spymaster's voice. "Glory to Axus. Glory to the empress. Amongst the gods we will rise."

"Glory to Axus," chorused Margus and Cobin in unison. "Glory to the Berru."

The three men left, and Peck withdrew from the rafters, his heart racing. Aaslo and the Endricsian forces were exactly where the Berru wanted them. Mory was exactly where the empress wanted *him*. And there was nothing Peck could do about any of it. He couldn't return to Mory lest he be killed. Mory would be distraught when he didn't return. Would he think Peck dead or would he think himself abandoned? Peck squeezed his eyes shut and gripped his hair hard enough that his scalp burned. He needed to find a way to get word to Aaslo. The Endricsians were sitting ducks in the old fortress. Most importantly, though, he needed to come up with a method of escape for him *and* Mory. Mory was the key. Without him, the empress would have to power the machine herself, and it sounded like she didn't have enough power to follow through on the plans the men had just discussed.

Peck released his hair and straightened. Yes, escape was the priority. It couldn't come too soon. But where would they take Mory? Would he be able to get Mory out of the cells the general mentioned? Where were these cells? Was there some kind of dungeon on the estate? Peck set off down the corridor, his steps as rapid as his heartbeat. He had to return to Mory before they moved him. If he failed, he would follow Mory to wherever they took him, and then he would find a way to save them both.

CHAPTER 21

THE DAMP, HEAVY AIR LEFT MOISTURE ON THE AGED TOMBSTONES, and the grass felt slick beneath her boots. Sedi swiped a hand over the closest grave marker, brushing the droplets away from the words inscribed there. *Markus Adleman, beloved husband and father.* Sedi remembered loving Markus, although she refused to allow herself any such sentiments now. She remembered the way he carried himself when he walked, always favoring his left leg. She remembered the way he held their firstborn son like a delicate glass ornament, and the way he cried when their third child was laid to rest far too soon. She couldn't for the life of her, however, remember Markus's face, nor could she remember the faces of the four occupants beside him—their children. She knew three of those children survived into adulthood, and two had reared children of their own, but she could remember little else. Time had stripped away the details of their lives.

Her gaze drifted across the extensive graveyard. Time had stripped *all* of these people from her life, for these graves, each and every one of them, were *her* people. These were her husbands, lovers, children, and grandchildren. Every tombstone marked the loss of a loved one, and each of them had claimed another piece of her soul.

Sedi had not visited her personal graveyard in some time, but she found that as she did, she was no longer filled with the dread she once had experienced upon entering it. No feelings of loss or abandonment assailed her—and that made her angry. Sedi was an empty vessel. She had locked away every semblance of love and joy that could be found in a companion and left them to rot here with the bodies of her once-loved ones. She had given up relationships long ago. The brief moments of love weren't worth the despair that came when that love was ripped away.

She didn't know why she'd come here, but she needed to think, and this is where she ended up. Sedi wandered between the graves, her thoughts drifting to the promise made to her, a desperate woman in, perhaps, the initial stages of grief-induced madness. Axus *promised* her an end, but she now knew he would not follow through on that promise. She felt angry, betrayed, and . . . relieved. Sedi paused midstride. Relieved? Why would she be relieved? All she had wanted for a very long time was to be through with this world, with this incessant existence. Suddenly, the thought of leaving saddened her. Despite enduring eons, she now felt there was something she needed to do—that something was unfinished.

All the doubts she had about Axus, about the Berru, about ending life on Aldrea flooded in, and her mind sought solace in something else, something she couldn't quite quantify. She thought of the enemy who continued to evade her efforts to destroy him. Aaslo was intriguing in so many ways, merely human, yet so much more. His power was unlike any she had seen even during her time with other First Order magi. His methods were natural yet crude in a way she hadn't seen for quite some time. She admired his drive to do what needed to be done regardless of being easy or convenient, even if his goals contradicted her own. His compassion, laced with morbid brutality, fascinated her. Aaslo was honest and straightforward with acerbic efficiency, so unlike the duplicitous Lysia.

And their kiss.

She had tried not to think about their kiss. She told herself it had only happened because they had both been drugged, but she knew the truth. She had been curious, and that curiosity had been rewarded—or perhaps cursed. That kiss awakened something she hadn't felt for a very long time, something she had hoped to never feel again. No, it wasn't just the kiss. It was Aaslo. *Aaslo* had awakened her.

Sedi's gaze traversed the endless gravestones of past loved ones once more, and for the first time in a *very* long time, a crack appeared in the armor around her soul. A trickle at first, then a rush; long-banished feelings assailed her. Not feelings of grief and sadness as she might have expected but of love and joy and happiness. As she read the names on the stones closest to her, she felt a resurgence of all the feelings she had held for those people in life. Tears began streaming down her face. As she tried to pull herself together, another niggling thought crossed her mind—a thought about Aaslo. The thought meant the world to her. Aaslo didn't seem to know it yet, but Sedi concluded that he and she were alike in one very important way. She was nearly certain that, by human standards, Aaslo couldn't die.

Aaslo leapt to the side and rolled through the forest detritus, deftly avoiding the swipe of claws before shoving his sword into the creature's black gut.

"Aaslo! Behind you!" shouted Myropa from where she hovered atop a mossy outcrop.

He lunged, sidestepping a tree, and spun just in time to avoid a nasty bite as a second little vight descended on him. They came from all sides now, at least twenty, from between trees and behind bushes. Myropa had already dispatched a good many, but she had been called away mid-battle. Having returned, he hoped she could rid him of the rest. Aaslo was tired. The fast and agile little creatures were difficult to catch. Plus, it seemed that anything less than a killing stroke would quickly mend, and the creature would be back on him a moment later.

Aaslo had been caught alone after leaving Rendvik Tower. He had walked to the copse of trees outside the gates to center himself and think through the tasks ahead. It had been sheer luck, as far as he knew, that Myropa happened upon him as the fighting began. A commotion to his right caught his attention, and Aaslo realized some of his wanderers had finally arrived from the fortress, carving into the mass of vights. Aaslo collapsed to one knee as three of the creatures jumped on him at once. One latched on to his human arm with its teeth and claws while another dug its talons into his scalp. The third couldn't find purchase against his dragon hide along his neck, and Aaslo threw it off.

A flare of brilliant light cast the forest into stark light and shadows, then the vights were torn away into a shifting rift in the air. Aaslo gripped his bleeding arm to his chest as the last of the vights disappeared. Myropa withdrew her power and hurried over to inspect the injury, but of course there was nothing she could do.

"Are you okay? That looks bad," she said with all the motherly intent Aaslo had missed over the years.

Aaslo winced as blood spurted from the wound. "I'll be fine. It will heal itself in a moment."

"You should see Teza. Injuries caused by vights' teeth and claws can become infected and cause death."

"I think it will be fine," Aaslo reassured her, "but I will check with her if it will make you feel better."

She gave him a tentative smile. "Thank you."

"How did you do that?" he wondered, referring to her help with the vights. "Where did they go?"

Myropa shook her head. "I don't know how I do it except that I somehow connect with the power of the Fates. The power tears a rent in space and sends them back to the Alterworld."

"Where did those come from? I thought you said it took an

immense amount of power to bring things from the Alterworld into ours."

"It does, but I think Axus is sparing no expense when it comes to you. He knows you have the depraved. I'm surprised he sent only vights, to be honest. He still underestimates you."

Aaslo clenched his injured hand as a shooting pain surged up his arm. "I don't know about that. He caught me alone. If you hadn't shown up, I would have had a more difficult time dealing with them. There were at least fifty of them to start."

She looked at him thoughtfully as the wounds on his arm began to knit on their own. "Still, I don't think they could have killed you."

"What makes you say that?"

"Oh, it's just a suspicion I've had for a while. Remember when you were buried under that building?"

"Which time?" he said with chagrin.

Her expression became tortured. "The second time. I came there to collect you."

"Collect me? You mean my soul? You were going to reap me?"

"Yes, I was sent to do so. It wasn't my choice, but I had been glad it was me and not some other reaper." She shivered, shaking away a painful memory. "Anyway, I couldn't."

"Because you are my mother?"

"No. I mean, it wasn't because I didn't want to, which I didn't. But I *tried*, and I actually *couldn't* pull your soul from your body."

"What does that mean?"

"I don't know." She shook her head. "With the way your body heals itself and the way you store other souls inside you, I think it might mean you're immortal."

Aaslo looked down at his bloody yet now unblemished arm. "You think *I'm* immortal? And you've kept this to yourself for how long?"

She appeared apologetic. "For a while I wasn't sure, and I didn't want to say anything if it wasn't true. I'm still not positive, but I think you should know it's a possibility."

"*I guess that means you'll have plenty of time to spend in your forest.*"

Aaslo held his hands in front of him as if seeing them anew, and huffed. "Okay, I'm not sure how to deal with that right now, but I don't see what difference this makes in the long run. Even if it's true and I am immortal, the gods can surely overcome that. They are all-powerful, after all."

"I'm not sure that's true," Myropa mused. "It was obvious Axus wanted to destroy me when he found out I had given you the depraved, but he did nothing. I don't think he *could* hurt me for some reason."

"But you said his power still affects you."

"Yes, but I'm starting to wonder if I don't have to be."

"What makes you think that?"

"Just something Disevy said. I don't know. I'm still working through it." Her thoughtful expression turned stony. "Axus has stolen more souls from the Sea. His power suffuses nearly everything in Celestria now, and I fear he is ready to take control. Not only that, but the Berru are readying for something. Their troops have started to march north. I hate to say this, but if you're going to do something, you'd best do it now."

"We have prepared as well as we can against the Berru. But Axus . . ." Aaslo left off what he intended to say because it didn't seem necessary. He was wholly unprepared to face a powerful god, with or without the shades.

Myropa exhorted, "You need to be extra vigilant now, Aaslo. Before you had the depraved, you were merely a minor irritation to Axus. Now that he sees you as a threat, I'm afraid of what he'll do. It's possible the gods *can* kill you. If you truly are immortal, he could torture you for eternity. You can't afford to get captured."

A chill ran up Aaslo's spine at the thought. Aaslo had endured much over the past several months, but he wasn't sure he could handle torture for any amount of time, much less eternity. He would surely become as mad as the depraved. Once that happened, would Axus finally have mercy and kill him or keep him locked away? If Aaslo had learned anything since leaving the forest, it was that there were worse things than death. Aaslo *knew* that Axus was one of them.

Aaslo rubbed his chest as he looked at Myropa. The squirming countdown within him had become nearly unbearable, leaving him with no doubt. "I know it's almost time." He spoke softly.

"Time for what?"

"It's time for me to go to Celestria and face Axus. I can feel it— here." He laid a hand on his chest. "If I don't go soon, I have no hope of prevailing."

Myropa's eyes filled with unspoken feelings. "I'm sorry, Aaslo. I never wanted this for you. As your mother, I just wanted you to live a long, happy life surrounded by friends and family. But, like Mathias, you were meant for something else."

"I was never meant for this. I fell into it by chance."

"I don't believe that," she said before apologizing for having to run off. Somewhere someone was dying, and she was needed. Between the attack and Myropa's revelation, Aaslo felt less settled than he had before going into the small woodland. So much for clearing his mind, he thought as he approached the fortress gate.

"You didn't need a clear mind, anyway. It would make you complacent. You thrive on discord."

Aaslo scowled as he made his way around a large group of men and women conducting drills outside the walls. "I do not. I've always preferred the peace of the forest. You know how much I dislike people."

"I know you've always made it a point to be as difficult as possible around people. What other explanation could there be?"

"It's not me, it's people who are irritating. If everyone was logical and took care of their business, there would be no problem."

"People have feelings, Aaslo. What about joy and happiness?"

"I'm happy in the forest."

"You're happy when your vixen is near." A satisfied chuckle rolled through Aaslo's mind.

"Why would I be happy about that? She's always trying to kill me. In fact, just last week she stabbed me through the heart."

"It was a love stab."

Aaslo's huff drew the sentries' attention as he passed the portcullis, barely noting soldiers and craftsmen installing the new gate. "That's preposterous. There's no such thing. It was an assassination attempt."

"You and I both know she wasn't really trying. I think it's her way of flirting."

"Well, that's a horrible way to flirt."

"No worse than yours."

"What's wrong with mine?" Aaslo spied Teza stalking across the bailey.

"Oh, Reyla, your pale skin reminds me of the bark of an ash tree."

Aaslo frowned. "It was an aspen, and I never actually said that to her."

"Only because you knew she wouldn't know what an aspen was."

Aaslo trudged into one of the many tents occupying the bailey and sat on his cot to shuck his muddy boots. "Of course she knew. I showed them to her enough times."

"Exactly, Aaslo. You had a beautiful, warm-blooded woman beside you, and you spent your time showing her trees."

As Aaslo removed his bloody shirt, he defensively replied, "She said she was interested in my work."

"She lied, Aaslo. She was just trying to impress you because you were a forester."

"I *am* a forester," Aaslo stated as he put on a mostly clean tunic.

"There are two points you need to take away from this conversation. One, you're terrible with women. And two, women lie. Sedi lies. Don't fall for her, Aaslo."

"I'm not *falling* for anyone. And it seems to me that Sedi has been the most honest person I've met. She's always been clear with her intent. She's never hidden the fact that she wants to kill me."

"Therein lies the lie."

Aaslo barked a short laugh as he scraped the mud from his boots and put them back on. "You think she's secretly in love with me?"

"I think she's interested in you, and I think you're happy about it."

"If that's the case, then this is a very messed-up courtship."

"Of course two immortals would be twisted in their ways. It's only natural."

Aaslo removed Mathias's sword from its scabbard and proceeded to clean and oil the blade. "First of all, we don't know that I'm immortal; and second, I'm not twisted."

"Aaslo, you walk around with a severed head in a bag and a corpse army at your back. You're definitely twisted."

Aaslo grunted but didn't argue. Mathias was probably right. Well, a little bit. At the very least, he wasn't normal, but normal people didn't battle gods. *Normal* might make him more friends, but it wouldn't save the world.

CHAPTER 22

THE MORNING AIR HELD A CHILL WHEN AASLO WOKE, AND HE KNEW winter was not far off. If he failed in his mission, though, no one would see the winter. His back cracked in several places as he stretched tight muscles, and he once again questioned his decision to sleep on the stone floor in one of the tower rooms rather than in his tent on the softer grass of the bailey. He made use of the chamber pot someone thoughtfully left then headed out to find breakfast. He followed his nose to the kitchens that they'd found in their exploration of Rendvik. This part of the tower bustled with soldiers and servants clogging the corridor. Men and women pressed toward the dining hall, while others pushed back as they tried to leave. Aaslo was about to give up and find his own food when a heavy hand landed on his shoulder.

"Hold there, Sir Dragon," said General Regalis. "Where are you going? The feast is this way."

Aaslo motioned to the crowd that choked the passage. "It didn't seem feasible."

Regalis laughed, but the humor didn't reach his eyes. He placed two fingers between his lips and issued a long, piercing whistle. The crowd quieted and turned as one to look. Regalis bellowed, "Make way! The dragon is hungry, and if you don't move, he may decide to eat *you*."

Aaslo cringed and Mathias cackled. The general and many of the soldiers had taken to calling him the dragon, and he didn't know how to stop it. There were a few chuckles, but some of the onlookers appeared to contemplate whether or not it was true. Still, the crowd parted, and Aaslo and the general passed into the dining hall outside the kitchens. The hall was large, but it had not been designed with a force of this size in mind, even with the majority of the army being stationed outside the walls to the north of the fortress. This kitchen served mostly officers and support staff, and of course, it lacked tables or chairs. Everyone who had a plate sat on the floor in a dense mass that made it difficult to navigate through the space.

Eventually, Aaslo was served a plate of eggs and potatoes with no seasoning, but it was hot and better than he had expected. When he finished, he handed his plate to a young man who collected them and turned to Regalis.

"So, General, how go things with the army?"

Regalis's expression sobered. "Hold that thought. We can talk about this privately."

Aaslo followed the general out of the dining hall and down the short corridor to the room with the lifts. Regalis opened the platform gate and motioned for Aaslo to join him. Aaslo hesitated for a number of reasons as his gaze turned upward to search for the ceiling he couldn't see.

"Come, Sir Dragon, Prophet Ijen assured me this is perfectly safe."

"And if you fall, you can sprout wings."

"I don't have wings," groused Aaslo.

"You most certainly do. I've seen them. They're made of fire."

"You don't need wings to use the lift," replied Regalis. He placed his hand on a large dial on the back of the platform. "We just select your level and pull this lever. I've used it several times already. It works perfectly."

Aaslo begrudgingly stepped onto the platform, and Regalis closed the gate to prevent any falls during ascent. Regalis turned the dial to the right, as far as it would go, then pulled the lever. The platform slowly began to rise then accelerated until the floors sped by in a blur. Aaslo tried not to look down, but his gaze traveled there anyway, and his head began to spin. He closed his eyes and steadied his breathing as the platform slowed.

"How did you ever climb all those trees if you're afraid of heights?"

"I'm not afraid of heights. I just don't like being dependent on magic to hold me up."

"Believe me, I'm with you," said Regalis, "but I am surprised to hear you say that, you being a magus and all."

As the platform came to a stop, Aaslo explained, "I'm still getting used to having power. I'd much rather depend on my own arms and legs."

He and Regalis exited the lift on the top floor of the tower and found Teza and Ijen standing together in deep discussion. They glanced his way but did not break off their hushed conversation.

Glass windows overlooking the vast expanse of hills and valleys lying between Helod and Mouvilan enclosed this level of the tower. The river that separated the two countries flowed southward in the distance, and the overcast sky threw a shadow over all.

General Regalis approached the northern window and pointed. There had gathered, beyond the base of the motte, an army of a hundred thousand Endricsian men and women, dedicated to the fight for life. "See, there's our army. It looks orderly, does it not?"

Aaslo saw the tents and wagons positioned in neat rows with plenty of room between to maneuver. Open spaces held companies drilling or practicing simulated battles. Supply stations were stacked neatly with crates and barrels, and even the horses were picketed in symmetrical rows or kept within the hastily built stockade.

Aaslo affirmed, "Yes, General. It is impressive."

"Almost as nice as mine would have been."

The general nodded. "As pretty a camp as I've ever seen, and yet it will not be enough."

"What do you mean?" Aaslo threw the general a sharp look.

"I mean this," said Regalis, crossing the room to one of the many oddities in the tower.

A brass pole as tall as Aaslo stood before each broad window, and a hollow ring about the size of a dinner plate topped each. Handles stuck out from the sides of the rings, and runes covered the rings and poles. The general chose the pole nearest the window facing southwest.

"What is it?" Aaslo watched with curiosity. "Are these the weapon?"

"You'll have to see for yourself." With a nod toward Ijen and Teza, the general explained, "They got them working less than an hour ago. You'll need to use your power to operate them. Use this one." He gripped the pole in front of him.

Aaslo didn't know what the device would do, so he looked to Teza and Ijen for direction. Their conversation ceased, and Ijen nodded to Aaslo. Satisfied that the device probably wouldn't blow him up, Aaslo filled the runes with power. The pole began to vibrate before settling into a low hum. Then the air within the ring shivered like ripples on a pond, and the window it faced showed an image that was not there before. At first, Aaslo had difficulty interpreting what he saw, then he recognized hills and trees. They were much larger than they were a moment ago.

"It's like this," Regalis instructed Aaslo. "Use the handles to move the apparatus side to side. Wherever the apparatus points will show in the window. Push the handles forward to make things far away larger. Pull them back to see nearer."

Aaslo played with the device for a few minutes, making things farther and farther away seem near. He even caught sight of an elusive herd of corvaks grazing between two copses of trees that had to be miles away. The corvaks spooked and darted away, and Aaslo panned away to see what startled them. That's when he saw cavalry coming over a hill.

"There, see? This is what I wanted to show you." Regalis pointed at the view on the window. "Look farther in that direction."

Aaslo pushed the handles forward, focusing on a black blob in the distance. It looked as though the earth had been scorched for miles and miles. His chest seized with the realization that it was not scorched earth—the black blob was an army. The farther he pushed the handles, the larger the army grew. He swung the device side to side to reveal still more army. In fact, he could not find the ends of it. Men, horses, war machines, and monsters from another realm covered the vast swath of hills and valleys. He saw monsters with sharp fangs and claws and monsters with long necks and tails and spikes running down their backs. Some of the creatures were wrought with muscle and as large as a house, while others, small and quick, darted between the legs of the larger creatures. Even the sky held horrid winged creatures that did not belong on Aldrea.

"Well, it looks like I'm about to have a lot of company."

The food soured in Aaslo's stomach as he looked out at the most dreadful sight he had ever seen. Regalis, too, looked at the window, and his dour expression mimicked Aaslo's own.

"Why didn't you say anything?" asked Aaslo in a quiet tone.

Regalis's voice was gruff. "I didn't want to tell you on an empty stomach."

"If you're going to vomit, I suggest doing it all over his boots."

"That is far more than five hundred thousand," murmured Aaslo. "How many do you think there are?"

Regalis shook his head. "It's hard to say. We cannot see the end of it. There could be a million, maybe more."

Aaslo looked at Regalis in shock. "How could they have so many? How could they bring them across the sea? And why did we not know?"

The general shrugged. "The intelligence has always been poor when it comes to the Berru, but it is apparent we vastly underestimated them." His flinty stare met Aaslo's gaze. "The situation is dire. We cannot win. We will be lucky to hold out for a few days once they attack."

Teza walked over and spoke. "We will hold out for as long as is necessary."

"Necessary for what?" replied Regalis.

"For you to unleash your dragon."

"For Aaslo to defeat Axus," Teza calmly stated. "If Axus falls, the Berru will have no reason to continue killing."

"That's a big assumption," replied Regalis, skeptical.

Teza crossed her arms. "It's an assumption I can live with. The alternative is too terrifying. Maybe we can't win, but we don't need to. We just need to hold them off."

Aaslo gripped the edge of the table. He looked into Teza's trusting eyes and saw hope there. She placed her faith in him, and he did not want to disappoint. Teza had become more than a travel companion to him. She was his friend, and Aaslo could not endure the thought of losing another friend. "If we cannot win here, I have no choice but to take the fight to Axus as soon as possible. I should leave immediately—before the Berru arrive. Every minute wasted now means lives lost later."

Regalis looked at him in disbelief. "You truly believe you can take on a god?"

"I believe that I must try."

CHAPTER 23

AASLO'S BODY SHOOK WITH THE SQUIRMING MASS OF URGENCY IN HIS chest as he stepped into the muddy quagmire churned up by the countless footfalls, wagon wheels, and hooves on the fortress grounds. The dampness of the air outside gathered on his skin, and he wiped his brow before the condensation could drip into his eyes. He secured his axe to the harness across his back then checked his sword. It was Mathias's, and it was only fitting that it should accompany him into the final battle. Of course, Mathias would also be accompanying him, since his head still rode in the sack tied at Aaslo's other hip. The weight brought him both comfort and misery.

Mathias's company was essential, though, as the task ahead would be daunting to say the least. Aaslo ate a filling meal, but not too filling. He drank a good amount of water but not too much. Though he'd slept as much as he could the previous night, he woke feeling groggy. As he checked and rechecked his saddlebags, Aaslo tried not to think about what he was about to do.

"You're stalling."

"I'm going into a complete unknown. It's pertinent that I have the right supplies."

"You won't be needing a bunch of supplies. You're going there to kill a god or die, not survive for months on end."

"You never know what you might need until you need it. An extra root won't rot the tree, but the tree may rot without the root."

"What does that even mean?"

"It means it's better to have it and not need it than to need it and not have it."

"What makes you think any of those supplies will be of use in Celestria?"

"I don't know that they won't be."

"Well, you've checked them five times. You have them. It's time to move. It's time to fulfill my destiny."

Aaslo patted Dolt's flank as he walked around the horse, checking his hooves. He made sure the bit was seated behind his teeth properly. Then he tightened the cinch on Dolt's saddle once again before releasing a heavy sigh. He *was* stalling, and it was unbecoming of a forester.

"Can Dolt even exist in Celestria?"

Aaslo froze. He hadn't considered that. It was possible the horse-that-was-not-a-horse *couldn't* exist within the realm of the gods; there was no way to know, and Aaslo thought his mount might be needed. He had no idea how big Celestria was or how far he would need to travel to find Axus. Dolt wasn't really a horse, though. He was a wind demon, a being that existed between realms. Aaslo figured if anything could exist in Celestria besides the gods it was Dolt.

"He's too stubborn not to exist," stated Aaslo.

"He's perfect for you." Mathias cackled, then abruptly sobered. *"Why are you really stalling?"*

Aaslo's first thought was that he was heading into near-certain death, but he knew that wasn't why. It wasn't that he was going to another realm but that he was *leaving* this one—and those he would leave behind. His gut churned as he found the truth hidden inside him. "I'm worried."

"Of course you're worried. You're going to face a god in his own realm."

"No, that isn't it," Aaslo replied with newfound certainty. "I'm not worried for myself. I'm worried for my friends."

"Since when do you have friends besides me?"

"Since I've been on this journey. I actually care about what happens to them. I won't be here to protect them, to help them. I likely won't see them again, and I'll miss them."

"I never thought I'd see the day when the great Forester Aaslo wanted to be with other people."

Aaslo scowled but didn't argue the point. It was true. He had never before wanted to be around anyone but Mathias, his father, Magdelay, and his intended. This desire for the others' company was new and a little disconcerting. But he couldn't stay, and they couldn't go with him. "I don't know how to say goodbye."

Mathias's voice was full of genuine concern. *"You need to work on that, Aaslo. It's one thing to carry someone in your heart. It's entirely different to carry them in a sack tied to your belt."*

Aaslo winced and mounted Dolt. He plodded over to his companions, who had gathered to see him off, but had quietly given him time to accept what he was about to do. He nodded toward Andromeda, stared at Ijen for a moment to see if the prophet might impart some knowledge, then tilted his head curiously at Teza's challenging expression.

"Don't die, Aaslo," she admonished. "Remember the goal is to kill Axus, not get yourself killed."

"I'm aware of that." He arched a brow.

Teza rested a fist on each hip. "And don't take too long." She waved a silvery hand at the army encampment. "Every minute Axus lives is another minute people will be dying here."

"No pressure, though."

Aaslo nodded in understanding. "I'll do my best. Just try to keep things together as long as you can."

Concern clouded her gaze, and she crossed her arms. "Don't worry about that. People want the security of being with the army. There won't be any deserters. I still think you should take the shades with you."

Aaslo shook his head. "No, you will need them here. The Berru are innumerable. Besides, I can draw on their power through our bond without their physical presence. Having them here keeps them out of Axus's hands."

Ijen reminded him, "Axus knows you have the shades, and he will do what he can to stop you before you reach him. You may find your way more difficult than anticipated."

"Is this prophecy?" Aaslo asked.

Ijen shook his head. "No, merely deduction. I *am* capable of thinking for myself, you know."

Aaslo grunted. "Well, I am not anticipating my journey being anything but extremely difficult."

Ijen sniffed. "More like impossible."

"Ah! Someone else who has faith in you."

Aaslo scowled at the prophet. "Not helpful."

With a final nod, Aaslo turned from his companions. He left unsaid so many things because he couldn't—*wouldn't*—accept that they would not be reunited. He summoned his power and opened a pathway. Even though he had never opened a pathway to Celestria, Arohnu and Enani's blessing placed the knowledge in his head. Aaslo's heart beat furiously as he prepared to enter the rift into the land of the gods. With sweating brow and clammy hands, he took a deep breath, lifted his foot to kick Dolt into motion, and—

"Wait!"

Aaslo's heart lurched. "What is it?"

"It's just that I don't know if you'll be able to hear me once you're there. I wanted to say thank you."

"For what?"

"For taking me on this journey."

Aaslo swallowed the lump in his throat and held back the tears threatening his eyes. He choked out, "You're welcome," then stirred Dolt to enter the portal.

CELESTRIA WAS SUPPOSED TO BE A MAGICAL PLACE, AND WHILE SURELY beautiful, it had no more appeal than the forests of Goldenwood. The brilliance of the colors that described *everything*, even in the darkness, failed to impress Aaslo. The ripples of moonlight sparkling on the stream were lost on him, and the heady nectar of flowers suffusing the air was but an afterthought. Enormous land masses with sharp, soaring spires, floating in the sky, dripped with waterfalls that made moonlit rainbows. Aaslo saw rolling hills, thick copses of trees, and a sky suffused with stars that looked like diamonds spilled across the night, but nothing about this place could break the dread pooling in Aaslo's stomach. Dolt shifted beneath him, then shifted again. Suddenly, the horse reared, throwing Aaslo from the saddle. He struck the ground atop his axe with a shout. Then he rolled over in agony as Dolt danced around him.

Once the damage to his spine had healed, Aaslo sat up to watch the quirky equine who seemed so pleased with himself. Dolt whinnied then paused. He swished his tail frantically before ducking his head. A pair of giant wings erupted from the horse's back. The great feathery things gleamed white in the moonlight but had large brown splotches. They were just as ugly as the rest of the horse.

"Holy buckets of gold, Aaslo. Your horse has wings!"

"I can see that." Aaslo blinked rapidly at the sight. "Do you think he grew those himself or was it something about this place?"

"Maybe he wanted to emulate his rider."

"I *don't* have wings."

"I beg to differ, dragon-man."

Aaslo wasn't going to complain about Dolt's wings, though, since now his mount could fly. He had taken the dragony changes to his own body in stride and, at times, with intense frustration, but somehow seeing Dolt with wings left him speechless. He could only imagine that this would be a great advantage, assuming Dolt ever allowed him to remount.

Dolt flapped his new appendages, growing accustomed to them, while Aaslo surveyed their surroundings. They were in a gully between two rocky hills. Thick green grass and low-lying plants covered the landscape, and shimmering boulders trailed along a stream bank.

A pretty little creature that looked to be a cross between a bird and a moth fluttered wistfully over a smattering of glowing wildflowers, but it seemed any other wildlife might have gone into hiding, and for good reason. In the distance, flickering lights illuminated the starlit sky. Aaslo heard explosions echo down the gully, and every so often the ground shook with the force, dislodging small boulders from the sharp rock faces.

As Aaslo stood watching the commotion in the distance, he felt a chill, as if something watched him. Not wanting to alert potential attackers, Aaslo casually surveyed the outcrops and shrubs. He didn't see anyone, but he could feel an ominous presence. The air, thick with the power of the gods, contained a subtler, more sinister presence overlaying that. Aaslo stepped closer to Dolt, hoping to snag the reins, but Dolt remained just out of reach.

"Behind you!"

Aaslo spun and ducked as a blade slid through the air where his head had been. At first, Aaslo could see nothing more than the swinging blade. The curved silver of the blade glowed with reflected moonlight. Aaslo backpedaled, shifting to his dragon sight—no, not one but *three* attackers. They wore black from head to toe, each wielding a curved blade mounted scythe-like on a long shaft. His assailants moved with inhuman speed. He dodged the next two attacks, but a third clipped his hamstring as he drew Mathias's sword. He limped back, but in the time he parried and dodged two more attempts, his leg healed.

Two attackers leapt at him from either side, and he rolled backward, dodging their attempts to take his head. He raised his sword in time to block the first strike, but the second came at his unprotected side too fast to avoid. The curved blade sliced into the flesh but glanced off his rib. Aaslo didn't have time to experience the pain before the blade swung around for another pass. He blocked the next strike and caught the haft of the first attacker's weapon as it descended. By then, the third attacker came at him. Aaslo knew he would be overwhelmed if he didn't put some space between him and the assailants.

Aaslo reached for his dragon power, and in an instant a ring of flames pulsed from him in every direction. The three assailants fell back, ducking and diving, to avoid the flames. Before they could recover, Aaslo drew his axe and threw himself at the first attacker. He hacked with the axe and stabbed with the sword simultaneously, impaling the attacker twice over. Before he could withdraw his weapons, though, the assailant vanished. Only a pile of black fabric remained. He had no time to consider what had happened before the second and third attackers were on him.

Swinging the axe with enormous force, Aaslo came within an inch of taking the second attacker's head. Unfortunately, the assailant dodged in time to avoid the first one's fate. The third barreled into Aaslo from the side, tackling him. Aaslo lost his grip on the sword but managed to bring the axe down onto the assailant's back. The attacker disappeared, leaving Aaslo tangled in black clothing. He lurched to his feet and turned to face his final attacker, who seemed undeterred by the demise of its comrades. The assailant came at Aaslo in a rush, and on a whim, Aaslo sent a blast of fire. When the fire cleared, only a billow of ash remained. He surveyed his surroundings with his dragon sight, breathing hard, but Aaslo saw no one.

Aaslo jerked when bumped from behind, and he spun, only to find a wet muzzle in his face.

"Thanks for nothing," he complained as he grabbed Dolt's bridle.

Dolt simply bobbed his head as if saying, *You're welcome.*

Now that he was closer, Aaslo surveyed Dolt's new wings. He realized the saddle's design didn't accommodate wings and it had been dislodged during their development. If he wanted to ride, it would have to be bareback. Even so, he used the blanket and several leather straps to create a sort of harness to wrap around the base of Dolt's wings, looping over Aaslo's legs. At least, he hoped, it would keep him from falling off and plummeting to his death.

"You could always fly yourself."

"What are you talking about?"

"You have wings, remember?"

"I was trying to forget. They're made of fire. I don't even know if they work."

"You'll never know unless you try."

Aaslo groused under his breath as he considered Mathias's suggestion. The fact that he had wings just reminded him he wasn't really human anymore. The more he tried to forget his *enhancements*, the more they were shoved in his face.

After several unsuccessful and, frankly, embarrassing attempts to mount Dolt without a saddle, Aaslo finally accomplished the feat. He secured his legs in the long loops of the harness and fixed his pack on his back. As he kicked his horse into motion, however, the idiot simply started walking. Aaslo had no idea how to tell Dolt to fly or even if the horse *could* fly.

"Dolt, *fly!*" he called out.

Dolt bobbed his head and kept walking.

"No, dimwit, use these." He patted the base of the wings.

The horse flapped his wings in response but kept walking, only now he walked in circles.

"Maybe if you show him how it's done."

"I am *not* flying," growled Aaslo.

"That's not very forester of you, Aaslo. A forester should accept what is and cannot be changed. You aren't being very accepting."

Aaslo huffed. Mathias was right, but he still couldn't make peace with the fact that his body was no longer *his*. It was something else—something foreign. He sighed. "I guess we're walking." Then, to Dolt, "Stop going in circles." Yanking the reins, he added, "Come on, you ornery beast. Go this way."

Dolt smacked him in the head with a wing, but at least he stopped walking in circles. They headed toward the fighting in the distance, as it seemed like the best place to start. Aaslo had no idea where to find Axus, but he knew Axus could find *him*. The attack by the three assailants hadn't been random. It had been targeted, and it had come immediately upon Aaslo's arrival in Celestria. He knew he would need to be extra vigilant, but vigilance was hard when he didn't know what to look *for*. Were the three assailants creatures created by the gods? Were they actually gods themselves? They had been excellent fighters but didn't seem particularly powerful. They hadn't used any magic and were thankfully averse to fire. He doubted his next opponents would be so easily overcome.

"It isn't that they were easy, Aaslo, it's that you're just that good."

Aaslo was taken aback. "What?"

"You can likely best any human opponent, magus or not. You've become a formidable warrior, and you have power beyond reason."

"I'm just a—"

"Forester? We both know that's not true. You've become so much more. You're probably more powerful than I would ever have been."

"*You* were the chosen one. *You* were meant to fight this battle."

"Not this battle. This war has become yours. You are powerful. Accept it."

"But is it the *right* power? Is it enough to go up against a god?"

"If it isn't, then I'll be seeing you soon."

This last, Mathias said with such cheer, Aaslo almost wished it to be so. Aaslo didn't seek death, though. Not in that way, anyhow. The only death he sought at the moment was Axus's. As Aaslo rode nearer the battle, the tightness in his chest unclenched. It was odd that as he got closer to battle, he became *less* anxious. The rocking of the ground and the booming in his torso became stronger as he rode, and Dolt began flapping his ugly wings as if considering taking to the air. Upon cresting a ridge, they came to a halt.

There in the distance, Aaslo saw the battle—or rather a *war*—underway. Three large buildings each topped a hill, and if he strained his dragon vision, he thought he could make out more buildings in the distance. Even though it was night, the constant barrage of magical strikes that streaked through the air illuminated the sky as if it were day. When one landed, the ground shook with the force of it. He noticed glowing people down amid the rubble. Some looked to be of normal, human size while others were massive like the giants of legend. They wielded all manner of weapons against each other, and they often fell beneath the blades and bludgeoners only to rise again.

Aaslo's heart raced at the sight of the vicious battle. He tugged on the reins, angling Dolt down the hill, and prepared to kick him forward when a deep, resonant voice stopped him.

"I wouldn't go down there if I were you."

Aaslo drew his sword and turned. Dolt wasn't so graceful, though, as he fumbled with his wings in an effort to turn his body quickly in response to Aaslo's prompting. A battle steed he was not.

There, upon the hill, bathed in the glow of the battle, was a god. He towered over Aaslo and Dolt, and his fathomless gaze belied the subtle hint of power radiating from him. Aaslo slowly lowered his weapon as he realized he knew this god.

"Arohnu." He gave a hesitant greeting.

Arohnu tilted his head toward Aaslo, but his gaze remained on the battle.

Aaslo asked, "Why should I not go down there?"

Arohnu shrugged. "What would be the point? You can do nothing. You don't even know which ones are on your side. You would just get yourself captured."

"You insisted I come here. What should I do?"

"You are here to face Axus, not fight in that pointless battle."

"Why is it pointless?"

Arohnu raised one eyebrow. "We are gods, Aaslo. We cannot die. At least, not by each other's hand."

"So, what? It's a distraction?"

The god nodded. "In part. We can be captured, even imprisoned. But, mostly, it's a way to keep the other gods busy while Axus attempts to steal their power."

Aaslo looked at Arohnu skeptically. "What about you? You are not fighting?"

"We all fight in our own way. I defy Axus by being here with you."

"Well, how do I find Axus?"

Arohnu gave Aaslo a knowing look. "Can you not feel him?"

Aaslo took note of the power he felt suffusing everything in Celestria. It was even stronger now that he was closer to the battle. Yet, still, a darker force overlay, something that didn't quite belong.

"You *can* feel it," said Arohnu. "I see it in your eyes."

"It's . . . *sinister*. Is that because he's the God of Death?"

"Oh, no. There is nothing innately sinister or *wrong* with being the God of Death. It's what he *does* with his power that gives it that dark, oily feel. He steals power from others. Power taken does not have the same feel as power given freely."

"So, if I follow his evilness, I will find him?"

Arohnu nodded again. "He knows where you are, though. You have not learned to restrain your power well enough to hide yourself. He would never admit it, but now that you are here, he sees you as a threat. He may seek to delay you, or he may try to avoid you, but thanks to his actions, he can no longer hide from you."

"Why isn't he going after Axus?"

Aaslo had been thinking the same thing, so he voiced Mathias's question. "Why is Axus *my* responsibility? You all are gods. Why don't you deal with him?"

Arohnu sighed. "It is as I told you before. He has gained a following. He has made promises. Too many other gods support him now." He nodded toward the battle. "They are busy *distracting* us from confronting Axus together. More importantly, we cannot end one of our own. We have tried in the past. The power does not allow for it. The best we could do would be to imprison him, and his supporters would free him. Our greatest chance of ending this is for *you* to face him."

"Can I win?"

"That remains to be seen, but I think you have a chance."

"Well, can I do it without dying?"

With a shrug, Arohnu told him, "Dying should be the least of your worries. If Axus defeats you, you will suffer a fate far worse than death."

"Lovely," muttered Aaslo. "Do you have any *useful* information?"

"Not particularly. Just know that you are not alone. There are others, others who care about you, who are fighting just the same. Do not despair."

"Easy for him to say. He's not the one risking eternal suffering."

"Must you say it like that?"

"What would you rather I say?" inquired Arohnu. "Have hope?"

"It's the same thing."

Arohnu gave him an odd look. "That's what *I* thought." He raised a finger and stopped as if listening. "I have called for you a guide. She will be here shortly. Good luck."

Then the god vanished, leaving Aaslo alone to watch a battle he couldn't fight atop a winged horse that wouldn't fly searching for a god who wanted to torture him for eternity.

He caught a flicker of motion in the corner of his eye. He hefted his axe and spun, prepared to fight. Myropa, his mother, stood before him, more solid than he had ever seen her. More solid, even, than in the pathways. She seemed surprised to see him, but her gaze went to the awkward wings that stood askew on his horse.

"He has wings!" she blurted.

Aaslo hooked his axe through the loop on his pack. "Not that it does any good. He doesn't know how to use them."

Myropa looked to the floating islands in the sky. "You will need them if you are to get where you're going." She stepped forward and brushed her fingers down the horse's muzzle. She wore a pleased smile, and Aaslo wondered how long it had been since she had felt the sensation. "Maybe he just needs to be asked," she said.

"I tried that," said Aaslo. "He didn't cooperate."

"But did you *ask* him, or did you *order* him?" She gave him a knowing look.

Aaslo huffed in frustration. "He's *my* horse. I shouldn't have to *ask* him to do anything. He's supposed to do what I say."

Myropa stroked Dolt's mane as she replied, "But he isn't really a horse, is he? I think he's more sensitive than you know, and he certainly has a mind of his own."

Aaslo shook his head, then addressed a more pertinent subject. "Where do I need to go? Where is Axus?"

Myropa's smile fell. She stepped up and threw her arms around him. When she pulled back, she whispered, "I don't want you to face him. I'm afraid for you."

He held her hands. "I know, Mother, but I have to, and it would be much easier if you show me where to go."

She dropped her gaze and nodded sadly. "I've never gone the long way. It is some distance from here, and you will need to fly to get there. Perhaps you could try again with Dolt."

Aaslo heaved a sigh, then through gritted teeth, he addressed his horse. "Dolt, will you please fly us to our destination?"

The horse released a series of snorts that Aaslo strongly suspected was a laugh. Then Dolt tilted his wings so that Aaslo could mount. Once seated with his pack secured in front of him and strapped into the harness, he pulled Myropa up behind him. He riffled through his pack and produced a length of rope, which he instructed Myropa to wrap around herself before securing it to himself.

Aaslo urged Dolt forward, and this time when the horse gained speed, he spread his wings wide and began to flap. After a few great gusts, the sound of hooves disappeared, and they took to the air. Dolt's mane whipped around in the wind, and Aaslo gripped it tightly just as Myropa held him. As they rose in altitude, Aaslo's stomach dropped, and he thought he might be sick. The foreign sensation of flying through the air so far above the ground and the sight of the clouds from above overwhelmed him. Closing his eyes and breathing heavily through his nose, he waited for the sensation to pass. After a moment, he opened his eyes again, and what he beheld was nothing short of amazing.

Celestria truly was a marvel. The moonlight and the stars bathed everything in a soft, silvery glow. To the east, an enormous structure twisted into the sky like an ancient, gnarled tree the size of a mountain. Spiky protrusions emerged from its curves, each tipped with a bright, glimmering light. To the south a sea of pillowy clouds was crisscrossed with glowing vines like a tangled net. The north held darkness so deep even Aaslo's dragon sight could not penetrate it.

Myropa stretched out a shaky hand and pointed west. "There," she shouted over the wind. "Axus's domain is there."

The hills and mountains Myropa had indicated were steep and sparsely forested, but between the clumps of trees, Aaslo saw another forest, one of crystals so grand some of them spanned the height of ten men or more. They jutted from the glimmering sand at all angles, their vitreous faces reflecting and refracting the starlight perfectly to cast a dazzling display of colors. As they drew closer, he noticed that at the crystal forest's center, atop of a foothill, lay a palace composed of a multitude of crystals in an array of colors and shapes. It glowed softly in the night like a beacon guiding home long-lost travelers.

"But it's so beautiful and inviting," he said in awe.

"Such is the power of death," replied Myropa, her voice tinged with anguish.

"She's not wrong."

"Beyond the palace and gardens, there in the mountainside, is Axus's maelstrom. Don't go there. It is the center of his power. If you face him there, you will not be able to withstand him."

Aaslo eyed the dark fissure in the rock face, which looked decidedly less inviting than the illuminated palace. He urged Dolt toward the palace, but he was pretty sure the horse-that-was-not-a-horse guided himself. Dolt's hooves clicked on the crystalline surface as he landed in a relatively clear area near their destination. Aaslo helped Myropa to the ground before he dismounted, then he drew his axe as he searched the immediate area for threats. The broad crystal faces of the pillar-like prisms reflected his image in the moonlight, and on more than one occasion he startled to action only to recognize his own face looking back.

When he rounded a large cluster of crystals, a heavy weight knocked Aaslo to the ground, pinning him. He struggled to budge the toppled crystal only to realize it not only moved, but it was attacking him. A thin shard stabbed into his chest. The lung collapsed and black splotches blanketed his vision. Aaslo worked to free himself in agonizing pain before he lost consciousness. He blinked rapidly, his dragon vision narrowing on his attacker. His assailant's body lacked the light he usually saw when looking at an animal, so Aaslo knew this thing to be different. Its body seemed to be made of crystals in the form of a scorpion. Its front pincers clamped onto Aaslo's arms as it withdrew the thin shard of its stinger from his chest.

Aaslo's blood poured from the gaping wound and sputtered up his throat as he wrestled against the monster. Then something massive crashed into the crystalline scorpion, throwing it from him and into the large cluster of crystals jutting from the ground. Aaslo blinked away the sweat and tears in his eyes as he watched Dolt smash through the monster, easily his equal in size. Myropa gripped Aaslo's shoulders and helped him sit up as they watched the battle play out. Every time Dolt's hooves struck the scorpion's crystal carapace, the crystals fractured with a resounding *boom*. Dolt abruptly reared back, and with one final, mighty blow, the scorpion shattered into a million flashing fragments.

Myropa pressed her hands to Aaslo's wound, but he gently pushed her away. "It's fine," he said as he finally took a deep breath. He tugged at his torn, bloody shirt. "See? It's already healing. It'll be good as new in a minute."

"I hate to see you hurt."

"Then she needs to stop looking, because you can't seem to stay out of trouble."

"At least I heal quickly," murmured Aaslo.

"Thank Arayallen for that."

"You think?"

Myropa stood back as he got to his feet. "Who else? The body is her purview."

Aaslo kept his eyes on the surrounding crystal forest as he collected his axe from where it had fallen. Meanwhile, Dolt approached and nibbled at his hair as if asking if he was okay. Aaslo patted the horse's neck, begrudgingly thanking him for the help. Then he collected his waterskin from his pack and drank deeply. He knew he could heal quickly, but he wasn't sure how long it would take to replenish the blood lost. When he finished, he replaced the skin in his pack. "Come. That battle was not quiet. They likely know we are here."

Aaslo readied his axe, gripping it tightly, as he led the way through the crystal forest toward the palace. As they went, he asked, "Who should we expect inside the palace?"

From behind him, Myropa thought before answering. "I don't know. I've never been there, but I would expect maybe a handful of lesser gods and minions."

"Minions?"

"They're soulless servants. They do only what they're trained to do. They have no will of their own."

Aaslo pushed a crystal branch out of his path, causing it to fracture. "When I first arrived here, I was attacked by three people in black. They did not seem to have any magic and disappeared when I defeated them."

Myropa stepped over the downed branch. "They were probably minions."

"And the lesser gods? How worried should I be about them?"

Myropa gripped his arm as her slippered feet slid over a slick surface. "Their powers are weak compared to the other gods. They have no dominions of their own. I expect it will be much like fighting an ancient magus. I don't know if you will be able to kill them, but you can at least incapacitate them."

"If they don't incapacitate you first."

"Will you be able to help me?" Aaslo scaled a steep incline then pulled Myropa up after him.

"Don't I always help?"

Myropa placed a hand on his back as he continued to lead the way. "I have no power over the gods, only creatures of the Alterworld."

"Why is that?" Aaslo stepped around a barrel-shaped prism in his path.

"I don't know. It's just something I can do. I don't even remember learning how to do it. But I will help if I can."

Aaslo paused at the edge of a courtyard leading to a palace entrance. As he surveyed the open space, devoid of crystals, he whispered, "I know you will, but I don't want you getting hurt. If things go badly, I want you to leave me."

Myropa whispered back, vehement, "I can't do that, Aaslo. You're my son."

"You're asking too much of her. Would you have left me?"

He turned to look at her. Her eyes glimmered with tears in the dark. Although Aaslo had never known her as a mother, he had come to think of her as a friend, and he couldn't stand the thought of something bad happening to her. "You can and you will. If nothing else, maybe you can find someone to help."

Myropa swallowed then nodded as she blinked away tears that abruptly froze and dripped from her eyes like the crystals around them. "I will do as you ask, but only as a way to help you."

CHAPTER 24

A GLOOMY FOG HAD SETTLED OVER THE HILLSIDE, LIMITING VISIBILITY to a mere dozen feet. Teza couldn't even see the river that flowed less than a mile from the fortress. She sighed and turned away from the tower window. She had no doubt the enemy would use the fog to hide their progress. Although she was certain the generals were on top of it, she felt the need to see to the preparations in person. She had pushed to be placed in charge of the army, and now she was beginning to regret it. Her muscles were tight with tension as she considered that as Mage General, she was responsible for every life under her command. The pressure was getting to her.

She finished putting on her armor, a surprisingly simple affair, thanks to the godly magic imbued within it. It locked into place, forming to her perfectly, giving her an ease of movement uncharacteristic of ordinary armor. It was also virtually silent, which made her grateful as she ran lightly down the winding staircase.

The command center in the grand hall of the tower keep was bustling. The generals, three of them in total, and Commander Andromeda hunched over a map on a table built of tree stumps and an old wagon bed.

General Regalis looked up. "Any sign?"

"No," Teza answered. "That doesn't mean they aren't there, though. With all the fog, I can't even see the river."

He grumbled, "At this rate, they'll be at our front gate before we even know they're coming."

"Don't worry about that." Ijen approached the table. "Teza and I set alarms along the route to the river crossing, not to mention a few other nasty surprises. We will know as they make progress."

"Ye be assuming they cross the river there," General Barbok commented. He was a Lodenonian who had spent more time at sea than on land yet had somehow risen to the rank of general.

General Nangent of Helod reached across Barbok and thumped the map. "They must cross here. There's nowhere else to cross without first building a bridge."

An alarm went off in Teza's head, and she knew the discussion was moot. "They've begun the crossing."

"I felt it, too," Ijen confirmed. "They will be here soon."

As the generals and Commander Andromeda barked orders to various pages and messengers, Teza spun on her heel, rushing to the bailey. Ijen matched her pace as they descended the stairs.

"What do you intend to do?" he inquired politely.

Teza gave him a sidelong look, breathing hard and wishing he wouldn't chat. She wasn't out of shape, but there were *a lot* of steps. "I'm going to find a way to see the enemy."

"I've been thinking on this, and I have an idea," Ijen began.

"Well, out with it."

"Loris Deretey and Jillian Mascede."

"The shades?"

He nodded sagely. "Yes, Loris's power is incendiary, while Jillian's is the opposite. We can use their powers to shift the atmospheric conditions to eliminate the fog."

"That would take a lot of power and wouldn't even harm the enemy," Teza pointed out. "I'm not sure it's worth the expense."

Ijen shrugged. "We could use shield wards to localize the effect. It shouldn't take that much power to reduce the fog in the immediate vicinity of the bailey and far enough beyond to force the Berru to cease their progress."

Teza mulled the advantages. "It's a good idea. We won't be able to see their entire force, but if we can at least see to the river, then we can enact our plan."

Having reached the bailey, Teza found the shades gathered in their own area of the barracks. The other troops wanted nothing to do with them. When Teza looked at them, she wondered if they shouldn't have been separated from each other as well. Echo and Avra both appeared the worse for wear, but at least they had not started flinging their power between them. Peter stood off to the side, plotting against all of them, and Jillian and Loris were wrapped around each other as usual. Aen ignored everyone until he saw Teza, at which point he leapt up and approached her excitedly. He appeared lovestruck as he gazed into her eyes, waiting for her to speak. Teza ignored him as she called out to Loris and Jillian.

After relaying the orders to burn away the fog, she hurried from the barracks as quickly as possible. When she was a few dozen feet away, ducking and dodging troops and supplies, she realized Aen was still with her. "Go back!"

He paused as if unsure about following her orders then grinned and stayed with her. A chill went through Teza as she understood how tentative her hold on the shades was. She tried to ignore him as she watched Jillian and Loris climb the steps to the wall. To her, they were mere shadows in the fog as they stood atop the bulwark to either side of the gate. She couldn't see what they did, but she began to feel a hum in the air that slowly built inside her chest like the cadence of a drum.

Aen became more alert, and Teza clenched her teeth as she considered the immense power being wielded by the two unpredictable shades. After a few minutes, moisture began to bead on her armor and droplets from the sky pattered on the dewy ground. Soon enough, she could see the two shades casting atop the wall until finally the fog had cleared. Then a horn blasted from one of the lookout towers. The enemy was within sight.

Teza hurried back up the steps to the tower. Ijen joined her in the foyer and entered the lift with her. Generals Nangent and Barbok stepped onto the platform along with a few pages. General Regalis did not accompany them as he had joined the troops in the field. With everyone aboard the lift, they shot to the top with urgency. After quickly accessing the magical viewers, they saw that the Berruvian army had indeed crossed the river and was still doing so. It was a narrow ford and would probably take two days for the entire army to cross, so they had plenty of time to activate their spell traps.

Teza held up a talisman she had linked to one of the spells she had erected at the river. The talisman was little more than a stick wrapped on each end with a piece of fabric painted with runes. She had only to break the stick and the spell would activate. She glanced anxiously at Ijen, then looked back to the image in the window showing a group of soldiers herding wolflike monsters across the river. Easily three times as large as a normal wolf, the beasts had wiry, jet-black fur, sharp horns protruding from their skulls, and spikes running along their spines. They sent a shiver along Teza's.

She placed her hands on either end of the talisman then snapped it in two. Instantaneously, men dropped as sharp spears of water surged from the river to impale them. The wolf creatures, loosed as their handlers fell, began to run, but the spears were many. Teza's spell continued for several minutes before finally running out of energy. Nearly everything crossing the river was killed, and the water ran red.

Once Teza's spell had dissipated, they waited for another wave of Berru to begin crossing. It did not take long, as their taskmasters appeared to be driving them hard. Teza could see several instances where men on horses whipped soldiers who didn't march fast enough or who got in their way. Teza knew the Berru had conscripted many

Endricsians into their army, and she hoped that given a chance those men and women would flee or turn against their oppressors.

When a large enough force was crossing the river, Teza said, "Do it."

Ijen brushed a spell over a murky sphere that fit in his palm before placing it in a small sack. Then he threw the sack on the ground and stomped on it. As the glass crunched beneath his boot, another spell was released. The water in the river began to oscillate, back and forth, in waves. Soon the waves were large enough to crest. The crests transformed, becoming sharp as razors, as they propagated through the throng of soldiers and monsters. The razors sliced through legs and torsos, taking both man and beast apart.

After the second attack, the forward momentum of the army stalled, and several magi came to the front. The magi remained safely on the bank as they inspected the river, and Teza smiled. Then she reached up and tore a leather thong from around her neck. This released the next spell, one that spelled doom for the enemy magi. The ground along the bank shivered, liquifying. As it began to swallow the magi, the less-than-loyal soldiers retreated to a safer distance. The magi cast spells, trying to save themselves, as they struggled against the liquid earth; the river formed sharp protrusions, stabbing through their bodies. Soon enough, the magi were dead and buried beneath the bank.

An hour later, Teza and Ijen had exhausted all their traps, and they had barely made a dent in the Berruvian army. Still, they had drawn first blood, so Teza counted it as a win.

AASLO TURNED TO THE ENTRY TO THE PALACE. LITTLE MORE THAN the vertex between two adjoining crystals, it had a glass-like door. On the other side, he saw the shifting shadow of perhaps a sentry standing guard.

Aaslo looked back to his horse. "All right, Dolt. You're up."

"What do you plan to do?" whispered Myropa.

Aaslo patted Dolt's muzzle. "I need you to use those powerful hooves of yours to break through that door. Will you do this for me?"

"*So much for subtlety. You might as well use your magic to blow the door apart.*"

Aaslo had considered doing that but decided to conserve his power. He hoped Dolt could and *would* accomplish what he asked.

Dolt bobbed his head up and down as if he understood. Aaslo

dearly hoped he did, because they would bring the whole palace down with the commotion. Then Dolt turned and walked the other way.

Aaslo hissed, "Stop, you ornery beast! The door is *that* way."

"He's Dolt. You knew this wouldn't work before you asked."

An abrupt pounding thudded in Aaslo's chest as Dolt's heavy hoofbeats surged across the courtyard. The horse collided with the glass door in a burst of light. The shattering of glass and a cacophony of shouts from within echoed through the cool night air, and Aaslo ran through the entryway, swinging his axe.

The first minion fell inside the doorway before Aaslo got a look at him. Surprisingly, although the minion had the body of a man, he had the head of a lamb. Aaslo didn't get a long look before fighting off another attacker who leapt over the staircase banister in the open foyer. Meanwhile, Dolt faced off with three assailants who slashed at him with crystalline swords. Dolt swung his wings to great effect, keeping his attackers at bay. Aaslo dispatched his own attacker quickly before turning and throwing his axe into the monstrous face of one of Dolt's assailants. Then he drew Mathias's sword and laid into another minion.

Aaslo didn't know whether to be relieved or sickened that none of the minions appeared human. Like the first minion, their bodies were human, but their heads were all manner of creatures, most of which he had never before seen. He killed two more before he spun to find all their attackers accounted for. Dolt had killed three, and they lay in broken heaps.

Breathing heavily, Aaslo sheathed his sword and retrieved his axe. He nodded to Myropa, who carefully made her way around the dead, then turned to the staircase. Blue-flamed sconces and lights glowing from the crystalline ceiling far above illuminated the steps. They had entered the palace through a side door into a grand foyer of silvery blue crystals that stretched floor to ceiling. The crystalline floor became treacherous once blood had been spilled. Soft blue light suffused the cavernous chamber from recesses along the walls and across the ceiling, and the seductive hum of a lilting melody filled the air. The broad staircase twisted and split into two directions before rejoining in the center at the top of the landing.

Aaslo took the path to the left with Myropa carefully ascending behind him. Dolt's clattering hoof falls could be heard on the staircase to the right. They met in the middle at the end of a long, broad corridor lined by tall glass windows on either side. A scarlet-and-gold carpet ran up the center of the hall, and dozens of glowing orange orbs, each the size of a peach, floated in the air over their heads of their own accord.

After a single step an arrow abruptly struck Aaslo in the shoulder. He jumped in front of Myropa to shield her and was struck by three more arrows in the torso and thigh. He yanked the arrow out of his thigh, and with a cry ran down the corridor toward the archers at the other end. He knocked several arrows aside with his axe but dearly wished he carried a shield as he took two more to his chest.

"Magic, Aaslo! Use your magic!"

Aaslo cursed himself for an idiot needing to be reminded of the power he wielded. He raised a shield ward then sent a bout of flame toward the archers, incinerating three on the spot. The remaining three jumped out of the inferno's path. Aaslo's chest felt shredded as he fought for breath against the arrows embedded there. While Dolt trampled two of the archers, Aaslo took down the last, then dropped to his knees and hunched over, struggling to breathe.

"Here, let me help." Myropa leaned over him, took the shaft of an arrow in her hands, and snapped off the feathered end. Then she shoved the arrow the rest of the way through his chest. Aaslo nearly lost his stomach. The second arrow had struck where his dragon scales met his flesh and had not gone so deep, and so she yanked it out the way it had gone in. It bled profusely. Myropa methodically dislodged the remaining arrows, while Aaslo focused on not passing out.

"You could have avoided this if you'd used your magic. So much for all that forester wisdom."

"I know," he wheezed. "I just didn't think of it in the heat of battle."

"Not remembering your greatest weapon will be your downfall."

Aaslo swallowed back bile as Myropa removed the last of the arrows, and then he could breathe again.

Myropa admonished him, "If you don't stop getting hurt, you might die of blood loss before we even find Axus."

"I thought you said I couldn't die."

"It was a hypothesis. I don't know that for sure."

"I forgot to use my magic. It doesn't come naturally, but I won't forget again."

"Which is why I encouraged you to practice your magic more."

Myropa looked at him with motherly compassion. "It was a painful lesson."

"That it was," he grunted as he regained his feet. His head swam, so he reached out to steady himself and caught one of Dolt's wings.

He thought the horse would dump him on his rear, but Dolt stood surprisingly still as Aaslo captured his balance. Aaslo removed his shredded, blood-soaked shirt and tossed it aside. The scales on his torso's left glittered in the warm light, and for a moment, Aaslo wished for his *entire* chest to be covered in the protective armor.

At the end of the corridor stood three doorways, all of which were too small for Dolt. Aaslo turned to the horse and removed the makeshift harness. "You can no longer accompany me, and I'm not likely to come out of this alive. Consider yourself free. Go."

Dolt gave him a withering look that told Aaslo he was an idiot and rolled his big, mismatched eyes. The horse turned around and stretched out his wings, filling the corridor. Aaslo got the feeling Dolt intended to guard their rear. He muttered a thanks as he took the central passage, and Myropa followed. Axus's malevolent power was drawing him to it. He felt the same seductive darkness when he used the power of death to raise his wanderers, only this seemed magnified, more, a mountain of concentrated power in one place—and that place was Axus.

Aaslo drew his axe, following the passage to where it ended at a stairwell curving up. The power of death coiled around him, calling to him, and his own dark power stirred. It wanted to consume it. He wondered if his own meager power over death could compare to that which Axus wielded.

It was hard to imagine facing off against a *god*, and his knees weakened at the thought. He nearly missed a step, and he stopped to steady his nerves. He did a quick survey of the powers inside him. There was the dark power of death, the nurturing power of Ina, and the fierce rage of the dragon—and the power of the shades. With the thought of those, his shoulders relaxed. Disevy had said the power of the depraved could potentially kill a god, and Aaslo felt the connections to the shades at his core.

Myropa looked up at him and laid an imploring hand on his arm.

Mathias pulsed in his mind. *"You can do this, Aaslo."*

With a steadying breath, Aaslo ascended the last of the steps to the highest landing in the tower. Axus stood before him. He had never seen the god before, but Aaslo had no doubt it was him. The power radiating from him made Aaslo feel that he was drowning in a sea of death. His knees buckled, and he dropped his axe as his hands broke his fall. Aaslo shook uncontrollably as he strained his neck to look up into the satisfied glare of the glorious god.

Axus stood with his hands clasped behind his back without a hint of concern for any attack. He wore no armor. His chest was bare, and a thick fur wrapped around his waist reached to his knees. His sandals laced up his calves and left no room for hidden daggers. So far as Aaslo could tell, the God of Death had no weapons at all save for the crushing power that brought Aaslo to his knees.

Aaslo heard a whimper behind him and managed to turn his head enough to see Myropa curled on the floor. As he watched, she forced her arms to stop shaking and met his gaze. Through clenched teeth, she spit out, "Fight it, Aaslo. You must *fight* him!"

Axus barked a laugh as he took a step forward. He closed the distance between them and looked down on Aaslo. "You are but an insect." Then he placed his foot on Aaslo's chest and, with minimal effort, pushed him over.

As Aaslo lay sprawled on the floor, Mathias sighed loudly in his mind. *"Get up, Aaslo. Now is not the time to lie around."*

Aaslo struggled to erect a magical shield around himself as he growled, "I *can't* get up."

"Of course you can't," declared Axus as he sauntered across the room, which Aaslo could now see held a single item at its center. It appeared to be a massive, glossy black stone that reached from the floor to the god's waist.

"You can *get up. It's all in your head."*

Aaslo reached for the first power to present itself, which happened to be Ina's nurturing power. It surged with joy at his call, and he managed to create the shield ward around himself and Myropa, though it did little to deflect Axus's power. Aaslo wondered if he wouldn't need to use the power of death against Axus. So Aaslo allowed the dark power to fill him and layered it against the shield. The crushing force of Axus's influence released him. Aaslo reached out and grabbed his axe as he leapt to his feet.

Axus paused in his pacing and frowned at Aaslo. "It is no matter. You hold no power against me." He flicked his wrist and thrust Aaslo to one side, slamming him against the wall.

Myropa shouted, "No!" as she hurried over to help Aaslo.

Axus warned, "Reaper, you are not welcome here. Return to Trostili and confess to your traitorous ways." He flicked his hand again, and Myropa vanished.

"What did you do to her?" Aaslo bit out.

Axus gave a frustrated growl. "What *can* I do to her?" Then he added, "I merely sent her away where she cannot interfere. I want to enjoy the things I'm about to do to you without listening to her sniveling."

Aaslo set his feet, allowing the power of death to fill him as he tapped into the power of the shades. They came alive at his core, as if waiting for his call. One by one, the power of each suffused him, and Aaslo became stronger and more aware. He experienced other unfamiliar things as well. He had always done what needed to be done, but never before had he felt a thrill for upcoming battle. Now, excitement, even elation, filled him for the chance to strike. To tear into something, *anything,* to rend flesh from bone, to crush anything and everything into pieces and scatter them across the land. The exquisite *need* to wreak havoc. Aaslo lashed out at Axus with brute force, pure and unrefined.

The blow swept the god from his feet to slam him against the wall, which fractured under the impact. Axus appeared shocked, but Aaslo gave him no time to recover before berating him with more powerful strikes. Axus rallied, surging to his feet and sending a blast of power back at Aaslo. Aaslo's feet left the ground as the counterstrike tossed him into a wall. The force threw Aaslo *through* the wall into an adjacent room before he slammed into another wall. With a groan, Aaslo recovered his feet and shook himself. Then he caught hold of a single strand of the shades' magic and released it on the god. A raging inferno scorched the room, but Axus's power deflected it.

Axus lashed back with a ball of black power. It smashed into Aaslo and began to eat his flesh. Aaslo's dragon roared with fury and sent a scorching inferno across his own skin. The black power burned away and flaked off into ash carried away on an air current.

Aaslo grasped another strand of power, and with its release on the heels of the inferno, a blast of sound shook the tower with a strength Aaslo feared would topple it around them. Great ruptures in the tower's structure caused the walls to crumble and the floor to buckle. A chunk of the ceiling crashed down between Aaslo and his foe, and the tower rocked on its base. Axus became enraged as his power pulsed against the wail. The god thrust his hands forward, the power again throwing Aaslo from his feet, except this time he did not stop. He crashed through an outer wall and fell through the air to certain death below. Abruptly, Ina's power of creation entwined with the dragon's inferno, and a massive pair of flaming wings sprouted from Aaslo's back. He instinctually and erratically flapped, slowing his uncontrolled descent. Then, slowly, he began to rise. Aaslo struggled in his direction for a moment, but soon closed in on the tower level where Axus awaited.

As he flew, Aaslo gathered the collective powers of the shades, allowing them to run freely, through him, as he directed the power at Axus. Then, as soon as Axus came into range, he released it in a torrent. The god struggled to rise beneath the deluge of power Aaslo poured out. Aaslo landed on the tower platform and stalked closer as he continued pressing the power onto Axus.

Axus knelt at Aaslo's feet, his face contorted in agony as his own power was overwhelmed. When Axus pushed back, Aaslo slammed it down with hardened will. Axus writhed on the floor before him, his suffering almost too difficult to witness. Aaslo drove every last bit of the shades' power into the god. He didn't let up as he released the final thread of power, and Axus froze. Icy frost spread through the room, covering the floor, walls, and ceiling. Aaslo didn't hesitate. He ran forward with a cry and slammed his axe into the frozen flesh of the god, shattering Axus's head from his body.

Slipping on the ice, Aaslo stumbled back in shock. Had he killed the God of Death? It happened so fast. Aaslo slumped against the glossy black rock at the room's center as he stared at the headless body in disbelief. Before he could catch his breath, though, a warm, golden glow began to pulse within the frozen shell of the god. It gradually spread throughout the body, escaping through the open neck. Aaslo closed his eyes against the incandescent flash. When he opened them again, Axus stood whole and unblemished before him. The God of Death wasn't dead, but he *was* livid.

Axus held out a hand, and power slammed Aaslo back into the dark rock behind him. Aaslo hauled his powers to the fore as he struggled against Axus's unchecked power. The god closed the distance, and Aaslo's body reabsorbed his wings as he squirmed beneath the power pinning him to the rock. Axus's face twisted in sadistic pleasure as Aaslo's arms and legs sank into the obsidian-like stone. Then the god was in his mind. Aaslo felt the icy dread of death and wanted nothing more than to embrace it. Axus whispered sweet promises: of release from a life of struggle, of the end of all pain and suffering, of eternal rest. No longer would he have to fight and suffer. He could be free of all that the world required of him. He could let go and join Mathias in the Afterlife.

The powers inside Aaslo awaited, eager to heed his call, but he no longer focused on them. The sweet seduction of death enfolded his mind just as the stone entombed his body.

"Aaslo, snap out of it! Fight back. You don't want to die this way."

"What other way should I die? This seems as good as any and better than most."

"Do you hear yourself? You don't want to die. You want to live. You want life to continue on Aldrea."

Aaslo heard Mathias's words, but thoughts of a distant world he could barely imagine at that moment provided little incentive to overcome the heady power suffusing his mind.

"You don't want Axus to win. He killed me, Aaslo."

Mathias's words came as a gut punch. Aaslo's vision cleared, and he faced a gloating, all-too-pleased Axus. Thoughts swimming, Aaslo wrapped his own power over death around his mind, shaking away the god's influence. Gritting his teeth, he resumed his struggles against the rock that enveloped all but his head. Now encased, he couldn't move or gain a magical hold on the glossy black stone.

Axus stalked toward him, growing larger as he did. The god loomed. "You may have broken my binding, but you will never escape this imprisonment. I have more important things to do than play with you. When I am finished ravaging your pitiful world and have gained control over all of Celestria, I will return to show you what happens to those who defy me. Until then, I will leave you with something to remember me."

He spread his fingers and placed his hand upon the black stone. It began to vibrate, sending pulses of sharp, shooting pain through Aaslo's body. Aaslo couldn't help the wail that escaped him as his nerves ignited with fire. Later, when he was too tired to scream, he realized the god had gone. The pain became a constant hum as Aaslo drifted in and out of consciousness.

"Aaslo . . ." whispered a sound he hadn't heard in some time. Or had he? He couldn't remember the last time the voice visited him. Pain exploded at the base of his skull and blackness engulfed him.

"Wake up, Aaslo."

There it was again, he thought as he drifted awake to a searing shock.

"Aaslo, fight it. Use your power."

Power. Did he have power? He couldn't remember.

"Use your power to block out the pain."

Was that possible? He would do anything to free himself from the unending assault on his nerves and muscles that seeped deep into his bones. He collected as much consciousness as he could and focused this so-called power. He could remember, now, that he did have some special abilities, but he still couldn't remember what they were. It didn't seem to matter, though, because another mind jumped to the fore. Consumed by anger, it wanted nothing more than to incinerate everything in its path. It longed for the hunt and the joy of consumption that followed.

Aaslo started to reach for that power when another slid into his grasping hands. This one tittered playfully as she whispered that *she* was the one he sought. Only she could bring the relief he desperately needed. Aaslo didn't care where the relief came from, only that it took away the agonizing pain. He latched onto the seductive power and drank it in. It unfurled and slid as soothing oil across his nerves, and for the first time in an unimaginable while Aaslo felt the cool void of relief.

After several minutes of basking in the void, his mind cleared, and Aaslo grasped his condition. His mind was free, but his body remained trapped in a small mountain of solid stone. Not just any stone, though. Aaslo felt something special within the stone, something unique to Celestria, something filled with the power of the gods. The powers of the shades had gone, exhausted in the fight against Axus—the fight Aaslo lost; but, he had other magic. He unleashed the dragon's power as he pounded it against the stone. He was rewarded for his efforts with a throbbing headache. He switched to the power of Ina, and when that didn't work, he tried the dark power of death. Nothing he brought against the stone worked to loosen its grip on him. He was well and truly trapped. Even Mathias remained silent as Aaslo hung his head.

CHAPTER 25

For two days the Berru had been outside the gates of Rendvik Tower. Teza didn't know what prevented their attack, but she had watched them erecting two connected rings made of stone atop a hillside beyond the mass of troops. Large pillars had been arranged in a circle, with fabric draped between them, hiding the activity within. She could only assume they needed the stone rings for some kind of ritual, but she found nothing in the book Aaslo had given her to determine what it might be. A few spies had been sent to gather more information, but, to her dismay, none had returned alive.

Teza drew her gaze from the stone circles and turned back to her own troops. Her armor reflected errant rays of light breaking through the clouds as she walked down the line, surveying the soldiers. She couldn't see the entire army, of course, most of whom were entrenched behind magical shields beyond the fortress's northern wall. Of all those who survived in Endrica, only these hundred thousand understood what was at stake. They were outmatched. Berru brought untold numbers to the field, and they had magi as well. But Teza had something the Berru didn't. She had the shades, a few hundred wanderers, and she had the *Contract*.

The Contract wasn't something that had been tested. Nearly every recruit in the army had accepted *The Contract* so that if—or when—they died, they would rise to serve again in Aaslo's undead army. Guided by Ijen, and apparently by Ina as well, Aaslo infused *The Contract* with power via ritual so that anyone who signed it while alive would be affected upon their death. Their power—their souls—would go to Aaslo so that they could become wanderers even if Aaslo wasn't present to claim them. How could they test it without killing one of their own? Ijen seemed confident it would work, and Teza had placed her begrudging trust in the prophet.

So Teza's army was greater than it appeared, but their greatest advantage lay in death, just as Ijen had prophesied all along. Down Aaslo's path lay death, and the world would never be the same. Teza's heart had already begun to mourn these hundred thousand souls, most of whom would be dead—or undead—by the end of the battle. If Aaslo fell before the battle ended, all would be lost.

Teza shook off the dark thoughts. She had to be strong, positive, before her troops. She had to show them the strength of the magi, the strength of Endrica, the strength of life. Despite her more and more frequent doubts that she wasn't fit to serve as mage general, she put on a brave face. She looked over to Ijen, who was busy scribbling in his book. With all the care and concern she could muster, she said, "Ijen, it could well be that we have very little life left. You need to put the book away and *live* for once."

Ijen turned his unfathomable gaze upon her. "The book brings me comfort. It gives order to what would otherwise be a chaotic world."

"Oh, I suppose that makes sense." She hadn't considered that Ijen might *need* the book of prophecy to maintain his composure.

With a nod, he closed his book, tucked it into his tunic, then strode away from her. Once he had reached his position, Teza turned back to the troops before her. She illuminated a magical, shining beacon above her and began to stride past the ranks of recruits in the bailey while Ijen did the same from the other end. She wanted to remind these brave soldiers that the magi were with them.

When Teza returned to her position on the wall, she looked across the battlefield once again. They had the upper ground, but the Berru seemed endless. The Berruvian regular troops were trained and armored, their magi rested; their lyksvight salivated hungrily, and the other *things*, the creatures from the Alterworld, were barely restrained. If the Endricsians somehow prevailed, this would be a battle for the ages. She would not shy away.

Each morning since they had arrived, the Berru took up positions as if to attack, and each morning they broke ranks an hour later. This morning wasn't any different, until a horn sounded across the field. The troops gathered behind Teza and atop the walls shifted uncertainly. Teza raised her silver fist, and a similar horn answered from behind her. This day, the Berruvian tide surged forward. Teza's heart thumped wildly as she waited until they came into range, then she dropped her fist and another blast resonated behind her. Arrows and flaming boulders swept through the air and into the Berruvian ranks. After the first volley, half a dozen horrifying creatures took to the air from the Berruvian encampment. The beasts looked like vultures with long, scaly tails, and they were twice the size. They carried round objects gripped in their talons, but Teza could not identify them until they began to drop from the sky. Upon impact with the ground troops, the bundles exploded, sending shrapnel flying for tens of yards in every direction. As the archers targeted the birdlike creatures, Teza and Ijen erected hasty shield wards above the soldiers.

The Berruvian swarm neared the moat when, from the other end of the line, Ijen gave Teza the signal she had been awaiting. They combined their powers to cast a spell utilizing the energy building in the clouds overhead. The energy raced across the sky then streaked toward the ground as a dancing troupe of lightning bolts that sizzled throughout the enemy ranks. Metal weapons and armor carried the energy over the field in a dazzling display of light and death. Hundreds fell and yet the swarm persisted. Teza breathed heavily, knowing she would need to rest before trying a spell of that magnitude again.

After several harrowing minutes, the Berruvian front line attained the moat. Endricsian archers targeted the men who rushed forward with heavy planks to span the moat, but as they fell, more men took up the task. Teza had ordered the shades to positions along the walls, and with dread she put them to use pushing back the enemy forces. Men at the center cowered as Echo released a blasting wail that ripped flesh from bone and tore apart the enemy's catapults. To the left, Peter Sereshian released the power of decay, and, with desperate cries, the Berru crumbled where they stood as their flesh sloughed away. To the right, Avra *disassembled* anyone who approached, blowing them apart into tiny pieces that drifted away on the wind.

The incoming wave faltered, but the fighting pressed on. Eventually the bodies of the dead clogged the moat, and a stream of men crossed to the wall. Hot pitch rained down on their heads, and soldiers screamed as they blistered and burned. Ladders and ropes were raised and pushed back by the Endricsians again and again until finally the Berru succeeded in gaining the walls. The nearly hundred thousand Endricsian troops stationed to the north of the fortress split around the structure to flank the Berru on both sides. The wanderers, the first line of defense, took the brunt of the attack, but Teza's people began to fall not long after. Teza and Ijen sent splintering attacks at the ladders, shattering them and sending the men plummeting to their deaths. A horn sounded from the tower, and Endricsian men and women rallied. The shades' powers of ice and fire spread across the field. Monsters and men froze where they stood or were reduced to ashes in seconds, blasted by a blazing inferno.

The battle raged, seemingly endlessly, as troops and monsters fought on in a gruesome dance of death and destruction. As the Endricsian troops fell, they rose again to fight in death, and so their numbers changed little. They eventually fought off those who had topped the wall and no more followed.

Just as the gates were about to be breached, a horn blast came from the enemy line and the Berru let up a little on their attack. They didn't fall back, they just didn't advance. It seemed they intended to stretch the battle out for as long as possible. A relative hush settled over the rear of the Berruvian force. During the lull, the Endricsian troops treated the injured, gathered supplies, and regrouped. No one tended the dead. They had lost nearly half their living forces. Teza's gut clenched for her people who had already died, but morbid hope surged through her as those fallen friends began to rise again in death to fight once more.

Tactically, the shades were their greatest loss. Just as the battle ebbed, all six weakened and—shockingly—lost their powers, as if they had been drained at once. The loss of their powers didn't appear to be caused by anything the enemy did, so Teza dearly hoped that meant Aaslo was to blame. She felt confident he would succeed in his battle against Axus. He had to. There was no other option.

THE BERRUVIAN FORCES LET UP ON THEIR ATTACK, BUT THAT GAVE Mory little comfort. His heart hammered like thunder as the guards grabbed his arms. The drums of death pounded in his ears and through his chest. The sudden rough treatment was an ill omen, and he knew something terrible would happen. He didn't protest as they dragged him from his tent, but they jerked and shoved him anyway. They didn't speak. They wouldn't even look at him. They prodded him, their eyes hard and empty, down the aisles between the neatly spaced tents and up the slope to the small hilltop. Mory had the unnerving sense that he marched to his death. He wasn't sure if he was terrified or relieved that Peck wasn't with him. He didn't want Peck to see him die again. It would break him.

Where *was* Peck? Was Peck even alive? Had they taken him to the executioner's block? No, it couldn't be. The empress said she needed Peck alive to ensure Mory's cooperation for *something*. She hadn't required anything of him yet, so Peck couldn't be dead. He hadn't seen Peck for weeks, though. He left their rooms at the Helodian estate to spy on the empress and never returned. Mory was sleep-deprived, although that might be due to his greatly diminished accommodations. The hard stone slab in the cell they moved him to wasn't ideal for sleeping. And it was cold, almost as cold as death, Mory thought. Perhaps Peck got caught lurking and they thought he had been trying to escape. Was that what prompted his transfer to the cells? Mory couldn't let himself believe that Peck was dead. Surely, if he were, someone would have mentioned it.

His suspicions were confirmed a few minutes later when they entered the ring of stones erected by the troops upon their arrival. Mory had never seen its like. Dark, diaphanous fabric hung between the pillar-like stones. The lengths of fabric swayed in the breeze and a soft, subtle light filled the circular structure from what little sunlight broke through the clouds. Gleaming, bespelled torches anchored to the stone pillars also illuminated the circle. Within, six wooden tables made a circle, each with a man or woman lying prone and unclothed upon its surface.

No one moved, and Mory realized they were all dead, their life's blood having been drained from their bodies to flow down ruts in the ground toward a small pool in the center. Within that bloody pool, steeped in red death, knelt Peck. They hadn't bound him, but his head hung in despair, and his bloodied palms pressed to his eyes as if blocking his sight could protect him from the horror he had witnessed.

Mory had seen death, though. He knew what came after life, at least in part. While he mourned the needless loss of human life, the blood and bodies didn't bother him. What did concern him was the slump to Peck's shoulders and his lack of awareness of his surroundings. Peck was never unaware. His constant vigilance had kept them alive all those years in Tyellí.

Pulling away from his captors, Mory splashed through the blood to crouch at Peck's side. Peck jerked away at his touch, but upon seeing him, threw his arms around Mory.

"Mory," Peck choked out. "I-I'm sorry, Mory. I failed you. I couldn't get you out. I don't want you here, Mory. It's not safe."

Mory shook his head. "I don't have a choice. The guards brought me."

Peck stiffened. "They're going to use you, Mory. They plan to kill everyone—every*thing*."

Mory shivered at Peck's frantic words. "How, Peck?" Peck only stared at him, and Mory realized, "This circle—it's filled with energy."

"What do you mean? What kind of energy?"

"It feels like . . . death. It feels a bit like Myra and a little like Aaslo. Like when I was dead. It's the energy of death, Peck."

Peck nodded and looked down at his bloody hands. "I know. They performed some sort of ritual, and they killed all these people. I don't know what they were trying to do, but—"

"Oh, we did more than *try*," came a sinister yet sultry voice. Mory's guards parted as the empress entered the circle. Her vicious smile absorbed all the life from the hilltop. As her bare feet carried her across the crimson-painted earth, the gauzy tatters of her dress soaked up the blood pooled around them. She stopped a few feet away, looking down upon Peck as if he were no better than vermin infesting her sanctuary. Then her gaze slid to Mory, and a spark of pleasure . . . no, *envy* . . . ignited in her gaze. She took a step forward and reached out to grip his chin, her black-lacquered nails digging into his flesh.

"I am ready for you, my sweet. There has been enough death here to power the machine." With a hard squeeze, she captured his gaze with her black eyes. "You will cooperate or this pitiful creature beside you will suffer greatly. Do you understand?"

Mory started to shake his head, but as her nails dug into his cheeks, he said, "Yes, just don't hurt Peck. I'll do whatever you want."

Peck rose to his feet, and Mory followed. Peck turned to him. "You need to fight this. I don't know how, but you need to fight. Don't worry about me, Mory. I'll be fine."

Peck said it with his usual assurance, but Mory knew the truth. Peck was trying to be reassuring and confident for Mory's sake, but nothing about this situation guaranteed either of them safety. In fact, the bloody corpses around them assured the opposite. Mory didn't call Peck out on his bluster, though. He thought that perhaps Peck needed to believe his own lies.

Lysia stepped around them and headed for a drape on the far side of the circle. "Bring them."

The two guards who escorted Mory, plus two more already in the circle, moved toward them. Peck and Mory turned and followed the empress without additional prompting. They exited the circle and entered another, this one devoid of bodies and blood. Although the foliage had been cleared in the center, weeds choked the spaces between the pillars, and errant shrub limbs poked into the circle. A strange structure built of massive stones, some twice as tall as Mory, sat at the center. Cryptic runes, as well as inlaid gemstones, wooden carvings, and even forms of glass, covered each stone. They stood in a ring around a central sphere that looked to be made of clear glass.

As they approached, the sphere rose into the air, and Mory noted for the first time a magus standing between two of the large, upright stones. He also saw that the bottom of the sphere was missing, and on the ground beneath was a pile of chains anchored to the stones.

"Secure him," Lysia ordered.

One of the guards came forward and grabbed Mory by the arm, wrenching him from Peck's grasp. When Peck lunged forward to grab Mory, another guard struck him from behind with a rod, knocking him to the ground. Mory was jerked around to face the empress as the guard used the chains and attached shackles to secure him in place beneath the hovering glass-like sphere.

The empress turned to look at him fondly. She spoke, her voice hollow and haunting. "You are intriguing. You aren't wholly alive. Did you know? Some small piece of you successfully shed the taint of life. In your resurrection was born a new creature, a being both cursed with the power of life and blessed with the power of death. Had you been born Berruvian, you would have held a place of honor in my court. Now, you will endure the greatest honor of all. Through *you*, all life in this world will be extinguished, and we shall ascend to take our rightful places amongst the gods."

Mory looked at Peck kneeling at the feet of the guard, only inches away from death. He tugged at the metal shackles that gripped his wrists and ankles. Then he met the empress's zealous gaze. "You're crazy. The gods will never accept you. You're only human. We're nothing to them. Whatever glory you think awaits you is just a dream, and that's all it will ever be."

The empress appeared unimpressed. She didn't seem to possess any feeling at all. She looked at him dispassionately. "It is easy to forget, given the taste of death in your aura, that you are not Berruvian. You could never understand because you are not worthy of the gift given to you. Such a pity. Such a waste."

Then she dismissed him completely. As she turned away, the glass-like sphere descended, encasing him in a vitreous cocoon. The sounds outside were sightly muffled, but he could still hear her words as she gave directions to her guards and the magus. Eventually, they all left except for Lysia and the two guards who stood over Peck as he knelt at their feet. Peck didn't seem to notice them. His entire attention was riveted on Mory, and, in his eyes, Mory saw nothing but stark fear. Peck wasn't afraid for himself. He was afraid for Mory, and Mory could do nothing to put Peck at ease.

Lysia turned back to Mory. "Now, we shall begin. Don't fight it. Your friend will suffer if you do. You are about to become the conduit for more power than has filled this world since its creation. It is only fitting that such power will bring about its destruction."

The empress began a dance with her hands. Dark tendrils of power emanated from her fingers, and a tremor ran through Mory. He couldn't just sit there and be used to bring about the end of all life on Aldrea. But neither could he escape. The dark power spread out and drifted toward the stones ringing the circle. It seeped into the runes, which radiated with an energy that seemed to suck light from the air around them. A throbbing reverberation thrummed through the air, invading Mory's chest and head, and the fresh yet acerbic scent filled his nose like the air after a lightning storm.

Mory's chains clanked as he tugged against them. He knew he couldn't escape, yet he felt inclined to struggle regardless. It was the same with the power that began to suffuse him. At first nothing more than a whispering tingle across his skin, it soon scorched deep into his bones. He fought it, pushed against it, with every ounce of will he could muster. A *snap* broke the air, and Peck cried out. Through his watery tears, the image wavered, but Mory could just make out the guard standing with a raised rod in one hand and Peck's hair gripped in the other.

Mory's vision splintered, making it increasingly difficult to tell the difference between the images conjured by his mind and those he saw with his eyes. He saw a city filled with brilliant souls and the luminous, delicate threads that connected those souls to their corporeal vessels. He could see Peck lying on the dark earth of the circle, bleeding and in pain. Behind him, the guard raised his rod again, but Mory didn't see it fall. Instead, he saw a forest suffused with vibrant coils of light, all of them connected like the veins of an enormous organism.

Peck shouted, and Mory saw his friend cowering on the ground, covering his head with bruised arms. Scenes of another place threatened to consume his vision, and Mory pushed against them once again. He needed to stay in the *here* and *now*, with Peck. He needed to fight against the power with which the demented empress attempted to fill him, and he needed to accomplish, somehow, the impossible. He needed to escape his bonds, escape the sphere, and save Peck. As he strained against his bonds and his heart hammered in his throat, he knew he could do none of those things.

Mory collapsed to his knees, the impact with the rocky earth reverberating up his body, the pain miniscule compared with that caused by the dark power's invasion of his body. Only within the mind-numbing visions did he feel relief. It was easier to let his mind wander than it was to stay in the present. Mory tried to stay with Peck, but as the pain increased, he found himself escaping into his mind. He wondered if it would not be long before he lost his will altogether.

MORY'S HEAD SLUMPED, AND PECK PEERED UP AT HIS ATTACKER through the space between his arms just as the rod descended on him again. He grunted with the impact but managed to keep his shout of pain contained. He shifted his gaze to the sphere that caged Mory. Inside, a storm of dark power attacked Mory from all sides. From what Peck could see, Mory appeared to be coming in and out of awareness. One minute he would be staring at Peck, his face contorted in pain, and the next his expression would be serene as he stared sightlessly ahead. Peck didn't know what the power was doing to Mory, but he knew he needed to get Mory out of that sphere.

Peck swallowed as he thought of all the ways he had failed Mory, beginning with getting captured in the first place. He had tried desperately to free Mory. He planned and plotted as he waited to remove Mory from the cells at the estate. Then he thought he could free him during the march from Helod to Mouvilan. He donned the dress of a Berruvian soldier and even managed to turn a few of the younger Berruvian soldiers to his cause, or at least what little he told them of it. With their help he got close to Mory's tent and had been about to enter when he had been discovered. He suspected one or more of his converts betrayed him, but of course he would never know. The guards roughed him up and brought him to the circle to witness the ritual slaughter of innocent people. Peck would never forgive himself for failing Mory. He would go to his death with a heavy heart and a tormented soul.

He shook as thoughts of punishment in the Afterlife assailed him. It would be a punishment well deserved. His life wasn't over yet, though. He still had time. His gaze went to the guard who towered over him. Only two guards and the empress remained in the circle. The empress possessed a dark magic that Peck couldn't begin to comprehend, and the guards were well armed with swords, belt knives, and of course the rod with which one attempted to bludgeon him to death. Peck, on the other hand, was beaten and unarmed. He had no idea how he would find his way out of this one, but he had to try—for Mory's sake. And, of course, for the world and the existence of life. But mostly for Mory.

The empress rounded on them. Her empty gaze remained on his face as she spoke to his guards. "Take him away and kill him. He is no longer needed."

Peck didn't fight the guards when they grabbed him beneath the arms and hauled him away from the circle. He glanced over his shoulder to see Mory slumped on the ground inside the sphere before the drape blocked his view and they walked through the second circle of sacrifices. Peck feigned a slip on the bloody mud and fell back into one of the guards as they crossed the space. As he surreptitiously slipped the man's belt knife from its sheath, the offended guard shoved him forward so that he stumbled and sprawled in the pond of blood pooled in the center of the circle. Somehow, Peck held on to his stomach as he tried to ignore the tangy iron scent that wafted off him.

The guard stalked forward, heavy boots splashing through the blood, and grabbed for Peck. This time, Peck turned and shoved the pilfered knife into the man's groin. With a choked groan, the guard doubled over. Peck quickly pulled the knife free and slashed the guard's exposed throat. The second guard stepped forward, but hadn't yet seen the damage Peck had wrought on the first guard. As the vacant-eyed guard toppled, Peck crouched and lunged with the knife, plunging it through the second guard's hamstring. The man cried out and made to draw his sword, but Peck, full of adrenaline, was faster. He yanked the guard forward, pivoted, and stabbed the man in the kidney. As the guard arched backward, Peck grabbed hold of his hair in a bloody fist and then shoved the knife into the side of the man's neck.

Peck breathed heavily; his arms began shaking as the second guard slid to the ground to join his comrade. He slowed his breathing, inhaling deeply through his nose, and immediately found it to be a mistake. The cloying, metallic fragrance suffused the fabric-draped circle, and Peck looked as if he had bathed in blood. His hand began to ache, and he realized he still clutched the knife in a death grip. He allowed his fingers to loosen as he stepped toward the drapery leading to the other circle.

Peering around the length of thick fabric, Peck saw that the empress was utterly enthralled with the sphere. She hadn't heard or noticed any commotion. He was surprised he had been successful. The two men had been members of the empress's personal guard, which meant they were probably two of the best soldiers the Berru had to offer. He had taken out *two* of them in a matter of seconds. He had had the advantage of surprise and desperation. While he killed them, his only thoughts were for Mory. He knew what he needed to do now. He had to kill the empress. It was the only way. And if that didn't work, well, none of it would matter anyway.

CHAPTER 26

SEDI SAT IN THE GRASS ATOP THE HILL AND WATCHED THE BATTLE between the Endricsians and the Berru play out before her. It was oddly peaceful beneath the swaying trees and among the birdsong, a brutal contrast to the battle below. It looked much like many other battles she had seen, except this one was vast and possessed creatures that had never before existed on Aldrea. Axus had imbued the empress and his incendia with the power to call forth creatures of the Alterworld, and it had only cost them the sacrifice of hundreds to accomplish it. Sedi had not stayed to witness those sacrifices. Even in her disenchanted state, she could not justify the slaughter of innocents for the sake of ritual.

Lysia was vicious and ruthless in a way Sedi had never been, nor had she wanted to be. She liked to think that she had retained some semblance of her former humanity. She had become a magus to save people, not to kill them. So how had she ended up *here*? How had she become so dismissive of death, and how had she come to an agreement with Axus?

Despite the brutal killing she witnessed in the battle, Sedi's mind felt clear for the first time in ages. A dark veil had been lifted from her consciousness, and she could once again see the future as something bright and vivid. Except, there would be no future. Axus would kill Aaslo. The Berru would destroy the Endricsians. Then Lysia would end the Berru. It was inevitable, and Sedi could only sit and watch it happen.

That last thought put Sedi on edge. She didn't like being helpless, lacking control. In fact, she never allowed situations like that. Sedi always had a plan, and she always had the power to carry through with that plan. Right now, she wanted vengeance against Axus for tricking her. It occurred to her that, thanks to Arohnu, she had the power to go to Celestria and face Axus. Of course, she would fail, and he would likely kill her, but that had been her goal all along. It was still her goal. Wasn't it?

With one last look at the humans battling for their lives, for all life, Sedi stood and brushed the soil from her pants. Then she opened a portal unlike any she had ever opened, for this one led to Celestria, the land of the gods. There were no long, illuminated hallways or passages and no endless pathways on which she might get lost. No, she stepped through and found herself instantly in another place, another world, but one no less entrenched in battle.

She found herself in a land of rolling hills, verdant forests, and grassy glens filled with both wild and cultivated flower gardens and placid streams. Mountains floated in the air like islands in a sea of clouds. It stood in stark contrast to the vicious power being blasted in every direction. Sedi dropped to the ground as a stream of pulsing light whizzed past to explode against the hill behind her. The blast sent dirt and chunks of rock flying, and a number of people—no, *gods*—cried out as they were struck. A once-majestic building topped the targeted hill but now lay partially in ruins. A low wall of stone surrounded the front, and she saw from her vantage that many glowing people took refuge behind it. Some of them threw attacks at other people who occupied a similarly destroyed building in the far distance atop another hill.

Obviously, these were gods, judging from the glow that emanated from their magical bodies and from their towering size, as well as the power they wielded. The distance between the two buildings rendered any human weapons or spells useless, and the destructive energy being flung about was immeasurably intense. Sedi briefly wondered if any one of these attacks might be capable of killing her. She could simply step in front of one and be done with it, but then she wouldn't be able to face Axus, and that had been her goal.

A dark shadow fell across her, and Sedi looked up to see a massive creature soaring above. Sharp protrusions tipped outstretched, leathery wings, and similar spiky protrusions ran along its head, down its long neck, and across its back to the tip of its sinuous tail. Each of the talons on the hands and feet of its muscular body were capable of eviscerating any prey. Even from a distance, though, its eyes captured her attention. The bright green orbs with slitted pupils reminded her so much of Aaslo that for a moment she thought he had been completely changed into a dragon. Sedi dismissed the idea even though some small voice in her mind whispered that she might not be wrong.

The dragon dipped low and spewed flame over the cowering gods on the other side of the wall behind her. Simultaneously, several gods released ranged attacks of their own on the flying beast. The dragon twisted, rolled, and dodged in midair, but two of the attacks ultimately landed, one of which clipped its wing. It tumbled from the sky to skid across the ground in a shower of grass and soil. A second dragon-like creature, this one black with two sets of wings, appeared from the broken building to attack the flailing and injured green-eyed dragon. As the two beasts fought, the gods continued their assault, forcing Sedi to run for cover. She headed for a cluster of boulders halfway around the hill but found them already occupied.

Taking cover anyway, Sedi stared at the woman who crouched behind the rocks, breathing heavily. She had short brown hair and fawn-colored eyes that were wide beneath her thick, dark lashes. Beneath her feminine, metallic-red armor, a golden gown flowed to her sandaled feet. Although her appearance seemed disjointed and impractical, the goddess somehow made it work. The goddess turned to Sedi with wide-eyed surprise.

"You—you are . . . what are you?"

Sedi tilted her head. "I'm a human magus. You are a goddess?"

The goddess's eyes turned upward as if trying to remember. "Yes, hmm. I don't think I know what that is. From which world do you hail?"

Sedi opened her mouth to speak, then thought better of it. Aldrea lay at the crux of the gods' war, and it was probably best not to draw that kind of attention. Instead of answering, she stated, "I seek Axus. Where can I find him?"

The goddess narrowed her eyes at Sedi. "Why do you want to find Axus? Are you for or against his cause?"

Sedi thought about the question. Since discovering his deception, she hadn't really considered herself to be on either side of the war. In fact, she had decided to stay out of it as a silent observer, but she did have her reasons for being here now. "I'm neither, and my business with him is my own. It's personal. Where can I find him?"

The woman grinned knowingly. "Axus has a way of making everything personal." She gave Sedi a once-over. "You are ill-prepared to face him. Your power is so . . . miniscule."

Sedi scowled. Besides Aaslo, Sedi was the most powerful magus on Aldrea, and she was by far the more practiced. Still, the goddess had a point. She was no god. "Are you going to tell me how to find him or not?"

"Can you not feel his power?" asked the goddess. "He is no longer suppressing it, and it is potent. Just follow the feeling of sweet release, of the endless void. Follow the taste of death."

Of course Sedi could feel the gods' power. It suffused everything. It was so strong that at times she nearly forgot herself. What she felt, however, was the combined power of all the gods, and she hadn't noticed any differences in the power until the goddess mentioned it.

As she focused on picking through the threads, she realized one dominated all the others, overbearing, almost forceful as it demanded attention. And seductive. Like a promise of liberation from the confines of a stifling and demoralizing life. She could feel it drawing her in, and for a moment she wanted nothing more than to succumb.

Sedi steeled herself against it and turned to survey the lands, looking for its source. She sensed the power emanating from one of the floating islands, a larger one covered in mountains and forest. At first, she despaired, as she had no way of getting to the island in the sky. Then her gaze slid to the scene before her. She had a brazen idea.

Sedi didn't look back as she ran to where the dragons battled and ducked behind a hill of displaced earth. The double-winged black dragon appeared to have the upper hand over the injured green-eyed dragon. The black dragon pinned the green-eyed dragon on its back, belly exposed, and its talons dug into the hard plates that covered the underbelly. The black dragon lunged forward to snap at the green-eyed dragon's head, and at the last moment, the green-eyed dragon swiveled its long neck to the side and clamped down on the black dragon's neck.

The green-eyed dragon pushed off the ground with its heavy wings and wrenched the black dragon's neck so hard that Sedi heard the snap. The black dragon sagged limply, and Sedi knew this was her moment. She wrapped the light around herself, rendering herself invisible, and hurried toward the struggling green-eyed dragon. She wasn't as confident in her ability to go undetected as she might have been before knowing Aaslo. He always seemed to find her, and she wondered if it had something to do with his dragon nature.

As Sedi neared the dragon, which was too preoccupied to notice her, if he even could, it managed to free itself from the black dragon's corpse. Sedi didn't delay. She ran forward, and using her magic, launched herself into the air. She landed atop the dragon's back, but he barely noticed. She settled between two of its back spikes, clinging to the one in front of her as she turned her mind to the next task. She put a lot of thought into what she had to do in the few minutes since this crazy plan presented itself. She needed to connect with the creature's mind in a way that allowed her to coerce it into going where she needed to go.

Making a mind link with an animal was not very difficult, but she had never tried it with a dragon, or *any* creature from another realm, for that matter. Sedi sent a wave of energy into the dragon's mind. It happened more quickly than she thought it would, as if the dragon was eager to connect. Sedi blinked rapidly as a multitude of foreign sensations and thoughts assailed her. She clamped down on these. She could not allow the dragon to take over *her* mind.

Of all the thoughts flooding into her, one thing became clear. The dragon was in pain. It was injured and needed time to heal. Sedi would use that to her advantage. She sent soothing feelings, giving the dragon a sense of calm reassurance. Then she encouraged it to think of places to heal, away from the battle. Once its thoughts came in line with that, she sent the idea to go to the sky island from which Axus's power emanated. The dragon didn't like that. It opposed the power of death. It wanted to live. Sedi again sent soothing thoughts. She tried to convince the dragon that it would go to Axus's island to heal, not to die.

After fifteen minutes of struggle, she believed she finally had the dragon. It took a few lumbering, limping steps forward, then launched itself into the sky. Pretty soon, she made her way toward a crystalline mountain range in the distance. As Sedi caught sight of the ground slipping by below, she wished she could have used the paths to shorten the distance. However, she didn't know how or *if* it was possible within Celestria. By the time she and the dragon reached the foot of the mountains, the sun had risen, and the vitreous faces of crystals within the rocks glimmered with dazzling luster.

The dragon set down in a frosted wonderland. The ground, the trees, the bushes, all were made of silvery blue crystal. Sedi could feel Axus's power in the foothills above her, but there was another power as well. The second power felt familiar and just as inviting, but for a different reason. It felt like Aaslo. Sedi's pulse quickened as she realized Aaslo might be facing off against the God of Death. She told herself her alarm came from potentially missing her chance for vengeance. It could not possibly be concern for the dragon-man who had intrigued her for so long and who kissed like he owned her. She pushed thoughts of their kiss away as she slid from the dragon's back. The dragon didn't even look her way as it limped into the crystal forest. As it moved away, their mind connection grew thinner until it ceased altogether. Sedi shuddered at the feeling of being alone in her mind once again and turned toward the crystalline palace in the distance. Then she quickly ascended the softly sloping foothills.

At the crest of a hill grew a garden that held numerous short plants made of crystal Sedi had never before seen. Raindrops hung suspended in the air as if frozen in time. Their solid, crystalline forms clinked together like glass as she strode through, causing those in her path to fall to the ground, where they created a sand that crunched under her boots. Sedi knew she was getting closer to the source of the seductive power, and it became harder to remain steadfast against it. Farther up the mountain, she saw a fissure in the rock face, a cave, and she recognized it as the crux of Axus's power. Curiously, though, Aaslo's power was not in the cave. It emanated from farther into the foothills, and as she stood frozen in place, she realized that power wasn't moving. It pulsed in and out as if engaged in a struggle.

Sedi looked to the cave, then looked in the direction of Aaslo's power. Whatever issue Aaslo had was none of her business. She was here for Axus. She needn't get involved in anything else. She would confront Axus. She might get in a few good licks to satisfy her need for vengeance. Then he would kill her, and her troubles would be over. It was a solid plan—one that didn't involve Aaslo in any way. So why, then, did she feel the need to help him with whatever trouble he had found?

Grumbling to herself, Sedi set off for the foothills. As she made her way through the dreamy crystalline forest, Sedi kept constant vigilance. She didn't believe in beauty without thorns, and she was certain that any place Axus frequented would have plenty. She wasn't wrong. As she came around a bend in the path, she stumbled upon two creatures fighting over the mauled corpse of a third. The creatures looked like wolves made of crystal, but crystal spikes ranged down their backs. They growled and snapped at each other, eventually tearing their prey in half. The smaller of the crystal wolves turned and ran with his prize into the crystalline forest, while the larger stood his ground and began consuming the carcass.

Sedi stepped carefully as she retreated and took a circuitous route toward her destination—a mesmerizing crystalline palace that shimmered in the sun's early-morning rays. The colorful sunrise reflected off its faces in such a way that it made her question if this could really be Axus's abode. How had the demented and conniving God of Death created a place of such beauty? But deep down, she knew the answer. Everything Axus did was seductive and enchanting. It was how he gained his power.

Sedi came up short when a woman materialized, seemingly out of thin air. The woman was familiar. While she had heard much about her, she had seen her only once in Aaslo's paths. This was Myra, or rather Myropa, Aaslo's mother, the reaper.

"What do you want?" Sedi demanded.

Myropa blinked at her. "I'm Myropa."

"I know who you are," Sedi growled.

Myropa's expression hardened. "Then you know I would do anything for Aaslo. I've been looking for someone to help. I sensed you and thought I'd take a chance. I know you and Aaslo have a complicated—and contentious—relationship, but he needs help."

Sedi narrowed her eyes at Myropa then glanced to the palace where she could feel Aaslo's energy pulsing in and out. "I can sense him nearby. His power has grown."

Myropa bit her lip. "Yes, he's not what he used to be. I think you know that. He's in the palace tower, and he's trapped."

"Trapped how? What happened?"

"I don't know. He and Axus fought. I didn't see it happen, but I could feel the power fluctuations. At first, it seemed like Aaslo had won, but then Axus's power resurged, and he *hurt* Aaslo." Sedi's stomach flipped at the thought of Aaslo being seriously injured, then she chided herself for the ridiculousness of the sentiment. Myropa continued, "Axus is gone now, and I returned to the tower to check on Aaslo. He's alive but trapped in some kind of rock. He can't get out, and he's in terrible pain. He needs help. I know you think of him as the enemy, but I also think you care about him. Please help him."

Sedi bristled at the idea that she cared about Aaslo. She didn't care about anyone but herself. Not really. She had come to realize it was the only way to survive the infinite life with which she had been cursed. But when Myropa said Axus had hurt Aaslo, Sedi's stomach took a dive. A hard rock had settled in her gut, and she felt the need to go to him, to see that he was well. Sedi realized what that sensation meant, and she swallowed hard against the fear. Did she have real feelings for Aaslo? And if so, would her mind survive those feelings?

Sedi's legs nearly buckled under the weight of the dread that suffused her, but she didn't want this woman, Aaslo's own mother, to see her weakness. She closed her eyes and took several deep breaths. Then she steeled her nerves and met Myropa's pleading gaze. "I will go. Show me the way."

Myropa beamed with joy as she grabbed Sedi's hand and pulled her along. They met little resistance, killing the few guards that remained. When they finally came upon Dolt blocking the door, the horse didn't seem inclined to let her pass. His strange, splotchy wings spread wide to block the entire hallway, and he gnashed and kicked at her every time she approached. Myropa pled with the horse to allow them through, imploring him to see reason. Sedi found the whole notion of pleading with a horse ridiculous, but she eventually stepped forward and gave the beast a slight bow.

"Dolt, you need to let us through," she said. "We are here to help Aaslo."

The horse lowered his head and turned his ears back as if he didn't believe her. He swept a wing forward and knocked her to the side.

Sedi rolled her eyes and pushed away from the wall. She was arguing with a horse. "I swear upon the graves of everyone I've known that I intend Aaslo no harm—for now."

Sedi initiated the mind connection with the winged horse. This time the connection was difficult. The power seemed to slip away from him. Before it fully disconnected, Sedi sent one penetrating sensation. It was her feelings for Aaslo—the feelings she had not yet defined but which terrified her.

Dolt bobbed his head a few times, then met her gaze with a direct glare. He finally dropped his wings and stepped aside. Sedi prepared a number of spells as she ascended the tower steps behind Myropa. She didn't know what she would find, but she hoped Axus would return so she could exact her revenge.

Upon arriving in the broken remnants of the tower, she found that Axus was not present. As Myropa had said, Aaslo was encased up to his neck in a small mountain of shiny, black rock. His face and hair dripped with sweat, his eyes were closed, and he appeared pale but vaguely conscious. Unfortunately, he was not the only being in the room. Three other *things* ambled aimlessly. They all had the body of a man but each possessed the head of some other beast, and they held various armaments. One creature with a long, furry snout and ram's horns turned to her and released a horrible screech as it raised a battle axe. Then the other two, one with the head of a bird and wielding a spear and a second insectoid being with a sword, immediately spun to face her with their weapons poised for attack.

Sedi hadn't bothered with the layers of light that typically rendered her invisible. She immediately remedied the oversight, disappearing from view and confusing her opponents. She cast an energy bolt at the ram, the first to reach the place she stood only seconds ago. At such close range, the shock of the blast shook her, causing her to lose hold of the invisibility spell. As the ram hurled backward to slam into the only standing portion of the wall, the bird jabbed at her with its spear. Sedi dodged and created a sword of light that she wielded with practiced ease. She danced over a pile of rubble as she parried the next thrust of the spear. The light sliced through the wooden haft, sending the metal tip clattering to the floor.

The bird fell back, and the insect lunged, clacking its mandibles as it struck out at her with its sword. Sedi huffed out a breath as her light sword rang against the enemy's blade. She ducked and spun as the bird recovered the spear tip and wooden shaft and attacked her, wielding both. Sedi backed away from both opponents, rounding the room as she checked the status of the ram lying prone but not yet dead. She raised a shield ward at her back as she scurried over part of the roof to the downed ram and thrust her light sword through its chest. Her opponents' weapons collided with her shield as she withdrew her light blade and turned to face them.

When she turned, she found herself only fighting the insect, since the birdlike creature had broken away to pursue the reaper. Myropa yelped as she ran around the circular room dodging its attacks, while Sedi squared off with the insect. Sedi breathed heavily as she leapt over a chasm in the floor and considered that Aaslo probably wasn't worth all the trouble. She didn't even know why she bothered to help him. Even as she thought that, though, a nagging voice in the back of her mind said she needed him.

With an angry growl, Sedi leapt toward the insect man. It stepped into her advance and brought its sword down in an overhead strike, which she ducked. It shifted, countering, and swung for her legs. Sedi jumped over the blade and released a cluster of magical sparks into the creature's chest with explosive effect. As gooey pieces of insect man rained down, Sedi set her attention on the bird Myropa had inadvertently distracted.

The reaper dodged the bird's attacks by keeping the stone encasing Aaslo between herself and the creature. Sedi caught Myropa's attention, and the reaper shifted, positioning the birdman's back to Sedi. Wrapping her light shield around herself once more, Sedi approached the bird from the rear. She thrust her light sword through its back at the same moment she used a beam of light to sever its head from its neck.

Sedi stood breathing heavily for a moment as Myropa hurried around the stone to Aaslo and placed her hands on either side of his face. "Aaslo, can you hear me? I've brought help." She glanced at Sedi nervously, then looked back to Aaslo. "Sedi is here. She says she will help you. Aaslo?"

Aaslo blinked his eyes open, and his gaze focused on Myropa. He smiled wanly. "I figured out how to get rid of the pain. It's not too bad now, but I can't release myself. This is not actually a rock. It's something else—something powerful. Wait. Did you say *Sedi* is here?"

Sedi stepped into Aaslo's field of view and gave him a wry smile. "It looks like you've gotten yourself into a bit of trouble. Why does it not surprise me that you'd need *my* help?"

Aaslo's brow furrowed as he frowned. "I fought a god and lost. Now that the pain is gone, this isn't the worst that could have happened to me."

Sedi chuckled and flicked a piece of insect man off her shoulder. "No doubt. You look terrible. It must have been a good fight."

Aaslo growled low, the sound emanating from his chest. "I used all the power I had. The depraved were completely spent." He swallowed hard. "I felt a shift in their power before it was gone. It somehow transferred to me. I think that with time, it will return, but it's mine now. The shades felt different before I lost them, though—their souls, I mean. It was as if they had been cleansed." He nodded toward the reaper. "Myropa checked on them for me."

The reaper wrung her hands as she looked anxiously at Aaslo. "They're just regular souls, now, I think. At least, that's how they feel. I'll be able to deliver them to the Sea once their bodies die—again."

Sedi raised an eyebrow as she considered the once-powerful depraved. If Aaslo had somehow seized their power for his own, then he possibly *could* rival a god—but apparently not Axus. She turned her attention back to the issue at hand. She chewed on an immaculate fingernail as she surveyed the rock holding Aaslo and fed just a bit of power into it in search of its secrets. "This *is* strange. It's unlike anything I've ever seen. It's like a prison for magic wielders. This might even hold a god."

Aaslo closed his eyes in defeat, and his chin dropped to rest on the rock beneath it. "You will not be able to break me out, will you?"

Sedi tilted her head. "No, but we might be able to overcome it together. You are much stronger than you were before. I could feel your power beyond the foothills, and even now you glow with a golden aura."

"But am I strong enough to overcome a god prison?"

She spread her hands. "We won't know until we try."

Aaslo set his jaw. "Then we better get on with it before Axus returns. But tell me, why are you doing this?"

"Doing what?"

"Helping me."

Sedi stared at him for a long, uncomfortable moment. Why *was* she helping him? He was the enemy, was he not? As Sedi looked at him now, she knew that wasn't true. In fact, Aaslo had become much more than an enemy some time ago. She steadied her nerves as she was forced to admit her thoughts, at least to herself. But how would she explain it to Aaslo? She didn't even understand it. She *had* tried to kill him numerous times. He had no reason to trust her. Especially for what she was about to propose. But she needed to try.

Sedi took a deep breath. "You are not my enemy, Aaslo. You never were. It was never personal. I had an assignment that I thought I needed to carry out. Only now my eyes are open to the truth, and I realize you mean something to me."

"What do I mean to you?" he asked cautiously, as if he didn't believe her.

Sedi's cheeks heated, but she answered truthfully. "I don't know, but I know you're important, and not just for your fight against Axus." Then, more quietly, she added, "You're important to *me*."

He scoffed, "Like I would believe that."

She sighed. "No, I don't suppose you would." After a moment's pause, during which she contemplated her heart and soul, her very existence, she said, "There is a place I sometimes visit to think. It's a graveyard. It's *my* graveyard. I've buried nearly every person who has meant something to me over the years there. I've been visiting it for nearly two millennia. At first, when I visited the graves of those I loved, I would feel only sorrow and grief. But after a while, I began to feel, well, nothing. I would put my lover or my grandchild in the ground and walk away feeling only emptiness. Then, I stopped loving altogether. I did not visit for a long time because I had no desire to revisit the past and no longer had anyone to inter. But recently, I went back. This time, I felt something, something I've never felt there. I felt love. The feelings I once had for those people visited me, and I again felt the joy of having known them.

"I would say I don't know what changed, but it would be a lie. I do know what made me feel again, and you did, Aaslo. You have awakened something that I thought completely and irretrievably lost. I *feel* things again. More importantly, I *want* to feel things again. I don't ever want it to stop, and now I know it doesn't have to. Because you're like me, Aaslo. You can't die—at least, not by human means.

"Axus may be able to kill you or imprison you forever, but it doesn't need to be that way. We could walk away now, go to another realm like the other magi, and live together forever. Neither of us would ever need to be alone. We would never need to feel the loss of the other."

"And what?" said Aaslo. "We just abandon Aldrea to its fate? Leave everyone else to die? You know I can't do that, Sedi. It may not have been my destiny, but I have a purpose, and I *will* see it through. I will face Axus one way or another, with or without your help."

Sedi looked at him solemnly. "If that is your choice, then I will join you in your quest. I will help you however I can. Please know that I am being sincere. My offer still stands. After all this, if we survive and you want to, we can be together."

Aaslo stared at her for a minute, but when he opened his mouth to speak, she cut him off. "You don't need to say anything." She had no need to hear his rejection. "Let us get on with freeing you, shall we?"

Aaslo looked as if he would say something but changed his mind. He finally said, "Okay, what do we do?"

"We should link our powers. I will guide the link since I know more about magic, rather than you fumbling in the dark hoping to find a solution."

From the look he gave her, Sedi could only imagine how much Aaslo disliked the idea of *her* controlling his power. She didn't like the idea of being linked to him any more than he did, but she could think of no other way. In truth, she wasn't even sure she *could* control the amount of power he seemed to be wielding, but she was eager to undertake the challenge. Before Aaslo came along, it had been a *very* long time since anything had challenged her.

She briefly explained to Aaslo how to link power with her, and once the connection was made, she took the lead. As she held the reins of Aaslo's power, she could feel he held back, but she couldn't feel how much. She first explored the stone, mapping out its power structure and searching for any weaknesses.

"I don't find any weak points in this prison except for the space you fill. Taking advantage of that, however, would probably result in you exploding."

Aaslo made an inhuman noise, more dragon than man. It sent a thrill through Sedi as it did every time she caught a glimpse of his animalistic side. Not for the first time, she wondered what it would be like if he just let go, let the dragon free. It occurred to her that she wouldn't mind experiencing a touch of that freedom with Aaslo. Sedi's cheeks heated at the thought, and she avoided his penetrating gaze as she continued exploring his prison.

Aaslo was right. The stone wasn't really rock. It was some kind of godly material that used a being's own power to imprison it. It seemed the more powerful the being, the stronger the substance held.

"I think I know how to release you," she muttered.

"Good, let's do it," he grumbled.

Sedi stepped back and shook her head. "It's impossible. It can't be done."

"But you just said you know how."

"Yes, I know *how*, but I can't do it."

Aaslo's aura flared, and Sedi felt her knees go a little weak. "What do we have to do? Tell me."

Sedi placed a hand on her cocked hip. "You wouldn't like it even if we managed to pull it off."

Aaslo spoke through gritted teeth. "Tell me now, Sedi."

She rolled her eyes and released a sigh. "Fine. We must drain your power completely. I have a feeling that would be impossible, since the stone will only grow stronger the more you use it. The only thing I can think of to do is have someone take the power from you." She spread her hands and looked around. "I don't see anyone here who can do that."

At first, Aaslo stared at her in disbelief. "You want to take away my power—the power I need to defeat Axus?"

"I believe it's the only way to release you. If you have no power, the stone will not be able to hold you. Besides, you won't be without power forever. It will begin regenerating once the link is severed."

They were quiet for a moment as Aaslo obviously mulled over her words. Finally, he said, "*You* could take my power."

Mirth danced in her eyes. "As much as I would love to drain you dry, there is no way I can hold that much power. I'm loath to admit that your power vessel has grown far beyond my own. That much power would destroy me."

"What about me?" asked Myropa softly. "Can I take some of it?"

Sedi looked at the reaper with skepticism before she nodded slowly. "It's possible. I'm not familiar with your kind of being. I don't know if you can carry his type of power."

Myropa lifted her chin. "I can bear the power of death."

Sedi eyed Aaslo sideways. "That's true. If you can take that much, it *may* be possible for me to harbor the rest if I first expend my own power. We will all be vulnerable, though. If Axus returns before it is complete, we wouldn't be remotely able to defend ourselves."

"Let's do this," said Aaslo. "I have no desire to spend eternity trapped in a rock."

Sedi was stunned. "You would do this? You would allow me to take all your power?"

Aaslo just looked at her matter-of-factly. "If that is what needs to be done, then we must do it. I can *feel* them dying."

"Feel who dying?"

"Everyone. All those men and women fighting for life. They signed a contract. When they die, their souls come to me. I am being inundated. Every minute we waste here is another minute in which people die. Yes, you could use my power to kill me afterward, but at least I won't die trapped in this rock."

Straightening, Sedi said, "I will not try to kill you again, Aaslo. I am on your side. I need you to trust me."

Aaslo gave her a hard stare, but he relented. "No, I believe you, Sedi. I may come to regret it, but I trust you."

Sedi smiled as a bubble of genuine joy burst within her chest. It was a foreign but not unwelcome feeling. Then she recovered her wits and shrugged as if it didn't matter to her one way or the other, but she was truly shaken. She had never done anything quite so daring as what they were about to attempt, and death by power overload did not sound like a pleasant way to go. Besides, taking Aaslo's power into herself somehow seemed . . . intimate, and she wasn't sure how she felt about that. Sedi's gaze fell on Aaslo's fatigued face. His mussed hair and mismatched eyes did nothing to detract from his allure. If anything, they gave him a roguish charm. All that strength made vulnerable by his imprisonment increased Sedi's desire to dominate him.

Aaslo cleared his throat, and Sedi realized she'd been staring. If the heat in his gaze indicated anything, she knew her own expression had made her thoughts quite clear. She averted her eyes as her cheeks flushed. She paced, thinking furiously about the best way to link their powers so that she could siphon Aaslo's *and* send a portion of it to the reaper. She would also need to maintain two additional spells while doing so. She had to expend her own power, thereby depleting her vessel, in addition to forcing the rock to release its hold on Aaslo.

Sedi eyed the open doorway and the bodies littering the floor. Despite her long-held desire for death, she didn't like being vulnerable. If an attack came once they'd started, she would have a difficult time fighting anything off. She didn't know if the animal men could kill her, but she hadn't come all this way to be killed by a minion. She wanted vengeance, and she would have it.

Once Sedi had her plan clear in her mind, she instructed Aaslo on how to allow for the flow of power from his vessel to hers, which would be made difficult by the black material feeding on his power. She wasn't sure how to link with the reaper, but Myropa assured her that she knew how to open herself. She rattled on about the Fates for a moment before Sedi cut her off.

"That's fine. Just do it, and we can get on with this."

Myropa's lips gave a moue of disapproval, but she didn't say anything, and Sedi knew she wouldn't. Sedi didn't know Myropa's history, but she knew the reaper wasn't one for confrontation. She briefly wondered if Myropa had ever lifted a finger against anyone in her life—or death, then dismissed the idea.

Sedi established the basis for the power transfer spell with efficiency and sent the questing end of the spell toward Aaslo and Myropa. Surprisingly, Myropa's connected first. Aaslo had a bit of trouble getting past his entombment. As he struggled to make the link, the stone began to migrate up his neck. His power wavered when it appeared he might be completely engulfed, but the progression stopped just beneath his chin once the link was finally made.

Next, Sedi began to drain her power into the stone of the tower beneath her feet and the air around her, creating a power vacuum within, which began to pull the power out of Aaslo. It hit her in a rush. Scorching fire. Demented darkness. All wrapped in a shell of growth and replenishment. The incendiary corona of the sun. Fresh rain and miasmic decay. Sedi collapsed as she struggled to contain it all. Then she felt a soft hand on her shoulder. It gripped her tightly and shook her with vigor.

"Send it to me!" shouted a voice in her ear.

Sedi shook her head and found the source of the voice. The reaper crouched beside her, yelling something about sharing power. Sedi abruptly remembered the connection with the reaper and immediately opened the channel. As the floodgate opened, the dark power rushed out into Myropa, and suddenly Sedi could breathe again. She stared at Aaslo in amazement. He had more power than she could possibly have imagined. How had he carried all of it and not crumbled under the immense pressure?

Sedi moved to regain her feet and found them stuck to the floor. Looking down, she noticed the glossy black stone flowed toward her and had already encased her soles. She scrambled up and yanked at her legs with all her strength, but they wouldn't budge. The material slid like tar up her feet, wrapping around her ankles. As Aaslo's power flooded her, so too did the black rock. Her gaze jerked to Aaslo and noted the rock around his face had subsided.

She struggled against her bonds as she also struggled to close the gates allowing Aaslo's power to flow into her. *No*, she thought. To free herself, she would need to reverse the flow of power. As she mentally prepared to do just that, grief impaled her. If she freed herself, she would trap Aaslo once more. He wouldn't be able to defeat Axus, and that was the only way to save both Aldrea *and* Celestria.

Sedi looked at the man who had defied her every attempt to kill him. The black rock encased her thighs, freeing his bare shoulders. She saw the dragon scales glinting across his shoulder and down his bicep. His sharp dragon gaze remained riveted on the open doorway, and his muscles coiled as if he might spring from the rock to protect them from attack. He was fascinating and *other*. He was also what the world needed. Sedi had a choice to make. Her or Aaslo. But could she do it? Could she sacrifice herself for *him*? Why should she? And what did she care about the world? She wanted nothing more than to leave it. Didn't she?

No, not really, she realized. Since meeting Aaslo, she had a renewed appreciation for life. But it wasn't life itself that drew her. It was Aaslo. She wanted Aaslo. She wanted him safe and whole and *hers*.

She glanced to the floor, where the reaper curled in on herself. Myropa struggled with the power Sedi sent to her, but she wasn't encased in the black rock. In fact, the black rock seemed to be ignoring Myropa altogether.

As the glossy blackness slid over her hips, Aaslo suddenly shouted, "Sedi, what's happening?"

She rolled her eyes. "You can see what's happening," she retorted. "Either you're encased, or I am. Which do you think I should choose?"

Aaslo roared his frustration. "Reverse the power. We'll find another way."

"No, I don't think we will," she replied. "As far as we know, there is no other way, and we're running out of time."

"Then reverse the flow and let it encase me," said Aaslo, reaching toward her but unable to move his legs. "I'll think of something else. There has to be a way. You and Myropa can escape."

Sedi crossed her arms. "See, here's the thing, *Forester*. *I'm* in charge of this power link, and I get to decide which way it goes. Consider this a lesson. You should never grant anyone the ability to steal your power."

His frustration evident, he bellowed, "But you'll be trapped— possibly even killed."

Myropa cried, "Let her do it, Aaslo. The world doesn't need her—or *me*. It needs *you*."

Sedi gave him a wink and a genuine smile as the black rock encased her shoulders. "But I'm not doing this for the world. I'm doing this for *you*, Aaslo, so you better appreciate it. I expect a promise in return. The first thing you do after you defeat Axus is come back here and get me out. Swear it."

"I swear," he said.

Sedi didn't see the last of the rock fall away from his feet. It was too late. The rock had closed over her head, completely encasing her. Her power abruptly cut off. Sedi couldn't breathe. Her lungs burned, and her bones cracked from the force of her spasms, since the rock didn't allow her to move even the tiniest fraction. As darkness enfolded her, Sedi thought of nothing but Aaslo and the lengths she had gone to in order to save him. A long-dead sensation filled her, and she accepted it. Sedi would have laughed if she had been capable of it. After so many centuries she had finally succumbed. She had fallen in love.

CHAPTER 27

AASLO CAUTIOUSLY LAID A HAND ON THE BLACK STONE THAT entombed Sedi. He could no longer see her. She had been completely consumed just as the power link between them had been terminated. His heart clenched, and sorrow momentarily swept him away.

"She isn't gone. She's immortal. She'll be here when you get back. Pretty soon she'll be up and trying to kill you all over again. And no doubt she'll be angry."

"No reason for her to be angry with *me*," muttered Aaslo. "She's the one who did it."

"Women don't think that way."

"What do you know of the way women think?"

"More than you."

Aaslo rolled his eyes. Then he tore away from Sedi's prison and looked toward Myropa, who wobbled a bit as she got to her feet. "Are you okay?"

She smoothed the silky fabric of her dress. "Yes, I think so. I couldn't hold your power, so I let it flow through the link with the Fates."

"You'll have to explain to me about these Fates someday."

"I would, but I'm not sure I understand them myself. They are a power outside the realm of the gods. They are not gods, themselves; they are older and, in some ways, more powerful. Even the gods must abide by the will of the Fates."

Aaslo stretched his aching limbs. "Then it's too bad we could not get them on *our* side."

"I honestly know nothing about their motivations or how their power works," replied Myropa.

Aaslo heaved a sigh. "We need to find Axus and end this."

"But he defeated you. The shades are gone. You no longer have the power of the depraved. What will you do?"

"I don't know, but I won't stop until he kills me."

"Now you sound like a proper hero."

"But your power is spent. Sedi and I took it all."

Aaslo shook his head. "No, I can feel it building inside me again.

It feels like a river connected to a vast lake of unimaginable power. The floodgates are open, and the power is just pouring in. My *vessel*, as Sedi called it, is almost full again."

"Hmm, that's what it feels like when I'm connected to the Fates. She said your power would regenerate, but I didn't expect it to happen so quickly." Myropa chewed her bottom lip and twisted the fabric of her dress between her fingers. "I know where Axus is. He's in his maelstrom, the nexus of his power."

Aaslo nodded solemnly. "Of course he is. What exactly is his maelstrom? How is it powered?"

Myropa shook her head. "I don't know. I'm not sure anybody but Axus knows. What I can say is that it consumes souls. They become trapped in there, and I'm pretty sure it feeds off them. It torments them until they're released."

"I don't suppose he releases them often," remarked Aaslo.

"I've never seen him release a soul. You must be careful, Aaslo. The power of the maelstrom is immense. It could suck you in, and you'll never escape. It's not something that can be fought."

Aaslo clenched his fists in anxious anticipation. Not only would he have to fight Axus again, he would now have to do it while resisting the maelstrom's pull. The problem seemed insurmountable.

"You've overcome insurmountable before."

"Never like this. What would you have done?"

"I would never have had to face this. I think it's time you stopped trying to fill my shoes and walk your own path."

"Fine. We'll do this *my* way."

He straightened and scanned the room for his axe. His heart clenched when he found it. The haft was a charred ruin, and the melted glob on the floor must have been the head. Unsurprising, the simple forester's axe hadn't been able to withstand the power of a god, but Aaslo was disappointed, nonetheless. He felt at his hips. He still carried Mathias's sword, and, of course, Mathias's head. He still felt guilty about the latter, but it seemed fitting that Mathias go with him into the final battle that would likely see them reunited very soon.

He turned to Myropa. "Very well. It seems I will have no choice but to face him in the maelstrom. Will you lead the way?"

Myropa nodded, then she slipped around him and padded out of the room. Aaslo looked back longingly at Sedi then followed. It became obvious Myropa had little familiarity with Axus's palace, as they had to backtrack several times. Once away from the gleaming structure, though, she had no problem navigating the crystalline landscape to the fissure in the side of the mountain. As they neared, Aaslo could feel Axus's power growing. By the time they approached the entrance, he was no longer sure he could face Axus. His doubt had grown to greater than his courage, and he faltered.

"I don't know if I can do this," he muttered as his hands began to shake. "He already defeated me once."

"And you're still alive."

"By mere chance. He won't make the same mistake again."

"You have the chance to redo the final battle, Aaslo. Not many heroes get that opportunity."

"I'm not a hero. I'm just doing what needs to be done."

"Sometimes that's all a hero is. Someone who does what needs to be done. Besides, you made it this far. I didn't make it out of Goldenwood with my head."

Aaslo took a deep breath but didn't move toward the opening.

"You can do this, Aaslo. I have faith in you. Myropa has faith in you. Sedi has faith in you. All the people on Aldrea have faith in you. Even the gods have faith in you. Have faith in yourself."

"Faith will not defeat a god."

"No, but you will."

Aaslo steadied his nerves and squared his shoulders. He drew Mathias's sword and summoned his power. This time, he held back nothing. A gleaming, golden aura surrounded him, and brilliant flaming wings burst from his back. He would go into the fight prepared.

Myropa embraced him one last time before he stepped through the dark fissure. When he emerged, he stood on a narrow ledge over a vast chasm extending far into the deep and soaring overhead. He could not see the chamber's farthest extents, but what lay at its center terrified him. A swirling mass of smoky, black, snakelike tendrils undulated between and around each other as a torrent of energy ripped through them. These carried the pain-filled wails of tortured souls, but the menacing cackle of a deranged god drowned out even that. Axus emerged from the maelstrom a beacon of terror, glowing with the glory of his post, and filled with the zealous joy of one who held all the power.

"So, you have come to face me again, puny bug." His eyes glittered with sadistic mirth as he spread his hands. "You are, of course, welcome here. In fact, I think I'll keep you here for all of eternity."

"What is this place?" asked Aaslo.

"This? This is my maelstrom. It is the glory that is me, the crux of my power, the very core of my being—my soul, if you will. Within it—within *me*—I harbor countless souls. All those terrible souls rejected by the Sea. Here, I punish them, *use* them, *consume* them. And now that you are here, I will consume your power *and* your soul. You will never escape."

Aaslo raised Mathias's sword and lunged at the dark god, plunging the blade deep into Axus's chest. A chime not unlike a forester's gong rang louder than the other sounds within the chamber. With fury on his face, Axus threw his arm up and around, wrenching Aaslo from his perch upon the cliff. His flaming wings flapped frantically as the center of the mass of angry power inexorably pulled him in. Aaslo cast every spell he could think of at Axus, to no avail. When he had exhausted his repertoire, he bombarded the God of Death with raw power. Axus laughed heartily at Aaslo's meager attempts, despite that they cost him. Then smoky tendrils of dark power wrapped themselves around Aaslo as energy lashed him. The attacks flayed his skin and laid him open, ripping his life's blood away. The maelstrom consumed him, trapped again, only this time, at the center of Axus's power, no one would rescue him.

Myropa paced anxiously outside the fissure. Part of her desperately wanted to join Aaslo, to ensure that he was well, but she knew if she did, she would be a useless distraction. She stood, in her palpable terror and grief, unsure of what to do.

A trill built in her chest; she was being called away. She couldn't go, though. She might be needed. How could she leave Aaslo to collect the souls of dead strangers? Her frustration mounted as the tingling sensation grew. She didn't have a choice. If she didn't go, the power of the Fates would rip her away by force. Tears flowed and shattered against the stone at her feet as her heart broke. If she held on for a few more minutes . . .

A dozen horses tied to her soul, galloping in different directions, abruptly wrenched Myropa away from Axus's mountain. In the next instant, it stopped. She clutched at her chest as she heaved in breaths she didn't really need. She found herself before a cottage at the edge of a summer meadow where it met a dense forest. Her body shook as she took in the cottage. It wasn't a large structure, maybe enough to house a single family. Vines ran up walls of rounded cobblestones in varying shades of grey and black. Four glass-paned windows graced the front, flanking a single wooden door at the center. A wood-shingled roof extended to one side to cover a large mound of firewood piled upon a wooden deck. Two empty rocking chairs sat to the side. The grass around the house was clipped but otherwise allowed to grow wild with flowers. There were no fences or pens for animals or outbuildings, but it was obviously lived in because smoke streamed from the chimney. To Myropa, this little cottage was absolutely perfect.

Unsure as to where she was, Myropa checked her sense of the power that made up the world. She was surprised to find that she was still in Celestria. The mystery grew, as she didn't sense the presence of any of the gods. She wondered if perhaps whoever lived here contained their power well enough that she couldn't sense it. She knew of only one god with that ability—Disevy.

Anger overcame Myropa. The god had kept himself aloof, refusing to become involved in Axus's war, while her only son put himself in danger to fight against Axus himself. If Disevy truly felt any concern for Celestria, would he not do something to stop Axus? Did he secretly hope Axus would succeed?

Balling her fists, Myropa stomped to the little cottage. She flung the door open and stormed inside. No one was there. As her gaze swept her surroundings, she noted that, inside, the space seemed larger. The comfortable living space at the front of the home drew her. The furnishings looked too fine for such a homely cottage. A red velvet settee sat opposite the hearth, flanked by two matching high-backed chairs, each with a plush footstool with carved lion's feet. A luxurious carpet in gold and red and brown spanned the space, lending it a warmth. Beyond the living area lay a neat and tidy kitchen with a wood-burning stove on the far side and long counters containing various cooking implements. It put her in mind of a place that held endless hours of love and laughter. A sleeping area with a large bed covered with a colorful patchwork quilt and several plump pillows took up the other end of the room. Small tables sat on either side of the bed, each holding a vase filled with fragrant wildflowers. She could imagine waking up every day next to Disevy in that bed.

Myropa's cheeks warmed. She shouldn't think of Disevy in that way. He wasn't hers. He was a god. And she was still mad. That brought her back to the questions at hand. Where was he? And what was she doing here? Someone forced her to come here when she needed to be with Aaslo. Was it coincidence, or part of a plan? Still, setting aside the fact that her son fought for his life—and the lives of everyone on both Aldrea and Celestria—she could feel at peace here. It was everything she never knew she wanted and needed.

Frustrated that someone obviously didn't respect her time or needs, Myropa set her mind to returning to Aaslo. She opened herself to travel back to him. Nothing happened. Something anchored her *here*. Myropa paced the plush carpet for several minutes as she tried again and again to leave. With an irritated huff, she fell back onto the settee in front of the crackling fire. Then she noticed a small side table that held a cup of tea and a book. Placing her fingers on the side of the teacup—it was hot. She picked up the cup and inhaled the silky fragrance of rose and soothing chamomile. She sipped and luxuriated in the feel of the warmth moving through her frozen body with a startling but not unwelcome sensation. Never before had any sustenance warmed her in Celestria.

The teacup settled on the saucer with a click, and Myropa picked up the book. Embossed in gold across its brown leather cover were the words *The Fates*. Myropa dropped the book, startled to understanding. This wasn't Disevy's cottage. He hadn't called her, and she didn't know if she felt relieved or irritated. If he wasn't here, then where was he? She looked back to the name of the book. *The Fates*. This was *their* cottage. Why had they called her? Were the Fates getting involved in this war? Or were they just getting her out of the way?

Stirred to curiosity, Myropa opened the book and began reading. After the first few paragraphs, she was confused. She skipped ahead a few pages and continued reading, which only added to her confusion. The book was about her, her life. She scanned as she flipped the pages. She skipped to the moment of her death, where the story abruptly ended. The final pages were all empty. While the book contained nothing more, she knew what it had been telling her.

Myropa looked around at the perfect little cottage with new understanding. Its quaint setting, its warm, luxurious décor, its homely appeal. It was all familiar because this was *her* cottage. The Fates were nothing but an illusion—*she was her own Fate*. That meant that the power that had kept her in the world, the power to send beasts of the Alterworld back to their own realm, the power that protected her from Axus's wrath, was her own power, and it had been all along. It also meant that the power that kept her there in that quaint cottage was also her own power, and she could overcome it. This time, when she opened herself to travel, she was not hindered. Her will was enough to break the bonds that tied her to the place. For the first time in life and death, she *knew* she possessed a strength even the gods could not overcome.

MORY FLOATED IN AN ENDLESS OBLIVION. HE WATCHED COUNTLESS eons drift by and felt nothing of their passing. Tiny stars winked in and out of existence, each one tethered to the world for a blink of an eye, but he had no connection to any of it. They were *other*, and he was—well, he didn't know what he was. His entire existence balanced on a precipice, and at any moment he might tip.

But which way? He couldn't remember what had been or where he might wish to go. He thought, perhaps, there had been pain, but it was gone now. Only this place that wasn't a place existed for him, a place between worlds—between *realms*. That was significant, somehow, but he didn't know why.

A jolt of power surged through him. Not *his* power. Someone else's. Dark. Demanding. And it sought something.

Mory blinked. An endless wave of blackness before him, a shroud so dark it absorbed light, snuffing it out effortlessly, mercilessly. That made Mory sad. He wanted to stop it, but he didn't know how. He was tiny, a mere afterthought, compared to the infinite wave of darkness. The power that wasn't his jolted him again, and he moved *toward* the dark wave. Mory began to panic, certain that if he reached it, it would snuff him out as it had the light. He struggled, but he had no power of his own. He didn't even know what he was. Some innate knowledge told him that he had to know what he was if he wanted to fight back.

He turned inward and was surprised. *He* was a tiny light, like the others. He glowed a faint blue but was threaded through with darkness like the wave. The dark power had attached itself to his darkness. A terrifying understanding rushed through Mory. The foreign power flowing through him was that of the evil Berruvian empress, and the infinite wave of darkness was Axus, the God of Death. Mory would become a conduit between them, used by them to snuff out the lives of all those souls swallowed by the darkness. He didn't want that darkness inside him, but he didn't know how to be free of it. But it was too late. They had succeeded. As the two powers connected, Mory began to grow. The dark wave that was Axus flooded into him, and he expanded to accommodate it. His light, his soul, wriggled and pulsed as he tried to stop it.

To Mory's horror, snakes of dark power filtered through him, reaching for the thousands upon thousands of lights. Every soul the tendrils touched became darkness itself, passing beyond the shroud. Mory became so full of the darkness that its insidious intent began to bloom in his mind. Then Mory *knew*. People were dying.

TEZA CRIED OUT IN HORROR AND TERROR AS PEOPLE BEGAN TO FALL on both sides of the battle, and this time, they did not rise again. Dark, sinuous clouds, physical manifestations of death, wafted across the battlefield in inky tendrils, reaching out of the nether for anything bearing life. Life forces stolen upon a dark, vaporous wind. As the miasma passed from one person to the next, they fell to the ground, their life forces claimed before their bodies surrendered. From her perch atop the wall, Teza watched it happen again and again. At first, it was only one or two, then a handful at a time. People who had not sustained mortal injuries died. Soldiers, warriors, and civilians battled with weapons and shields, but failed to see the death that swept in and dragged them away. No armor could stop it.

It no longer mattered that half her force of a hundred thousand was already dead, and the Berru would soon tear through the wards and the gate. Her time as mage general was at an end, for she could do nothing about the death sweeping unimpeded across Aldrea. Aaslo had failed. The prophecy played out as Ijen had said it would. Everyone would die.

THE BRIGHT SUN SHINING OVER SOUTHERN LODENON ALL DAY WAS now obscured by a quickly forming grey haze. Lily gathered her sack holding a schoolbook and pencils and hurried home down the street. It looked as if it might start raining at any minute, and she didn't want to get soaked. She wasn't the only one running, which made her way more difficult. Shoppers and stall workers in the market scurried back and forth across the dirt road, finishing their last-minute purchases or securing their wares.

Someone tripped over Lily, knocking her over, sprawling into the dirt. She thought at least it wasn't raining yet. Dirt was easier to brush off than mud. When she looked up, she saw something she didn't understand. A dark tendril swept down from the sky, curling toward a man crossing her path. When it touched the man, he stiffened and fell.

Lily crawled over and placed her hand on his chest. He wasn't breathing, eyes staring vacant, lifeless, at the pitch-black sky.

As Lily lay there in shock, more black tendrils fell from the sky, striking other people in the market. People began screaming and running. A woman tripped over her. Lily stood on shaky legs, her schoolbag forgotten, and ran for home. There, ahead of her, a tendril surged toward a woman who had dropped her basket of laundry. Lily ran faster, knocking the woman out of the way. The tendril simply curled around Lily and caught the woman anyway, and the woman died instantly. Lily wept furiously as she searched the sky for the tendril that would come for her.

Across the Endric Ocean, on the northern shore of Berru, a fisherman named Onguin stood looking north, across the water, at a vast storm staining the sky black and grey. As he dragged his net into his boat, he watched the storm grow. It quickly spread across the ocean, and clouds began to accumulate above him. He shivered and hoped it wouldn't rain before he could dock. He took his seat and began rowing for shore, but he knew he wouldn't make it in time. The clouds, nearly as dark as night, gathered faster than he had ever seen.

As he watched the sky, a tendril of black smoke curled down. His heart lurched as it flew toward him, then clung. His pulse raced, and then it stopped. He drew no breath, held no thoughts. His body slumped into his lonely fishing boat, his soul wrenched away.

Peck ducked as a black tendril of power swept from the sky and plunged into the Berruvian guard by the stone circle's entrance. The man fell, dead. Peck shook himself, then with practiced stealth, shifted through the shadows lining the stone circle. The now-blackened sphere at its center fully held Empress Lysia's attention. The dark power connecting her to whatever spell she cast swirled around her in a tornado born of soot. The now-loose ends of her long black hair and the gauzy shreds of her dress danced and snapped in the tumultuous wind, her eyes alight with zeal and power. She stared into the sphere with a malicious grin. Peck could no longer see Mory within the dark power the sphere contained. He didn't even know if Mory still lived, but he couldn't think about that at the moment. He was no longer doing this just to save Mory, nor was he doing it for

Aaslo. The simpler days of struggling for the right to exist for him and Mory were gone. Now he was fighting for Aldrea—for life, for *everyone*. He had to focus on his task.

With the empress's back to him, he stalked forward on silent feet. The hand gripping the knife started to tremble, and he paused to still it. With mounting tension, his muscles contracted, and he sucked air into his tight chest. Then, Peck surged forward through the vortex of power and plunged the knife into the empress's back. As the dark power scattered, out of control, Peck released the knife and fell back onto the grassy earth. The empress turned and lurched. Her face contorted into vile hatred as she pointed a craggy finger at him. Power began to gather around her once again, and Peck's heart stuttered. He had failed, and now she would exact her revenge. He would die, as would Mory.

The black power snaked toward him, and he dodged its icy grip. Leaping to his feet, he sped toward the empress. He spun to her rear and yanked the dagger out. She released a terrible cry as he backpedaled. He lunged again and slashed her across the chest, then danced away. The empress shouted for her guards, but of course none came. He had either killed them, or her spell had. He knew now what the machine that held Mory did. It killed, plain and simple. It didn't matter which side you were on, whether Berru or Endricsian—when those smoky tendrils dropped from the sky for you, you were dead.

The empress sent a burst of power toward him, and Peck slammed into one of the stone pillars, causing it to rock on its base. His ribs and back ached as he crumpled to the ground. He rolled to the side, narrowly avoiding a javelin of dark power, and forced himself to his feet. He continued to dodge her attacks, which grew slow and unfocused. He could see a black smoke wafting off the woman toward the sphere. The empress was alone, injured, and her power committed elsewhere. Peck would only have one chance.

He briefly considered throwing the dagger at her, but Peck hesitated. If he missed, he would be without a weapon. Instead, he dodged inky tendrils as he slipped in and out of range, inflicting cut after cut on the enraged woman but failing to land a killing blow. Crimson soaked through her filmy grey dress in a number of places, and with her pale complexion and black eyes, she truly looked a horror. He inflicted another cut across her hip; she raked him down his neck with her pointed nails. It was a minor wound, and he ignored the burning sting as he spun and stabbed her with the knife again. It glanced off her shoulder blade, and she yelled for her guards once more, her voice barely more than a wheeze.

Peck danced away, but his heel caught on a rough patch, and he fell. The empress rasped a cackling laugh as she rallied to send a surge of dark power at him. He tried to roll, but he was too slow. Tendrils of death dug into his flesh, and Peck screamed. The power wrapped around his heart and lungs, and his vision darkened. His attention turned to the blackened sphere. He knew Mory was inside, and he knew Mory was suffering. Mory would die a terrible death far too young because Peck had been too slow.

He blinked past his darkening vision and caught a glimpse of the empress standing over him, triumphant. In a final bid for Mory's life and for all of Aldrea, Peck drew on the last of his strength and threw the dagger. He didn't see it land. His vision had gone, and his mind began to splinter. Then, the power digging into his soul dissipated. Peck sucked in lungsful of air as he sprawled on the hard, rocky earth. As his mind cleared, he abruptly remembered where he was and lurched to his feet. There, before him, lay the empress, her eyes vacant and her power extinguished. The dagger was buried to the hilt in her chest, and her black eyes stared, unseeing, into the dark sky.

CHAPTER 28

AXUS'S MAELSTROM SURGED AROUND AASLO AS AN OUTWARD FLOW of power snapped back at him. Whatever had drawn on Axus's power abruptly ceased, and because of that, the god's dark power became more focused—primarily on Aaslo. He felt it pull him in every direction at once, as if he would fly apart into a million pieces. Every thread holding him together unraveled simultaneously, and it was all he could do to keep them contained within his vessel. The multitude of powers that resided within him each vied for dominance, but he couldn't figure out which he needed most to fight the torrential forces assailing him.

"You're overthinking, Aaslo. Don't give up!"

Beyond the storm, demented laughter raged. Not the wild glee of mania, but the joy of satisfaction, a celebration of victory. Axus had won. Aaslo was trapped, would be torn asunder, and Axus would rain death upon Aldrea from his kingly throne above all other gods. Aaslo knew Axus wouldn't stop with Aldrea, either. He would take each and every world, in which the other gods had placed their power, until he claimed everything. He would leave nothing to chance. He wanted *all* the power. Aaslo wouldn't be able to stop him. Arohnu, God of Prophecy, had been wrong to place his faith in Aaslo. He simply didn't have the strength to defeat Axus. He couldn't even escape the maelstrom. In death, he would be trapped within it, tormented for all time.

He whispered, "I'm sorry, brother. It looks like I won't be seeing you in death after all."

"Brothers in all things, Aaslo. I have faith in you, and I'm never wrong."

"You were often wrong." Aaslo's face was damp with tears of anguish, both physical and mental. The maelstrom rendered his flesh from bone, and even his dragon scales started to peel away. As the searing power of death ripped across his skin, he sought escape within himself. He held the thousands of souls inside him close, wrapping them around himself in a cocoon of infinite, soothing energy. If he could just hold on to this bit of power, he might retain some piece of himself. A futile battle, though, he knew. Even now, the bonds threatened to untangle.

Then a new sound reached his tortured ears.

"Aaslo! Aaslo, listen!"

He parsed out her words.

"Aaslo, can you hear me?"

Myropa. His mother. Come to him in the moment of his death. A fitting end, he supposed. He felt glad for her presence, although saddened that she would have to see this. He had no way to respond. It hardly mattered. He was at his end.

"I understand now," she called through the tempest. "You have the power, Aaslo. It's in you. It *is* you. It's *all* of you. The soul is *infinite*, Aaslo. Infinite power!"

He already knew that. He had no idea how to *use* that to his advantage. He could feel the limitless extents of every soul bound to him, but it was a different kind of power—the power of life, existence, directionless, unfocused. It wasn't the kind of power that could be used for spells or attacks.

"That doesn't mean it's useless."

As Aaslo tried to sift through the powers available to him, Myropa's words echoed in his mind. *"It's all of you."*

He began to come apart at the seams, but he wasn't ready to let go just yet. If he was going to die anyway, suffer for all of eternity in Axus's maelstrom, then he truly had nothing left to lose. He turned toward the nurturing power of Ina, the destructive power of the dragon, and the seductive power of death.

"That's right, Aaslo. Use them."

He shed the thin veneer of control he had maintained over each of them and opened himself to all of them. He embraced the heat absorbed from the fae magma monsters, the strength visited upon him by Disevy, and the raw power granted him by Arayallen. He drew on the power of thousands of souls shared by his wanderers. To these he added the immense destructive power of the depraved he had somehow stolen for himself. Finally, holding back nothing, he unleashed his own soul, that piece of the veil that had been ripped away during his birth. He used that infinite, unparalleled, directionless power to bolster those that he could affect with his will.

The dragon unfurled its thick, leathery wings and took flight, releasing a raging inferno as it soared unchecked. Ina cackled endlessly as he accepted all that she was into himself, allowing her nourishing power to stretch beyond his limits. The dark power of death slithered into every crack and recess of his mind and body, connecting him to everything that ever was and was no longer.

Aaslo allowed these powers to consume him, and in that moment, he was no more. All that had made him human burnt away in a blinding eruption of golden light, and only his consciousness and the infinite power of his soul remained. All the powers became one. *His* will, unbreakable. Golden rays pierced the maelstrom, disrupting its turbulent flow, impaling the incessant, destructive power driving the madness within it. In that moment, he understood. The maelstrom wasn't a construct created by Axus to torture souls. The maelstrom *was* Axus. The core of his power. Every soul he claimed within it made him stronger.

And he had tried to consume Aaslo.

Aaslo directed his infinite power into the maelstrom, tearing it apart eddy by swirling eddy. As he did, those souls trapped within began to slip away. Aaslo wasn't worried, though. He sensed another power—familiar but far away. Then he recognized Mory. Somehow the boy had connected with the dark power that was Axus, and those escaping souls fled down that connection into Mory. Aaslo used that connection to siphon the souls from Axus's maelstrom, pulling them one by one from their prison, and feeding them to Mory. Axus roared in anger, lashing at Aaslo, who was beyond his reach. When Axus's assault had no effect, Aaslo felt the dark power shudder, and he knew what Axus felt. *Fear.*

Aaslo used the golden light of his power to rip the god apart from the inside, piece by piece. Axus tried to fight, but for every soul liberated from the maelstrom, he lost strength and power. As each person who signed *The Contract* died on Aldrea, Aaslo's power *grew.*

A dark howl echoed through the chamber as the maelstrom rose in fury, but Axus had no chance. Aaslo shredded the god's very being until not even the thinnest thread remained.

Within that hollow, cavernous chamber, Axus was unmade.

MORY DIDN'T KNOW WHAT HAPPENED TO THE DARK WAVE OF POWER that was Axus, but within the last several minutes, he had been inundated with gleaming souls escaping from the death god's clutches. The tiny lights shone brightly as they wandered aimlessly, and Mory began to panic. He knew these tiny lights were souls, and if they weren't claimed, they would be lost in the void for eternity. But if *he* claimed them, he would become responsible for them. It would be his duty to care for them until he could pass them on to someone worthier. He couldn't allow them to be lost. He decided to claim them *temporarily*, and reached out. They came, filling him with their power.

Suddenly, the dark wave, that shroud of death that consumed everything, was torn to pieces, shredded until not a tatter remained. It happened so quickly that Mory wasn't even sure he had witnessed it. Then the void started to suck him in. In Axus's absence, a vacuum had been created, and the open connection Mory had once held with the dark god drew him into that hollow space. Mory didn't try to fight it. He burst at the seams with the power of the millions of souls that Axus had tried to claim, and Mory needed that extra space to expand into.

As Mory filled the void, he noticed that it was not completely empty. Within the cavernous space gleamed a golden light. As the light brushed him, he recognized its power. It felt like Aaslo. As soon as he had the thought, the light took shape. After a moment, that shape became recognizable. It *was* Aaslo. He appeared as he had when they had first met. Both his arms were human, as were his eyes. He was wholly and completely human, and yet *not*. Now, he bore a greater power. He radiated it, surrounded by a golden aura.

He bore the power of a god.

Aaslo looked at him in surprise. "Mory, I am glad to see you are well."

Mory peered down at himself and realized he had, in fact, managed to re-form himself. His body was whole once again, but he wore a set of golden robes that matched an aura emanating from him.

"I am," he said, turning his hand over. "But I think I am changed."

Aaslo clenched his very human hand that had once been a dragon's fist. "As are we both."

"Not just that." Mory's voice filled with awe. "I think we're—"

"Gods?" Aaslo finished his sentence.

Mory swallowed and met Aaslo's troubled gaze. "Is that possible?"

"Not quite," a new voice spoke, deep, filled with strength, power, and authority. Mory and Aaslo turned to see the newcomer striding toward them through the void as if taking a casual stroll.

"I recognize you." Aaslo's voice filled with surprise. "You're Ord, the old man who gave me mead back on Aldrea. Except, you look younger."

The man's perfect smile shined brightly as he grinned. "You remember. Allow me to introduce myself properly. I am Disevy, God of Strength and Virility."

Aaslo's eyes widened. "The mead. That was when you blessed me."

"So it was." Disevy sounded pleased. "But you have come far since then. You are now a god in your own right."

"And me? Am I a god?" asked Mory.

Disevy shook his head. "Aaslo was already in the process of ascending long before his fight with Axus. I don't think he realized it, but he had become immortal upon first acquiring the power over death. You, on the other hand, are not quite there, but you could be." He laid a firm hand on Mory's shoulder. "Axus was destroyed, and you have claimed the souls he harbored in his maelstrom. If you accept his role, you too, will become a god."

Mory couldn't help but shiver. "Role? What role?"

"Someone must shepherd the souls of the dead and take custody of those not meant for the Sea of Transcendence."

"The souls of the dead?" Mory didn't like where this was going. "Wait, you're talking about death. You want me to become *Death*?"

Despite Mory's alarmed shout, Disevy regarded him with patience. "It is not a matter of what *I* want. It is what *you* want. You have been drawn into the position of God of Death, and as such you gain your power from the passing of souls across the void and by harboring those who do not enter the Sea within yourself. You can choose not to take the role."

Aaslo interjected, "Axus's maelstrom was a place of pain and terror. Mory doesn't have the countenance for that. He is not cruel like Axus. He could never punish people in such a way, regardless of what they'd done in life."

Mory reeled from the idea of becoming a god. He hadn't thought about having to punish anyone. "Aaslo's right," he blurted. "I'm not cut out for this. Why can't Aaslo be the God of Death?"

"He could," said Disevy with a nod. "But I believe Aaslo has a different destiny." He directed a contemplative look toward Aaslo. Then he turned his powerful gaze back to Mory. "The maelstrom was Axus's chosen approach to dealing with the souls of those rejected by the Sea. You can determine your own way. Perhaps yours will be more compassionate. It is your prerogative just as this place is your prerogative."

"What do you mean?" said Mory. "Where are we?"

"We are in Celestria, and if you accept your role, this will be your dominion."

"But nothing is here."

"That's because you have not yet created it. Here, in your dominion, you will be all-powerful. Whatever you dream can *be*. You must make your own home here."

"But what about Peck? Can he come here with me?"

Disevy slowly shook his head. "I'm afraid your friend Peckett does not have the power or the will to exist in Celestria, but you may watch over him."

Mory despaired. In order to become a god, he would have to leave Peck behind. He would need to become his own man—his own *god*.

Disevy waved, and a large yet shallow pool materialized. Rounded boulders and cobbles lined its sides, and its surface was perfectly smooth as if it had never been touched by the wind.

Mory's eyes widened. "Where did that come from?"

Disevy smiled. "You created it."

"No, I didn't," Mory said defensively. "I don't even know what *it* is."

"It is a viewing pool, and you created it with your desire to see your friend. It is a fitting first creation for someone who has just ascended. You will do well here. Do not worry about Peckett. You may visit him from time to time, if you like, in Aldrea and at the Sea when he passes beyond the veil."

Mory's heart tumbled into his stomach. He hadn't yet had time to consider that he was immortal and that Peck wasn't. Peck would eventually die.

Disevy saw the realization in Mory's expression, because he looked at Mory with compassion. "Death is not an end. You will come to know this better than anyone. With time, you will understand your power and find joy in watching the soul's journey through life and death, and, if you like, rebirth."

Mory rocked back on his heels. "If *I* like? You mean I have the power to reincarnate someone?"

Disevy smiled with a twinkle in his eye. "You will be the God of Death. It is your prerogative."

AASLO LISTENED RAPTLY TO DISEVY'S EXPLANATION OF MORY'S NEW-found powers. It was strange that Mory should suddenly become a god, but perhaps no stranger than his own ascension. At first, he thought Mory unsuited for the role of the God of Death, but the more he thought about it, the more he considered it a good choice. Mory was sharp, intelligent, kind, and compassionate. In his youth and innocence, the hardships of life had not yet jaded him, even though he had seen and experienced enough darkness to understand the need for rules and punishment. The boy was level-headed, even-keeled, and driven, which seemed like appropriate traits for a god. Aaslo knew even the infinite passage of time would not change the boy so much that he would ever seek dominion over Celestria. Nor could he imagine Mory wanting to claim all the lives on any world for the sake of power. Mory was, perhaps, the perfect person for the role of God of Death.

"I think you should do it, Mory."

"What? Really?" replied Mory.

"Sure, Death already belonged to a would-be conqueror, why not put it in the hands of a child?"

"Yes, really. I think you are the perfect person for the job. You're good-natured, compassionate, and dedicated. You're loyal and honorable. People respect you because you're dependable and respectful in return. You care about others and put their needs above your own desires. You aren't covetous and haven't been jaded by time and trials. You will learn and grow with time."

Mory's gaze darted between him and Disevy and he swallowed hard before looking toward the pool. Aaslo knew Mory wanted to see Peck again. He wanted to know what Peck thought of this idea. But it seemed he wouldn't get the chance. He had to make *this* decision on his own.

"What if I say no?" he said.

Disevy's voice was calm and comforting as he said, "You have grown beyond your earthly vessel. Your human body died. Once you release those souls you're harboring, your soul will be taken to the Sea of Transcendence."

"You mean I'll be dead. I *am* dead," said Mory.

"In essence, yes," confirmed Disevy.

"I'll never see Peck again. I don't even know if *he's* alive. I can't make him go through that again. If I die, it will destroy him."

"Then you accept?" asked Disevy.

Mory took a deep breath before nodding. "I—I guess so."

"You must be certain."

Mory blew out another breath. "Okay, yes. I accept."

Disevy looked to Aaslo. "He is very nearly there already. I believe *you* have the power to tip him over the edge."

"You think *I* can raise him to a god?" said Aaslo in surprise. Disevy simply stared expectantly, so Aaslo turned to Mory. He opened himself to the immense power that suffused him when he defeated Axus and released it into the boy. A blinding aura consumed his mind, and Aaslo lost himself for a time.

"Are you ready?" came Disevy's deep voice.

Abruptly drawn back, Aaslo realized Mory was no longer beside them. The boy had moved to the viewing pool and stood watching it intently. A bright, golden aura surrounded him.

Aaslo pulled his gaze from the boy. "Ready for what?"

PECK KNELT BEFORE THE EMPTY SPHERE, HEAD HUNG LOW, AND TEARS dripping from his chin. Mory was gone. All of him, his entire body, had been consumed or destroyed or *something*, and he was gone. Peck could feel nothing but the agonizing pain of loss and emptiness. A hand landed on his shoulder, and he did not rouse.

"You are hurt."

Peck heard the voice, but he didn't recognize it. It wasn't Mory's, so it wasn't important.

"Please, Great Emissary, allow us to heal you."

He heard the voice again; it wasn't speaking to him. It spoke to someone called Great Emissary. Mory wasn't the Great Emissary, so again, it wasn't important. He felt a tug at his elbow, which caused him to shift his weight. The small movement reminded him that *he* still had a body. A surge of something—panic? Anger? He wasn't sure—flooded his system, and he lurched to his feet, backing away from the source of the voice.

He blinked blood and tears from his eyes as he took in the courtyard. A dozen guards and three magi in long black tunics stared at him uneasily, with the empress's body at their feet. Peck glanced at the empress, then at the men and women who blocked his exit. He expected to see anger and judgment in their expressions. Instead, they peered at him expectantly. Peck looked to the bloody blade sticking from the empress's chest. He thought he might be able to get to it before they caught him, but then what? He couldn't fight them all. The head magus, the one named Cobin who had been in the stone circle at the beginning, followed his gaze and seemed to know what he was thinking. The man cleared his throat and then looked back to the guards and magi behind him.

"Leave us," he commanded.

The others shifted uncomfortably, sending furtive glances at Peck before shuffling through the rustling curtains draped between the standing stones. While they left, Peck inched his way closer to the buried blade. The magus frowned and watched Peck thoughtfully before speaking. "There is no reason for you to fear me. I am not your enemy."

Peck halted a few feet from the blade. His hand twitched with the need to reach for it. "You are Berru. Of course you are my enemy."

The magus nodded. "That was true before." He spread his hands to indicate the body of the empress at his feet. "But no longer."

Peck shuffled another step closer to the blade, but the magus didn't move. "You expect me to believe that?"

"It is true," the magus stated simply. "You see, in Berru, there is only one way to ascend to the throne, and that is to take it from whoever occupies it."

Peck's eyes widened. "You mean *kill* them?"

The magus nodded. "Indeed."

Peck momentarily forgot about the knife as his gaze returned to the empress. When he met the magus's gaze again, he saw expectation. Peck's stomach flipped. "Are you saying that *I'm* now the emperor?"

The magus gave a tight smile. "I'm glad to see our new emperor is sharp." Peck suddenly remembered the knife and glanced at it again. The magus shook his head. "Take it if you want. You do not need it. I will not harm you."

"Why not?" blurted Peck. "You are a magus. You could easily kill me and become emperor yourself."

Peck wrenched the knife from the empress's body, and the magus allowed it. Peck didn't attack right away, though. He knew the man likely had a shield ward or some nasty spell prepared. The man stared at the body of the empress for some time before he spoke. "I was at Lysia's side for nearly eight years, and in all that time I never once had the daring or courage to steal her position. For one, it is detrimental to one's health to be emperor," he scoffed. "But also, Lysia had a way about her. She was meant to rule. That didn't mean I agreed with all her choices, but I found myself unwilling to move against her.

"You came here with no weapons and no power, but you had ideals and a desire to survive. You succeeded where I could not. You now bear the title and power of the emperor, and the only way to rid yourself of it is to die. I do not envy you."

"But I can leave. You all go back to Berru and find someone else to be emperor."

The magus shook his head sadly. "It doesn't work that way. You should not look at this as a punishment. Look at this as an opportunity.

Berru is a fractured empire. Lysia's ambitions would have led to the death of *everyone*, yet now we will live. We need someone to lead us in a new direction, to help us find purpose. Your destiny is *our* destiny."

"My destiny? Last year I lived on the streets stealing purses and running from the boss's thugs. I'm no longer that scared thief. I have the honor of being second-in-command of the scouts in Aaslo's army. I know the glory of fighting for something greater than myself, and I know what it means to lead, but I'm no emperor. I wouldn't even know where to begin."

The magus smiled. "Of course, you will need guidance."

"And that guidance will come from *you*? You want me to be your puppet with a target on my back while you sit comfortably on your secret throne?"

"Not at all. I will merely offer counsel. You will be emperor in truth. Whatever you decide cannot be worse than killing everyone in our empire."

Peck gripped his knife like a lifeline as he thought through what the magus had said. The man had a point. Lysia might have held her empire with an iron fist, but she had intended to use that fist to crush everyone. He couldn't do worse than that, could he? Peck always thought himself ambitious, but he had only aspired to be a first-rate cutpurse. Never in his life had he considered ruling over anyone. The closest he had come was in caring for Mory. The thought brought him up short, and he raised the knife to point at the empty sphere. On a choked breath, he said, "Where is he?"

The magus looked at Peck sadly. "I truly do not know what happened to him. The empress was blessed directly by Axus. Her power was a mystery to me."

Peck's breathing became ragged, and he backed away until his legs struck something solid. He glanced down and took a seat on the stone he had found. "I need to think."

The magus nodded his understanding. He pointed to an opening in the curtains. "I will be just over there when you need me."

Peck set the knife on the stone next to him and pressed the palms of his hands to his eyes, trying to hold back his sobs. As he sat like that, a soothing warmth overtook him. Then a hand came to rest on his shoulder.

Peck jumped and exclaimed, "I said I need to—" His shout abruptly ended when his eyes landed on Mory, who stood in front of him, whole and shining like a beacon. Peck froze in shock but managed to utter, "M-Mory, what is this?"

Mory grinned and shook his head. "Sorry, I'm still new to this power. I don't know how to suck it in like the others."

Peck gripped Mory's shoulders with the intent of never letting go. "But—what power?"

Mory spread his hands. "Look at me, Peck. I'm a god! Can you believe it? Since Aaslo killed Axus, I'm the new God of Death."

Peck's eyes could not be any wider. "Aaslo *killed* Axus? And you. You're a *god*? How?"

Mory scratched his nose and sat on the stone next to Peck. "Apparently, I sort of got dragged into the role because I was connected directly to Axus's power when he was killed. It wasn't completely by accident, I suppose. They gave me a choice. I was *almost* a god, and Aaslo raised me the rest of the way."

Peck could only stare in shocked silence.

Mory squirmed uncomfortably. "I was watching you, Peck. I saw you crying over me, and I heard what the magus said about you being emperor. I need you to know that I'm okay. I'm better than okay. I can create anything, and you never have to worry about me again. I'm immortal." He paused, but when Peck didn't say anything, he added, "I think you should be emperor, Peck."

"You do?"

Mory nodded. "You'll be a good emperor. You've always been great at thinking things through, and you're a different man than you were, a decent man. You understand honor, loyalty, and friendship. You'll do right by the Berru, and, most importantly, you won't let them attack Endrica again. It's better you be emperor than leave it up to them."

Peck's chin wagged soundlessly as words escaped him. Finally, he admitted, "I guess that makes sense."

Mory grinned at him. "Good, and I'll do what I can to help. You don't need to worry about dying, Peck. I'll take care of you when you do. You'll see. It's not so bad.

"I heard how you became emperor. People are going to try to kill you. If you don't want to die too soon, you'll need to be strong. I'm going to bless you, and I need you to accept it."

Peck was so overwhelmed that he didn't know what to say. He had so many questions, and each one seemed as important as the last. In that moment, though, the only thing that really mattered was that Mory wasn't dead. He was alive. No, he was better than alive. He was a god. And it seemed like from here on out, Mory would be taking care of *him*.

CHAPTER 29

Disevy laid a heavy hand on Aaslo's shoulder. "There is much to be done. Celestria is in shambles. The other gods will have felt Axus's demise. The fighting has stopped, and rebuilding efforts are underway."

"So soon? But it just happened."

"Things are different here in Celestria. We do not dwell on what was when the sands shift. And, we can do many things at once. I, myself, am currently rebuilding the Fifth Pantheon as we speak. But there are issues to be addressed."

"That's well and good," said Aaslo, "but I want to know something. You lead the Fifth Pantheon and Axus was your subordinate. Why didn't *you* stop him? Why didn't *you* kill Axus? Why *me*?"

Disevy held his hands behind his back and sighed in much the same way Magdelay had done when she taught him and Mathias. "It's true that I couldn't get involved or your part in the second prophecy would never have come to fruition. But it's more than that. I believe that, had I gotten involved, I would not have been successful. Although he corrupted himself in the process, Axus gained quite a bit of power from the souls he stole and from those he kept in his maelstrom.

"As for why you? It needed to be someone Axus didn't see as a threat, someone who could get close to him. Axus was vain. He never considered that you might be capable of defeating him. Who would have believed that a simple human forester could kill a god? No one could have seen that coming—except, of course, Arohnu."

"I certainly didn't see it coming."

"Me neither," murmured Aaslo.

"Now there are other things that need doing. Those who were loyal to Axus must be punished."

"And you want me to be involved?"

"It is only fitting. Aldrea was your world. It still is if you wish it to be."

"I can go back to Aldrea?"

Disevy surveyed the empty space beneath their feet as they walked through the void. "Mory became a god because he was drawn into Axus's power, consumed by it, as Axus died. Therefore, his role here in Celestria is set. He is the God of Death. You, however, are different. Your power is something new, and some of it is directly tied to Aldrea, to all the worlds, actually. I believe you will find that you may exist in any of them as easily as you exist here in Celestria. Perhaps God of Worlds would be a fitting title." Aaslo frowned, and Disevy shrugged noncommittally. "We can work on it."

Aaslo squinted and noticed land coming into view in the distance. They had come to the edge of Axus's—no, Mory's—realm. A figure hovered at the edge. As he approached, he saw his mother. She looked different in a way that he couldn't quite put into words. She glowed with vitality. She seemed powerful in the way he had always imagined her when he was a child. A look of concern graced her face, but as he got closer that concern morphed to joy.

"Aaslo," she exclaimed as she held her arms out for his embrace. Putting his arms around her, he found he felt less awkward this time, reassuring him that with time, it would come to feel more natural. She pulled away to look at him. Stroking her hands down his arms, she said, "You are whole again. Your arm—"

"I think," Aaslo said, furrowing his brow, "I think I did this to myself. I can control how I appear now."

Her gaze seemed to take in the space around him. "You are one of them now, aren't you?"

Aaslo glanced at Disevy before saying, "It would seem so. And Mory, too."

Disevy stepped forward quickly, as if he could no longer hold himself back, and took her into his arms. "Did you finally find your truth, my love?"

She smiled up at him as she returned his embrace. "I believe I did. I understand now. There are no Fates. I *chose* to stay in this world in the only way I could. I became a reaper and assigned myself to Trostili because I somehow knew he would connect me with Aaslo. The only reason the gods had power over me was because I allowed it. It was all the power of my soul. And I know, now, that I am strong."

He placed his palm on her face and stroked her cheek with his thumb. "Now that you understand, will you choose to stay with me, sweet Myropa?"

Myropa glanced Aaslo's way as if seeking permission, then turned back to Disevy. "I will stay with you for as long as you will have me."

"Then you will stay for eternity," said Disevy just before he crushed his mouth to hers.

Aaslo shifted uncomfortably and his thoughts turned to a different woman, one to whom he had made a promise. "I need to go. I must release Sedi from her prison."

Aaslo didn't wait to be acknowledged before striding down the hillside to the former site of Axus's palace. It was no longer there, having been unmade with the god himself, but Aaslo could see the black stone pilar that encased Sedi standing atop the hill. Somehow, he knew exactly what he needed to do. All the powers and blessings he had received combined to form one god power that he used to crack the stone. He fed his power into the fractured prison, and in the same way that he unmade Axus, he unmade the stone. As it fell away like sand, Aaslo caught the unconscious Sedi.

Aaslo cradled Sedi to his chest as he knelt in the black sand. After a moment, she gasped and then sputtered and coughed as she tried to catch up on her breathing. Her eyes fluttered open, and she looked up at him. Bedraggled and worn, she gave him a genuine smile. She blinked lazily then jerked as her vision cleared and she noticed Aaslo's attention. She appeared uncertain.

"You kept your promise."

"Sedi, I'm glad you're okay."

Her gaze traveled over his face and down to his torso. "I see you're no longer a dragon."

With a thought, enormous, red, flame-tipped wings burst from Aaslo's back. Heated air rushed around them as the wings stretched and flapped. Sedi's eyes widened when the wings disappeared as quickly as they had appeared.

"I am very much still a dragon—perhaps more so now because I am one with it. I accepted it. I can feel the fury and the instinct to hunt, but a strong desire to make things grow and heal tempers it. I feel *more* now—more of everything. I feel . . . passionate."

Sedi's eyes dilated as she swayed toward him. "Is that so?" she whispered.

And it *was* true. As he gaped at this stunning woman who had transitioned from enemy to ally, Aaslo felt a surge of emotion fill him. Sedi may have tried to kill him, but she also helped him; and when the end came, she risked her soul to save him—to save everyone. She had overcome the madness of time and phenomenal loss and found in herself the drive to persevere, to endure. She was brilliant both in mind and skill, and the way she had defeated her demons and rallied to his aid left Aaslo in a state of awe. Aaslo could only stare as his enhanced emotions crashed against each other like waves in a turbulent sea.

Aaslo pulled her closer, and she leaned into him. A pleased rumble shook his chest. His woman wanted him.

"Your woman?"

With his roiling emotions unfocused, Aaslo's baser instincts took charge. His desire to dominate warred with his need to provide. He wanted to hunt her, to possess her, and at the same time worship her. All he knew for certain was everything he felt revolved around Sedi.

She whimpered, and Aaslo realized he had allowed his godly power to escape him. He reined it in, and her shoulders relaxed.

Her voice husky, she asked, "What do you feel passionate about right now, Aaslo?"

"You."

The word escaped him before he knew he spoke, but she rewarded him with a glorious smile that shone brighter than all the power of the gods combined, and he found that he didn't want to take it back. Then Sedi's smile slowly dropped to a frown.

Her voice choked as she said, "I have done terrible things, Aaslo. I thought I was doing good, but my mind wasn't right. Somehow, you cured me, but it doesn't change what was done."

Aaslo pulled her closer. As her arms wrapped around him, he rubbed her back soothingly. "It's okay."

"No, it's not," she sobbed.

He took a deep breath. "You're right. It's not, but it will be. You have all of eternity to make amends."

"I don't know if I can."

"You can and will, and I will be by your side if you'll allow it."

She pulled away and looked up with tear-filled eyes. "Truly? After everything that's happened, you wish to be with me?"

Aaslo grinned down at her. "So long as you don't try to kill me."

Sedi huffed a watery laugh. "As if I could. You are a god now, are you not? You cannot be killed."

Aaslo raised a brow. "That's not precisely true. I did kill Axus."

"Aaslo Godslayer."

Sedi wiped away her tears then gave him a devilish grin. "You'll have to tell me how."

He laughed with genuine mirth. "I think I'll keep that to myself. Can't have you getting any ideas."

Aaslo's laughter faded. Mesmerized by her glittery gaze, he leaned down and pressed his lips to hers. Tentative at first, Sedi quickly succumbed and deepened the kiss. Aaslo felt as though his world burst apart as all the passion he had held back flooded the kiss. When they finally parted, they were both breathing heavily.

"Well, this is rather uncomfortable."

Aaslo pressed his forehead to hers as he stroked her face. "The truth is, Axus unmade himself when he started stealing souls and using them for his own designs. He corrupted his own power. It turned dark and oily, and it left him vulnerable. It's because of this that I could unmake him as I did."

"You'll have to tell me the whole story."

"I will, but first, I have something I need to do. Will you wait for me?"

She pulled away. "I'll wait for as long as you need." Then she graced him with a coy smile. "But don't think I'll be worshipping you now just because you're a god."

"I wouldn't dream of it," said Aaslo as he stepped away.

ARAYALLEN'S JAW HUNG SLACK AS SHE STARED TOWARD THE HORIZON where once soared a range of majestic crystalline mountains. They were gone. Not covered by a haze or crumbled into vast plains, but vanished, as was the seductive power that they radiated. She shook to her core as she realized what that meant. Something unimaginable had happened. A god was dead. *Axus* was dead. So mesmerized by the sight, or lack thereof, she didn't notice as Trostili sidled up to stand next to her.

"My love, can you forgive me *now?*" he pleaded.

Arayallen shook herself and turned to him. "Your cohort is dead, and now you seek my forgiveness? You think I will so easily forget your betrayal?"

He raised his hands before him and donned an expression of innocence. "What betrayal? What did I do to warrant such anger?"

She balled her fists at her sides as her power flared. "You started a war to kill *all* life on Aldrea and take over Celestria!"

"That wasn't me, my love. That was Axus. I only ever sought to serve you."

Her voice rose to a screech. "How was working with Axus serving *me?*"

He took her shaking hands in his. She tried to tug them away, but he held firm. "My love, I am the God of *War.* I know how to wage one, and I *always* win."

"But you lost!" she cried as she jerked her hands away.

"Did I? Are you so sure?"

"What do you mean? Axus is *dead*. He was a god, Trostili, a very powerful one, and he is somehow dead."

"Can you not be certain that that was not my plan all along?"

"You were on *his* side!"

"My love, *I* placed the forester in the chosen one's path in the first place."

"What?" she huffed in disbelief.

He nodded sagely. "It's true. When I learned of the Aldrea Prophecy, I knew I couldn't let it stand. The chances were too great that the chosen one would fail, and Axus would become too powerful if that happened. So, I went to Arohnu, and I pressed him for a second prophecy, albeit a darker one—one that assured that Celestria, if not Aldrea, could survive Axus's aspirations. *I* made sure the forester and the chosen one met so that the second prophecy would have a chance of success if the first one failed."

His convincing words started to persuade her, but then she remembered his theft. "But you stole my *wind demon* and set it after Aaslo."

"Yes, I stole your *wind demon*, true, but I did it to help the forester. He needed a powerful companion." She opened her mouth to argue, but he raised a finger to continue his point. "*And*, don't forget, I designed the armor intended for the forester but that ended up in the hands of the healer. Also, *I* guided the reaper back to her son, hoping she would choose to help him. And, *I* suggested to Axus to make the deal with the human magus Sedi, who was an important part of the second prophecy. I did all of this while standing beside Axus in his circle of trust."

He pulled Arayallen into his embrace as she stared at him, dumbfounded. "So, you see, my love, I have only ever been on your side."

Teza blinked away the sweat that had trickled into her eyes as she peered across the field through the haze. There, among the butchered, mangled corpses of monsters and men, a shining beacon glowed with the roiling flames of the sun. Suddenly, around the battlefield, the monsters burst into flames. Their screeches and wails churned the gut until they were finally silenced. Around the beacon the fighting stilled, and that stillness spread across the battlefield like wildfire. When the wave reached her, Teza felt something strange. All the fighting spirit left her, and peace and calm took its place. She saw that others around her seemed to feel the same. Once the fighting had ceased, the glow subsided until Teza's eyes could focus on the figure within—Aaslo. To her surprise, he appeared fully human save for the aura surrounding him; well, and the flaming wings that stretched behind his back.

A voice, *his* voice, rang in her head. *"Axus is dead. The empress is dead. There is no glory awaiting you in the Afterlife. Cease this fighting and return to your homes."*

Shaking herself from her stupor, Teza let her gaze rove across the battlefield. The swirling vortex of power streaming from the machine to blacken the sky had vanished. The terrible machine within the stone rings to the south no longer pulsed with power, and the smoky tendrils that indiscriminately snuffed out lives had ceased reaping. So much death had visited this place. Both sides had heavy losses, only on *her* side, the dead hadn't stayed dead. Wanderers meandered through the gruesome battlefield as the Berruvian army attempted to regain some semblance of order. The same was happening on her side of the field and within the walls of the fortress.

On the battlefield echoed the shouts of *"The empress is dead"* and *"Axus is defeated."* With their leaders' demise and the loss of their monsters, the Berruvian soldiers began to panic in the face of the flaming god. The tide rolled out as the Berru broke and ran for the river crossing. The fight, it seemed, was over.

Teza returned her gaze to Aaslo. The glow steadily subsided, and the golden aura of power had almost disappeared as he neared. Teza half knelt in the bloody dirt at the base of the wall. Her magical, god-inspired armor was scuffed and dented, and she was drenched in sweat and filthy, yet in that moment she felt as though she ruled the world.

"Is it truly over?" she asked as Aaslo stopped in front of her. "Did we win?"

A disheveled Ijen joined them as Aaslo reached a hand down to help her up. Aaslo stepped forward and shocked Teza with a hug. Then he stepped back and confirmed, "We did. Axus is gone, and Mory has taken his place as God of Death."

Teza's brows rose as surprise shook her. *"Mory* is a god?"

Ijen moved gingerly as he took out his book and flipped through the pages. Then he began penning something into the margins.

Aaslo's mouth curled at the corners, and Teza thought perhaps it was his version of a smile. She had never seen it before, and it was startling. "Mory's not the only one. It seems I, too, have ascended."

She blurted, "You mean people can just *become* gods?"

Aaslo shook his head. "It's not so easy. We became gods via some very specific circumstances that could not be easily reproduced, if at all."

Ijen commented, "This does make an exciting conclusion to the story."

Aaslo sighed with exasperation. "I told you before, this is not a story. It's my life."

Unsure of what to say, Teza asked, "Well, what are you god of?"

Aaslo shrugged. "I'm not sure. I suppose time will tell. Now that I'm immortal you're all stuck with me."

"Then you're staying?"

He nodded. "Yes, I'm not yet ready to leave this world." He patted the sack at his waist. "Besides, I'm hoping to convince Mory to give Mathias another chance at life." Aaslo's eyes lost focus for a second, as they often did when he listened to something in his head. The smile returned and he shook himself. "Thank you both for all your help and support, and not just with the fighting and the army. I thank you for your help with this." He laid a hand over his heart. "Ever since I left my forest and lost Mathias I've been in a very dark place. Having you around helped me retain a little bit of sanity. You kept me from complete and utter despair. I am in your debt."

Teza, having no words, threw her arms around his neck and hugged him tight. With tears in her eyes, she said, "Thank *you*, Aaslo. You saved the *world*. You killed a god! There is no debt between us. God or no god, you're family now, and I will love you like a brother."

"Thank you, Teza. Then I will count you as my sister."

Teza jumped as Ijen snapped his book shut and walked away. She turned back to Aaslo with a cheeky grin. "I guess now that we've won, someone will have to follow through on all those deals we made." She batted her lashes at him sweetly. "What do you think, *brother*? Isn't a little godly blessing in order?"

Aaslo barked out a laugh, and Teza knew that all would be well.

THE SEA OF TRANSCENDENCE, WITH ITS FROTHING SWIRLS OF LIGHT and hypnotizing ebb and flow, mesmerized. Aaslo had never seen its like in all his travels—travels he would never have had if not for Mathias. The sack at Aaslo's waist felt heavier than usual as he traversed the silken sand to stand at the shore's edge. The sky was a dreamy pink and deep blue like the moments before the sun set fully and the stars first make their appearance. The foamy rush of waves provided an endless cadence that soothed the nerves, and the glowing play of lights in the depths lent the place a welcoming feel.

Aaslo inhaled deeply and a strange combination of salt and nectar greeted him. Then he turned and walked along the beach until he reached a rocky outcrop that jutted into the sea. He sat in the dry sand beside the rocks and pulled his sack into his lap. Then he removed Mathias's head from its confines and placed it on the rock beside him. He stared at his brother's face, so perfectly preserved yet devoid of even the slightest glint of life. This was not Mathias. This was but a shell, a last vestige of an age long past. Aaslo got to his knees and began digging in the sand. When he felt the hole was deep enough, he lifted Mathias's head and placed it inside. He stared at it for a moment more, then covered it over. He didn't need it anymore. He was ready to say goodbye.

He sat again and watched the waves peacefully sweep across the shore. No birds cawed from the sky, no crabs scuttled across the sand. No long grasses swayed in the breeze and not a single fish flitted about in the depths. A place devoid of life yet full of potential. The water wasn't really water after all, but an endless pool of souls ready to be born again or exist in the Afterlife, whatever that was.

"You won't be joining me here, will you?"

Aaslo glanced to his right and found Mathias lounging against the rocks beside him. He jerked at the sight of his brother whole and well, momentarily at a loss for words. Mathias brushed his golden hair out of eyes that shone with energy. He tipped his strong jaw up to the sky and wore a wan smile as he glanced toward Aaslo. Mathias had always been full of spirit and drive, but at this moment he looked at peace. Emotions inundated Aaslo. Joy and relief warred with sorrow and despair. So overwhelmed, he had almost forgotten the question. Mathias raised one eyebrow expectantly and grinned at his open mouth.

Aaslo finally cleared his throat. "No, I don't think I will. Not for a long time, anyway. Not unless someone figures out a way to kill me."

Mathias grinned, and the golden flecks in his blue eyes twinkled. "I always knew you were stubborn, but I didn't realize you were too stubborn to die."

Aaslo returned Mathias's grin. "It's a forester's prerogative."

Mathias laughed at that, and Aaslo joined him. They laughed for a long time, and it wasn't because Aaslo was particularly funny. It released them from all the strain and terror that had befallen them since leaving their hometown of Goldenwood. When the laughter finally died, Aaslo looked at Mathias. "Were you really there? Were you with me the whole time, or was it just my imagination?"

Mathias shrugged. "Am I here with you now? You understand the soul is infinite. Did I choose to refuse death and stay behind to haunt you? Or did your soul refuse to let me leave? Was it simply the power of a memory? The real question is: Does it matter?" He reached out and punched Aaslo in the shoulder, eliciting a glorious ache that Aaslo had been missing. "I would never leave you to have an adventure on your own. Brothers in all things, remember?"

Tears filled Aaslo's eyes, and he nodded, knowing Mathias hadn't really answered his question. "I remember. I could never forget that."

Mathias nodded toward the spot where Aaslo had buried his head. "I'm glad to see you moving on, Aaslo. It's not healthy to be carrying a severed head everywhere you go. People will think you're deranged."

"I couldn't let you go. I wasn't ready to say goodbye, but after everything that happened, I realized I finally could. It seems I don't need to, though. Now I can come here to see you when I need to. You'll be here, won't you?"

"Perhaps for a time. I've been toying with the idea of another life. Maybe one that doesn't get cut so short."

Aaslo nodded. "You deserve it."

"You deserve to be happy, too, Aaslo."

A small smile played across Aaslo's face. "I think I've found some happiness."

Mathias's eyes glinted with mirth. "You've chosen the vixen, then?"

"Sedi challenges me. She's intriguing—"

"And enchanting." Mathias waggled his brows.

"And we're both immortal."

"I suppose that's important now. You're a *god*, Aaslo. How great is that?"

Aaslo rubbed the back of his neck as the stress of added responsibility reared its head. "It's certainly different. What do you think I should do with my newfound godhood?"

Mathias grinned. "You could cover the whole world in forests. Then you could travel and never leave your precious trees."

Aaslo chuckled but he choked, overcome with emotion. "What am I going to do without you? You were my brother. You were always there. And now you'll be gone, and I'll be alone."

Mathias laid a hand on Aaslo's shoulder. "You like being alone."

"Never *that* alone. Never without you."

"You'll learn to accept it and move on."

Aaslo dug his fingers into the sand as he considered the suggestion. He said, "I don't want to be alone anymore. I understand, now, that the connections between people, between souls, are important. They make us stronger."

Mathias looked at him with surprise before nodding appreciatively. "You're not alone, Aaslo. You have people now. You have Peck and Mory, and a sister in Teza, even Ijen, and we can't forget the vixen," he said with a suggestive grin. "Plus, there are the other gods—a whole new family." After a pause, Mathias became serious again. "You made a good hero, Aaslo."

Aaslo shook his head. "No, you were the hero. I just did what needed to be done."

"Said like a true forester."

IJEN AWOKE IN A STRANGE CHAMBER. HE DIDN'T KNOW HOW HE HAD gotten there or what he had been doing before being taken. However, he knew of only two ways he might have come to be there. Either someone had rendered him unconscious and taken him through the paths, or one of the gods had planted him there. Either option told him that the reason for him being there must be important.

From his prone position on the floor, he saw dark timbers crisscrossing the ceiling, and the floor on which he lay was of some rich wood Aaslo would be able to identify, but with which Ijen had little experience. A few mismatched carpets of fine quality dotted the space, but unfortunately none were under him. Several dark wooden tables and cabinets sat in view, but he couldn't see what they contained from his vantage. As he stood, his head swam. He shook off the dizziness and surveyed the room. Although it had no windows or visible sconces or lamps, it was well lit in a warm and inviting kind of way. He realized it might be a library of sorts, or perhaps a museum. Shelves stacked with books and scrolls stretched from floor to ceiling along the walls. Strange artifacts, or relics, dotted tables and short plinths spaced haphazardly about the expansive room.

Ijen turned to the nearest shelf and selected a book from the many stacked upon it. It was perhaps as thick as his thumb and had a dark brown cover. Upon opening it, he could not read the language in which it was written. He placed it back on the shelf and selected another and then another. He quickly realized that, of those he could read, each and every one contained a prophecy, although none were a prophecy with which he was familiar. He replaced all the books then turned to the rest of the long chamber.

Two rows of black stone plinths ran up the center of the room. Over each floated a gilded tome illuminated with golden light by some unseen source. The rows of plinths created an aisle leading to the end of the room, where two final plinths stood side by side. The one on the left was illuminated, while the one on the right stood dark and empty. Ijen inspected a few of the plinths as he progressed down the aisle and noted each had a bronze placard atop its surface inscribed with the name of a prophecy. He followed the aisle to its terminus, where he stood before the illuminated plinth. The placard beneath the book that floated above it read *Aldrea Prophecy*. With surprise, he reached out but quickly changed his mind. The Aldrea Prophecy was no longer relevant. He turned to the empty plinth. There atop the plinth sat a placard, and across its bronze surface read *Book of Aaslo.*

Ijen's brows rose toward the ceiling. He had never heard of this room, but it seemed to be a place where all the prophecies of the world, perhaps many worlds, resided. His prophecy would hold prominence here. Of course, his prophecy had held great importance to *him*, since it had occupied his mind for nearly his entire life, but it never occurred to him that it might have been as important as the Aldrea Prophecy. After all, down Aaslo's path had lain death, and death was not something to which most people aspired.

Reaching into the fold of his tunic, Ijen pulled his book from the pocket that he had carefully sewn. He held the book before him as his gaze caressed the familiar worn green cover. It would be strange to not have the book's weight pressing against his heart. Ijen began to shake as he considered parting with the book. He had never been anything without the prophecy. Everything he had done in his life, every thought and dream, had been related to it. Without it, he was barely a person. Without it, he had no relevance.

His fingers nearly vibrated, and his breath came in short pants as he laid the book atop the plinth. As soon as his fingers left it, the book gleamed brightly, rose to float above the plinth, then settled into the soft glow held by the other books. The book had changed. Its cover, pristine and unblemished, was a vibrant forest green with gold embellishment. Ijen was suddenly overcome with the need to take it back, and he reached for it. A flash in his peripheral vision caught his attention.

Glancing over, Ijen noticed a short table beyond the plinth, atop which lay an unobtrusive book nearly as thick as his clenched fist.

Ijen stepped up to the table and picked up the book, not knowing what to expect but knowing it was for him. He opened the book, revealing smooth, blank pages. Each awaited visions of the future, something new and untold.

As he stared at the first creamy page, an image came to mind, consuming his thoughts. Sights, sounds, and smells assaulted his senses, and beneath everything lingered certain *knowing* that almost always accompanied prophecy. Ijen withdrew his pen from his pocket and began to write.

EPILOGUE

I turned as a rush of cold wind blew in through the open door. Excited murmurs filled the room as the newly arrived couple closed the door, shook snow from their jackets, and kicked off their boots. The man turned, then paused upon seeing the sea of curious faces looking his way. He grinned, and two of the children vacated a bench as he came to sit among them. The woman smiled as she, too, joined them. "It's all clear. There has been no sign of lyksvight for a fortnight, but the wanderers are keeping watch anyhow."

It had been nearly a century and a half since the Grave War ended, but pockets of lyksvight remained scattered across Endrica. They would attack unwary travelers and even enter the settlements on occasion. The chaos between kingdoms, and the many factions that vied for resources and power after the Grave War, made it difficult for the patrols to hunt them down. Between the lyksvight and the greed of unsavory folk, the world became a dangerous place. For this reason, the wanderers continued to keep vigil, especially when the sun had set.

Beside me, young Corin looked up at his older brother. "Do you need to go keep watch now?"

His brother turned his milky gaze to the boy and shook his head once. Then he croaked, "I stay."

Corin grinned broadly and hugged his brother before jumping up and rushing over to the couple. He threw his arms around the man and climbed into his lap. "Thank you for keeping my brother with me, Aaslo. I need him."

Aaslo patted Corin on the head and muttered, "I know. That's why the dead remain here. They like to take care of us."

Corin pulled back and looked at Aaslo with a critical eye that seemed comical on such a small child. "Are you really a god?"

Aaslo looked over at me and sighed in defeat. "Telling stories again, Leydah?"

I grinned. "Only the best stories, Aaslo. History is important."

Aaslo shared a look with Sedi beside him, then turned his attention back to Corin. "I'm a forester."

CHARACTERS

Aleena—woman in community house
Corin—young boy in community house
Maydon—Corin's older brother
Aaslo—forester of Goldenwood
Jennilee—girl in the community house
Garus—an older boy in the community house
Sedi Tryst—ancient magus
Lysia—empress of Berru
Pithor—former leader of the Berruvian army
Margus—general of the Berruvian army
Cobin—head magus of the Berruvian army
Dolt—Aaslo's horse
Mathias—the chosen one; Aaslo's best friend
Myropa (Myra)—a reaper
Mory—a young thief turned scout
Anderlus Sefferiah—marquess of Dovermyer
Hegress—cavalry and infantry general for the marquess
Teza—healer
Ijen—prophet
Daniga—scout leader
Peck—thief turned scout
Broden—co-leader of the Cartisian Yellowtail Clan
Hennis—co-leader of the Cartisian Yellowtail Clan
Aria—former Great Oryx hunter; Cartisian
Greylan—Dovermyer guard
Rostus—Dovermyer guard
Andromeda—Pashtigonian captain of the Queen's Royal Army
Queen Tilly—Pashtigonian queen
Crisius—Empress Lysia's deceased lover
Ibris—Pashtigonian One God
Trenton—injured soldier
Avra Bouver—ancient magus/shade, academic
Brother Yarrow—monk at the Temple of Earth and Ash
Arohnu—God of Prophecy
Enani—Goddess of Realms

Elias—Pashtigonian warrior
Loris Deretey—ancient magus/shade, health and wellness
Aen Ledrian—ancient magus/shade, humanitarian, first prophet
Peter Sereshian—ancient magus/shade, magic for profit
Sir Elridge—knight from Uptony
Brent—soldier in Aaslo's army
Merc—soldier in Aaslo's army
Vincent Regalis—greater army general
Captain Evan—leader of tower contingent
General Barbok—Lodenonian general
General Nangent—Helodian general

DEFINITIONS

Argontian Warriors—six massive statues erected on the southern
   peninsula of Helod
vizens—flying creatures of the Alterworld

NOTE FROM THE AUTHOR

I hope you enjoyed reading this final book in the Shroud of Prophecy series. Visit www.kelkade.com to sign up for my newsletter and receive updates and news. Please consider leaving a review. Also, check out my other ongoing series, King's Dark Tidings.

ABOUT THE AUTHOR

KEL KADE lives in Texas and occasionally serves as an adjunct college faculty member, inspiring young minds and introducing them to the fascinating and very real world of geosciences.

Growing up, Kade lived a military lifestyle of traveling to and living in new places. These experiences with distinctive cultures and geography instilled in Kade a sense of wanderlust and opened a young mind to the knowledge that the Earth is expansive and wild. A deep interest in science, ancient history, cultural anthropology, art, music, languages, and spirituality is evidenced by the diversity and richness of the places and cultures depicted in Kade's writing.